Sebastian Three

Sebastian Three

Conquest of Power

Elizabeth Johnson

Aldage Books Publishing Limited

Dedication

I dedicate this book to God Almighty for the inspiration, love, and the confidence He gave me to pursue my heart's desires. Thank you, my Father, for your unfailing love.

To my family, especially my three wonderful boys, Josiah, Jesse, and Jaden who encourage me every day to follow my passion.

To my editor, Diann, thank you.

And to all those that read Sebastian One and Two, who nudged me forward with their amazing reviews as they waited for the next instalment.

I thank you all for your endless support.

Prologue

"S," Hanna called, stopping a few yards from him. He didn't acknowledge her call with a reply. Before now, when she called him "S" it made him smile inwardly, but not this time. He felt betrayed by her, and he felt justified in that feeling.

"Please, let me explain," Hanna begged. Sebastian sighed; he couldn't bring himself to face her; doing so would only remind him of the inevitable, not that it helped to look away either when it was all he could think about. When he didn't respond, Hanna decided to carry on with her explanation regardless.

"I'm sorry. I wasn't thinking, or should I say, I wasn't thinking about your feelings when I brought him with us. All that was on my mind and still is even now is how we can come out on top of all this chaos. I know we have been doing well on our own, but I feel another set of hands in this war won't hurt us." Hanna tried to reason with him. Sebastian scoffed, not wanting to respond. He was afraid she wouldn't like what he would say.

Hanna pleaded, "Please love, look at me; I know it's difficult for you right now, but can you try and put that other business with Hector to one side. Try and see it from my viewpoint." Sebastian, forced himself to face her, and the expression on his face was unyielding.

He chuckled softly, "I am glad you can separate the two. I think that is probably because it was you that kissed him. You know what I see, each time I look at you or . . . him, the image of the two of you at it. You gave me no time to process it all, and then you throw him in my face. Perhaps you're right but I can't reason like you do now and I can't see beyond this problem." He paused and moved two steps away. Then he said, "I know we were not together then, but I would think you would know if you care about me like you claim you do, that he was the last person you could have done that with. So, pardon me if I can't work hand in hand with your new boyfriend." Sebastian could see he was hurting her, but she couldn't be as hurt as he was at that moment. He began to walk away, and Hanna hurried after him. "Wait, please, it's not like that," she said. "I don't know why it happened either but my head wasn't right then; I really missed you and I was lonely . . ." She tried to explain, but Sebastian cut in.

"So, you run into his arms instead?" he asked. "Did that make you feel better?" he demanded. Hanna bit her lip nervously as she tried to hold back her tears.

"I can't imagine you with someone else let alone him. Why him Hanna? You knew how I felt about him. If I meant anything to you~even if we were not together~you should have considered that. You won't admit it, but, right from the beginning, you have carried something for him. You tell me it is not true, but each time I say we must do something about him, you are against it. So, forgive me if I am not doing what you want right now. If you never wanted anything to do with me again, then you should have carried on with whoever pleased you, but you tell me you wanted me still and then you . . . do that with him and as if you haven't punished me enough you bring him here to my face. I'm sorry I can't do this, and talking about it makes me nauseous. I need to be alone I . . . I never thought there would be a day that I wouldn't want to gaze upon your beautiful face, but right now, I can't bear to look at you," Sebastian said, and walked away.

Chapter 1

Thomas

Thomas yelled as he rattled the solid steel cage where he was locked. "Get me out of here, do you hear me? Get me out of here now! Nicholas, you coward! Come down now and fight me! Come fight me and we shall see if you survive, you coward. Stop hiding behind Mason; you did this; you did his dirty work for him; now it is time to face the music. Come here now and face me you pile of shit, come down here and fight me, I have decided your fate and I will rip you apart as you did her." Thomas pulled hard at the door, but the steel won't budge.

Famished and tired, he knew he was using his last strength as he barked. Darkness surrounded him, and he couldn't see beyond his hands. He was aware that it was because his body desperately needed blood. Seeing in the dark was one of the perks of being a vampire. He wondered how long Mason had had him locked down here. How long had his body been without food? He had been conscious for hours and had spent all that time yelling and wasting his last strength calling for Nicholas to come and fight him for killing Margret the woman he loved. His memories returned and he remembered the terrible moment when he saw Nicholas break off Margret's head. It felt like he was reliving the moment again, he again experienced the pain he had felt as he saw her body smash on the ground. His heart stopped when she died. He couldn't process or understand the reason why Nicholas would do such a thing to him even if he were just carrying out Mason's order. He didn't know why Mason felt so threatened by Margret, why he had to have her killed knowing what she meant to him. A fresh rage filled him. Thomas knew he couldn't fight Mason. Doing that would mean he was suicidal, but he knew that if he were well fed, he could defeat Nicholas. If anyone had predicted that he would one day see Nicholas as his enemy, he would have ripped their tongue out, but now Nicholas had done this to them and Thomas found his actions unforgivable. Now all he wanted to do was to avenge Margret.

Nicholas and Henry were like his brothers; he took them under his wings. He taught them all they knew; he loved and trusted them with everything he had and he would have died for them if need be, but the betrayal felt like a sword in his heart. Thomas knew Henry had nothing to do with Margret's killing, but since he had woken up, no one had come to see him, knowing it had been long since he fed and to top up the treachery, they had the audacity to lock him up for days rather than face him and face up to what they had done.

Thomas looked more pale than normal; even though he couldn't see well, he could feel his skin drying out. He knew he must have gone at least three days since he last fed, and prior to this, he had always fed every day. Thomas had always thought he was Mason's right hand; being treated this way was ridiculous. Mason may be his master, but he didn't have any respect for him at the moment, and with Margret dead, he felt he had nothing to lose.

Angered, Thomas called: "Mason! You get down here now and speak with me. Is this all I am to you? You get my woman killed and you cower away unable to face me. Get down here now and bring that traitor with you; let him come and face me and tell me why he killed his own mother. Do you hear me? Get down here

2

now Nicholas, you rotten heap of dung. Come fight me, coward! I will snap you in two with my bare hands."

"Calm down before he takes you up on your offer; you are in no shape to fight." Thomas heard Sebastian's voice, and he knew he wasn't alone; he had known since he first became conscious, but for some reason, the rage he was feeling inside coupled with the lack of food made him unable to focus on anything other than his anger. Thomas was quiet for a second; he knew he had offended Sebastian, but he had to do so because he had followed Mason Benedict's orders. Mason had said he had to bring Sebastian back to Mexico; it was for the good of their kind. He was sure that was the same lecture Mason must have given to Nicholas, but that was neither here nor there. Thomas remembered snapping Sebastian's neck and taking him to the jet just before he witnessed the terrible killing of the woman he loved. He recalled how he threw Sebastian down just as he saw Margret's body hit the ground. All he wanted to do was kill Nicholas, and he would have done just that if someone had not stopped him. By deduction, he knew that the only person who could have stopped him from killing Nicholas was Henry, and he didn't thank him for it.

He turned toward Sebastian, "How long have you been there listening to me yell and you say nothing? Why now? Why speak now?" Thomas questioned Sebastian.

"I had no desire to speak with you until now. And I do not need to be amused by the pleasures of your morbid rantings. I am fed up of seeing you shriek and shake, making threats you cannot carry out in your present state, and then you fall unconscious because you have not fed for em what is it now five days. Yeah, I have suffered five torturous days of your delirious state of mind, slipping in and out of consciousness. And each time you come to, you resume the same behaviour that leaves you wasted. It's embarrassing seeing someone I once respected without any control. You've not had blood for five days. I suggest you stop ranting. You are weak because Mason made sure you were drained so you wouldn't harm his pet, Nicholas. So, you will do well to calm yourself down and stop making empty threats you can't carry out. You are in no shape to fight anyone, stop howling or Nicholas will have no choice but to take you up on that offer." Sebastian paused just a little to allow himself a breath; he was equally tired, but not like Thomas who had no control. He could tell by Thomas's breathing that he was getting under his skin, but he didn't care.

Sebastian said, "Don't get me wrong, I am not mocking you. What am I saying~oh yes~I am mocking you. You, treacherous, untrustworthy friend. I guess the joke was on me; we were never friends. I always knew that, but I gave you a chance and you blew it when you brought me here." Sebastian waited for Thomas to respond.

"What do you want me to say? That I am sorry? I don't know. I like you or I should say, I liked you, but I am a soldier, and I take my orders seriously," Thomas said. Sebastian scoffed.

"Then why make threats at Nicholas? He is a soldier like yourself. He carried out an order too," Sebastian stated.

Thomas was quiet, and then he said, "It's different. It's not the same. I loved Margret. I only just met her and in that short time, she was everything. Nicholas knew it; you all knew it," Thomas responded.

"You don't deserve my pity, but I pity you, you know what? Scrap that, I feel for you for Margret's sake. I know what it feels like to lose the person you love. I know that pain all too well, so I don't begrudge you for wanting to avenge her death, but Thomas just shut up and think. We've been down here for five days. If we want to get out of this cage, it's time we engage our brains. I can't very well think with you ranting on like a mad man. I am equally enraged. I brought Margret here; she was my family. So, if you want justice for her as I do, shut your mouth and use your brain." After speaking, Sebastian got up from the corner of his cage and walked to the front where he hoped that Thomas would be able to see him. He could see Thomas holding on to the bars of his cage. They had been put in separate enclosures.

Sebastian had woken up almost immediately they placed him in his cell. After they had drained Thomas's blood, Sebastian would be next, but he put on a show. He heard Mason's voice at the top of the stairs saying to let him be. "Leave him alone; it doesn't matter. He is not strong anyway; he feeds on animal blood, and we are not in any danger from him. Make sure they are not fed until I give the order." Mason had said his piece without coming to face him. Sebastian knew then that Mason was ready for the next stage of his plans whatever that entailed. He still didn't understand how all this had anything to do with Hanna.

"How come you sound sane? If what you say is true, that we've been here for five days, then you too would have been here like me without food. Your disposition marvels me; how can you cope?" Thomas asked astonished to hear how collected Sebastian seemed to be.

"Hmm, wouldn't you like to know. Now that I am aware we are not friends, why should I tell you anything? It's my little secret. You may be here with me; it may look like we are in the same predicament; that doesn't mean our fate is the same. For all I know, Mason leaving you here with me may be a way to con me so I can confide in you. This may all be a show to make me feel like they have turned on you. Not that there is anything to tell. I am just saying. I don't trust you, I don't trust anyone. Your loyalty will always be to Mason. Perhaps you planned it all together, the killing of Margret, the one person I had left who would always have my back. Did you really love Margret, or was it just a show, Thomas? Did she mean anything . . ."

"Shut your bloody mouth and sit back in that filthy cage." Thomas roared interrupting Sebastian "I loved her," he bellowed with every strength he could muster, "I loved her with all my soul. I loved her with every fibre of my life, you fool." Thomas was tired; he could see Sebastian's reasoning, but he wasn't here to seek allies; he just wanted vengeance for Margret, the same thing he knew Sebastian would also want. "I have existed for more than seven centuries, and in all that time, I never found anyone like her. I loved her from the moment I laid eyes on her, and I loved her more than I could ever love my wretched soul. How dare you think I would wish her harm. How dare you accuse me of such a hideous crime. Do you not understand the pain eating away at me at the thought of never seeing her, holding her again? Can you not see what it has done to me, and that is why I must avenge her; that is why I must kill Nicholas myself with my own hands." Thomas said weakly.

"All right, I believe you but stop howling; you are going to faint again, I can see it coming . . ." Sebastian said, but before he could finish his sentence, Thomas staggered backward.

Sebastian advised, "You are running on fumes; you need to sleep and preserve your energy; if you don't listen, at this rate, I don't think you will be able to speak the next time you awake."

Thomas sat down in his cage and practiced breathing in and out to stop himself from fainting, but there was nothing in his body; his body was suffering from withdrawal; he could feel his body going into shock and then he fell backward and went unconscious again.

Sebastian sighed. At least now that Thomas was at rest, he would be able to think. The only thing that had kept him sane was seeing Hanna's face when he almost died at the hands of Zacchary. That gave him the will to live. It felt so real, like she had been there in person, just like when he had seen her at the beach the other time. These sightings gave him hope; it meant she still cared. It seemed that she always appeared when he was in trouble; he didn't know what to make of it. Did she still care or was that her way of making sure he was suffering as she had intended? Considering the two options, he didn't know which to believe, but he told himself when he eventually escaped from Mason's clutches his only purpose would be to find Hanna and try to convince her again that they belonged together as he had intended before Thomas dragged him here.

Sebastian hoped that the time spent away from Hanna would have made her realize that she was as unhappy as he was and perhaps she would be willing to forgive him now. Wishful thinking, he told himself, but then if he didn't dream, what else was there to do? The alternative was unbearable and following in Thomas's footsteps didn't look very appealing. Sebastian wondered if Mason had eyes on them. He had looked around for cameras and couldn't find any, but he wouldn't put it past Mason to have eyes where he couldn't see.

He also knew if Mason did have eyes on him then he would be wondering why he had not started to show signs of weakness like Thomas had been displaying. Thanks went to his mother, Elizabeth, who had taught him how to survive without blood for extended periods of time, an act he had now mastered. Sebastian knew if it came to it, he could painfully endure two to three more weeks without blood. That would be a hard stretch, and he hoped it wouldn't come to that, but he already had plans to feign blood deprivation at seven days. At ten days, he would fake unconsciousness. Maybe Mason would panic and get him blood. The more blood they gave him, the better would be his chances of escaping. Sebastian looked at Thomas's inert body and then returned and sat in the corner of his cage again.

About twenty hours later, Thomas stirred a little, and his movement distracted Sebastian from his thoughts. Sebastian was working on a plan; he wasn't sure how it would work, but he knew that if he wanted out he would have to get Thomas on his side. That was going to be a hard task since he knew Thomas was foolishly loyal to Mason, but there was a crack now, and he thought that Margret's killing genuinely grieved Thomas. If that was true, then perhaps he had a chance at widening that crack and turning Thomas into an ally. Thomas made a faint groan, but his body did not move. Sebastian knew that without blood, there was zero chance that Thomas would be able to function, let alone help him. He wondered if Thomas had anyone amongst Mason's minions that felt loyalty to him. Sebastian remembered all the faces at the banquet table when Mason had thrown a banquet for him; they must have all been laughing their heads off including Thomas, knowing what was coming next. He wasn't fooled; this situation didn't surprise him, but he just didn't know how quickly Mason would turn on him. And now that he was here, his only hope was to try and turn Thomas against Mason if he was to have any chance at coming out of this alive.

"Are you still there Sebastian?" Thomas asked faintly.

"I'm sure you know I am," Sebastian responded. Thomas sighed slowly.

"My breathing is hard and controlled; my throat is parched and dry. You can sense my sufferings from my speech as I can sense yours," Sebastian added.

"Yes, I can sense you," Thomas said "But you are still in control of your body; you have not lost consciousness once. I don't know how you've managed to do that. You are, after all, a vampire, even though you feed on scum; that animal blood you drink is the reason your body should have already shut down." Thomas was bewildered by Sebastian's strength.

"Perhaps there is something else I am missing, like how are you able to single-handedly kill a seven-hundred-year-old vampire?" Thomas asked rhetorically. Sebastian could tell Thomas was beginning to scrutinize him, and he didn't want that; who knew where it would lead. The last thing he wanted was for Mason and his minions to find out that he could walk the sun. That would only confirm that Hanna could give them what they were after.

"Well, Thomas, what can I say? That was pure luck. Zacchary was going to kill me; I knew it, and for some reason, I wasn't ready to leave this world yet," Sebastian said as he pictured Hanna's face shimmering to the surface on the battlefield.

"Maybe the answer lies in my diet~you know~the animal blood you call scum. You should try it sometimes~. Anyway, I am tired. I've been fighting to stay in control. The last thing I want is for Mason to drag me out of here unconscious. Whatever he has in store for me, I must be awake to witness it," Sebastian said.

Thomas chuckled as he bounced Sebastian's explanations in his head for a while and decided there was nothing more to it.

"You must feel like a right pig's ear, not knowing what to expect and when to expect it," Thomas stated.

Sebastian sighed, but he didn't respond. To get Thomas on his side, he needed him to fill the silence, so that when he suggested the idea, it would feel like the sensible thing to do. After a moment had passed, Thomas continued. "I know I shouldn't speak, but the silence drives me insane." He tried to control his breath so Sebastian could hear his words. He didn't have the energy to speak loudly.

"I tell you what: I think it's about time Mason stopped playing this game with me," Thomas said, and then he was quiet again.

Sebastian knew it was time for him to begin sowing the seeds of doubt in Thomas.

"Do you blame him? You and I know why he's left you here. I don't approve of favouritism, but I quite understand it. You've been shouting the odds and telling whoever cares to listen, how you will rip Nicholas apart. Only a fool will feed you and leave you to carry out your threats. Come to think of it, Nicholas must be more important to him than you are. If he left you to your devises, Nicholas would be dead meat by now. So, my thinking is that Mason wants you to calm down so he can explain to you why it was necessary to have a son kill his own mother. It's demeaning for you being locked down here, but I bet it wasn't particularly personal. He probably didn't know how much in love you were; neither do I want to believe that Mason knew that Margret was Nicholas's mother. Because if he knew, then I wonder what kind of a villain he is and to what gain? I also wonder if Nicholas even knew that he had been ordered to murder his own mother. Anyway, that is neither here nor there. What is done is done. We can continue to cry about it or together we could decide to fight our way out of this nightmare." Sebastian made an end of his speech.

Thomas did not respond, but Sebastian could tell by how hard Thomas was struggling to control his breathing that he had hit a nerve.

An hour passed and no words passed between them. Sebastian feared that Thomas wasn't taking the hint. He knew he had to try another way.

"Tell me one thing please. I know we aren't true friends, but since you are here, could you shed some light on why exactly I am being held in this confinement? You are or were Mason's lieutenant. You must know what he has in store for me? You've told me you know about Hanna, but what I don't get is why you think holding me captive will help you get what you need. You care to explain?" Sebastian asked as he rose from where he had sat for the last twenty-one hours. Thomas chuckled quietly, and Sebastian held his breathe. He was hoping that Thomas would shake something lose, something that he could use to aid him, to get Thomas on his side.

"Oh boy, I know what you are doing; if I had the energy, I would bump you for thinking you can pull one on me," Thomas responded Sebastian held his tongue and hoped that Thomas would say something else.

There was a long pause and finally, Thomas spoke again. "Although I agree with one thing you said, if Mason left me to my devices, I would tear Nicholas from limb to limb and leave him his carcass to deal with and I am still going to do just that immediately when I get free of this cage." Thomas paused to gather his strength before continuing his talk.

"I don't owe you anything Sebastian, but since it is clear you may not survive this ordeal, whatever it is Mason has planned for you, I will tell you all that I know—that much I can help you with. Move closer boy; can't speak loud at all; you might just catch what I am saying if you strain well enough." Thomas paused before he began speaking, Sebastian could feel Thomas struggle to breathe, and if he didn't need answers desperately, he would have told him to save his strength, but he had to take his chances when he could get them.

"It's a long story," Thomas began, "I don't know the half of it. What I know is that before your existence, there was an oracle and as I recall, it was something like this—if I remember rightly. I wasn't meant to hear it, but I overheard Mason speaking to his wife Annemarie on her dying bed, and she said that the vampire that saves him would lead us to the light." He stopped again to regain his strength. "Yeah, that is all I know, and you happen to be the one that saved him. You do know what it means for us to only walk in darkness. It's been more than seven centuries for me. I can't even remember what the warmth of the sun felt like on my skin. No witch alive or dead had such power to make a vampire a daywalker. Not even Mason's wife and there was no witch as powerful as she was. To be told that we are not utterly condemned to walk the dark world, that there is power here on this human earth to make someone like me a daywalker lifted our hearts greatly. When it comes down to it, I will always choose to walk the day. You feel betrayed; so you should. If by your sacrifice, we all get the gift of the sun, then you would have done something significant for our kind with your life. I don't know what that girl of yours is capable of, but Mason says she is the cure and if keeping you here will bring her to us, then it is what it is." Thomas finished speaking dragging out the last word as though he were about to fall into another deep sleep. Sebastian chuckled loudly and purposefully. "You must be a fool then; I thought you were wiser. If it is true and she can make you walk the light, do you think she is powerful enough to make all of you daywalkers? Did you ever ask yourself what happens if all of this is one big lie, or if Mason has his own agenda? I mean you were close to him, and look where you are now. Let me tell you what is going to happen if in fact you think my Hanna can make vampires walk the light. When Mason gets hold of her, he will use her powers for himself only. Why share when he can have it all to himself. That is if she is really that powerful to make vampires daywalkers. As you said, no one can do it; I think this is wishful thinking. Why you choose to follow him baffles me when you can do so much on your own. Look at how he has degraded you. Can you not think for yourself, or is that beyond you as well?" Sebastian jabbed at Thomas purposefully to get him angry.

"Watch your filthy mouth now boy!" Thomas warned.

"What? Did I touch a nerve?" Sebastian poked and tutted, knowing there was nothing Thomas could do to him, not in his weakened state. Thomas's breathing became even more strained. Sebastian wanted to anger him enough to make him think, not get him to shut down.

"Listen, I mean no offense, I just get tired of your passivity in all of this. You want to walk the light as much as Mason, as much as any vampire out there, and if there is a cure and Mason thinks holding me here will get him Hanna, then think, why not use me yourself, and I will be willing to help you if you help me. I will ask her to make you a day walker, but to do that I have to make it out of here alive, and you need to help me," Sebastian said.

It was Thomas's turn to laugh, "I may be a fool at Mason's hands, and I see your points, but don't you ever think you can play me. If she is as strong as I have heard, the moment I help you escape, what guarantees do I have that you are not going to get her to kill me anyway. I like my odds better with Mason; as soon as he becomes a day walker, I will be next . . ." Thomas said, but Sebastian cuts him off.

"I believe wisdom doesn't come with age; if it did, you wouldn't be so naïve. Stop dreaming and look around you. Nicholas comes before you; you are starving down here, and the one vampire that killed the love of your life is up there having the time of his life. Wake up, will you and see that I am giving you a once in a lifetime chance. If you don't agree now and I escape and believe me, I will find a way, I always do, this deal will be off the table. You will become an enemy, and I can assure you that I will fight and kill you and any other vampire that dares think they can harm Hanna. But all that doesn't need to happen if you help me," Sebastian said heatedly. Thomas laughed softly.

"Oh boy, believe me, you may have been lucky to kill one old vampire; don't mistake me for him, but for argument's sake, let's say I believe you. You've told me yourself that she doesn't want you, remember? Why would she do anything you ask?" Thomas questioned.

"If you believe that, why then use me to lure her here? You must believe that I matter to her; I didn't think I mattered anymore until recently, and I want the chance to find that out. Help me and we could both get what we want; if she favours me when we find her, I will request that she help you on the condition that you never return to Mason, and he never finds out. I don't know why you would want to anyway; if this is how he treats his friends. I'm not looking for friendship either. Just partnership. And after this is done and I make good on my part, we don't have to see each other again." Sebastian stated.

Then he went back to the corner of his cage and sat down leaving Thomas to ponder what he told him. Sebastian hoped that Thomas would agree to a partnership and if Thomas bit, then the next thing would be to convince Thomas to get someone he trusted to sneak him some blood, and he knew the exact person for that job. Then out of nowhere, Thomas said, "I have been thinking; you make a lot of sense. Although I've tried to persuade myself that what you say is not true and if you had told me this before Margret was killed, I would have probably cut out your tongue myself before forcing it down your throat, but now I see the errors in my allegiance, and I may very well regret this, but count me in, I hope you have a plan?" Thomas said.

Sebastian smiled knowingly.

"Did you hear me?" Thomas asked; he wanted confirmation.

"Yes, I heard you, Thomas," Sebastian responded.

"So, tell me, boy, how do you plan we do this?" Thomas probed.

"You need to feed; sooner or later Mason is going to send someone down here, and we both know who he will send. Henry. Get him to sneak you some blood and assure him you are over Margret; he may not believe, but get him to sympathize with your situation," Sebastian said.

"Sounds like a good plan, but you forget one thing. What if Henry refuses? I can only ask him the favour if Mason allows him to come to me. Your plans are full of holes; in another twenty-four hours, I won't be able to talk anymore; my body will shut down. For this plan to work, it will take a miracle."

"I know; I have considered that possibility, but I think Henry loves you, and he is loyal to you. He will come; he won't want to see you suffer more than he thinks you should. I dare say he could even defy Mason on your behalf. If he comes and you can't speak, then I will speak with him on your behalf. Let's just hope you mean more to him than Mason," Sebastian said.

"Well that doesn't fill me with a lot of hope, but at least it's a plan," Thomas responded.

"Yeah, we will see if it works," Sebastian answered.

14

Chapter 2

Mason Benedict.

Mason sat in his room and watched his two prisoners; he knew he had played this wrong. He couldn't hear what they were saying, and the last thing he wanted was for Thomas and Sebastian to come to some alliance. Thomas had been his right-hand man for a very long time, and this wasn't a good way to treat him for being a loyal subject. However, there was no easy way of explaining his reasons for ordering Margret's death. It was a selfish call, and at the same time, he knew it was the right call. Mason wished Thomas hadn't fallen so deeply for her, but any alliance Sebastian could have he had to topple it before it ever became a problem. Knowing now how much Margret had meant to Thomas, he could not take the risk of allowing Thomas his freedom.

Thomas is the best fighter he has by a mile; Nicholas was strong and could hold his own, but he didn't stand a chance with Thomas when he was at his strongest. If he ever allowed the fight, and Thomas killed Nicholas, then he would have to avenge Nicholas by taking Thomas out. Nicholas had acted on his instructions. Nicholas was too important to him; Annemarie, his wife, had raised him as her own son, and he had promised Annemarie that he would ensure his safety until he could restore her back to life and they could be a family again as they once were.

The situation was bad enough; Mason wished Sebastian had not brought Margret with him to Mexico; then he wouldn't have had this problem on his hands.

Annemarie had said that he needed to do all that was in his power to ensure everything went to plan. He wasn't going to let Margret get in the way of that either, and wasn't going to allow his liking Sebastian to stop him from gaining Hanna's powers. He twisted the ring on his finger; Annemarie had poured out her powers and her soul into the ring, and all he must do was gain a drop of Hanna's blood to activate the power in the ring and bring his wife back to life.

Mason wondered what Sebastian was saying to Thomas; he noted that Thomas hadn't been screaming *Murder* as he had done the past days. Mason knew that Thomas needed blood desperately, but what baffled him most was Sebastian. Sebastian looked okay; there were no signs of his body going into shock even though he had not fed in a while. Mason wondered how long it would take for him to shut down. He quietly noted that in this, Sebastian was stronger than any vampire he knew. He had never met a vampire whose body didn't shut down from lack of blood, and he pondered how long it would eventually take for Sebastian's body to shut down. There was a knock on his door.

"Come in," he said, motioning with his hands. He turned from the television device to face a worried looking Henry.

"What is it?" Mason asked Henry looked behind Mason to the screen where he noticed Thomas lying immobile. He quickly shifted his eyes back to Mason.

"It's Nicholas, Master," Henry said.

Mason was quiet; he knew Nicholas had not been himself since they returned. He had already planned to chat with him.

"What about him?" Mason asked as he moved closer to Henry.

"It seems he's gone mad; he won't stop ranting and rambling on about Margret. He's not making any sense to me," Henry said.

16

"Tell me, what exactly has he been saying?"

"Something about it being her fault for keeping him in the dark; I don't understand; I thought you might," Henry said, and Mason looked away for a moment. He thought about the possibility of Nicholas knowing Margret was his mother and quickly dismissed the idea. He couldn't possibly know; Annemarie had wiped his memory after he brought him home when he wouldn't stop crying for his mother. Mason turned his face toward Henry before speaking.

"And what makes you think that I would know?"

"I'm sorry Master," Henry quickly added, with a bow. "I just assumed you could help him; he is hurting; I have never seen him like that. He won't let me near him. I don't know how to help him. If she meant so much to him, I don't understand why he killed her," Henry explained.

Mason looked past him not wanting to give anything away, and then he gracefully turned his back and flicked his hands to dismiss Henry. "If that is all, you may go; I need to think."

"If I may speak freely Master?" Henry asked.

Mason turned toward him; he knew what this would be about. Knowing how close Henry was to both Nicholas and Thomas, Mason knew that Henry's next concern would be Thomas.

"You may," Mason responded. Henry hesitated to speak. He knew he had to be careful with his choice of words.

"What is it? Out with-it Henry, I have other pressing issues to get on with," Mason pushed.

"It's about Thomas; it's almost seven days since you . . ." Henry couldn't bring himself to finish his statement. Mason's eyes pierced him expecting him to finish what he started. "I just feel like . . . we need to feed him before he shuts down completely," Henry said; he paused and waited for Mason to respond; when Mason did not, Henry continued speaking.

"He seems calm now; perhaps he's had time to think. He knows he can't harm Nicholas. He knows you won't permit it; I won't allow it either," Henry explained.

"Hmm, I know. I have thought about it as well, but until I am sure that there will be no risk to Nicholas's life, it is impossible for me to release Thomas—not when there is a chance, he still carries a grudge. I am not one to take chances," Mason paused for a moment before continuing.

"I know I can't keep him locked up forever; the longer he stays down there the more fervent he will become in his tumultuous rage to end Nicholas. However, I will give him a chance to reason differently. You will go down and chat with Thomas on my behalf. See for yourself his state of mind and report back to me and I will make a decision on your findings," Mason ordered.

Henry felt relieved; he didn't like that there was chaos amongst them; he wanted everything back to normal. Henry smiled when Mason told him he could go to Thomas; he was hopeful that when he explained to Thomas how penitent and shameful Nicholas was about the killing of Margret, perhaps Thomas would change his mind about wanting to avenge her, and things could finally get back to how they were before the unfortunate event took place.

Henry was annoyed at the fact that they hadn't been able to celebrate the killings of two of the brothers, Zacchary and Anton. Their deaths were a great victory because they had been after the brothers for centuries. However, instead of revelling in their recent victories, Nicholas had to go and do something dumb. No matter how he tried to rationalize it, Henry couldn't understand the reasons behind such brutality towards Margret, when Nicholas knew exactly what she meant to Thomas, and now they had to fight amongst themselves. Nevertheless, he loved them both and it wasn't right for him to take sides. Neither could he watch them both suffer from the consequences of their actions. Henry also was aware that Thomas always knew what Nicholas meant to Mason.

He was aware that threats at Nicholas over a woman or anything at all would not go down well with Mason. Only a vampire with a death wish would dare do that. Mason turned his back and moved toward a painting of a beautiful redhead woman in his room; he trailed his finger over her cheek. Mason stared into the eyes of the woman in the painting and sighed.

"You may leave now," he said to Henry without moving from where he stood. Henry bowed and retreated from his presence.

A few moments later, Mason turned his attention back to the screen where he observed both Thomas and Sebastian. Mason observed that Sebastian was back in the corner of his cage.

Truth be told, he was in awe of Sebastian; the discipline his mother had instilled him set him apart from the rest of them. Watching him all those years and particularly these few days made him wish he didn't have to do what he needed to do. Mason knew he could not allow such feelings to destroy plans that had been set in motion for centuries. The only other person that had ever come close to changing his mind was Elizabeth Francis, Sebastian's mother; she almost had his head and his heart turned.

However, the ring had power over his will; Annemarie had put a clause that made it impossible for him to love another no matter how much he desired it. An image of the last time he held Elizabeth in his arms flashed into his memory, and he quickly pushed it out. This was not the time to reminisce; what was done was done, and now that they were here, it was time to carry out the rest of his plans. He allowed his mind to feel how joyful it would be when he eventually had his wife Annemarie by his side and to top it all, to walk the day. Mason smiled; he knew it was time to let Sebastian know exactly why he was holding him prisoner. It was time he knew the part he played in all of this. And time he told Sebastian the whole truth, including how his mother, whom he had almost fallen in love with, ended up dead.

****

Henry approached the steel gate above the dungeon where Thomas and Sebastian were being held hostage. Two vampires were stationed at the entrance as guards just for good measure. They nodded as a sign of respect when they saw Henry. Normally, after Mason, Thomas called the shots, and when Thomas was not around, Nicholas led and then Henry. It was the way it had always been, but Thomas was being held prisoner, and a majority of the vampires felt sorry for him. They don't really know what took place, but Thomas's yellings and ravings had filled them in on what happened. They all met Margret when she visited, and no one dared to question Nicholas about why he killed her, but each one of them knew that if Nicholas had done it, then he must have been ordered to do so by Mason and Mason must have had a reason for wanting her removed which brought their allegiances back to Mason.

"Open the gate; I need to check on Thomas," Henry requested. The two vampires looked unsure.

"Master said not to let anyone enter," one of the guards explained. Henry looked at both with a little hint of anger at the lack of respect they showed him.

"If it was Thomas or Nicholas standing here, would you hesitate to do as they requested? I will not ask again. Open the gate," Henry ordered, and the guards refused to respond. Henry knew that if he explained to them that Mason had asked him to come that they would obey, but he was annoyed by the evident lack of respect they had for him when in his mind, he felt that he was equally as important as Thomas and Nicholas. Angered by their disobedience, before they could blink, he reached for their necks at the same time and snapped them.

Their bodies hit the floor simultaneously, and Henry moved them out of the way. He hoped that when they woke up they would have found a new sense of respect for him. He then proceeded to open the gates, making a loud crashing noise. Thomas heard the noise; he drew a deep breath and filled his lungs with Henry's scents. Finally, he was grateful that someone was coming; he had lost all hope until just now. A part of him told himself he was hallucinating, but then he heard Sebastian rattling his cage to try and get his attention.

"Someone's coming," Sebastian whispered. He hoped that Thomas's body had not shut down. He heard Thomas breathe in slowly and he took a deep breath of his own in relief, grateful that Thomas was still around. Sebastian got up from where he sat; he could tell by the scent who their guest was. He smiled to himself; he knew that Henry would come as he had predicted; his eyes darted towards Thomas. All Thomas had to do was play nice, so that Henry would get him blood; nothing was more important right now. The closer Henry got, the more relieved Thomas felt, even if Henry didn't bring him any blood he was just happy to see him. He always knew that Henry would come, and the fact that he had not come sooner could only be because of Mason.

"Come to gloat, you rascal?" Thomas asked breathlessly. Henry walked down the stairs and stood in front of Thomas's cage.

"You really have seen better days," Henry scoffed,

"This colour looks good on you," he joked, but observing how depreciated Thomas looked saddened him. It reminded him of how they first met. Thomas's dark hair had changed to gray; his skin looked very rough, paper dry and aged; his eyes were tired. He knew what that felt like; it had been a while since Henry had seen a vampire look like that. The only other times had been when they had tortured vampires in the past for information by depriving them of blood. However, never in a million years did he expect to see Thomas in such a state.

"How are you?" Henry managed to ask Thomas. Henry tried to keep his voice a little cheerful. He could smell Sebastian from where he stood, but he refused to acknowledge him. He had been briefed by Mason immediately when they arrived of what was to take place and as much as he liked Sebastian, he believed Mason had to do what he had to do for the benefit of their kind. Henry knew that he had to detach himself from Sebastian the moment he was briefed. The way he saw it now, Sebastian was that one sacrifice that needed to be made for the good of his kind. Although he had told himself that he was not going to acknowledge him, seeing him made it difficult, but he remained undeterred.

"How . . . do you . . . think I am? How come . . . I am red . . . uced to this? I think . . . we are . . . all for . . . getting that . . . it was I, who was wronged?" Thomas questioned; his voice sounded very feeble. He wasn't really expecting a response. He knew Henry didn't have the answers, and the question was really for Mason, but he had to vent his anger anyway.

"All I can say is that I am sorry; you know I love you, and I respect you, and I also love and respect Nicholas. I don't know why he did what he did to you, and perhaps if I were in your position, I would be feeling very murderous, but I am not and I don't know what it truly feels like to love a woman, but I love you both, and I don't want to lose either of you so I propose a solution and as hard as this may be for you, this is the only way forward in this situation. Otherwise who we are and what we stand for will become fractured," Henry said; he wanted to add something more, but he hesitated as he noticed Thomas struggling to stay focused. "This has to stop, and you have the power to stop it," Henry added.

"How?" Thomas questioned.

"Apologise.," Henry responded, and then he added, "I know this is difficult for you, but you need to do what is necessary to get out of this. I need you back, and so does Mason. He does not want to lose either of you. You know what I am getting at, don't you? Thomas, you have to forgive Nicholas. It is difficult, but you must try. I don't know if it will count in your decision to absolve him of what he did to you, but he is not well. It seems like he has gone mad with guilt; he isn't feeding, and he is really in a bad place. What he did to you, he suffers greatly for; why kill him as well?" Henry stopped speaking and waited for Thomas to reply, but he was quiet.

A lot was going through Thomas's mind, like the deal he had made earlier with Sebastian, the guilt he would feel when Henry saw he was working against them. He considered what Henry said about Nicholas being in a terrible state, but Thomas couldn't bring himself to forgive. Remembering the last time, he saw Margret being ripped apart by Nicholas; he knew there was no way he could feel any compassion for Nicholas. However, Thomas also knew if he were to get a chance at freedom, he knew he had to play along and pretend that all was well. He would have his revenge, but first, what he needed more than vengeance now, was blood. A drop, a bag, anything to keep his body from shutting down.

Thomas opened his mouth to speak, but he let out air instead; it was becoming too difficult to form words. Henry knew what that felt like; he had gone through this very treatment at the hands of Thomas when he was newly made. Henry had been made by a woman he dated briefly as a human. Then one day she announced that she was leaving suddenly. She had said she was giving him a parting gift. On her instructions, he closed his eyes and the next thing he felt was a deep bite that left him in agony. The next few days were a nightmare.

The hunger for blood drove him crazy and he lost control. He killed anything and any human he met. It was brought to Mason's attention that a vampire was on the loose and no one came forward to claim him as their own. So, Mason had sent Thomas to manage the situation. The orders were to kill and destroy, but then Thomas found him and brought him back against Mason's behest to destroy all the newly made wild vampires that were bringing the awareness of their kind to the knowledge of humans. To break him, he had locked him up for days, and as he remembered, he didn't last five days before his body shut down. What he remembered most of all was the pain he felt in every cell in his body when Thomas finally gave him blood to revive him.

Henry allowed the memory to fade, and then he turned to face Thomas and whispered, "I brought you a present, but you must be careful; Mason is watching. I wasn't sure he would release you even after I had come to see you. You know that I know what you are going through. Here, come closer," Henry said moving closer to Thomas's cage. Henry knew where the hidden camera was, and he used his back to block the view of the camera so Mason wouldn't see what he was about to do next.

Thomas used every energy to force himself toward Henry who carefully pulled a blood bag from under his shirt. "Here drink a little," he said, handing the bag to Thomas, who grabbed the little bag of blood from Henry and quickly and greedily scoffed it down.

Sebastian was aware that Henry had refused to acknowledge his presence, and it didn't bother him. It only confirmed what he knew to be true, that whatever trouble Mason planned to rain down on him he probably wouldn't survive, which made him more determined to escape. He could smell blood, and that gave him hope. If Thomas got strong, then there was a chance that he would make it, that is if Thomas didn't betray him. What Sebastian wanted more than the world was one last chance to be with Hanna, and he didn't want it to be here in Mason's domain being used as a pawn to kill her. He knew now that it was a terrible thing he did when he came here asking for Mason's help with killing the brothers Anton, Hector, and Zacchary. His stupidity had somehow resulted in Margret's death and now his captivity. The only gain he achieved was the death of two of the brothers and if he made it out of here alive, he promised himself to hunt and kill Hector himself before coming back for Mason.

"Give it back; if I stay here too long, Mason will suspect, if he doesn't already. That should hold you until Mason says it's okay to release you; it shouldn't take too long now, but you must help your cause; just tell me now that you forgive Nicholas and all will be well," Henry said, grabbing the empty blood bag from Thomas.

"Remember, you mustn't show any sign that you have fed or I may be joining you here," Henry warned. Thomas gasped in relief.

The smell of blood made Sebastian hungrier, but he knew he had to control himself. There was no getting away from the whiff of blood that had filled the room. Human blood had a stronger scent than animals' blood, especially since it had been ages since he saw any kind of blood. His body raged inside; he felt like breaking through the cage and ripping the blood bag from Henry's grasp. However, Sebastian knew any movement from him could ruin things; he had taught his body control over the years and that was what he would adopt now.

Thomas licked his lip as every trace of blood on his mouth disappeared.

"Sorry I couldn't get more. So, what do you say? Have you had a change of heart about not killing Nicholas? What should I tell Mason?" Henry asked. Thomas, still licking his lips, felt his taste buds come back to life as he felt a sudden injection of life flow through him. He was grateful to Henry, and he knew, for now, he had to keep the peace if he wanted out of his cage so he could continue to enjoy such pleasures of life as he had become accustomed to. It felt like he hadn't eaten for centuries; however, he knew he had to be careful so as not to give Henry away. Thomas knew Henry was waiting for his answer. His tongue loosened a bit and he took a deep breath to welcome his old self back. He still needed a lot of blood, but what he got was better than nothing.

"Henry, what you are asking is a lot, but, because I know how much Nicholas means to you, I will spare him. On the condition that he keep away from me." Thomas responded to Henry's request for forgiveness. Henry considered Thomas's response and smiled.

"It's not what I want, but I understand, and I can live with that for now. I will tell Mason, and I think he will regard it as good news, for now. I am positive that this change of heart should facilitate your release soon," Henry mentioned as he smiled at his friend.

"Hmm, I hope so. I cannot take this poor treatment of my person any longer. Make sure you tell Nicholas, personally from me, to keep away; upon my release that is the only way there can be peace," Thomas reminded Henry.

"Understood. I must make my leave now. Hopefully, after I relay your change of heart to Mason, I will see you soon," Henry stated.

"Yes, I'm looking forward to freedom myself," Thomas responded as Henry retreated, avoiding Sebastian entirely, an action that didn't elude Thomas. However, Thomas understood why Henry wouldn't bring himself to befriend Sebastian any longer. If he had been in Henry's place, he would have done the same. But, now that he had seen that Mason had no respect for him whatsoever, his allegiance had shifted and, now in Thomas's mind, it was every man for himself.

Chapter 3

Hanna Greene.

Things were clearer now; reading Sebastian's letter and journal made her even more sure that she wanted to be with him at any cost. She had been sick with worry not knowing what had befallen him. Nothing else mattered now but this need she felt inside to be with him. Thoughts of him and the fear of never seeing again invaded her mind constantly. There was no denying the obvious; she loved him. If it were possible, she felt the more her heart yearned for him, the more she was assured that she loved him more than ever she thought possible. Was it because of the guilt that she had punished him for a crime he did not commit? Or the fear that her punishment may now have led to his death? She couldn't bear to think of the latter being true. All Hanna wanted was to find him, to nestle herself in his embrace, and fill her lungs with his scent. To hear his low chuckles, and feel her heart skip a beat each time he said her name. Hanna was sure now that if everything else in her life was a lie, his love for her was true and she would do anything within her powers to get him back. It didn't help that she couldn't use her powers to find him.

Something had changed; it used to be easy to locate him. All she had to do was think about him if she wanted to know where he was. However, since the day of that horrible accident, that dreadful day she saw him dying in that field, she lost her access to him. Why? She wondered. It had been almost three weeks and nothing. If he were dead, it would explain a lot of things; it would explain why she couldn't locate him, but the thought of that even being remotely possibly true killed her. She couldn't bring herself to accept that possibility, not without seeing his body.

The letter he had written her was morbid; it pointed to the obvious, the vision on the field was another reminder she was wasting her time, but Hanna hoped he had survived. Perhaps seeing her on that field may have helped him want to fight to stay alive. Hanna was hoping against hope to see him again. She had read his letter repeatedly; some words could barely be read as her tears had soaked through the ink. Reading that letter brought her no joy, but as if she wanted to punish herself for neglecting him for years, she tortured herself each time she read it until it was so painful for a single tear to pass through her eye.

It made sense to search for her birth mother now, but without Sebastian, Hanna didn't have the will to do anything else or to even want to live life. Every day she focussed on tracking him.

She laughed out, in frustration, at the irony of her situation; the two people she considered precious to her were beyond her reach, and with all the power she possessed, she had no idea where to start.

Now that everything was out in the open, it was up to her to stop letting anything get in the way of her love for him. Three years was a long time to lie to one's self, she thought; if the truth be told, the moment she decided to walk away from him she had stopped living and now, she would fight and give her life to get back what she had thrown away. The times she spent with Sebastian were the best days of her life. And now she needed him as one needs air to breathe. At the same time, when she had thought he was responsible for the death of her birth mother, she wanted him to suffer. She understood why; it was because she knew that by his revealing what he had done, what he thought he had done, she had to make him suffer for destroying what they had and what they could have been. She would have preferred that he had denied it all.

Hanna wondered, if by some miracle, he still lived, she wondered if after Sebastian found out the truth, if he would still look at her or want her like he used to. Would he forgive her for putting him through all that pain? Or would he reject her and do unto her as she did to him? Thinking about it clearly now, she thought, Sebastian had protected her and provided for her all her life and at the first sign of trouble, she had repaid him by abandoning him. The madness that was Sebastian consumed her day and night. To feel closer to him, Hanna decided to go back to where it all started. She drove to the house she shared with him briefly in Grosmont Yorkshire. Going to Grosmont was difficult; it was where she had first fallen madly in love with him and where all the chaos in her life began. The only other time she had been back here since she left with Sebastian to go to France, was when she had to come help Suzan, Hurrit, Denali's sister before she was taken to join the rest of her wolf family in Scotland. The whole tribe moved into one of the Scottish forests to live out their lives in their wolf forms. Hilda would be next; she would soon turn eighteen, and Hanna knew she had to ensure that she was also taken to the Scottish forest. Hilda had made some threats the last time she saw her. If Hanna recalled, her exact words were, "The next time I see you, one of us is going to die." Hanna had not taken the threat seriously, although it had remained at the back of her mind. The town held too many bad memories, all wrapped up in her fondest and most loving memories of falling in love for the very first time. Her parents Joan and Joseph had died here too, and she never got to say goodbye.

However, this was not the time for that; she pushed the thought from her mind. She could only deal with one thing at a time, and priority number one now was finding Sebastian.

Driving into Sebastian's driveway, her mind took her back to the first time he drove her to his home. Her heart began pounding hard against her ribs, and her eyes watered; she felt so close to him here. She got out of the car and turned to face the house. Hanna imagined him standing outside, welcoming her with open arms. Her heart raced wildly and saddened at the realization that it was all in her head. Hanna took a deep breath as visions of him faded. She then went in search of the house key. After a few minutes, she found the key hidden under a plant pot. Using the key, Hanna turned the doorknob and stepped inside. The house smelled a little dusty, but Sebastian's scent still filled the space. Everything was clean; it didn't look like he had returned since the last time they left together for Paris. Hanna stepped into the living room, walking over to the sofa she used to sit on, she rested her body and gently coiled her feet on the couch she looked over at the empty chair where Sebastian usually sat.

Her eyes clouded over and pain-filled tears again rolled freely down her cheeks. She didn't bother to wipe them away. She couldn't stop herself even if she tried. If only she knew what to do; her instinct had made her come here; she couldn't stop crying. Being in his house, smelling him everywhere, was too much of a punishment. She ran upstairs to his room, opened the door, she walked toward his bed. She had spent time here in this bed with him wrapped snugly in his embrace, and she wanted to remember exactly how it felt.

Hanna sat on the bed and ran her hands over the bedspread as though it were him. Her eyes shifted to the chest of drawers in his room. She got up and opened it; there were some plain T-shirts neatly folded. She reached in and took one and held it close to her nose. His scents filled her up again. It was more than she could take; she tried again to find something in her mind, but she got nothing. The realization that she may never see him again struck her fresh; her heart felt like it would explode from the sorrow that suddenly consumed her. She had thought coming here would help; instead, she was going into a depression.

This was too much; Hanna found it difficult to think of a solution to help him and herself. She went back to the living room and sat on the sofa. For the first time in a long time, she felt powerless. She got up from the sofa and went over to Sebastian's chair; she knelt in front of it and tried to imagine him in it, sitting in front of her, like they had done the day that she had first told him that she loved him.

She closed her eyes and allowed the memories to pour in, her heart longing for his presence and at that moment, his face flashed before her. She opened her eyes in astonishment; never in a million years did she think that would work. She had just seen him, and this was no memory. It felt as though he were allowing her in, like a shut door was suddenly opened. This was unbelievable; hope surged through her. Hanna closed her eyes again and repeated the memories of him that connected her with him moments ago; this time, his face became clearer than the last time she saw him. She noticed he was in a dark confined space, and his body coiled into a ball; he didn't look well.

She was bursting on the inside with joy, not at the fact that he was suffering, but because he was alive; she had feared the worst, but somehow fate had decided to turn things around for her. Unsure of what to do, she whispered his name.

"Sebastian, Sebastian!" she called out. At first, there was nothing; Hanna wondered if she had imagined seeing him because she was so grieved in her heart. "S," she tried again, and then his eyes flung wide open.

Chapter 4

Sebastian Francis

He didn't move, but he was aware of her presence; he wasn't sure if he was due to his restless mind, but he had heard her voice, called out his name, but he thought he had imagined it, and then he heard her call him "S." He had never thought he would hear her call him that again. Confused, he opened his eyes; Sebastian wondered if he were hallucinating; the lack of blood easily explained it. He didn't move; if this were Hanna, he had to be sure. He had made a deal with Thomas, and since Thomas's release, it seemed that Thomas has reneged on their plans. Sebastian had been counting the days since he was imprisoned although now he has lost count as he is unable to tell day from night.

Mason Benedict had come a day after Henry visited and had given a heartfelt apology to Thomas, and then had him released. Sebastian had no chance to speak to Thomas after his discussion with Mason. Henry had helped Thomas out of the cell, and Sebastian kept looking at Thomas for a sign to show he was still on board, but he gave him nothing. All he saw was his back, and then he disappeared. After Thomas's departure, Mason then turned his attention on him and smiled.

"You don't have anything to worry about, Son; whatever you had planned with Thomas is over now that he is out. He knows where his loyalty lies," Mason said. Sebastian hated the way he called him Son; however, he refused to honour Mason with a reply. Now that they were at this point, there was no longer need for pretentious pleasantries, and he wasn't going to give Mason his attention.

Mason noticed Sebastian's deliberate attempts to ignore his presence.

"A lot must be going through your mind; believe me, I never wanted to get close to you. It would have been easier for the two of us if we were complete strangers; then you would not be feeling betrayed. However, I had to do what I must to preserve my happiness. There were times when I almost gave up on my plans because you fascinate me. I almost did love you as a son, but the truth is that you are not my son; even when I reached out, you always made it clear you wanted nothing to do with me. So, then it made it easier to see you as a pawn in all of this." Mason said. Sebastian looked up and met Mason's eyes but said nothing; then he looked away.

"I know this is hard to hear, but you deserve the truth. Ultimately, your joy was never going to make me happy. It's meant to be every man for himself in this world, but I have a bigger and better plan for our kind. What must happen for our kind, is greater than you and I and it comes at a cost. Now, you must wonder where do you fit in all of this?" Mason asked rhetorically before continuing to answer his own question.

"You are here because you are needed. It is your destiny to help your kind walk the light. It is in a way an honour to be the one to lead us to the child of power" Mason paused to see if Sebastian had any words for him. The mention of the child of power roused Sebastian's anger, but Sebastian knew there was nothing he could do. He had not fed in a while and even if he had, he stood no chance against Mason. If he showed rage, he would be losing the reserve energy his body was surviving on. A glare was all he could manage, the sight of Mason disgusted him.

"You must have a million questions for me. Go on ask me. I can tell by the look on your face; ask me anything and I will answer truthfully," Mason said. Sebastian was quiet. Mason chuckled when Sebastian refused to respond. "Have it your way then." As Mason proceeded to leave, Sebastian spoke.

"How long had you been planning this?" Sebastian asked, and Mason turned toward him; he had a wicked grin on his face, and it made Sebastian wish that he had the strength to overpower Mason. He imagined himself bursting out of his cell and wrapping his hands-around Mason's neck, and not letting go until his head was detached from his body.

"Ah, he speaks. Very clever question. Well, let's put it this way. Before you were ever made. It's been a long time coming, and it's nothing personal. However, since you asked, and I do not have to pretend that you are my guest any longer; I will tell you the truth." He paused before continuing.

"I fell in love with a human witch; it's a funny story actually. She had been sent by a rival to kill me. Then, every strong vampire had to have a powerful witch by their side. Annemarie overpowered my sorcerer and was going to kill me next, but she had never met me before, or so she thought. I always knew to watch my back; I knew her mother, who was, in her lifetime, a very powerful witch. I had told her mother then that I would look after her daughter should anything happen to her. Annemarie was only a teenager, not older than sixteen in human years then, and she was very beautiful. I loved her the moment I saw her. When her mother passed, before I could get to the child, my rival had taken Annemarie and he had groomed her to become his weapon. I had to prove to her that I was a friend and not a foe. It was not easy to make her see things my way. We spoke about things at length, I reminded her of her mother and the promise I had made to protect her. It was a miracle when she eventually saw things my way and together we took out my rival. Since then we became a team, but the

34

difference was that I was in love with her, I had been since I first saw her, although I hid it from her. Years passed and she grew more beautiful and as she grew, my love deepened for her. It was even more painful to watch as suitors came for her. It took all the strength I had not to rip in two every man that dared look at her. It got worse for me; she accepted another man's proposal of marriage and came to tell it to me. I couldn't bear the thought of her in another man's arms. She belonged to me, but I couldn't stop her happiness. I mourned her loss even though she had not yet married the human. I kept my distance because I couldn't bear seeing her so happy and knowing that I was not the reason she was joyful. Time passed, and we didn't see each other for a while. A few days before her wedding to this human, she came to find me. I had gone to sulk, and the first thing she said to me was, "Would you have let me marry that man when you knew I belong with you?" Mason paused and looked on longingly into space as though his mind had transported him back in time. He took a deep breath before continuing.

"I didn't know what to say; I got up from where I sat, happy to see her, but not quite understanding what she was saying." He smiled,

"When I didn't say anything, she looked annoyed; I didn't want that, but I couldn't find the words to make her understand what she meant to me." Mason shook his head and wrapped his fingers on the bars on Sebastian's cage as he let his mind take him to his past.

"So, she said, I have seen you fight wars Mason Benedict. I have seen you at your best, and no one comes close to your fierceness. You to me are the bravest, but darling how you cower when it concerns me. I love you. I have loved you for a very long time, and it saddens me that you can't tell. I have waited for you to let me know that you want me, need me even. When you wouldn't tell me how you felt, I have unwillingly allowed men to come to stir you into jealousy in hopes that perhaps you would tell me that you want me, that you need me, that you love me because I love you a great deal." Mason paused again.

"I felt like I was flying as she spoke those words to me; it felt like a great symphony; my heart, my being, my mind rejoiced. All I heard was that she loved me. I found myself moving closer to her until there was no space between us. I wanted to carry her, and hold her and thank her, but I couldn't find the words to express how much I was feeling." Mason laughed softly,

"Then she asked, 'Do you love me, Mason Benedict?' I looked at her; she was so delicate, so beautiful, and I said, from the very first day I saw you, my love. I have been sick daily with love for you; you are my world; you are all I want and need. She laughed, and for the first time, I held her in my arms like I had always dreamed. Since that day, we were inseparable. We got married shortly after, and together we did everything and conquered all our enemies together. Her powers enabled her to cheat death for so many centuries; she was the greatest and most powerful witch, but soon we ran out of luck. Her powers began to dwindle; we had used every magical being we could lay our hands on to keep her alive. There was nothing else we could do. I couldn't imagine the world without her in it; I told her if she died, that I would end my existence, but she told me that there was a way, but I had to be patient; she had heard a rumour; someone had spoken of a child and I had to go and find out the truth. So, I began to travel in search for answers and one day; I ran into a man that foretold the birth of the child of power and a vampire of purity and of a love so rare. Love so rare?" Mason paused and then scoffed,

"What makes your love for Hanna more special or rarer than my love for Annie? Anyway, I now had hope of a future with Annie. I rejoiced greatly; I knew now that we had a way, even if it meant waiting for centuries for that child to be born. I was prepared to do my part, to do anything to reunite myself with my love. I returned home and told Annie what I had heard; she believed, so I believed even more. Annie used the last of her powers to forge a ring, and the ring held the essence of her life and the powers she possessed and all we had to do was wait. Then she died. It was hard losing her, but I knew if I planned it right, we would be together again. So, I waited, and now we are here. So now you understand what drives me. You have loved too; you know how that feeling takes over your being. I would do anything; I would cross anyone; I would destroy anything that stands in my way just so I could be with her again," Mason said as he stared down at Sebastian. All Sebastian felt in his core was hate; he didn't give a hoot about Mason's dead witch or their love; all he heard was Mason's desperation to use him to get to Hanna so he could use her to bring his evil wife back.

"So how did you know I would be the one to target?" Sebastian questioned

"Ah, that. The child of power would have a weakness, a vampire who had not been tarnished with human blood, a vampire of purity. Mason stopped to laugh at that one.

He continued, "I must say that was the part I found difficult to believe; until you, I had never met a vampire that did not feed on humans. To find you, I had to play the long game. It was not a coincidence that you found me locked away in that dungeon; I had been waiting for you for years; I had to set a trap and you fell into my lap. If I am sincere, I liked you and I . . . I . . . liked your mother as well. But, she wasn't my Annie; she tried to make me forget and I would have, but you returned the ring to me. Do you remember?" Mason asked showing Sebastian the ring on his finger.

"I could have loved your mother, but the ring--once you gave it back to me--it fought against my will to love your mother. Your mother was beautiful and I liked her a lot; there were times I thought I loved her. She didn't know about my quest. We met each other behind your back. I insisted you were kept in the dark about us. At first, it wasn't serious, but Elizabeth wanted more than I was willing to offer. She almost had me; she declared her love for me numerous times, and I was very fond of her, but I am not one to be unfaithful. Loving Elizabeth would have been a betrayal to Annie. How could I love her when my heart belonged to another? I finally made up my mind about your mother; she served no purpose; she distracted me from my mission and so she had to die. I needed you closer than I needed her and I took care of it." He paused to see if Sebastian had anything to say in response. He could see the rage on Sebastian's face as he tried to process what he was being told.

"You killed all those humans to avenge your mother when in fact it was I that took her life so you could become mine." Mason stopped to see if Sebastian now understood what he had revealed.

Sebastian got up from where he sat; his hands shook in fury, but he knew what Mason was doing, and he wasn't going to give him the satisfaction. First, he wanted Hanna, the woman he loved and now, he'd just told him, he murdered his mother. Mason stepped back as Sebastian held the bars of his confinement tightly; his jaws were clenched and his eyes brewed with anger.

"Who are you? She cared about you and you murdered her for it. Why would you do that to her or to me? Sebastian asked through gritted teeth.

"You know who I am. I just told you. I don't have anything particularly against you; I just need to do what I have to do. You ask who I am. I am what I need to be when I need to be what I need to be. It's that simple," Mason responded.

"You said she loved you; that isn't a crime. You're a hateful cruel sociopath; why did you have to kill her over a dead witch that you may never see again?" Sebastian asked bitterly.

Mason's jaw tightened, and he rubbed his hands on his ring to stop himself from getting angry.

"You are well within your right to be angry, but your anger serves me no purpose; neither does it make me remorseful. I did what I had to do. Elizabeth~as beautiful and gentle as she was~she was not Annie; she tried; she almost made me reconsider, but the ring, in it is Annie's soul. It always keeps me focused. Plus, Elizabeth was . . ."

"She was what?" Sebastian pushed.

"Elizabeth sheltered you and wrapped you in her cocoon. Your path had to go dark; she raised you on animal blood; you were unspoiled and that served its purpose to a point. You had to be who she raised you for our paths to cross, but that was done now. The next agenda was for you to meet the child of power, but that could not happen with her mothering you the way she did. You had to go dark, so I came to town. I killed her maker; I was responsible for all the killings that caused the panic. I had eyes everywhere; I had been watching you. It's only proper; you were too important to my cause for me to allow her to take you from my grip. So, when you went hunting your squirrels, I showed up. She was surprised to see me; she thought I had changed my mind about being with her, but of course, she was wrong. I convinced her to come out with me; I remember, her eyes glowed with joy at my sight, which brought a smile to my face. She looked exceptionally stunning, especially that night; if I weren't strongly committed to my cause to reunite with Annie, I suppose that night she could have changed my mind. I couldn't resist caressing and touching her fair face; I knew it would be the last time I saw her, and it saddened me. For a moment, staring into her beautiful eyes, I felt like I could love her too; I felt something in my core for her, but then my fingers, my hands, started to shake and my eyes drifted toward the ring, and my mind snapped back to its senses. I was reminded that I belonged to another." Mason paused shortly, it felt as though for the first time he was remorseful, but he didn't want Sebastian to see it.

Sebastian's breathing raged wildly; the more he heard the angrier he became. He knew he had to control himself or his body would go into sudden shock; he didn't want Mason to get that satisfaction.

"At last, Elizabeth was in the way; she had to die. I remember the yearnings in her eyes as she looked at me. She lifted herself up on her toes and pressed her lips on mine . . . she kissed me." Mason placed his hands on his lip as though he could still feel her lips on his. "Her eyes were closed; she looked perfect. Then I knew it; I had to do it then. It was quick and painless. I can still see the shock in her eyes as they flew open and her life drained away. I ended her." Mason stopped speaking and walked over to the wall opposite Sebastian's cage, and then he leaned his weight as though he felt relieved now that he had finally told the truth about Elizabeth's death.

This was all too much for Sebastian; he could tell that Mason was telling the truth, but he didn't want to bring himself to believe it.

"If what you say is true, how come I never smelled you there?" Sebastian asked.

Mason laughed, before speaking, "I have lived for over two thousand years' boy; I know how to mask my presence. I compelled a bunch of humans to your home; I knew you would be very eager to avenge her death, and I provided you an avenue to do what you needed to do to bring you to the other side." Mason paused to draw a deep breath before continuing his confession.

"Ah, I thrust a stake in her heart so you would think that the humans had killed her, and then I set her body on fire. When I sensed you running home like I knew you would, I compelled the humans to run away so you were convinced of their guilt. And now we are here; listen, thinking about it now, I admit to myself that I did love your mother, but I don't think it was enough. It's either that or whatever Annie did made it impossible to see a future with another woman. My point is if I could do that to a person I love, I would stop at nothing to get my way," Mason stated.

Sebastian laughed softly; he was beyond angry, and he knew now that the only way he would be okay was when he killed Mason himself.

"Why do you laugh?" Mason asked.

"I laugh at you and your pathetic, ludicrous excuse. You obviously do not know what love is. Love isn't what you think it is. Oh, maybe you once knew, but that love you crave is done. My mother should never have involved herself with you; she knew better, but she always thought the best of everyone. You, you never deserved her love, and that is why I will make sure that you pay for every pain you have caused." With his fist clenched tightly to his cage, his nose flared up in anger, Sebastian snarled as he continued to speak. "Now, listen here, you old, vile, spiteful viper. I will die before I let you touch a strand of Hanna's hair, and you will not use me for your gain. Oh no, you deceive yourself, but I promise you this, so you listen good and listen carefully. I will be free of you and then I will come back and destroy everything that you have built or own. I will kill everyone that answers to you until you have no one left. And for my mother's sake, I will take from you the very corpse of that evil witch you claim to love, and I will destroy her body together with any hope you had ever dreamed of having a future with her. When I have done this, Mason Benedict, I will return for you. I will rip your head from your neck slowly so you feel every ounce of pain you have caused me. I will split your body open from limb to limb and tear you into tiny pieces before dumping you at the bottom of the ocean. Look at me very well Mason Benedict; you think you know evil; think again. This is not a threat; it's a debt I owe you, and I will pay you back every single evil coin you have dealt me," Sebastian warned. Mason began laughing; at first it was a low chuckle that gradually turned into a full-blown laughter.

"You mock me. I expected better from you. Pray tell, how do you suppose you will do all that locked away in this dungeon? I commend your spirit, your resolute stoutness, but my boy, may I remind you that every vampire here is at least older than you by six centuries. Do not let your recent victories cloud your judgment. You are far too disadvantaged for your threats to count. I have dealt with stronger and worthier opponents in my lifetime. Trust me; I would not lose any sleep over you." Then he began to chuckle again as he started to walk away. He stopped by Sebastian's cage and shook his head before resuming his laughter, and then he took his leave.

"Laugh all you like, but remember I owe you a debt Mason," Sebastian warned as Mason's steps faded away.

Chapter 5

That was twelve days ago; since then, no one had visited, not even Thomas. It had been almost three weeks, and the lack of food had begun to take its toll. Sebastian had no strength left; he had nothing in reserve; his body would shut down soon and he knew it. He had been going into spasms every now and then; the next shock could knock him unconsciousness. Mason was experimenting on him; he had never seen anything like it, and he wanted to see just how long Sebastian would last. All hopes of Sebastian escaping had vanished; reluctantly, he had started accepting that Mason had won. Not knowing what would happen from there on, his mind went to Hanna. He tried to picture her face, her smile; if he died here and she lived, it would be okay, he thought, although he would have loved one more moment with her. Just as his mind was filled with memories of her, he heard her voice call his name twice. It was all in his head, he reckoned. Sebastian's eyes were closed as he tried to welcome the inevitable, but then, she spoke again and this time around, she called him "S."

In his weakened state, excitement surged through him; Sebastian wondered if he were hallucinating again. He knew troubled minds conceive desperate ideas that bring about all sorts of imaginations, and he was sure that he was hearing things that weren't real.

"S. Can you hear me?" he heard her voice again, and this time, his hope was raised. His eyes opened wide, and he blinked once in response to her voice. He could hear her, but he couldn't feel her presence; he looked about him carefully not wanting to alert anyone that someone was communicating with him. Sebastian was not sure what to expect; he knew Hanna's voice, and she was the only one that called him "S." What did she want? he wondered, not that he wasn't grateful, but his mind began to race, wondering all sorts of things. For some time now he had refused to think about her, not because he didn't want to, but the pain of rejection and the realization that he was going to be used to lure her to her end troubled him.

"Hold on my love, I am coming to get you," Hanna said.

"No!" Sebastian mouthed; he didn't want her there and he didn't want to give her away. He was convinced this was Mason at work; this was all he wanted, and now he was going to get his way. However, there was something different in her tone. He thought he had heard her call him, "My love." Something had changed; the last time he checked her birth mother was still dead, and he had been the one responsible. He laughed to himself. He knew it now; he was hallucinating. Then suddenly, before he could finish his thoughts, a brightness filled his cage; it reminded him of the time he had thought she died and he wanted to kill himself. Before he could make sense of what was happening, he saw her standing in front of him. His mouth opened in astonishment, but there was no time to waste as Hanna, grabbed his hands and said, "I am taking you home now S." Sebastian had seen her disappear from his presence before when he lay on the beach after she came to rescue him from beneath the ocean, but after that day he never thought he had a chance with her again; nor did he think she would come and save him again. That could only mean one thing; she still cared he concluded.

One minute he was in a cage and the next he was on the floor of his home in Grosmont Yorkshire.

Sebastian looked on in disbelief; if he had tears in his eyes, he would be crying right about now. Hanna's eyes looked tearful; her face was just a few inches away from his and being this close to her felt like paradise, but he still wasn't sure any of this was real.

"Wake up," he murmured to himself repeatedly. The thing with desperate minds is that they can conjure up any situation they want; surely that is all that was going on here. He wanted her face to be the last he saw before he became unconscious, and he must have slipped into another world where things were just as he wanted them. Sebastian shook his head in disbelief as Hanna leaned over him.

"No, no . . . you are not real; go away . . . you . . . you can't be real," he whispered. Hanna held him closer to herself, pulling him up so that his head rested on her lap as she wrapped her hands around him to comfort and assure him that she was, in fact, the one with him.

"It's me, my love; I'm real. I'm real. I am okay; I am here with you, am here now," Hanna reassured him; he stared at her as she tried to calm him. His mind began to feel at peace as he started to believe his reality. Suddenly, his body began to seize.

Hanna panicked, "What's wrong S, what happened to you?" her eyes were fearful; she had never seen him look this frail. Sebastian was too tired to speak, but he knew if she were real then before they could both talk about anything, first he had to feed.

"I . . . I . . . need bl . . . ood," he managed to say. Hanna looked around, not knowing what to do; she brought out her wrist for him to feed on and placed it next to his mouth.

"Sebastian, listen to me; you have to feed on me; there is nothing else here; okay; do you understand? Drink from me," Hanna said, pushing her wrist in front of his mouth. Sebastian grabbed her wrist with his hands and pushed it away.

"No! No, never, never Hanna, never," he said breathlessly; his voice was harsh with disappointment.

"But you have to feed; I don't mind, and I don't have anything else to give you," Hanna insisted.

"I said . . . no. Go, find me a dog . . . anything . . . but not . . . you," Sebastian insisted. She was frustrated but saw his determination not to touch her blood.

"Okay wait. I will be back shortly. I will find you something," Hanna assured him gently as she placed his head on the rug and rushed out. She got into her car and drove away. She had no idea where she would find an animal, but she knew she had to find him something fast.

She drove from street to street, aimlessly looking around. *What was she doing?* she wondered. She would not take him someone's pet and if she couldn't do that, what was next to do? Then she remembered an animal shelter not far from the town centre. She had gone there once with her father Joseph when he bought her dog, Stone. Hanna drove straight there and parked her car in front of the shelter. There was a man at the reception area; he was on the phone when she entered. She waited impatiently for him to finish speaking; all the while she worried about what could be happening to Sebastian if she didn't arrive with something soon. When he finished, he smiled at her, and Hanna nodded in response and without wasting time, she said. "I need a dog."

"Hmm, okay, um, do you know the type of breed you want?" Hanna shook her head; she felt terrible coming to a place that was meant to be saving animals from violence; the irony of it ate at her, but she had to help Sebastian feel better.

"Am not sure; any will do I guess; I want two," Hanna replied trying her best not to look guilty.

"Okay, since you don't know the breed you want, do you mind coming with me? I will show them to you and you can pick the ones you like," the man told Hanna who shrugged and followed him out back to where the dogs were kept. As they approached, the dogs began yelping, barking, and wagging their tails. She looked from one dog to the other; they all looked too adorable for her to take to their death. Heavy guilt filled her up. There was no way she could do it; she stopped in front of their coop and patted their heads as they jumped up and down in their cages.

"I can't do this," she admitted to herself.

"Sorry, what did you say?" the shopkeeper asked.

"I'm sorry, but I have wasted your time; I need to go," Hanna said as she ran out of the shelter to her car. In the comfort of her car, Hanna broke down. She felt helpless, but she knew those dogs weren't the solution to helping Sebastian. She wondered what would happen if she couldn't get the blood to him. Worried and sick with guilt, Hanna drove away quickly before she changed her mind.

Not knowing what to do, Hanna parked her car near the woodland and began walking the woods. She remembered Sebastian once told her he hunted there for squirrel sometimes. If she found one, she reckoned killing a squirrel wasn't as bad as taking him a rescued dog. After walking around the woods for about twenty minutes and finding nothing, Hanna knew she had left him for too long; she revisited going back to the animal shelter, but then, she pushed it out of her mind again. Disappointed, Hanna tried to retrace her steps to her car; then she heard a sheep's *baa* and then she remembered there was a farm close by. Better a sheep than a dog, she thought. She rushed back to her car and drove to the farm. Hanna knew she must convince the farmers to sell her a couple of sheep, and she was positive that with the right amount of money they will be willing.

As Hanna arrived at the farm, a man was tending to the pigs. She parked her car and walked up to the man.

"Hello," she said to the farmer; he stopped feeding the pigs and turned his attention on her.

"How can I help you, Miss?" he asked.

"Sorry to disturb you; I was driving through and I saw your farm," Hanna said; the farmer looked at her without saying anything. Hanna knew she still needed to tell him why she was there.

"I don't live far from here; I was just wondering if you don't mind my looking around," she asked.

"Sorry, Miss, this farm is not open to the public," the farmer said in his thick, northern accent.

"Oh, I'm sorry; I didn't mean to pry; I was just curious. I 'll go now," Hanna said, half expecting the man to extend a welcoming hand, but he turned and resumed feeding the pigs. Hanna knew she couldn't leave without at least taking one animal with her.

"Erm . . . sorry, I don't mean to keep disturbing; I actually forgot to ask; I just wonder. Are any of these animals for sale?" Hanna questioned.

"Sorry Miss, I only work here, I'm not the owner," the man replied without turning towards her.

"Oh, okay, but um suppose I was interested in getting my hands on some of your animals—how do I go about buying a lamb or two—say for two hundred pounds. Do you think the owner will consider my offer?" Hanna pushed with hopes that she would get lucky. The man turned to face her as though he felt insulted, and started to walk away. "Five hundred?" Hanna asked desperately. The man stopped and faced her, his eyes narrowed curiously.

"Why would you want to pay five hundred for a lamb?" he asked.

"Oh, not one lamb; I need two," Hanna clarified.

"If you want two, then you will have to pay a thousand pounds," the man said trying his luck now that he had seen how desperate she was for the animals.

"A thousand pounds for two sheep?" Hanna asked. Bewildered, her voice went high, and suddenly recognizing the man's greed, she knew she had no choice; she drew a deep breath.

"Okay deal, but you have to make it quick." The man reached out for the money; Hanna took out her purse and counted five hundred pounds in fifties. Before placing it in the man's hands, she said. "Half now, and half when you deliver the two sheep; I am parked out front."

"The agreement was for two lambs, not sheep," the man said.

"It doesn't matter which it is; I don't care either way. If you want this money, then make it quick. I just need two animals; it can be goats, or oxen, two sheep or even one of these dirty swine although I would rather not deal with those, just as long as they are farm animals. Do we have a deal?" Hanna asked as she held the money out in her hands.

The man reached to take the money from her.

"Okay give me the money. I will see you in thirty minutes." Hanna handed the money to the man.

"One more thing, could you please, tie them up so they can fit in my boot?" The man nodded and Hanna went back to her car to wait.

Thirty minutes passed and the man did not show; another fifteen minutes flew by and still he was no show. Hanna worried; she began to think that she had been swindled. She wondered if he noticed how desperate she was to get her hands on the animals. Hanna came out of her car and thought about going to the farm to find the man when she saw him pushing a cart toward her.

She sighed in relief; she had been gone from Sebastian too long, but it was better to show up late than to go back empty handed in this case. She smiled. As the man approached, Hanna opened her car truck and the man stopped in front of her.

"You took your time. I thought you had swindled me," she joked as the man began loading the animals into her boot.

"I seriously considered it, but you were in luck; I spoke to my father about selling the sheep and he said *no*. By the way, my father owns the farm. He said to give you a couple of calves. You said you weren't choosy, and they were going to be disposed of anyway," the man said.

"Thanks," Hanna said and added. "I'm glad you decided not to swindle me." She shut the door to her truck and she then gave him the balance of the money and she was going to enter the car when the man asked.

"What do you need them for anyway?" he asked Hanna who looked at him not knowing what to say.

"I ask only because you are not really particular about what animal you get," the man continued to probe.

Hanna smiled, "I don't mean to be rude but it's none of your business; you got your money they are mine now," Hanna said, the man shrugged his shoulders nonchalantly.

She got into the car while the man counted the money. Happy that she had something, Hanna drove quickly to Grosmont house. Opening the boot, she tried to lift one of the calves from the boot, but it was incredibly heavy. She wished Sebastian weren't so predisposed. She wondered if she needed to use her powers to get the animals inside. She laughed at the ridiculousness of it, but she knew there was no other way. She held onto both calves and imagined where she wanted to go and in an instant, she appeared in the sitting room with the two animals. She ran straight to Sebastian; his body looked paler than when she had left him; she shook him; he managed to open his eyes, but he could not speak. His mouth opened slightly; she knew she had to kill the animals right away; drain them of their blood and feed it to him. Sighing, she ran to the kitchen and obtained a knife. She took the knife sharpener and sharpened the blade of the knife. Then she took a bowl and a towel and returned to the sitting room. Looking at the animals, her stomach turned, but then she took one look at Sebastian and she knew she had no choice. She wondered how she could make it painless for the animals; she turned her attention to the first animal and regrettably said.

"Feel no pain as you depart; be at peace for your soul gives life again." And then she placed the towel over the face of the calf and killed it, making sure the blood drained into the bowl. The animal didn't jerk or move in pain and she had drained all its blood. She moved to the other animal and did the same as the first. When she had finished draining the blood, she dragged the lifeless carcass to the kitchen. While in the kitchen, Hanna searched and found a funnel she would use to pour the blood into Sebastian's mouth.

Chapter 6

Hanna placed the funnel in his mouth and began pouring the blood a little at a time until every drop was gone. She had first thought that she would be able to save half of the blood, but his body was not responding, so she decided he needed all of it. She wondered how long it had been since he last fed. After she had poured the last drop of blood, Hanna waited for him to move, and then suddenly, she saw the veins on his face begin to pop, as if he were in pain; his eyes rolled, but his body remained still. Hanna wondered if there was anything she could do to help ease his pain. His eyes warned her to stay away, so she stepped back and watched in horror as he endured the pain that was consuming him. It brought back memories of all the times she had seen him punish himself, and she felt guilty. She turned her back and stepped away because she couldn't face seeing him that way; but then, she heard him say her name.

"Ha . . . nna, Hanna. Please, don't leave," Sebastian begged; consumed with pain, he panicked when he thought she was leaving again. Tears clouded her eyes, and she returned to him swiftly.

"I'm here my love; I am not going anywhere," Hanna said as she knelt at his side. Sebastian's body felt like it was on fire; every cold dead cell struggled to regain life and strength from the blood flowing down his body. However, because Hanna was near him, the pain felt bearable. He wanted her close to him as if his life depended on it. He wanted to look at her beautiful face and get lost in her big, beautiful, dreamy blue eyes. He noted that he had heard her call him "My love" three times.

Although he was in pain, he felt like shouting for joy. It didn't make sense that she was here now after three years; she was acting like the Hanna he knew before his confession to her in France, but he wasn't complaining; he was just not sure why she finally decided he was worth her forgiveness. Hanna placed his head on her lap again and her heart skipped several beats as her body touched his. She drew a deep breath and held herself together not wanting to give away how she was feeling inside knowing that he would be able to hear how fast her heart was beating. If things were different, and he weren't so frail and in pain, she would be asking his forgiveness now after which she hoped that he would be willing to take her back. Some parts of his body were already looking alive, but it seemed that he still had a long time to go before fully recovering. There was a lot they needed to talk about, a lot of healing to make up for the pain.

Hanna stared at him and weaved her hands into the locks of his head that lay on her lap. Sebastian closed his eyes; this was too good to be true; he didn't want to open his eyes and wake up to find that he had made it all up in his head. The more he felt her hands move freely over his hair, the more he assured himself that this was real. After many hours, the pain subsided; Sebastian's body gave in to sleep against his will. When he finally woke up, he took in his surroundings, noting to himself that he was still indeed at his house in Grosmont. Hanna had placed a cushion under his head to support him, however, she was nowhere to be found. Then, something disgusting hit his nostril; he recognized that smell very well; it was the smell of human food. He smiled and sighed in relief. It felt like all his Christmases had come at once. The smell of human food meant that she was still around. He sat up not knowing what to do and wondering whether or not he should go to her. It felt awkward not knowing what to do; what came naturally to him was the feeling of wanting to be next to her, but *What if she isn't ready for that yet,* he thought. Wanting to see her, he got up and walked cautiously to the kitchen and saw the carcass of two animals lying on the kitchen floor, one was missing a leg.

The missing leg was cooking in a pot; Sebastian smiled; still wanting to see her, he walked toward the stairs; he could hear the shower, from where he stood. In that instance, he became aware of his dirty clothes; he really didn't want to see her again in such a state. He walked up the stairs, and as he made his way to his room, memories of the times he shared with her here came rushing back, and it made him happy that she was here with him now. The shower stopped before he reached the door to his room; that was when he realized that she had been using the shower in his master bedroom. Not wanting to put her out, Sebastian went into another room and turned the shower on. He washed from top to bottom, after which he dried with a towel and found some spare joggers he had left in the bathroom chest a while back. Although he had no clean top to wear, Sebastian was happy that he had thoroughly washed the dungeon dirt from his hair and body. He felt like his old self; not wanting to be indecent before Hanna, he waited until she went downstairs before going into his room to get a top. As he entered, he saw her personal belongings scattered on the floor of his room. It looked like she had been staying in his room for a while. Sebastian opened his chest to fetch a t-shirt; the door to his room flung opened and there she was.

His body froze at the sight; she looked so beautiful. Her hair was still wet and swept back; he found it hard to breathe, and he didn't know what to do. Now that she was before him. Hanna stared at him; she knew he was beautiful to look at but she had never seen him bare chested, and she loved what she was looking at.

"Sorry . . . erm . . . I . . . I didn't see you downstairs. I panicked," she explained. Sebastian managed a smile. "You look...good, for someone that has been through hell and back," she added. She noticed he was just staring at her and it made her heart jump. This was her man in front of her, and all she wanted in that moment was to bury herself in his embrace. However, she knew she couldn't do that—not after all the ways he had suffered because of her. Hanna waited for him to say something, but he just stared at her; she wasn't sure now that he was okay with her here, or if he wanted her gone.

"Erm, I'll go now and leave you to yourself," she announced and turned on her heels. Not understanding what she meant by, "I'll go now," Sebastian feared that she meant she was leaving him again.

"No!" he managed to say,

"Please, stay," he begged.

She smiled. "I'm not leaving the house, I'm only going downstairs," Hanna said. Happy he still wanted her around.

"Okay, I'll see you, sooner than you think," he said; she nodded and then paused to admire him again.

"l will be waiting," she said before turning on her heels.

Sebastian wore his top and sat down on the bed in relief. This was really happening; she was being nice to him. While he was ecstatic at the turn of events, he also knew that Mason would have realized that he was no longer a prisoner and he knew they both had a short time to disappear and plan how to defeat him before he would find them. Sebastian chuckled with satisfaction. It felt like old times again, him and Hanna against the world.

He waited in his room for a while; he could hear her eating; he waited upstairs until he was sure she had finished before going to join her. Hanna was washing up when he entered the kitchen, and the dead animals were still on the kitchen floor. Without saying a word, he picked them up and took the carcasses out back in the garden and buried them.

When he returned, she was seated on her sofa like old times; he wondered where he should sit. She looked at him carefully; she couldn't believe he was standing so close to her; neither could he. Sebastian would have preferred to be sitting next to her, but this was still too new and neither of them knew yet where they stood with each other. Sebastian sat on his chair facing Hanna as they did in the past. They looked at each other; it felt awkward as they both waited for the other to speak. Hanna knew she was the one that should start the talk, but she didn't know where to begin. Noticing the awkwardness in the room, Sebastian started to speak. He cleared his throat; she looked away not able to cope with being so close, yet so far from him. She wondered if he would ask her why she came back.

"You look well Hanna, still as beautiful as I remember," Sebastian said and wondered if that was the right thing to have said.

Hanna smiled. "Thank you, you look good yourself I'm glad those two calves didn't go to waste," she joked.

Sebastian laughed softly, "Thank you, Hanna. I should have started with that. I don't know why you helped me; this is not the first time you have done so, but I am very thankful you came for me."

Hanna nodded and then there was another awkward silence. To break the silence, Sebastian asked, "How long did I sleep?"

Hanna cleared her throat before speaking, "Twelve hours!" she said,

"Twelve hours!" he repeated; she noticed his forehead creased as if he were thinking, and then there was silence again. This was not what she wanted, and she could see he was struggling to understand why she had returned and been so nice, but she knew he was too polite when it came to her to ask pushy questions.

"You are probably wondering what am doing here?" Hanna said out of nowhere. Sebastian looked at her; he really wanted to know what was happening; at the same time, he was dreading it, in case she didn't want the same things that he wanted. But he reminded himself that he had heard her call him My *love* before he slept, or perhaps he imagined her saying it; he wasn't sure.

"Among other things, but yes I am shocked that you came to help me. That you are here . . . even but um," Sebastian said, but paused when he noticed Hanna get up and walk toward him. He felt her hands on his hips as she knelt in front of him, her eyes penetrating his. It felt like déjà vu; he could hardly hold himself together, but he didn't know what she would say this time around.

"S, I am here because I want to be here. The past years were hurtful without you, and I know it was my fault; I left and I caused you a great deal of pain but . . ." Hanna said, confused. Sebastian got up and pulled her up with him. Then he said.

"Please Hanna, don't kneel; you were just in your decision to walk away. I did you . . . wrong. I lied to you; you trusted me and I let you down. I deserved the pain and much more for what I did to you."

"S, listen to what am saying. I was annoyed with you and for a really long time, I felt justified in my anger toward you, but at the same time, I missed you so much that it hurt to breathe; it hurt to think about you and all the pain you were going through. Do you understand what I am saying?" Hanna paused to gauge Sebastian's reaction.

He smiled awkwardly, still not understanding what changed, and why she was different with him now.

"That was all in the past darling; you are here now. That is all that matters," Sebastian said although he wanted to know the reason behind her sudden change of her heart. Thinking back on it all, he knew Mason was to be blamed for the monster that he became. He was sure that if Mason had not killed his mother, he wouldn't have gone dark; at the same time, it was a blessing in disguise as that led him to Hanna.

"Sometimes, I wished, that you had hidden the truth from me because if you did, we both wouldn't have suffered as we did, but then I think that I would have found out and still reacted the same way," Hanna continued. Her closeness, her smell and the feel of her breath next to his skin made it difficult to resist holding her close and kissing her. It tormented him; Sebastian removed himself from her and walked over to the window. Hanna closed her eyes as he walked away; her heart tumbled in pain at the distance he placed between them.

"So, what's changed now? You still know the truth. I killed your mother. I'm still the same Sebastian you didn't want in your life three years ago," he pushed. He could tell that his question made her feel uncomfortable and that was not what he had intended, but he needed to know what was happening before he started to live in hope of a future with her.

"You didn't kill my mother; that's what changed," she said and waited for him to say something.

His eyes looked confused, and scoffed. "I was there, and I know what a dead human looks like," Sebastian responded sympathetically. He wondered if she was lying to herself to make it all right in her head to be with him. As much as he needed her in his life, he didn't want to be with her if she had to pretend that he hadn't done what he did. Hanna walked toward him.

"I know you think it was her, but the woman you killed was not my birth mother," Hanna revealed. This revelation changed things; Sebastian looked doubtful, but on the inside, he felt a sudden relief wash through him.

"How can you be sure? How do you know this?" Sebastian questioned.

"It's a long story S. I'm still getting my head around it. But the long and short of it is that the woman you killed wasn't my mother. She and her mistress had stolen me from my mother. Her mistress placed my mother in a mental hospital for eighteen years of my life. So, except you found her in that hospital and killed her; I want you to know that you did not kill my mother," Hanna explained. Sebastian was in a daze; he could hardly digest all she was saying.

"You mean the woman I killed was not your birth mother?" Sebastian repeated again to be sure. Hanna nodded in agreement.

"But the woman I killed could easily have been your mother?" Sebastian questioned further.

"Yes, that's true, but she wasn't, and you didn't kill her. In a way, I have a feeling you saved me from an ill fitted fate," Hanna said.

Sebastian smiled with joy. That was the first time he had felt he could smile and mean it. He knew this new revelation changed things. "So where does this leave us?" he asked as Hanna closed the gap between them.

"I don't know S. I was angry at you for so long. I was angrier with myself because I couldn't get over you. I watched you suffer, but I missed you every single moment of every day. I wanted you more than I wanted to live, but I was too stubborn to see past what I thought you did. I am here now, and I'm sorry for the pain I caused us both. I'm sorry for how I treated you. I want you back. I need you in my life to feel complete. It's selfish what I ask, but I will beg, if I must, because I know what I want and it's what I have always wanted since the very first time I saw you. Do you think you can ever forgive me and love me like you once did? Please, do we still have a chance? Because without you S, I make no sense," Hanna pleaded.

Sebastian couldn't believe his ears. He wanted her. He needed her close to feel alive, but the only way he knew he could tell her how much he needed her was by showing her. He pulled her closer with one swoop of his hand until her body pressed against his chest. Their breathing grew ragged as their bodies touched. Sebastian placed his free hand on her cheek and brushed the hair back from her face. Burying one hand in the back of her head, and placing his other hand on the small of her back, he held her closer to him. Her lips brushed against his, and he wanted to kiss her as he had imagined during the time apart. He could feel Hanna's eagerness, but he didn't want to rush. He was going to savour the taste of her lips. Gently he kissed her a second time; the touch of his lips on her burned within her. She moved her lips urgently against his, and he couldn't resist the passion that built between them.

Hanna pushed herself into him; there was no room left between them and still, she felt like she wanted to melt into him. Her moan as they kissed drove him crazy inside; they were both going mad with desire for one another. He could tell by the way she kissed him that she had missed him as much as he missed her. It felt as though they had never kissed before; she pressed her hands on the back of his neck and curled her legs around him. The need to take it further built into a crescendo; Hanna could feel Sebastian's body trembling with need, and so was hers. This wasn't how he wanted her, not rushed, not in this madness that consumed them. Sebastian knew it was because they had missed each other so, but they needed to stop before things got out of hand.

Sebastian's body tensed, and Hanna sensed his reluctance to continue, and together they came up for air and chuckled at the ridiculousness of how much they had missed each other. She climbed down from him and tried to keep a good distance between the two of them. Being so close was madness; Sebastian tried to move away; he could hear Hanna's heart pounding hard against her chest, and that didn't help.

He wanted to get away because seeing her this close drove him insane with desire for her. As he walked past, his hand brushed past hers, and Hanna grasped his finger. He felt weak at her touch. Before he could blink, they resumed kissing again, moving until they found the sofa. Hanna moved his top away so she could feel his skin next to her; he helped by casting it to the ground.

Sebastian's heart warmed at the touch of her body on his skin; he was going crazy; he had never felt so out of control with the need to make love to her. His body wanted her, more than it craved blood. but somewhere at the back of his mind he knew he couldn't go that far; this wasn't the right time. She must have felt him against her and she didn't loosen her grip on him, but he wasn't sure they were ready for this now. Not now, he kept telling himself. Not now. At the back of his mind, he knew Mason and his minions would be on a hunt for the two of them. Sebastian unwillingly broke away, and Hanna pulled him back to her; he kissed her for a minute more, and then he got up and put a little distance between them before speaking.

"That was incredible. Now I know how much I have missed you, Hanna Greene," he said breathlessly. Looking at her as she sat on the sofa drove him mad.

"You are brutally . . . irresistible," he added. Hanna rose from where she sat and went to him.

"Don't, please," he pleaded, and she laughed knowing what she was doing to him.

"I promise I won't bite," she said, and he laughed softly.

"You little . . . temptress. You know what you do to me. Why torture me so?" Sebastian asked.

"I do not take pleasure in your pain S, just the burning desire to be close to you," she said; he wanted to move away, but he couldn't resist. Sebastian opened his arms and she lay against his chest. He gently held her to him, and they stood in each other's arms for what seemed like ages.

Then Sebastian spoke, "You have no idea what you mean to me Hanna, or what losing you did to me. But I'm happy now that you're here, back in my arms."

Chapter 7

Sebastian picked Hanna up and took her back to the sofa; she giggled as he carefully placed her on his lap. Hanna wrapped her hands around his neck and planted kisses all over the side of his face. As good as he felt inside, Sebastian knew that he had to bring Hanna up to speed with the situation they were both going to face soon. It felt wrong to spoil the moment, but he knew he had no choice.

"Hanna," Sebastian called, and she pulled back to look at him.

"Yes, don't tell me you are already getting sick of me," Hanna teased.

Sebastian chuckled. "That can never happen," he reassured her.

"Great, because I find that I can't help myself around you," Hanna said.

Sebastian laughed softly, and then said, "I can clearly see that." He joked.

Hanna hit him playfully on the chest. Sebastian sighed softly. He wished they didn't have a war to fight, but it was time Hanna knew everything that he knew about Mason.

Hanna felt his body tense, "What's wrong?" she asked.

"I'm sorry darling, but we have to talk," Sebastian said.

"About what exactly?" Hanna asked. She wasn't stupid; she knew there was a reason she found him in a locked cage, but she wanted to enjoy this happy reunion before they had to deal with whatever else was after them.

"I'm sorry love; you are clearly enjoying yourself, using my body as a prop, but darling I hate to say it; we've got a big bad wolf coming after us, and we need to plan. We have to destroy the wolf or be destroyed," Sebastian said, Hanna creased her forehead.

"Really, it's that bad?" she asked with an eyebrow raised.

"Yes, Love. I wish I had better news, but as we speak, I know they will be on the search, and we don't have long now."

Hanna got up from Sebastian's lap and sat next to him.

"Okay, I'm all ears. Tell me all about it," Hanna said.

"I don't know if you recall. I mentioned I had a friend that was going to help me fight the brothers. Do you remember? When I went to Italy to fight the brothers?" Sebastian paused to check if Hanna recollected him mentioning Mason. Hanna nodded, and Sebastian then went on to explain all that had happened between him and Mason. Hanna listened attentively as Sebastian recounted all of Mason's plans and his confessions. He told her about Mason's plans to use her to resurrect his dead wife Annemarie, not forgetting the plan to use Hanna to make all vampires day walkers. Hanna's eyes widened with anger as she listened to all the things Sebastian was saying that this Mason had done and was planning to do.

Sebastian mentioned what happened between Nicholas and Margret and that Margret and Thomas became lovers and how somehow Mason had gotten Nicholas, Margret's birth son to kill her. Sebastian also told her of the alliance he had formed with Thomas when he was held a prisoner by Mason and how Thomas did not follow through after he gained his freedom. Hanna got up in frustration as Sebastian narrated his escapades. He also mentioned the details of his last visit to England and how he, Thomas, Nicholas, and Henry had killed two of the brothers, Anton and Zachary. Sebastian stopped to see how Hanna took that news because those two were the ones responsible for the deaths of her parents Joan and Joseph. He noticed that she looked happy to hear of their demise, but when he revealed that he was disappointed that Hector had escaped, he observed that she couldn't meet his eyes. Her reaction to Hector bothered him; there was something about Hector and Hanna, and he couldn't quite understand what it was. However, he had bigger problems to attend to first, after which, he hoped to deal with Hector so he wouldn't be a problem in his future with Hanna.

Hearing Sebastian talk about Hector brought back recent memories of the time she spent with him when she went back to Harrogate in search of her mother. Hanna remembered the kiss she had shared with Hector and she felt ashamed that she had allowed herself to be that vulnerable. She knew she should tell Sebastian about it now, but she also knew he wouldn't take it well even though at the time they were not together. In Sebastian's world, Hector was the enemy, and there was no making him see Hector any differently. Although she felt no love for Hector, she had come to see him as a friend not a foe and she didn't know how she could explain that relationship to Sebastian. Hanna didn't like keeping the truth from Sebastian, but she didn't see how telling him about the kiss would help their relationship.

Sebastian detected a change in her countenance; Hanna was going red with guilt, and she excused herself immediately and went to the kitchen. She opened the tap and allowed the water to run. Leaning over the counter, her mind went to the day Hector had entered her room. Hanna didn't want that memory to return; it was bad enough that she had to keep it from Sebastian but reliving it in her head was a big absolute no. She splashed cold water on her face, and as she turned, she noticed Sebastian was by the door.

"What is it, Hanna?" Sebastian asked curiously. He could tell that something was eating at her since he mentioned Hector. Hanna bit her lower lip as she always did when her nerves kick in. She shook her head and turned off the tap.

"Hanna?" Sebastian called concerned; she turned toward him, her back to the sink. "It's nothing," she said,

"I don't believe it's nothing," Sebastian pressed. Hanna smiled nervously; she knew she had to get it together.

"I'm just exhausted S, I'm tired of all the fighting, but I know we don't have a choice. It's us against them. I just need a little time to be mentally ready." Hanna hoped Sebastian bought it. It was mostly true. Sebastian narrowed his eyes; he wasn't quite convinced, but he wasn't going to push. The timing was not right for him to argue with Hanna about Hector.

"Okay, I know I have burdened you with so much information, but, my guess is that Mason would already be on his way. And this house and every other house I own won't be safe for us to stay in. He has eyes everywhere; at the most, I think we only have twenty-four hours or even less before they catch up to us. We should prepare and leave this place at once. Thomas, Henry, and Nicholas have all been here. We have to find somewhere safe, put our heads together and come up with a plan," he said.

"I agree; we could do that, or we could surprise him by taking the fight to them," Hanna suggested. Sebastian shook his head disapprovingly and stepped into the kitchen.

"No, I don't think we should go there, not yet. He has the body of the witch there; if we go back now, it could be a trap. We will be handing ourselves to him on a platter of gold. Listen, let's find out what is going on first, and I really don't know how we can do that because almost all the vampires swear allegiance to Mason. We need lookouts so we can always be one step ahead. When we know what we are doing, then we will go and take that witch's body," Sebastian declared.

"That sounds like a great idea, but what would we do with her body?" Hanna questioned.

"Destroy it; I don't know; set it on fire; hack it to pieces; grind it into smithereens; feed it to the dogs; anything to make sure that witch stays dead so he could never bring her back again," Sebastian said leaning his body on the island in the middle of the kitchen.

Hanna walked to him and placed her hands on his chest.

"After we do that, tell me, what would you want us to do next?" Hanna enquired.

Sebastian coiled his hands around her waist. "After destroying the witch, we will go back for Mason and his minions and kill them all. Until Mason dies, we won't be free to live our lives," Sebastian assured her. Hanna took a deep breath and looked down. She looked depressed.

"Hey, look at me. It's okay. We can do this, together. I promise you, we can destroy Mason," Sebastian reassured her.

"How do you suppose we would achieve that? You told me there are more than twenty aged vampires with him at all times," Hanna questioned.

"That's true but they don't have you; do you understand what I mean?" he asked.

"Hmm, am liking it. So, we roast them all," Hanna added.

"No, not all of them, I promised Mason a real special treatment."

"Ah, I don't know. I worry about you facing him alone; you said he is very strong. Why not let him roast too, dead is dead, right?" Hanna suggested.

"Yeah, but I will sleep better knowing he died at my hands. After all, he's done to me, I would like to pay him back my own way," Sebastian insisted. He looked at Hanna, and he could tell she was worried.

"Don't worry your pretty head, darling, he's had it coming. Destroying his dead wife's body will be the first blow; without her, he is not as strong. Don't worry; no matter what happens, I promise to keep you safe even if it kills me," Sebastian said,

"S, you don't have to worry about me. I can take care of myself. It's you I'm worried about; I don't want to lose you again," Hanna said.

"And I worry about you, love. I know you can take care of yourself, but it doesn't stop my worrying. I fear losing you forever. I would rather be dead than have you hurt or used in any way. Do you hear me?" Sebastian insisted. Hanna nodded in response.

"It's going to be rough for a while, but we will be fine in the end, I promise you," Sebastian assured her as he lifted Hanna's head to meet his; his eyes smiled lovingly at her. He wanted to kiss her again, but their last escapade left him reeling with desire. So, he kissed her on the forehead instead.

"Hanna, we have to start packing. I promise you, they are on their way here as we speak."

Chapter 8

Mason Benedict.
Eighteen hours earlier

Mason found it interesting that despite not feeding Sebastian for weeks, his body had not shut down. He wanted to know how long he would last before his body conceded like every other vampire. His little experiment was distracting him from proceeding with his plans. But his curiosity got the better of him, knowing if he didn't carry out his little experiment now, by the time he began to torture Sebastian to lure Hanna out, and he dies, he may never know just how long he can last without blood. The oracle had said that through his pain, she would be weakened. However, Sebastian looked close to giving up. That would make an astounding three weeks of functioning without blood. He almost felt like clapping for Sebastian because he was so impressed by his ability to control his need for blood. He wondered if Sebastian could last another week without food. But then again, the poor, smug bastard might just go another week to spite him. Angered by the thought that Sebastian was mentally strong, Mason decided to put a stop to his experiment. The next day would mark the beginning of the next phase of his plans. Mason had moved his wife Annemarie's body to the banquet room; her body had been prepared for her rebirth so to speak. Iggy and two other female vampires saw to it; she was dressed in white, and for someone who was supposed to have been dead for centuries; she looked like she was sleeping.

Mason ordered Henry to get a little blood ready—just enough to make Sebastian conscious in case his body shut down. He wanted Sebastian to feel the pain that would be inflicted on him. Mason was planning to torture Sebastian emotionally, but he wanted him conscious enough to know what was been done to him. He had a sorcerer lined up to help ease his work. Everyone had gathered around including Thomas and Nicholas. Mason made a little speech about the beginning of another phase and how everything they had been working toward was about to come to fruition.

****

As Mason spoke, Thomas was reminded once again about his little chat with Sebastian and the deal they had made. Somehow the boy had won him over; all he wanted now was to get out from underneath Mason. Thomas knew he had to play nice, although, since his release, Mason had apologized to him for the ill treatment. Thomas thought it better to get along until he could come up with a plan to help free Sebastian, but for some reason, it seemed that everywhere he went Patrick followed. Thomas knew that Mason had put Patrick up to it, to watch his every move. Annoyed that he was being monitored, Thomas confronted Mason about it. Mason then explained that he asked Patrick to watch him because he wasn't sure Thomas had really gotten over wanting to hurt Nicholas. Thomas bought his explanation, but deep down he also knew that Mason had lost the trust he once had for him, and he feared the real reason could be because in Mason's mind he was afraid of the bond Thomas now shared with Sebastian since they were prisoners together. To take the heat off him, Thomas knew he had to win back Mason's trust. To do that, he had to keep the peace until Mason again believed in his loyalty. There was no point in declaring a war he knew he couldn't win on his own strength. However, Henry was right about Nicholas; he had seen what killing Margret had done to him. Even though Nicholas was already suffering, Thomas vowed to still avenge Margret's death someday. The way he saw it, there could be no forgiveness until he'd taken an eye for an eye.

****

Mason called the sorcerer Anchor forward and requested that his wife's body be brought into the room by Iggy and two other female vampires. Soon, as the girls disappeared, one of the guards rushed in with Henry. They looked alarmed; Henry bowed his head in reverence, and Mason beckoned him over to him. Henry moved hurriedly towards Mason and whispered something in his ear. Mason's eyes widened in fury. Thomas could tell something had gone horribly wrong, and he knew it had to do with Sebastian. He almost wanted to laugh out loud in relief. How the hell did that boy manage to escape, he wondered, but before he could finish his thoughts, Thomas noticed Mason's eyes darting toward him.

"What have you done?" he asked angrily.

"I don't know what you mean?" Thomas replied. He was immediately fearful of what Mason might do next. The only other time he had seen that amount of fury in his eyes was when his wife Annemarie was dying, and he could do nothing about it.

"Don't mess with me; do you think me a fool. Where have you hidden him?" Mason questioned moving swiftly toward Thomas while others looked on in shock and horror. It was the first time that Mason had raised his voice and showed any kind of annoyance toward Thomas in their presence.

"With all due respect, Master, I don't know whom you are referring to," Thomas responded.

"I am referring to the boy Sebastian! Where is he? Where is Sebastian? You will tell me the truth, or I will rip out your tongue;

70

you dare betray me after all I have done for you? I made you next in line to me and you choose him over me, over all I am willing to do for our kind? Tell me where you hid him, or I will rip you apart this minute," Mason shouted, grabbing Thomas by the throat and lifting him up with one hand.

There were muffled whispers of horror amongst the others. Thomas knew he couldn't fight Mason here; there were too many vampires loyal to him. Even if there weren't all these other vampires around he didn't really stand a chance with a vampire more than three time his age. Thomas knew the only way out of this was to convince Mason of his innocence.

"I didn't help him; I am loyal to you. How could I have helped him when you've had someone watching me since my release, and why would I be on his side when I have been by your side loyally for centuries?" Thomas pled his innocence. Still fuming, Mason released his hold on him and turned his attention to the rest of the vampires; a few stepped back in fear. Everyone looked away afraid that they would be next in line for his anger. If he could do this to Thomas, no one was safe, they thought. His eyes caught Iggy's as she returned with the other female vampires carrying his wife's body. They laid her down, and Mason moved toward her, stopping by Annemarie's corpse. He took one look at the lifeless body of his dead wife and his anger rose to a greater height. Just when he thought everything was going according to plan, one of his own betrayed him. He thought. "You! It was you," Mason accused pointing at Iggy. "You were seen with him the last time he was here; did you help him escape?" Iggy stepped back fearfully; she had heard him accuse Thomas as she was bringing the body and was thankful the anger was not directed at her. However, no sooner had she made her appearance than he shifted the blame to her. Now all eyes were on her, and she knew that whatever was going to happen it wasn't going to end well. Someone had to pay, but *Why did it have to be her?* she thought.

"Bring her to me," he commanded.

Henry and Patrick grabbed Iggy and dragged her to Mason.

"Tell me, where is he? Where did you hide him?" Mason pushed for answers. Iggy was shaken and unsure of her fate because she had never seen him so enraged.

"I . . . I . . . I don't . . . I don't know. I swear . . . I don't know. I didn't help him," Iggy tried to say.

"I don't believe you." Mason hissed.

"I watched you drool after him like a lost puppy. I ask you again, where have you hidden him? Tell me and I will spare you?" Mason cajoled.

"I swear to you master, I don't know . . . I swear . . ." Before Iggy could persuade him of her innocence, Mason lifted her with his hands and squeezed her neck tight until her head fell off her body. A few of the vampires gasped in horror as her body dropped to the ground. They couldn't believe how quickly he had sentenced her to death, and fear consumed them. Everyone looked away afraid that if their eyes met with his, they could be next. Mason flung her head to the ground and moved angrily toward the rest of his subjects.

"Where are the guards, I appointed to watch him?" he barked, and two fear-filled vampires stepped forward. "Tell me? How did that blood-starved degenerate escape without your knowledge? Who helped him?" he demanded. The two vampires looked at each other, puzzled, and then their gaze fell on Iggy's lifeless body. They knew at that moment that they could be next to die.

"We don't know Master; we never left our post," one said, shaken, not daring to look Mason in the eye.

"So, you are saying that he disappeared into thin air, just like that. I didn't think you were all useless; tell me what good are you to me when you can't even keep an eye on that weakling," he said as he wrapped his hand around the neck of the guard that spoke. Everyone cowered in fear knowing that his time on earth was over.

"I swear to you Master, we never betrayed you; we stood guard until you instructed that we gather here for the ceremony." The guard blurted out as he fought to save his skin. Just then as though lightning struck, it dawned on Mason that something else might have been in play. Annoyed that he didn't think of it sooner, he dropped the guard muttering the word "Useless." He took another look at his fear-filled subjects, and then he dashed out of the great hall and went straight to his quarters.

Mason was sure he would prove himself right as soon as he viewed the surveillance tape. Playing the tape since the last time he had seen Sebastian, he noticed Sebastian's mouth move as though he were speaking to someone. However, there was no one else in sight, and then, in a moment, the room brightened; he couldn't see anything at this point. It was very fast; one minute Sebastian was lying on the floor and then the next, he was gone and everything returned to normal.

He knew then who it was that had come for him; never in his whole existence had he seen such power displayed before his eyes. He played the tape repeatedly in hopes that he would be able to see Hanna, but the light made it impossible to see anything. She had come and complicated things for him because he had underestimated her powers. Mason always knew she would come, but he had thought he needed to put Sebastian through torture to get her to him. Now he saw his mistake; not feeding Sebastian was the wrong move; it triggered him emotionally to call for her, and now he had lost his only pawn in this game to conquer her power. That made him smile; it had been a long time since he'd fought a worthy opponent, and he knew whatever this was and however it would end, it would not be easy, but he was sure in the end he would win. Now that he had answers, he marched back into the great room, where his scared subjects were still awaiting his return.

"We have to find Sebastian. All of you divide yourselves into three groups. Nicholas, you and four others will come with me;

Thomas, you will head the second group, and Henry you will lead the third. First, we will take the jets and fly out to England, France, and Italy. If we don't find them there, we will search the whole world for him if that is what it takes, but he must be found. Patrick, call all the eyes we have on the ground; tell them to keep an eye out for him. If and when he is spotted, I must be informed immediately. Now, we have work to do; let's get to it." Mason ordered and everyone bowed in respect, then, he looked around as if he had forgotten something.

"Patrick," he called.

"You will remain here; keep your eyes on my wife's body, and your ears to the ground. Guard her with your life, or you will answer to me." Remembering Sebastian's threat to him; he knew he had to take it seriously.

"We mustn't take anything for granted," Mason added. Although he would have loved to do things differently, he was at war now, and to win he would do everything in his power.

Chapter 9

Sebastian and Hanna Greene

"What happens now? Where do we go?" Hanna asked as she watched Sebastian put a few things in a bag.

"I have no idea, but I know we need to leave this house now," Sebastian responded, and then he opened a drawer and brought out two-colourful-wigs.

"What are you doing with those?" Hanna questioned curiously. Sebastian chuckled softly as he examined the wigs.

"Wigs darling, I got them a long time ago, back when you lived with Joan and Joseph. I always thought if the worst happened and I had to take you away, it would come in handy one day and I think that day is today." He sighed regrettably. "Here, this one is yours," Sebastian said as he tossed a long, red fringed wig toward Hanna.

Hanna smiled and wrinkled her nose as she took in the scent of the wig. "It smells funny."

"Yeah, sorry about that. I doused it in some animal skin back in the day to mask your scent, and it's been lying here for years unused. It's disgusting I know, but the stinkier it is, the better for us. You will need this as well." He walked over to her and placed big round spectacles on the wig.

"Do I have to wear those as well? I don't think I can get used to this stench," Hanna complained.

"I know, regretfully darling, that's not the only thing you have to get used to. I have a few glad rags and a pair of sneakers for you to change into as well," Sebastian mentioned. Hanna shook her head in horror. He reached into the same drawer and retrieved a bag wrapped in cellophane tape. He allowed a claw to grow on his little finger and pierced the bag. Hanna covered her nose as the horrible stench filled the room.

"Don't tell me I have to wear that, please S, anything but that," Hanna begged with her nose wrinkled. Sebastian smiled; he wished she didn't have to, but he really needed their scent masked.

"Sorry love; if it makes you feel any better, I have one for myself." Sebastian burst open another bag and threw the clothes on the bed. They stared at their new outfits and then began to laugh. Then Sebastian picked up his clothes and made to leave the room to allow Hanna to change clothes. "Hurry up love. I will be waiting outside the door," he said as he closed the door behind him.

Frustrated, Hanna took off her clothes, and put on the smelly, long, blue denim skirt and the white t-shirt Sebastian said she had to wear. Then she packed her hair in a low bun before placing the wig over her scalp. She stood before the mirror and examined herself; she didn't look hideous, she thought; apart from the stench on them they fitted well. She looked at the big round glasses on the bed before carefully picking up the spectacles and placing them delicately on her face; and finally, she wore the sneakers. Carefully examining herself, Hanna thought that she looked different and smelled like a swine's puke. She picked up her packed bag and made for the door. As she opened the door, the image before her made her giggle; she thought she looked silly, but he looked stupid.

"I really don't like you in that. You don't look like you at all," Hanna said.

"That's the point, love," he said adjusting her glasses.

"However, I don't know how you manage to still look sexy in that," Sebastian stated.

"You lie; I feel and look silly," Hanna argued.

"I completely disagree; you are beautiful even in those. Is there anything you cannot pull off?"

"You will say anything to make me feel good," Hanna sighed and then turned to face Sebastian. He sniffed the air close to her temple.

"I dare say that even the swine smell works wonders on you," Sebastian joked. Hanna shook her head and kicked his legs.

"Ouch!" he said, pretending to be hurt.

"Now that we have our disguises, what's next?" Hanna asked.

"Now, we leave through the back door and make our way through the garden into the woods. I had a little storage area built back there for days like this. I store things there that we can live on should we ever need to run," he said, Hanna shook her head in wonder.

"Is there anything you didn't prepare for?" she asked Sebastian, and she smiled.

"Well since I met you, I've been prepared for all kinds of stuff. Then I thought I was being paranoid, but now am thankful for that paranoia. Anyway, let's go. You ready?" Sebastian asked. Hanna's eyes sparkled with trust and pride.

She just couldn't believe how meticulous he had been in the past about protecting her and all she wanted to do was throw her hands around him and tell him how grateful she was to have him in her life, but that could always wait, she thought.

"Yes, after you," she said. Sebastian smiled and drew her to him.

"First, I would like to kiss you again if you don't mind. You look too ravishing in your new guise," Sebastian said slowly as he devoured her with his eyes. Hanna's heart pumped quickly. She couldn't deny him the kiss, and she wanted him to kiss her again. If truth be told, it was all she had thought about since their last session.

"May I?" he asked.

"Yes" she replied faintly. He placed his hands on her face and removed her glasses, and then he said, "You always take my breath away Hanna Greene, even with your red wig on." Hanna wanted to smile, but then he moved closer and grabbed her waist, pulling her close and holding her to him protectively. As he bent his head toward her, Hanna could feel his eyes watching her; her heart raced, beating hard against her rib. Touching his lips on hers, Sebastian waited for a reply. He felt her lips move softly against his, and a rush of heat spread through his chest and engulfed his whole body at her touch. He responded swiftly, his lips melting into hers, and circling hers as the kiss deepened. Hanna's heart swelled as Sebastian tightened his hold on her and caressed the back of her head with one hand. Sebastian could hear the beating of her heart, and he let out a moan. The trouble with kissing him, she thought, was that she could never get enough of him. Hanna held him closer to her as though her life depended on it; she wanted him like this forever; she didn't want to let go, but she also knew they were both wasting precious time here, with Mason on their tail. Mason! That was the last person she wanted in her head at that moment. She pushed him out of her mind as the passion of the kiss consumed her.

It was a kiss to last a lifetime; tears fell from Hanna's eyes to Sebastian's cheek. He pulled back instantly.

"What's wrong love? Are you hurt? Why the tears?"

"I'm sorry; I was so happy, but then I became sad, and the way we were just now, it felt . . . I felt scared. You know this war. What if we never get to be together like this again? What if one of us dies?" she asked.

"Shush . . . don't talk like that, I know you are scared. I am too, but look at us. Who knew we would ever get back together? This is all I want, you. You are my dream and my reality, and nothing can get between that not even Mason. I won't allow it," he said. Hanna looked up at him and managed a smile. Sebastian wiped her tears with his thumbs.

"We would make it together or die trying, but that is totally out of the question. We cannot think like that, darling. We must be positive. Look at me Hanna; we will defeat Mason and everyone that poses a threat to our happiness. Darling, this will pass, and we will get a chance to live as normal as we want. When we die, it won't be because of a war. Do you hear me, Hanna Greene?" Sebastian asked, delicately caressing her cheek and wiping away her tears. He placed the glasses back on her face.

"Cheer up love; we've got this in the bag," Sebastian assured her. Hanna's smile widened, and she nodded approvingly.

"Okay S, I believe you," she said.

"Good," Sebastian responded and kissed her on the temple.

"Now, do you have all you need in that bag?" he asked, and Hanna nodded.

"Good, let's get out of here."

They left the house through the back door, and Sebastian asked Hanna to remain hidden in the garden while he scouted their surroundings for spies. Satisfied that no one was watching, he returned for Hanna, and they quickly crossed his land into the woods. After walking silently for fifteen minutes, they came to a little shed, almost impossible to see, camouflaged and covered by a mystical angel oak tree with branches spreading wide and reaching to the ground. Sebastian reached into his pocket for a key; he then walked to the shed and snapped the branches covering the entrance with his hands. He opened the shed, switched on the light and beckoned Hanna to join him.

The first thing Hanna saw was a car concealed by a covering. There was a deep freezer and stacks of canned goods and bottled water all over the floor. Sebastian removed the dusty covering to reveal a black luxurious Audi with tinted windows.

"I'm going to start the car; the battery may be dead, but I have another stashed here just in case. Meanwhile, darling, could you please load the boot with some food, and I will join you as soon as I fix the car," he said.

"Okay, but how do you suppose you are going to drive that thing out of here? I didn't see any roads around here S," Hanna asked.

"I will push it out; it's only a short distance to a little side road. Don't worry love; I have got this," Sebastian assured her.

"Cool, I better start loading the food then," Hanna said and began loading the food ranging from sunflower tunas, baked beans, kidney beans, peas, tomato soups, sweet corn, pineapple chunks, sweetened milk, canned drinks and other things.

"Wow S! There is so much food here; we can't take it all; it won't fit the car," Hanna said commending his efforts; he smiled as he tried to start the car. Hanna could hear the futile efforts as the car sputtered to life and died, but she didn't want to comment on it as she was hopeful that Sebastian would sort it out. She concentrated on filling the truck with all the food and water they could carry.

When she was done, Hanna turned her attention to the freezer. Sebastian noticed her eyeing the freezer as he fiddled with something in the bonnet. Hanna then took deliberate steps toward the freezer; Sebastian went back to the car and started it again and it roared to life. Hanna smiled in relief before she could lift the lid of the freezer. Sebastian was at her side. He placed his hand gently on the lid and said, "Now, you don't really want to see what's in here."

Hanna looked at him questioning. He smiled and then retrieved a cool bag from behind the freezer; her eyes followed the bag, but Sebastian was not going to satisfy her curiosity.

"Why don't you go wait in the car? I will join you in a minute," Sebastian suggested moving his head in the direction of the car; Hanna reluctantly left his side and walked toward the car. Sebastian waited for her to get inside before he began loading the bag with the animal blood bags he had preserved in the freezer. Sebastian blocked Hanna's view, and he smiled to himself because he knew she was dying to know what he was putting in the bag. He wondered how long it would take before she began nagging him for answers.

He threw the bag on the back seat and closed the car door.

"Okay, sit behind the wheels and put on your seat belt, please. You are going to steer the car, and I am going to push us out until we get to the dirt road, and then we would be out of here. Hanna nodded affirmatively; her mind went to the bag and she wondered what he was hiding in it and why he wouldn't let her see it. As Sebastian began pushing the car out of the shed, Hanna considered opening the bag, but then she decided against it. Sebastian pushed until they got to the dirt road he spoke about. Then Hanna moved to the passenger seat, and he got inside the car and began driving. They didn't speak for a while; Sebastian concentrated on the road, and his mind strategized over plans to win the war. Now that he knew how powerful and dangerous Mason was, Sebastian knew there could be no mistakes.

"What was in the freezer?" Hanna asked, breaking into his thoughts. Sebastian smiled, keeping his eyes glued to the road.

"Wouldn't you like to know, Ms Nosey?" Sebastian teased.

"Am not . . . nosey. Call it curiosity. Just tell me and save me the time. You know I won't stop asking, and I really don't want to lower myself to snooping," Hanna pushed.

"Well then, why don't you have a guess? What could I be hiding from you?" Sebastian asked looking pleased with himself.

"I don't want to play that game, it's ridiculous. I will find out eventually, so why not save us the hassle and tell me?" Hanna insisted. Sebastian smiled softly and then he sighed before speaking.

"Okay, I'll tell you. Back when your life was in danger, when the brothers Anton, Zacchary and the other one came spying for

Isobel," he paused for a moment; he didn't like mentioning Isobel's name; neither did he want to say Hector's name but it was necessary.

He continued, "I toyed with the idea of taking you from your parents so I could keep you safe. I lived on paranoia; that was when I had the shed built and I stocked it with food for you and for me. It was meant to be a lifesaver in case of a day like this. Wherever we hide, the last thing we want is to be seen by one of Mason's eyes," Sebastian explained hoping now she understood.

"So, it's blood you stored in there? Why didn't you want me to see it?" she asked.

"I don't mind if you see it. I was only playing with you, and it worked. For a minute there, you had to agree that you thought about something apart from Mason even if it was just briefly. Sebastian stole a quick glance her way and caught her rolling her eyes. He chuckled; he loved teasing her.

They were quiet again, and Hanna looked out the window as Sebastian sped down the road.

"You know I haven't gone to see my parents. I never got to say farewell to them. All this time, I stayed angry at you. I just couldn't see past my hurt to bring myself to go see them. I blamed everyone but myself," Hanna said. Sebastian didn't know what to say. This was a touchy subject, and he had just got out of the dog house himself. He placed his hand on hers to comfort her. Hanna looked at their hands and smiled softly.

"But, I have thought about it, and even though they lied to me, they loved me. They took me in when they didn't have to, and I paid them back like this. They loved me and died because of me and I don't even know where they are buried," Hanna lamented. Sebastian still didn't know what to say; he kept his eyes on the road, but it pained him that there was nothing he could do to help.

"I did the same with you; you were good to me; you loved me and I threw you away," She continued.

He was not able to hold his tongue. "Stop it," Sebastian said, and he pulled the car to the side of the road. Turning to face Hanna, he placed his hands gently on her shoulders and said, "You can't torture yourself over things beyond your control. We all have regrets; I regret a lot of things, but giving you to your parents isn't one of them. I promise you Hanna, when all this is done, I will take you back to Grosmont and together we will find their graves, say our goodbyes and thank them but before that, I will avenge the last of their killers. Let's focus on one thing at a time; Mason dies first; then Hector goes next. Then we can come back to pay our respect to them."

Hanna's body stiffened as thoughts of Hector dying made her uncomfortable. Sebastian noticed the tension in her body and immediately knew it was because he mentioned Hector's name; it annoyed him that she reacted each time Hector's name was mentioned. However, now was not the time to voice his concern.

Hanna looked away, unable to face him as the mention of Hector's name brought back memories of times shared, especially the kiss. Sebastian sat upright in his seat; he sighed and his jaw clenched; he felt a little jealous that Hector had some kind of hold on her. He questioned whether he had any real reason to be jealous of Hector all those times spent apart he wondered if their paths crossed.

Hanna noticed that Sebastian's body language had changed. He resumed driving with his hands wrapped tightly around the wheel. They drove for miles, and he was very quiet. The silence was killing her; she knew she should tell him the truth. She also knew he would go mad, but then she would explain that it meant nothing and that she had not been in the right space in her head, but deep down she feared losing him. Hector was the last person he would accept into her life, but she didn't hate Hector like he did, and she didn't know how to make him aware that she didn't want Hector dead. The silence made her uncomfortable and it made her feel guilty for some reason. Hanna knew she needed to say something to him to stop the awkwardness, but nothing came to her. So, she leaned toward the window, placing her head on the head rest and pretending to sleep until eventually sleep claimed her.

Chapter 10

Mason Benedict.

Twenty hours later

Arriving in England, Mason and Nicholas were driven in a black limousine to his twelve bed apartment in Kensington Palace garden. The other four subjects in his group rode in a different car. Mason had a lot on his mind; he had just spoken with Thomas and Henry, who updated him on their search for Sebastian. Thomas was heading the search in France, while Henry and his group would handle Italy. Mason knew Sebastian wasn't foolish enough to return to places where he could easily be found, but all the same, he still had to check; no stones would be left unturned. With all that going on, he worried about Nicholas who was still grieved about killing Margret. The news had reached him that Nicholas now knew that Margret was his birth mother. He never thought it would come out, nor did he expect her death to affect him this way. Mason had thought the only person he had to deal with was Thomas; he never factored in Nicholas's feelings, and now it looked like Thomas was doing much better than Nicholas. Mason wanted Nicholas to be strong; he wanted him to have a sound mind. How was he to send him to war if he allowed the death of a woman he barely knew to cut him so deep?

When they arrived at Mason's home, he instructed the chauffeur to drive around the block. Nicholas looked up at Mason; he knew what was coming; Mason was going to try to straighten him out. However, he knew no amount of talking could save him from the curse he carried. There were days when he tried picking himself up, but there was no getting better when images of a childhood long forgotten kept playing in his head on a loop and dragged him down again. He saw his mother, with the look of pleasant delight, kissing him as she tucked him into bed at night, saying, "Mama loves you, Nicky, never forget it." His young self giggled happily, as he wrapped his hand around his mama's neck. "I love you too, Mama," he said and then his mind jumped back to the moment when he separated her head from her neck, and the bitter hatred he felt for her then and he was sickened all over again.

"Nicholas, my boy. Look at you; you look frightful; you waste away when there isn't a reason for it," Mason said. Nicholas looked down respectfully not able to meet his eyes.

"Why suffer yourself? You mean a lot to Annie, your mother; for her sake, I will do anything—even pardon you for anything. You've mourned that woman enough. Get yourself together; we have too much at stake. I need you, but I can't have you this way. You killed a woman; she is not the first vampire to have died at your hands so why this foolish madness?" Mason rebuked. Nicholas gradually lifted his eyes to meet Mason's before voicing his question.

"Did you know who she was before you ordered me to kill her?" Nicholas asked.

"What?" Mason pretended that he had not understood what he meant.

"Margret, did you know that Margret was my mother?" Nicholas asked again calmly.

"What nonsense, Mother! You already have a mother my Annie she raised you from a boy until you became a man," Mason said; Nicholas refused to back down; his eyes penetrated Mason's.

Mason could tell that he wasn't going to drop this stupid matter, so he said. "Yes, I knew, but it had to be done. I couldn't ask

Thomas to do it; he was already bewitched by her. I didn't trust that Henry would not tell Thomas of my plans. The only other option was you; I know it sounds heartless, but you didn't know who she was. Margret would have spoiled things for us; if I had told you who she was, she would have taken you away from me, from your real mother Annemarie. Just because a person brings forth a child does not mean they qualify to be called *mother.* She abandoned you; I saved you and Annie raised you; never forget it," Mason argued.

"But she was my real mother, Margret . . . Margret, the woman I killed. I remember now; there was an accident; she tried to save me; we were shipwrecked. She tried, but the water, the current, it drove us apart. Then she came back after all those years, my mother came back, and you made me kill her and now I am cursed. I don't deserve to live. She loved me even though she never said it I could see it in her eyes; that's why she never fought back. You made me kill her. How could you do this to me? I blame you for her death. I blame myself for never wanting to fail you. I know that Thomas will never forgive me. He loved her; she meant the world to him and now when he looks at me, all he sees is a pile of shit. I have lost his respect, and all I feel inside is nothing; I don't have the will to live; I don't want the things you want any longer. I don't want this war; I just want to sleep. I want to sleep a very deep sleep and never awake," Nicholas lamented,

"Nonsense, you are grieving. I see that now. You clearly need more time. Had I known asking you to kill her would affect you so, I would have asked Henry to do it; never mind. I will give you more time; think more on what you really want; the next time I speak with you, I shall not tolerate any more of this ungrateful talk," Mason said without empathy. The car stopped in front of his home. Giving Nicholas one last look, Mason stepped out and was met by one of the four subjects in the other car.

The vampire bowed and then whispered into Mason's ear. After speaking, he stepped back and waited for Mason's instructions.

Mason looked from him to the other three standing in a straight line on the side of the house.

"Where is he?" Mason requested.

"He is in the other car?" the vampire replied.

"Bring him inside at once," Mason ordered as he walked gracefully toward the door draped in a long black leather trench coat; the door opened and another subject bowed and stepped aside; he held the door until Mason entered the hallway. The rest of his subjects filed in after him. Two other subjects opened a huge set of heavy double doors, curtseying as Mason made his way into a spacious great room. The room was sparsely and beautifully decorated with luxurious tapestry and huge Persian rugs. The edges and cornices of the walls were decorated in pure gold. The ceiling was incredibly high with tall windows draped in velvet dark curtains. There was a high chair, made of dark wood, and the ankles of the legs had rings of brass; the same design was featured on the arms of the chair. The back was cushioned and lined with dark red velvet. Mason took deliberate strides and climbed two steps before sitting down. The chair looked like a throne; the rest of his subjects stood a considerable distance away. As he sat in his chair, he tapped his fingers impatiently on the edge of the arm.

Minutes later, a woman entered and presented him with a goblet. Mason took a couple of sips and sighed with contentment before placing the chalice on the luxurious, ancient stool next to his throne. He looked from one end of the room to the other. Nicholas had joined the others. Mason noticed him standing on the edge of the wall still looking remorseful. Seeing him that way irritated him; he didn't like the way his talk had ended with Nicholas. Thomas and Nicholas had been his most loyal subjects, but now he wasn't so sure. Everything changed since he ordered the death of that woman; he wondered if he would still have wanted her dead if he knew that her death would have such a strong hold on them. It bothered him deeply that they were so flaky, not as loyal as he thought they were. Frustrated, Mason picked up the chalice and threw it across the room in anger. The crimson content splashed across the room staining the luxurious tapestry on the wall. He got up at once and began pacing the room. Fury ruled his spirit; he knew what he had to do. He had done it once before and he knew now that he would have to do it again to both Thomas and Nicholas if they proved themselves disloyal or useless to his quest. When a faithful dog rebels and bites its master, then its day to die has come, he thought. He stopped pacing and turned to look at his subjects; everyone had bowed their heads including Nicholas. He forced his eyes away from Nicholas and allowed himself some calm. This was not the time to worry about things he could not change; he had other pressing matters on his mind, and he was grateful for that.

He had been informed of a sighting, and he couldn't wait to hear the good news.

"Bring the human to me at once," he yelled and returned to sit on his chair. The heavy doors opened and a vampire walked in pulling the human by his collar and throwing him across the room. The human slid on the floor until his body came to rest under the steps leading to where Mason sat. Mason looked from the human to the vampire in annoyance; the vampire looked down in shame.

"Careful now; we must be wary of acting like animals. We are civilized and we must behave as such. He is our guest after all and not a dog." He got up and walked toward the human. "There now," he said, lending a hand to the human and helping him up. The man looked at him in fear; Mason and every vampire in the room could smell his fear.

"Settle down," Mason said and looked up at his subjects.

"Bring our guest a seat," he commanded. The double doors opened again, and a chair was brought in and set in the middle of the room. Mason gestured to the man to sit, managing a smile to encourage the human to do as he requested. The man trembled as he walked over to the chair and sat down.

"Better," Mason said looking from the human to his subjects.

"This is how we treat a guest; we must be gentle at all times," Mason said returning his gaze to the human.

"Do you want something to drink?" he asked, and the man shook his head in disagreement.

"Good, I feared that you would say yes and I am sure we do not have a drink favourable to the human palate." He smiled at his own joke, and a few others giggled. Suddenly looking serious, he said, "Jokes apart, I was informed that you have something to tell me." The man shook his head again.

"Surely you can speak. Is he dumb? Does he not have a tongue to speak with?" Mason questioned the room.

"I don't know, I don't . . . know . . . what you . . . want from me?" the man finally blurted out.

"Oh, there you go, he does have a tongue." Mason's eyes darted to the vampire who brought the man to him.

"What is this? You told me that he has useful information," he questioned.

"Yes Master, he does. If you allow me a moment to explain, I will make it clearer," the vampire said.

"Go on, you've wasted my time enough," Mason urged.

"An informer, I hired, called and told me that he overhead this human bragging about how he sold two calves to a blond human girl for a thousand pounds. The girl, the one we want, is meant to be blond and the farm where the human works is close to one of the houses Sebastian owns," the vampire finished talking and bowed his head respectfully.

"I see, and is there any truth to this?" Mason turned his attention to the human. The man looked at him nervously and nodded his head.

"Speak! Use your tongue. It is polite to do so," Mason ordered the man.

"Y . . . yes, I . . . I . . . sold tw . . . o, two calves; she wanted la . . . lam . . . bs at first . . . then she said . . . for me to give her she . . . sh . . . sheep but . . . but, instead, I gave her . . . two . . . calves and . . . she took them and . . . paid me so much money for it. If it were goats, I had, she would have taken it as well. I . . . thought her request was strange . . . that's all," the man explained.

"Hmm, strange indeed. You've done well. You may go now," he said to the human who immediately got out of the chair, and began walking fearfully toward the double doors. All eyes were on him; as he reached the doors, the doors opened, and he turned around slowly half expecting someone to pounce on him; but everyone remained where they were. Quickly, he hastened out of the room and the doors shut once again; Mason smiled and returned to his seat; then he said. "See that the human doesn't become a problem." He gestured to the vampire that brought the man in. He bowed respectfully and exited the room.

"Get everyone in here," Mason called out. About fifty vampires waiting in the hallway came in as commanded. Only five came with him from Mexico; however, he had twelve other subjects that resided in his homes in England and kept him abreast of every situation with regard to that territory. A few others flew in at his request from neighbouring territories. News of hope had spread like wildfire that Mason would end the curse of darkness and make them all day walkers. A lot of vampires had started arriving, eager to show their support and give their allegiance.

"Welcome all of you; if you don't know by now, I have been fighting to end the constant circle of darkness. We are creatures of the night, but I have found a way to put an end to that circle. Nothing of worth is achieved without sacrifice; to do this, we must sacrifice one of ours." There was a low rumble amongst his subjects as those that didn't know who he spoke of wondered if it were one of those presently gathered.

"Rest your minds and be not fearful; I do not speak of anyone standing here. However, I will need all hands ready to fight along with me as we fight for our freedom. It would not be easy, but I assure you if we are agreed, we will conquer powers beyond your dreams." Mason paused to look at his subjects; they seemed pleased with what he was saying. Then he continued, "We will rule the day and live to revel in the sun as the humans do. We are superior to humans, and the time is now to live as we were meant to do." His subjects cheered happily at the prospects of a future they had only dreamed of.

"However, the power to walk the day lies in the blood of a young powerful girl, but never you fret. She will be conquered; her weakness is one of our kind. His name is Sebastian, Sebastian Francis." He paused again to gauge his subject's reaction and to check if anyone apart from Nicholas and his crew from Mexico know whom he was referring to; they all seemed fine and clueless about Sebastian.

"He is different from us; he feeds on animal blood." There was a roar of laughter at the thought of drinking disgusting animal blood.

"Order," Mason commanded, and everyone was quiet immediately. He waited a moment before speaking again.

"Do not underestimate him; he is stronger than most. He is young, but he did single-handedly kill a seven-century-old vampire. Maybe it's the animal blood that strengthens him, or perhaps it's the girl. I am not sure now, but do not be alarmed. We will defeat them both. We have new information that tells me they are here in England. Now, call Thomas back from Italy, and send for Henry in France. I want every one of our kind here in England. The more the merrier. we will fight together until we are victorious. Tonight, we will begin the search. Split up and go to all the houses he has or has ever owned in England and report back to me. Tell all the eyes that we have on the ground to be more vigilant. He must be found soon so we can put an end to a dark era and live as kings. Now off you go," Mason said, and everyone including Nicholas filed out of the room. "Nicholas," Mason called; Nicholas turned to face him. Mason got up from his chair and met him at the door. Then he whispered, "Go to your room; you are no use to me in that state," he said and walked into the hallway and up the stairs leaving Nicholas behind.

Chapter 11

Sebastian and Hanna Greene.

"We've been driving for ages; where are we now?" Hanna asked, waking from her slumber. Sebastian took his time before answering. Hanna noticed that his body language had calmed from before, but he still had a lot on his mind. She could not tell if it was because of their current situation or because of the issue he had with Hector.

"I am taking us to the house I gave to the family of one of my caretakers in the eighteen hundreds; the house was passed down from each generational caretaker to the next. Now it lies empty; the only surviving family died a few years ago; to my knowledge he had no living relatives or tenants, which means under my agreement with the first caretaker, the house comes back to me," He glanced at Hanna, and said, "You look well-rested."

"Do I? Well, I don't feel it. How long did I sleep?" Hanna asked.

"About three hours, I'd say," Sebastian responded

"Three hours!" Hanna exclaimed.

"Yeah, at first I was worried. You didn't make a sound. I feared something was wrong, but then you began to snore loudly, and I was glad to hear it. Who knew hearing you snore would be so entertaining."

"What! That . . . that can't be true, I do not snore," Hanna denied.

"Well, I have been told that most humans can never hear how loudly they snore when they are at it. You, darling, sounded like a train wreck; oh wait, that isn't right. Let me think; it was more like a dinosaur snorting vigorously," Sebastian said and Hanna narrowed her eyes shamefully unsure if he were joking or telling the truth.

"I tell you what; it was guttural," he continued teasing.

"Deep with rasping and high-pitch yawning's at intervals. If I should be so bold, I will call it a mixture of music and pure comic at its best. I wanted to laugh so badly my ribs hurt, but I kept it together for your sake. I didn't want to wake you," he said

"Really, I feel so embarrassed," Hanna said covering her face with her hands. "I' m sorry. That must have been awful to listen to. I still can't believe that is true," Hanna said, horrified.

Sebastian looked at her and began to chuckle.

Hanna turned and peered at him through her hands. He was laughing at her, and she wasn't amused. She hit him on the shoulder.

"You think it's funny to laugh at my expense. I am glad you find my shame amusing," she said furiously; she was annoyed but wasn't sure why. Surely the fact that he was laughing because she snored shouldn't be enough reasons to offend her, she thought. Sebastian knew he had to tell her the truth; he had lied, but he only did it to make her laugh. Now that he thought about it, he alone had found it funny.

"Darling," he called. Hanna refused to respond.

"Hey, look at me," he called. Hanna turned to face him; he smiled and her heart melted.

"I am sorry," he apologized. "I was only messing about; you know I like to play with you, and you make it so easy to get at you. Do you really believe what I said? Listen, love, you slept like an angel; not one guttural sound from you and that's the truth," Sebastian said, caressing her cheek with the back of his finger.

Hanna sighed. "You can be cruel S. I believed you," she said, and Sebastian chuckled softly.

"Sorry, I couldn't resist. I knew you would bite, but you do know I wasn't trying to be cruel," he defended. Hanna smiled.

"I know; I was just embarrassed is all. Don't mind me. What you described sounded horrible, but I should know better than to believe you," Hanna said. "Anyways, according to you, I slept for three hours, and you are still driving. Where exactly is this house we are heading for?" Hanna asked, looking out the window to see if she could tell where they were.

"We are in Wales; somewhere in Pembrokeshire. The house is a little remote cottage at the edge of a sea cliff with spectacular views of the sea. You will love it there; it's very peaceful, and I think for now we will be safe there. We should get there soon. Five minutes at the most."

"You said 'safe'; how can you be so sure?" Hanna asked.

"I'm not sure, but I hope that we will be safe at least for a while. No one can be sure of anything, love, but, for now, it will do. We need a place to think and strategize; at the most, I think we can stay there for a week. At the least, we should be all right there for the next forty-eight hours."

"Okay, I really need to use the loo," Hanna said.

"Can you hold it for a couple of minutes? I am turning into the coastal path now." Sebastian steered the car onto a side road and drove for a few minutes before turning off the road and stopping the car next to a white stone cottage. It was dark around, and the sound of the sea hitting the rocks could be heard. Hanna stepped out of the car and took in the air; apart from the splashing of water, it was very quiet. There was no other house around, but she could see a thick woodland to their right. If someone was hiding in there, they wouldn't know, she thought. Sebastian walked toward the back of the house while Hanna waited by the car; a few minutes later he came back with a set of keys. He opened the door and cautiously stepped in and smiled in relief. He had been afraid he would not be able to enter because he wasn't sure the house had not been willed to another human against his agreement with his late caretaker's family.

"Hanna, come on in. The loo is on the top of the stairs on your right." As Hanna ran up the stairs to relieve herself, Sebastian began unloading all their food in the kitchen. Hanna joined him, and together they placed everything on the kitchen counter. Sebastian then placed the blood bags in the freezer, taking one out and placing it in the microwave to warm.

They switched off the outside light and placed a cover on the car so as not to give themselves away. Sebastian poured the contents of the blood bag in a teacup and drank it, and Hanna opened a can of beans poured it in a pot and heated it. While Hanna ate, Sebastian busied himself with the wood burner. It was very windy and cold, and although Hanna didn't complain, he wanted to make the place warm and cozy for her. He sat on the love seat and watched the fire begin to crackle; Hanna came and sat next to him, curling her legs on the chair and leaning against him.

"I wish the world could leave us alone; I would have really loved it here with you. You're right; it's so peaceful and beautiful here," Hanna said.

"I know. The simple things in life give the most joy," Sebastian responded.

"Yeah, it's true. But it's wishful thinking to believe we can have a life this simple, you and I," Hanna stated, and Sebastian turned to face her.

"No, it's not, we deserve to be happy. We've been through so much and we just got back together. We have so much living to do; now that we are together again we will live our lives as we want because I believe we are more determined to succeed than they are. If I were a gambler, I would bet on us," he said. Hanna smiled.

"I will too," Hanna said. Sebastian smiled as he looked at her in her red wig. "What! Why are you smiling?" Hanna asked.

"It's the wig; it suits you, but I prefer you with your hair. May I?" he asked; she smiled and nodded as he pulled it off her head.

"There, much better. I wish we didn't have to do this," he said looking at the fire and realizing that he didn't put enough wood for it to burn all night.

"Aren't you forgetting something?" Hanna asked, looking at his blond wig.

"What?" Sebastian asked, hunkering down to put more wood on the fire. He sat back down, and Hanna looked at him.

"What is it?" he asked again,

"You still have yours on," she joked; he pulled it off his head and threw the two wigs into the fire. They watched as the fire consumed them.

Then Sebastian turned to her and said, "Now, I think you should sleep. I will make the bed upstairs for you unless you want to stay down here by the fire. Tomorrow we can begin planning for battle."

"I think I have rested enough; I don't need any more sleep," Hanna said. "If you have any ideas, I would like to hear."

"Are you sure?" Sebastian pressed.

"I can't sleep anyway; the quicker we do this the better," Hanna assured him.

"Okay, I think by now we can assume Mason will already have all his subjects and their human informants looking for us. He wants his wife back and he wants to walk the day. The more he preaches that to his subjects, the more the support he will get, which means anywhere you and I consider home will be under heavy surveillance. Believe me."

"I do," Hanna said.

"We cannot trust anyone but each other; do you understand? We must assume everyone and anyone are ears and eyes for Mason," Sebastian warned.

"Okay," Hanna agreed.

"While you slept, I was thinking; we need to stay a step ahead, and the only way I see us doing that is by returning to Mexico."

"What!" Hanna exclaimed. "But you said it would be dangerous for me to go back there," Hanna stated.

"I know, but he won't think we would be so foolish. Can you take me back the way you brought me out? I am going to take that dead evil witch he calls his wife and destroy her body so he can never bring her back. Let's see how he likes it when I destroy her as he killed my mother. If she is destroyed, then he will not need your powers anymore to resurrect her, although he would fight us harder then, but that is to be expected. Of course, we must assume that her body will be guarded," Sebastian explained.

"Okay, but, what if it's a trap? Like you suggested earlier?"

"Then at the first sight of trouble we leave. I know it's dangerous, but we have no choice," Sebastian explained. Hanna nodded approvingly.

"I agree, but I don't know how to get back there. I was only there because I saw you. I just can't go back on my own. I need something to lead me there," Hanna explained. She was letting him down.

"Really? There must be some other way! What if I describe it to you, will that work?" he asked,

"I don't think so; I have to have a perfect mental picture of the place in my mind for me to go there," Hanna said. She paused when she saw how disappointed Sebastian looked; she felt as though she was letting him down.

"It's okay, I will think of something else," Sebastian said.

"Wait. Let me try something; give me your hands and think of the place, I am connected to you, meaning, I can see what you can see if I want. I should be able to see what you see in your mind's eye," Hanna said, "But I'm not promising anything. Fingers crossed," she said again.

Sebastian placed his hands in hers and said. "I'm all yours; let's hope it works."

Hanna closed her eyes and tried to focus on what Sebastian was thinking, but she couldn't see anything.

"I don't know if it will work. I can't see anything," she said.

"Just keep trying," he encouraged. She released his hands and took a deep breath.

Then she placed both her hands on his temple and after a few seconds, she said, "Yes, now I can see what you see."

"Oh good. Just to be sure, I am standing in the foyer, do you see it?"

"Yes, I do, I can see the windows and the sea views, and um wait, a grand piano."

"Yes, that's where I am now," Sebastian confirmed excitedly.

"Are you ready to do this?" Hanna asked.

"Absolutely."

Chapter 12

Then just as though they were never in Wales, their bodies faded from view, and they both appeared behind the grand piano in the lobby of Mason's house in Mexico. Sebastian opened his eyes and smiled in wonder.

"Hanna, you did it," he whispered as she turned around to see for herself. They both smiled with relief.

"Okay we have to be quick. I think Mason keeps her body in a room close to his; it's a bit of a distance from here. I can't hear anyone, but we should be careful. I'm sure he won't leave the place empty; someone will be on guard here. Just stay close," Sebastian warned and Hanna nodded and followed him closely. They couldn't hear anything. As they approached the corridors, they waited to see if anyone was around, but no one showed; neither could he sense anyone. Then Sebastian and Hanna walked down the corridor toward the room where he stayed the first time he was there, before he was taken prisoner. The room next to his was Mason's; he checked to see if there was another room after Mason's, but there was none.

"What is it?" Hanna asked quietly.

"I don't know; I had thought that he would keep her in a room next to his, but there is nothing here, just walls." Sebastian touched the walls to see if there was a secret passage, but there was none.

He turned to look at Hanna, "I don't know what I was thinking," he said sadly.

"Or maybe, she is in his room. What better place to hide her?" Hanna suggested. Sebastian's eyes brightened with hope.

"Ah, why didn't I think of that? Let's see." He pushed on Mason's door and it gave way. They stepped inside and there was nothing in the room. He had never been inside Mason's space. And he never visualized the place so empty. Sebastian turned and looked at Hanna and he said, "I don't like this; something feels wrong. I think we've walked into a trap." Then he sniffed about in the room. "Let's get out of here now," Sebastian said.

"Not so fast," a voice echoed through the room. Sebastian grabbed Hanna's hands, but before she could zoom them back to their little cottage in Wales, a bald man appeared out of nowhere and shoved Sebastian away from Hanna.

"I always knew you would show up here. At last, we meet," the bald man said; it was the sorcerer that Margret had met in New Orleans.

"Who are you?" Hanna asked. Sebastian got up from where he had fallen and charged toward the bald man only to be shoved back into the wall. Hanna's eyes shot toward the man in anger. "Leave him alone," she yelled and she heated him up so that he was unable to breathe. The man yelled and grabbed his throat, muttered something in a mysterious language and recovered quickly.

"Not bad, not bad at all. I see you are a little spitfire, but little one, you are no match for me," the bald man said. He continued to speak incantations, and then he reached into the air and began to pull Hanna to him by some force. Hanna felt a force around her like a pair of invisible arms pulling at her. She pushed back with her own force returning the energy that pulled her to the bald man. The force hit the man like a lightning bolt on the chest and sent him flying. His back hit the wall and he fell to the ground.

Hanna turned to check on Sebastian, who was now on his feet. The bald man saw that Hanna was distracted and quickly used it to his advantage. He spoke to his hand and it began to grow, elongating into spirals. Each finger became a snake head. The heads hissed as they made their way toward Hanna and Sebastian. Sebastian heard the snakes coming for them and alerted Hanna; she turned around; her face was disgusted at the image before her and her anger turned to wrath.

"We'll see about this," Hanna said. The snakes drew cautiously close, surrounding them so that there was no path left to escape. Her eyes went from the snakes to the man who had conjured them out of his body and she said, "Let fire engulf and burn this evil soul to hell." As she spoke, a wild fire broke out; the hissing increased from the snake heads as they retreated from the fire consuming them.

The fire raged wildly burning the snakes; the bald man tried to control the situation; he got on his feet and shielded himself with a cloak that seemed to stop the fire from getting to him. Hanna, seeing that he was about to escape, raised her hands and the sorcerer was lifted off his feet. He struggled to free himself, as his feet dangled in the air, he uttered incantations of his own in attempts to stop what was happening to him.

Sebastian looked on in amazement as he knew the sorcerer was about to get what he deserved, but before Hanna could say another word, a gray smoke filled the room, and the bald man's cloak dropped to the floor and the man disappeared. Hanna and Sebastian looked at each other. "Something tells me that is not the last we will see of him," Hanna said and Sebastian nodded in acknowledgment.

"Let's find that evil witch and get out of this place," Sebastian said. The fire Hanna had started was spreading around the room. As they turned toward the door, Patrick was standing in the doorway with a stake in his hands. Before they could blink, he threw the stake; Sebastian pushed Hanna out of the way and bent backward; his head missed the weapon by an inch. Smoke began to fill the room; Hanna coughed, and Sebastian turned; she was okay but before he could get up, Patrick reached for him and landed a big blow to his face sending him across the room where the fire was at its strongest. Patrick followed Sebastian before he could recover and punched him repeatedly. Hanna could not see very well because of the fire; the smoke was getting into her lungs and she began to cough loudly. Sebastian heard Hanna's cough, and he knew they had to leave at once. He managed to push Patrick off him. But, Patrick landed on his feet and charged towards Sebastian once again. This time Sebastian was prepared; he resisted Patrick's blows with his own strong ones. Drawing strength from Hanna, Sebastian remembered he was able to defeat Zacchary when the thought of never seeing Hanna again was too unbearable to accept and now having her in this fire engulfed room, he knew he would do anything to ensure they got away safely. Patrick was equally stubborn; defeating Sebastian meant praises from Mason, and he was going to do whatever was necessary to be victorious. Hanna moved closer to where the two wrestled with each other, seeing Patrick's huge body looming over Sebastian's; she shoved Patrick toward the fire by flicking her hands and held him down with her eyes so that he could not move.

"S, are you alright?" she asked without taking her eyes off Patrick.

"Yes, I'll live," he responded. Sebastian rose and walked toward Patrick; the fire had caught on his clothes, but nothing was going to stop him from what he was about to do. Sebastian was angry because Patrick had thrown the stake toward Hanna; it could have killed her. Sebastian picked the stake from the floor and drove it into Patrick's chest. He yelled out in pain. Then Sebastian stood on Patrick's shoulders while Patrick was still screaming and said, "It's time you retired. Go to hell."

In one swift turn, he broke Patrick's neck and tore his head off. He turned to look at Hanna. He knew she may not like the savageness with which he had ended Patrick's life.

"I'm sorry you had to see that, but we have to send them a message; you'd better look away." She shrugged nonchalantly. She felt when you were at war, everything was fair game. Holding on to Patrick's head by his hair, Sebastian kicked the headless body into the fire. "Let's get out here," he said to Hanna as they walked out of Mason's room. The fire burned ferociously. Sebastian closed the door to keep it at bay for now.

"What do you need that for?" Hanna questioned pointing at Patrick's head.

"This will come in handy soon enough," Sebastian replied.

"What now?" Hanna probed.

"Now we find that witches body and get out of here." They began to search from room to room and encountered no other vampire. Sebastian suggested looking in the basement, and upon getting there, they found a few dozen humans held captives as prisoners for food. Sebastian remembered seeing them when he had first visited. Then, he couldn't help the situation, but now, nothing could stop him. He opened the gates and compelled them all to leave. Men and women ran out of the building. A few animals that Mason had collected to impress Sebastian were also in cages. Sebastian released them all and led them out of the building into the open island. Still holding onto Patrick's head, he found a bag in the foyer; he placed Patrick's head inside. The fire had spread from Mason's room into other quarters, and still, they hadn't found Annemarie's body.

"Maybe she is not here," Hanna suggested and she could already see the disappointment on Sebastian's face.

"Maybe, but there is one last place we haven't looked." Sebastian hurried into the banquet room with Hanna following closely behind. As he opened the door, a smile spread across his face; he turned to look at Hanna and sighed with relief.

"There she is," Sebastian said. Annemarie's body lay in an open glass coffin. Having found what they came for, they walked cautiously toward her.

"How long did you say she has been dead?" Hanna asked in astonishment as she stared at the beautiful body of the woman.

"I don't know; centuries they say. I think more than seven hundred years," Sebastian said; he knew why Hanna asked the question.

"Wow, she looks like she is sleeping, like she just died this afternoon," Hanna voiced in wonder; they both stared at the body of the red-haired beauty, and then Hanna looked up at Sebastian.

"Okay let's do this; hold my hand and put one hand on her corpse," she instructed. Sebastian nodded and did as she had said.

"I have to be careful. I don't want to touch her in case it's a trap. Who knows? Touching her could mean transference of power," Hanna suggested.

"Yes, very wise counsel," Sebastian agreed. He put his hands through the handle of the bag that contained Patrick's head, so the bag dangled on his arm, which gave him room to hold Hanna and then he placed his free hand delicately on Annemarie's dead, cold arms, and then he said, "Wait, can you do one more thing before we go?"

"Anything S. What would you like me to do?" Hanna asked.

Sebastian smiled and said, "I know it's already on fire, but I don't want to leave any stone unturned. I want you to burn it all to the ground until there is nothing left but a pile of ashes."

"Well, you asked, and I will grant you the pleasure," Hanna said, before making the pronouncement on Mason's resident.

"Let fire devour from top to bottom and consume everything in its path leaving nothing but the ashes of this foul place." And

106

immediately, fire broke out everywhere. Sebastian smiled with satisfaction and looked at Hanna.

"Very well done darling; now let's get out of here," he said; she agreed and in an instant, their bodies faded from view as both of them and Annemarie's body reappeared in the living room of their cottage in Wales.

Chapter 13

Hilda Denali.

Arriving back in England, Hilda had never felt better. She could feel the power coursing through her body, charging like an electric current, and it took all the self-control she had not to test her powers on passers-by. As she walked through the Heathrow Airport, she found she could think of no other person but Hanna. Her mind was focused; all she needed to do was find her enemy and detonate her newly found powers on her. But nothing could be done without first becoming the head of her tribe. Then, together, they would unleash war on Hanna so that her people could be free of the curse of the wolf. She got into a black cab that took her to King's Cross Station where she boarded a train home. She sat alone on the journey, impatiently tapping her hands on the sides of her seat, once, twice and then thrice in a rhythmic fashion. She enjoyed how her powers glowed within the surface of her skin. The heat brimmed with a red glow, and she felt ready for battle. To win she had to be patient, but she had no patience; just the urge to destroy everything in her path until she came up victorious.

Arriving home, she stepped into the castle she once called home and was met by her guardian who seemed very relieved to see her.

"Hilda, where have you been?" her guardian asked, and Hilda said nothing; she looked the woman over, sniffing the air around her before entering the hallway.

"I have been looking for you everywhere. Where did you go young lady?" The guardian pressed her for answers but got none.

"Answer me, will you? You disappeared for almost two weeks and waltz in here without any explanation. I was worried. I had to call the police, Hilda," Hilda stopped to look at her; she felt nothing for the woman; no compassion; neither was she grateful for her concern. She had been dying to try out her powers; she felt the buzz to jab a little on her guardian to keep her quiet, but then she thought of the tribe members she needed to speak with. Without her guardian, there was no getting to the elders of the tribe. Hilda decided for now to control the urge to shut the woman up.

"A missing person's case was opened and then they showed me CCTV footage of you boarding a plane to Africa. Why did you go to Africa without telling me? You are my ward and you show no regard for me. You cannot behave like this Hilda. Your mama and papa left you in my care, and I take that role seriously until I do not have to anymore," her guardian rebuked. She followed Hilda closely up the stairs and down the corridor to her room. Hilda forcefully restrained herself from unleashing her powers on her guardian; she found the woman insufferable. When she got to the front of her room, she turned; coiling her fist into a ball, Hilda lifted her hands and acted as though she was about to touch the woman's skin. Her warm palm glowed red. The guardian noticed the change in the girl she had cared for these past years. Her eyes widened in horror, and she flinched with fear; she noticed that Hilda's eyes sparkled with enjoyment at how sorely afraid she was; then Hilda spoke.

"I have had enough of your intolerable nagging. I am not a child that I should report my every whereabouts to you, and I am not yours that you should demand it of me. Now leave me, woman, before I have a change of heart." Hilda then smiled sadistically knowing from now onwards she was in control and her guardian now knew it.

"Now, I have a little job for you, busy bee. Make yourself useful and gather all the elders of the tribe to me. Every single one of them must assemble here; I have news for all of you. While you are at it, I also want all the boys and the girls that are yet to turn; we are going to fight for our freedom and everyone will be needed," Hilda ordered. Her guardian remained where she stood still in shock, unsure of what she was seeing and if, in fact, she was now under Hilda's command. She blinked once and tried to fight back.

"I will not do such a thing. Who do you think you . . .?" Before she could complete her sentence, Hilda interrupted her.

"No, the right question is this: Why are you still standing there?" Hilda yelled, and her guardian noticed Hilda's face distort briefly; the woman gasped in horror; she stepped backward immediately and lost her footing, but she quickly scrambled to her feet as she tried to run. Hilda reached out and pulled her toward her with the force of her powers. Her powers charged within her and she felt great; she wanted to make an example of the woman, but she knew she had to control herself. She needed her for now, and while she was still useful, she would control the urge to burn her alive. Her guardian felt her body move toward Hilda who had taken control of every ounce of her being. She wanted to speak, but her tongue clung to the roof of her mouth. Then Hilda blew a gray fume up her face and the smoke spiralled down her guardian's nostrils. Her eyes rolled and then closed shut. The next time she opened them, she looked more willing to obey.

"Now go; see to it that all my wishes are carried out," Hilda commanded and released her hold; the woman fell to the ground but got up immediately. She was more agreeable to Hilda's desires.

"Yes, I will see to all you have requested at once," she said. Hilda, smiled and dismissed her with a wave of her hand.

Hilda waited until she was alone in the house before stepping into the bath; her body was heating up and she could feel herself losing control. To calm herself, she ran a cold bath; as soon as she got in the bath, she noticed her body heating up the bath; each time she thought of Hanna, the water boiled over. She knew she had to find a way of controlling her powers; the angrier she got, the more her body glowed crimson red. It made her feel great and all she wanted to do was to unleash all that energy on someone, but it couldn't be just anyone she knew. She had always been an angry girl. It was her anger at her parents for failing her family that led her to this path and now she wanted nothing more.

Where all the so-called elders of the tribe had failed, she was sure now that she would prevail. She laughed out loud at the thought that her mother had had access to the source of her power and she chose the coward's option. She was grateful that she was different, and that she had the strength to do whatever it would take to destroy Hanna and the curse that had plagued her tribe for centuries. When she succeeded, they would all be grateful that she did everything possible to save them, she thought, and, if not, then she would kill them all for being so ungrateful, she concluded. She got out of the bath and wore a red dress that fitted her body perfectly. The dress reached her ankles; she let down her jet-black hair and wore red lipstick to match her dress. Hilda stood in front of the mirror and observed herself; her skin glowed under the silk gown. She closed her eyes and took a deep breath, and then she lifted her hands above her head, and a force of energy began to build. Smiling, as the power tingled within her, she pulled her hands down and out of nowhere, as though she had birthed them from her palms appeared two glowing fireballs.

Hilda laughed with content, and then she aimed the fireballs at the mirror, shattering it. Still not content, she brewed more fire from her palms and targeted every object in her room until everything in it was consumed. Suddenly feeling famished, she made her way to the kitchen. Her little display of power had left her feeling weak. She opened the fridge to find food. There was a roast beef covered in foil, some cheesecake, eggs, milk, butter, steaks marinated and prepped for cooking later. She picked up the roast beef and sniffed it but the smell turned her stomach. Her eyes darted toward the raw beef steaks in the fridge; they were more appealing. Without thinking, she grabbed and began to devour the raw meat until there was nothing left. Still, she felt hungry. She rummaged through the freezer and found some frozen uncooked chicken, sausages, and beef. She placed her palm on the meat to melt the ice and then sat on the kitchen floor and gulped them down her throat. Hilda closed her eyes in enjoyment and licked her fingers as she consumed the last of the meat. Her guardian returned just in time to watch her devour raw meat. The shock of what she witnessed coupled with what she had experienced earlier became too much for her; she dropped to the ground and her heart stopped. Hilda wiped her mouth and examined her teeth with a kitchen spoon. Then she walked to the corpse of her guardian and scrutinized her for a moment before stepping over her dead body as she left the kitchen. She could already feel the presence of her visitors; now that she had eaten, she felt more at ease. She hoped to keep it that way, at least for now.

A few men waited for her in the living room.

The men looked stout; she counted six of them as she walked into their midst. She could feel their anxiety as they questioned within why they had been summoned by a little girl. Her father may have been the head of the tribe, but they all knew that it was his devastating colossal failure that had cost them all their families. The curse jumped a few people, but almost every member of the tribe had a family member that was already living life as a wolf or was about to lose a loved one to the curse.

"Welcome," Hilda said, looking from one face to the other.

"Thank you for honouring me with your presence. This is an urgent meeting, and I will not take your time as I do hope you wouldn't waste mine either," she said. She heard a few of the men murmur to themselves, wondering by what authority she chose to speak to them in such a manner. Choosing to ignore them for now, Hilda continued. "Gentlemen, please sit; we have a lot to talk about," Hilda said gesturing to the sofas.

"What gives you the right to summon us to you; we will not sit until you have told us why you called us here," one of the men said; he had gray long hair with streaks of black.

Hilda smiled and said, "As you all know, my father was and still is the head of the tribe even in his present state and in his absence or demise the power passes on to his heir. As it stands both Hurrit and Suzan cannot take on that role as they have both succumbed to the curse, so that leaves me. I am his only living human heir which makes me the head of the tribe; therefore, by that authority, I have asked for your presence here." Everyone was quiet, she knew they couldn't argue the fact unless they were looking for a fight, and she was ready to make an example of any rebel if given the chance.

"Now that we have established the facts, gentlemen, please sit down and let us talk," Hilda said; she gestured to the seats again.

The grey-haired man stated, "Your father may have been the leader, but that right was revoked when he failed this tribe. Your family no longer holds the power to head the tribe when you have brought us nothing but shame and pain, defeated by a girl that should have been sacrificed for the good of the tribe. You should hang your head in shame for what your parents did, and as I understand, you will soon join them; the sooner the better. When you turn, the oracle will be cast and a new leading family will be chosen from among the six of us. Anyone of us will be better at leading this tribe than a little-spoilt brat that doesn't know if she's coming or going." His statement caused the others to laugh hysterically. Their disrespect angered her; they do not understand what I offer she said to herself as she tried to remain calm. She reminded herself that they were not the enemy.

"You laugh, and you mock me, but I will disregard your outburst for now because I understand that you are hurting. Like me, you lost loved ones; you lost all hope, but I am here now to make it all better," Hilda said; moving closer to the grey-haired man, she kept her hands hidden behind her back and told herself to be patient.

"I will even disregard your total lack of respect for my family, who, if I may remind you, have headed this tribe for centuries from one generation to another." She paused to look at them. "However," she said looking from the grey-haired man to the others, "for your sakes, I will pardon your impertinences; I pray you hear me now and listen well. I will only forgive these insubordinations once; any more show of contempt before me will have severe repercussions. Believe me, I am not the enemy; I have called you here to try and 'rectify,' as you call it, my father's failures, and I need your help to do that." Hilda paused to hear their response; the men looked at one another and began to laugh again.

"Look at her. She is really serious. She wants to head the tribe," the grey-haired man said pointing at Hilda.

"My dear, what can you do that your father did not try and fail?"

Another jeered, and said, "Amal, give the little girl the feather; she is desperate to rule." A few of the men clutched their stomachs and the laughter roared. Hilda looked on in disgust; she had warned them, she told herself, and now she had to teach them a lesson.

"I have heard it all. Now, let's go; it is clear we have wasted our time coming here," the grey-haired man said. He turned to face the rest of the men who were still clearly amused. As they turned to leave, Hilda, pulled Amal, the grey-haired man, toward her with the force of her power. His body moved toward hers until he was standing at her feet; he tried to move but he couldn't; he soon realized he was no longer in control of his own will. She lifted her hands higher raising him above the ground. Then she looked from him to the others who looked on in shock and horror at what was unfolding before their eyes. They were sorely afraid; she wanted them to know who it was in control.

"I warned you. I warned you all, and now I have to teach you to be respectful. I am your leader, whether you like it or not. Do you still think me a joke?" she asked. They shook their heads in response, unable to form words. She returned her gaze to Amal, the grey-haired man.

"What about you? Do you still want to mock me?" The man shook his head aggressively.

"What? I didn't quite catch that. Use your tongue" Hilda said.

"Please forgive me. I'm very sorry" Amal blurted out.

"Yes, you will be sorry," she said and looked from him to the rest of the men who cowered in fear of what would happen next.

"I told you. I will only forgive once. Now you force my hand, and I have to teach you to never forget that I am the head of this tribe." She looked at the man and formed a fist, and then when she opened her hands a ball of fire appeared.

"I may be a girl to you but I am more powerful than you. I will burn that tongue that you berated me with." She opened his mouth and shoved the fireball down his throat. The man staggered and his body shook aggressively as the fire made its way down his body; his eyes popped out as the others witnessed the horrific punishment Hilda doled out to their friend. His body ignited from within. Amal yelled out in pain; his skin began to crack open as the fire sparked, visible beneath his skin and in an instance; his body crumbled and dispersed into a cloud of smoke. Hilda took a deep breath, opened her mouth, and the smoke from Amal narrowed vertically and entered her through her nostrils and her mouth until nothing was left.

The men were too petrified to move; they trembled with their mouths wide opened. Hilda turned to them and asked.

"Does anyone else oppose my leadership?" She asked, looking from one terrified face to the other. The other two that had spoken up to mock her suddenly found the use of their feet and tried to run, but then Hilda flicked her fingers and they fell.

"Wait," she said. "Must we go through this again? I don't want to hurt you," she said moving closer to the men. "I want to set our people free; I want to break the curse. Is that not what you all want?" She asked rhetorically knowing she wouldn't get an answer. Hilda offered her hand to one of the fallen men.

"Get up. Don't be afraid. You are not the enemy. He had to die. I warned him, but he chose not to listen. Tell the others what you saw me do; tell them I will fix everything where my father failed. I am not my father; be thankful for that. Things clearly have not gone how I wanted, but still we must make do. I want all tribe members in the woodlands of Scotland living as wolves returned home; I want a gathering of every member of the tribe here in my home for those about to be turned as well as their families. A new sacrifice shall be made on the next new moon, and I assure you, Hanna will be killed, and I will use her blood to cleanse this tribe and restore every man, every woman, and every child to their families as it should have been. Am I understood?" She asked, looking to ensure they were hearing and understanding what she said. The men nodded eagerly in acknowledgment. They bowed their heads in obeisance. Looking at all the heads bowed before her, she smiled with contentment. She had them where she wanted. She had hoped it would be easier to gain their support; however, she did what she needed to do and now she was a step closer to building the army she needs to win against Hanna.

"Okay, you may leave as soon as I depart." As if in show of power, Hilda turned on her heels and dispersed into a swarm of bees and flew away until she was no longer visible.

Chapter 14

Sebastian and Hanna Greene

Sebastian carried Annemarie's body to the back of the house and carelessly threw the corpse on the floor. He turned to look at Hanna who watched from the kitchen window. He picked up a keg of petrol and doused it on the corpse. He silently wondered if Mason already knew that his precious dead witch's body was missing. Thinking about his mother and how she had been killed by Mason because of this dead witch, Sebastian sighed, and then he lit a lighter and threw it on the body. The fire broke out immediately. He smiled as the fire burned and said, "This one is for you mother." His thought went to that time when he swore he would avenge her because Mason had led him to believe that the humans killed his mother.

"And for all those I . . ." he couldn't bring himself to say the word *murdered*. "I'm sorry; it's not enough, but I am," he said. Sebastian closed his eyes and forced the memory out of his mind. He then went into the kitchen to pick up an axe; he had promised Mason that he would pay him back for his evil deed, and he was going to make sure he fulfilled his words. As he entered the kitchen, he noticed Hanna's face looked confused when she saw him with the axe.

"I already told you what I would do; look away if you don't have the stomach for it," he said as he was about to step out the door.

"No S, that's not what I'm shocked about," Hanna said pointing to the corpse Sebastian had burned with fire.

"What then?" He asked.

"Look S. Isn't that something?" Hanna said astonished.

"What! I saw it . . . I burned it with fire . . . did you not see it? I . . ." Sebastian was lost for words. The fire had died down, and the body was restored to the way it was before he doused it in petrol. Sebastian ran out to inspect the body.

"This can't be," he muttered to himself. Hanna rushed outside to meet him. Sebastian turned to look at her and then looked down at Annemarie's body. "I saw it burn. I don't understand. It's impossible," he protested.

"Well, you did say she was a powerful witch. What do you want to do with her now that it's clear she can't burn?" Hanna asked.

"What if you try burning her with your power?" Sebastian asked.

"I don't know; I am wary of using my powers on her. If what you say is true and they need me to resurrect her, what if using it on her brings her back? I think we have enough enemies as it is. Let's not empower them by waking the wicked witch," Hanna joked. Sebastian swallowed hard.

"You are right, I guess. I am going to rule out burning from the list and get on with chopping her into bits," Sebastian said, raising the axe high.

"Wait," Hanna said.

"What? Do you want to say a prayer for her? I think it's too late for that, darling," Sebastian joked.

"No, that's not it. I just think chopping her up is barbaric. S, just throw her body into the sea. He can't bring her back if he can't find her," Hanna suggested.

"I don't like taking the risk of leaving her in one piece. I say we cut her up and scatter her about so she can never be put together," Sebastian pushed. Hanna's forehead creased at the suggestion.

"No, I don't like it, but if it puts your mind at rest, have at it," Hanna said and walked back into the house.

Frustrated, Sebastian dropped the axe; he looked at the body and said. "You will go to hell in one piece because of her, we both know you don't deserve it, but hey, she always wins." He went inside, walking past Hanna.

"What are you going to do?" She asked,

"Just wait and see," he responded. He returned later with a heavy chain and tied it around Annemarie's feet; he then tied the chain around a heavy rock. Rolling the rock toward the cliff, he dragged Annemarie's body on the ground until he was at the precipice.

"Now, see if you can escape this one," he said to the corpse as he pushed the rock and Annemarie's body into the sea. He heard a big splash as the rock and body hit the water simultaneously, and he watched as the body immediately sank to the bottom.

He felt triumphant. He had one over Mason, although he wished he had hacked her up and burnt her to smithereens. Still, it was a victory where he was concerned.

Re-entering the cottage, Hanna had a cup of tea in her hand. Sebastian smiled with satisfaction as he opened the freezer to fetch a blood bag. He warmed it in the microwave and poured the contents into a tea cup. They both stood leaning their backs on the counter, enjoying the contents of their tea cups.

"You still haven't told me what you plan to do with that head?" Hanna asked referring to Patrick's head.

"Ah that one. I'm going to place it where Mason is sure to find it," Sebastian answered.

"Hmm. Do you know where yet?" Hanna quizzed.

"Not sure. I'm still thinking but leaning toward Grosmont. That's the most recent place we would have been seen if anyone saw us, but it could be risky. If he decides to go, I'm hoping we will be back there before he arrives, so I can reunite him with Patrick's head." Sebastian smiled with amusement.

"Why does he have to see it?" Hanna asked.

Sebastian looked at her and said, "Darling, by now he will be raising hell, gaining supporters. He has a great army of vampires. All I want to do is put fear in them; make them think that perhaps if I can kill Patrick then maybe the rest will consider keeping their own heads. I doubt it will help, but we are winning and I want to continue doing so." He grinned.

"Please don't tell me you're enjoying this?" Hanna teased.

"Not even remotely, but we are at war, and we must conquer by any means possible," Sebastian replied.

"I agree," Hanna added.

There was silence as they ingested their drinks.

"Does that taste nice?" Hanna asked.

"What?" Sebastian asked looking up from his cup.

"I mean, drinking from a bag instead of directly from the animal?" Hanna explained. Sebastian shrugged.

"A beggar they say has no choice. It is what it is. I can't go hunting. It's too risky. Too many eyes working for Mason, both humans and vampires alike. Even those that never supported him as ruler will come now that they think he has all the answers. Imagine existing in the dark for thousands and hundreds of years and suddenly there is a promise of light, hope of walking the sun . . . just imagine how they will flock," Sebastian said, and then he looked away unable to meet her eyes as he suddenly realized they may not win the war, not with the number of supporters Mason would gain.

"What is it?" Hanna asked.

Sebastian looked at her and smiled faintly. Then he tucked a stray hair behind her ears and said, "Darling, it scares me; we would be facing a great army. Thousands more would have joined

Mason by the week's end. We can't fight them all; I don't know what we can do. I don't want to lose you; I don't want you hurt." He paused; he was being negative; if they were to have any chance at all, he knew he couldn't allow himself to think that way.

"Never you mind; we will destroy them all, and you and I will be the only ones standing," he said, and Hanna responded with a smile of her own.

"I like this thinking better," she said.
"You and I against the world," she added. Sebastian placed his tea cup in the sink and turned on the water to wash it. Hanna also placed hers in the sink and admired Sebastian as he washed the cups and gently put them away. She had denied herself his love for three years, and she would do anything to ensure they remained together. As he dried his hands with a kitchen towel, Hanna went to him and asked. "Tell me S, what do we have to do to remain standing?"

Sebastian looked at her; he could tell he had worried her earlier; he pulled her into his arms and kissed her forehead gently. "We have to kill Mason; when we kill him, we destroy his army. Without a leader, they will fight amongst themselves, and they will go back to their lives and put it all behind them as though it was just one big fantasy," Sebastian said, still worried, but he tried to hide it from Hanna. Killing Mason won't be easy, he thought; how were they to get him alone when they didn't know where he was?

Hanna looked up at his face and said, "Then that is what we will do. We will find Mason and kill him, but if we don't and we die, it's okay too. I will leave this world knowing that I loved you, and you loved me . . ."

"No darling, don't say that." Sebastian held her face gently between his hands. "Never say that; don't forget we will be the last man standing. Mason must die, no matter what the cost."

Hanna blinked; she knew she had to be strong for the two of them. She could smell his fear, but he was doing a good job of covering it up. They both had to be brave for one another until they won. Sebastian looked at her as if he could see her very soul; as if he hadn't seen anything as beautiful before, and he wondered what he did to deserve her. Hanna smiled warmly; she loved it when he looked at her that way. Sebastian traced his thumb over the bow of her lips. Her eyes gazed into his longingly; then he placed his lips on hers gently; she closed her eyes immediately; they touched and she welcomed the electric feeling that sparked all over her body. The passion between them intensified, and Sebastian's body turned warm; he wanted her more than he had ever wanted anything. He knew now wasn't the time, but since their reunion, each time he looked at her, his body craved hers, and for some reason, the talk of doom earlier made it feel imminent. The need to make love to her and touch her in places he'd only imagined became increasingly disturbing.

"I'm sorry Hanna, I can't," he said as he broke from their kiss. She held him back.

"Wait. Don't go. Just a few more minutes," she said.

"I'm sorry love, I can't. I want more than this, and I can't ask you if you are not ready, but kissing you drives me nuts with want," he blurted out. Hanna's mouth formed an o as she realized that they had gotten to the point where things needed to move to the next stage and as much as she was dying inside to go there, she knew she couldn't. They had a war to fight. She knew better, but she couldn't help herself; it was selfish of her to keep kissing him when she hadn't told him what she would lose if they made love. Each time she kissed him, her father's words played at the back of her mind.

"I should warn you, he is your weakness; if you should ever have carnal knowledge of him, you will lose all your powers and return to humanity." It was time she explained this to him.

"S, don't go, please. We need to talk," she said and tried to pull him back to her, but he broke free.

"Sorry love. we will talk later; I just need to get away from you for a moment. I will take a shower and join you soon," he said and disappeared.

Frustrated, Hanna went to the living room and sat down awaiting Sebastian's return. While she waited, she thought about how to gently let him know that they would never be able to go beyond kissing as long as there was evil to fight. Hanna wondered how he would take the news; it was not easy for her as well; the temptation was too much, living alone with him, kissing him, wanting him and knowing she couldn't have him. If only they didn't have Mason after them, then she would trade all her powers to be with him that way even if it was for only one night.

Sebastian returned smelling exquisite; he felt better, but he also felt a little embarrassed for making her uncomfortable earlier. He should have better controlled his urge, he thought. However, he also knew that it was only natural to feel that way for the girl he desired. He sat next to her and smiled awkwardly.

"I'm sorry about before; I shouldn't have said anything; I didn't mean to pressure you. I don't know what I was thinking. I mean, look at you; you are stunning, and there has not been a time when I haven't wanted you. Each time I look at you, I get the urge to kiss you, but I know that is unreasonable. It can be frustrating, but that is no excuse for my behaviour. I never want you to feel pressured by me if it's not what you want. Forgive me, darling, and forget I said anything," Sebastian said placing his hands on hers. Hanna nodded and looked away; she knew she couldn't let him take all the blame when she was also at fault. She had to tell him the truth now.

"There is nothing to forgive S; what you describe is the same way I feel about you. I want you too, more than you know, but we can't. I mean if we were both normal, if we didn't have vampires after our lives, that is what we should be doing. The sad thing is we may never get to be together that way. We just can't; we have too much to lose if we do. I should have told you something a while back. You must understand by now that our lives are intertwined; we both can't seem to exist without each other; that is why Mason needs you to apprehend me. What I am trying to say is, you are my weakness S and if we didn't have so much at stake . . . you know, but we do," Hanna said unable to tell him exactly what she wanted to say. She feared that he might lose interest in her.

"I don't understand? What do you mean by that?" Sebastian quizzed, Hanna stood up and walked toward the window. Sebastian got up and went after her.

"Tell me what you wanted to say; make me understand," he entreated her.

"Sebastian, if we ever . . . erm . . . if we both, you know," Hanna said trying to find the right words. Sebastian narrowed his eyes as he came to the understanding of what she was getting at; he held her hands as he tried to help her voice out what he thought she wanted to say.

"Are you talking about us having carnal knowledge of each other?" he probed. Hanna looked at him and nodded.

"What will ensue if that happens?" he probed further. Hanna closed her eyes and then sighed before speaking.

"I will lose all my powers and return to humanity," she said dejectedly looking at him to see if he was disappointed.

Sebastian's forehead creased with confusion.

"Why didn't you tell me?" He asked.

"I don't know; I guess a part of me was afraid," Hanna replied.

"Afraid, of what? Of me? Why would you be afraid? I thought you knew by now that you could tell me anything," Sebastian said annoyed that she kept a secret from him. If anything, he expected her to know by now that he was on her side and nothing could come between them.

"I'm sorry. I felt insecure; afraid that I would lose you. You know my mom used to say that all men have needs, and you are a man even though you are a vampire. Clearly, she was right; you want more; you need more from me, and I can't fulfil your needs. I was afraid that if I couldn't offer that . . . that you may look elsewhere, so I decided that telling you wasn't the best option, for now. But I always knew that I would one day, and now, I guess . . . it is time you knew," Hanna explained.

Sebastian looked at her with disappointment etched on his face. He wanted to say something; he opened his mouth, but he decided against saying it. He was too annoyed at her for thinking him so shallow.

He didn't know how else he could explain to her or show her how much she meant to him, and he thought that by now she knew and that she trusted him more and gave him more credit. He walked away before he said something he would regret.

"Wait S, where are you going?" Hanna asked, but Sebastian refused to answer. "At least tell me that I am wrong?" she yelled after him.

He stopped in his tracks without turning to face her and said, "Hanna, it's a pity you don't already know that." Then he walked out of the cottage through the back and walked towards the cliff.

An hour passed, and he didn't return. Worried, Hanna put on her shoes and went outside to look for him. She searched around the woods surrounding the cliff and couldn't find him. She didn't like how they had ended their talk. Not being with him for an hour felt like a decade, and she wondered how she had survived without him for three years. She wanted to yell his name, but she stopped herself. Sebastian had said nowhere was safe; calling for him could expose their whereabouts. After searching for half an hour, Hanna returned to the top of the cliff and looked down. Did he go for a swim, she wondered or had something happened to him? She was panicking, and she knew that wasn't going to help. She inhaled slowly to normalize her breathing, and then she closed her eyes. If she couldn't find him physically, then she would locate him through her mind.

"Sebastian," she voiced.

"What are you doing out here Hanna Greene?" She opened her eyes. His voice came from behind her. She spun around quickly. Relief filled her face.

"I looked everywhere for you; where did you go?" She asked as she hit him and pushed on his chest with her fist. He caught her fist and held her to him.

"I took a walk, I'm sorry; I didn't realize I was gone that long. I lost track of time," Sebastian explained. Hanna struggled to break free, but Sebastian held her closer to him.

"You knew I would be worried; were you trying to punish me?" She asked. Tears gathered around her eyes. Sebastian noticed, and it pained him he had made her worry, but even more that she thought him capable of wanting to hurt her.

"Listen, Hanna," he held her face so she could hear what he was going to say. "I'm not who you think I am; all I want to do is love you; I want to make you happy. If I had met you when I was human, I would have married you, and we would have made lots of little Hanna's. Perhaps in another life. Understand this: It is you I want; it's your love I need, and I can be with you forever if life permits without the need to fulfil fleshly gains. Hanna Greene, I only have eyes for you; ours is no conventional love. Next time, have a little faith; trust me a little more, and always know that I will never intentionally hurt you."

Hanna allowed the tears to spill freely down her face now. "I'm sorry. I don't know what I was thinking. I'm sorry," she said; Sebastian smiled softly and wiped her tears with the back of his hands.

"You weren't thinking; come with here." He pulled her into his embrace. "Let's go back inside before someone spots us," Sebastian said.

Chapter 15

The next day, as evening approached, Sebastian sat on the sofa and Hanna laid her head on his lap supporting her head with a cushion. She closed her eyes as Sebastian massaged and stroked her hair and scalp. "Darling, I think we should go back to Grosmont now; I want to place Patrick's head there for Mason to find," Sebastian said.

Hanna opened her eyes. "Okay, I just think, doing that will make him fight us more aggressively. And if he already does not know about his wife's corpse, when he finds that head he will know we have her. Is that wise?" Hanna asked.

"We don't have a choice; he must already know by now anyway. The sorcerer that escaped must have told him we were in Mexico. I think if his minions see what we did to Patrick, it might instil fear to a degree. I don't know; it may end up being a genius idea or the most foolish thing I could ever do. All the same, we have nothing to lose now. It's win, win either way," Sebastian said.

Hanna got up and looked at him and said, "Well, since we have nothing to lose, we do as you say. Maybe it will work to our advantage somehow. He will definitely rage over the loss of his wife's corpse, and that will make him reckless. We need to get him on his own and end this once and for all," Hanna said.

Sebastian, nodded before answering. "Yes, but he won't come alone. He will have Thomas, Nicholas, and Henry amongst others and those three are dangerous fighters. I don't know how I can defeat them." Sebastian mentioned thoughtfully.

"What if I level the playing field, make you equally as strong or even stronger?"

Sebastian looked at her doubtfully. "Is that even possible? How would you go about doing that?" He asked.

"I don't know; the idea just popped in my head; it could work or go wrong so fast, but I would feel safer if I knew I did something to protect you from dying," Hanna assured him and got up, pulling him up to her.

"Wait, what . . . um . . . are you doing it now?" He asked, confused.

"Yes, time is of the essence; I don't know why I didn't think of it before. What I am thinking is this: I will put a shield on you so that your body becomes impenetrable and unbreakable so that if you ever find yourself in a situation where I can't help because my hands are full, you will be safe," Hanna explained. Sebastian smiled.

"Well, won't that be something? If you can do that darling, that will definitely level the playing field," he said, but then she looked troubled again, and he wondered if he had celebrated too quickly. The look on her face meant that there could be unacceptable consequences to their plan.

"Okay, Hanna, tell me. What is it now?" He asked, hoping for the best but reluctantly preparing himself for the worst-case scenario.

"There is also something I should have told you long ago, and I didn't because I never thought we would be in this situation," Hanna said and bit her lower lip. Sebastian noticed how nervous she was, and he wondered how bad the consequences were. He took a deep breath and braced himself for the news.

"Say it love, whatever it is we can handle together," he said lifting her chin up to him so he could look her in the eyes.

"There is no easy way to say this, and believe me, I wish there were other ways, but when I strengthen you, I will be taking from my powers to make you stronger. That means a part of me will go in you. It's not going to affect me now or anything like that, but should Mason get his hands on me or if I become incapacitated, the only way I can regain my powers will be . . . erm . . . it will be . . . to erase . . . erase you . . . from my life. If I do that, I will regain strength, but my memories of you will fade."

"What! Darling, I don't understand. Erase me? What does that mean?"

"I will have to draw from the strength I put in you; it means taking back the light I put in you as well. If I do that, I will be strong again, but it will mean sacrificing our love S; it will mean that I won't . . . I won't . . . remember you or the love we shared. It will break the bond that joins us, but I will become even stronger for it," Hanna tried to explain.

Sebastian had looked helpless before she spoke; he already knew it was going to be bad news, but he wasn't expecting it to be this bad. He looked up at her.

"Is that all?" He asked. She shook her head,

"No, there is more, I'm afraid; once that happens even though I won't remember who you are, you may still have memories of us. I don't know how it works exactly. I don't know if this will be instant or a gradual process, but that is pretty much it," Hanna explained and watched his face to see how he was taking the news. Sebastian looked stunned.

He smiled awkwardly, "I need to sit down, erm . . . do you mind if I take a seat?" He asked and sat back down, but then he got up almost immediately and walked towards the kitchen as if in search of something. Then he stopped abruptly and turned toward her.

"And it can't be reversed after the battle is won?" He asked. Hanna shook her head,

"No, I won't know you anymore," she said forlornly, sadness creased his face.

"So really, the joke is on us. We may never have a future, because I will be nothing to you. Hell, you may even kill me because you won't know that we are on the same side," Sebastian said trying to make sense of the bombshell she just laid on him.

"This is only as a last resort; I never mentioned it before because I never thought anything would even make me consider doing it. You should remember; this is not only about us, S. If I let Mason take me, all those vampires will become day walkers. Imagine what that will do to the humans; think about it; we sacrifice our love, our future to save humans," Hanna explained.

Sebastian nodded, "I get it." And then he chuckled sadly. "You know when I first met you, I'm talking about you now, not the little you." He paused and looked at her. "When you told me you loved me, I thought . . . it can't be real, clearly, you were too good to be true, and I was right. Sometimes, I pinch myself because I still can't believe that I get to have you in my life. The minute I met you, I was alive again. I became hopeful because . . . of you. But this, what you just said, if it ever happens, it will be . . . like dying all over again; it will feel like living in a meaningless world, like drowning in an endless pit vast and void. Why would I want that? Why would anyone?" He chuckled awkwardly, and then he was quiet.

He looked down and then he said, "I already know that feeling, but I also know I can't be selfish; it can't just be about me and what I need. So, if that is what it will take to win this war and keep you and the humans safe, then that is what we will do." He made an end of his speech. Hanna didn't say a word; they both knew the pain of not being in each other's lives. Tears clouded her eyes and spilled down her face.

Sebastian went to her and comforted her, pulling her into his arms. What he failed to say was that after she had done that, he would make sure he died in that battle. The way he saw it, it was better to be dead than to live his life without her a second time. And it would be okay because no one would miss him; she wouldn't even know him.

"It's all right love; let's just make the best of what we have now. We both know that nothing of worth is gained easily," Sebastian consoled Hanna, holding his own grief in.

"We must all play our parts to keep the world from darkness. Let's do it. Put the shield on me," he said.

"Are you sure?" Hanna asked. Sebastian nodded.

"I am," he replied.

"Okay, stand over there." Hanna wiped her eyes dry with the back of her hand. She took a deep breath and stretched her hands toward him. In that moment, Sebastian became afraid; he suddenly felt that when they went to Grosmont, they may not return together depending on what they met there.

"Wait!" He said and pulled her to him again; his heart ached for her touch, and his mouth found hers, and he kissed her with desperation and passion. It felt as though he were imprinting and embedding the memories of the softness of her lips, her taste, and smell into his mind. And then, as suddenly as it started, he pulled back and said, "Remember even if it is just for now, that I have loved you with everything Hanna Greene."

Hanna smiled; she could tell what he was thinking after the news she gave him. However, she knew she would do whatever it took, break down every wall, if necessary, to ensure they would both come back alive.

"And I have loved you, too, Sebastian Francis. We will make it back in one piece, but if we don't, I have a feeling that in another life, if there ever is one, that we will find each other again, and I will be your wife if you will have me." She smiled.

He laughed softly. "And we would make loads of beautiful children together. I would probably . . . hassle you all the time and you just have to put up with me."

They both laughed; then Hanna continued. "If we die in battle today, tomorrow or many years from now, it is okay, because you found me, and we lived and we loved with all our hearts."

Sebastian swallowed hard and then traced his hands on her lips. He created enough distance and said, "Okay, now I am ready; make me unbreakable."

She smiled and nodded approvingly. "Brace yourself, this might hurt a little," Hanna said as she stretched forth her hands.

Sebastian yelled out in pain as every bone in his body began to break. He dropped to his knees, losing control of his legs. His body glowed like metal burned in a furnace. He could feel his bones melting and moving inside him as the pain increased. He rolled on the floor helplessly willing for her to stop, but Hanna continued; she glowed as deposits of her powers strengthened him. His bones remoulded, and his skin gained power. The glow died down, and she put her hands to her sides. He didn't move; his eyes were closed; she walked towards him and knelt beside him.

"S, it's done."

Chapter 16

Hector Sayers.

It had been four weeks since Hector lost his brothers in battle, he found their loss difficult to accept. He'd never been alone since Anton made him a vampire and now he'd lost two of his brothers in one day. And the only thing left to do was get vengeance; he had thought it impossible before to fight Thomas, Nicholas, Henry, and Sebastian on his own; but it seemed like Lady Luck was on his side. He heard from an ally that Sebastian was being hunted by Mason. And the news of Mason making all vampires day walkers had brought out almost every vampire under the rocks to England. They were all signing up to join his army. The excitement and promise of a better life had brought about talks of great celebration after victory. The centurion festivity was to take place immediately after the child of power was defeated. Every vampire that wanted the gift of light had been charged with finding Sebastian because when Sebastian was found so also would the child of power be found. This wasn't the news he wanted; if Mason were hunting Sebastian it would make it harder for him to find Sebastian and avenge his brothers. And the more vampires who joined Mason's army, the more untouchable Thomas, Nicholas and Henry would become. He needed allies if he wanted to succeed, which was easier said than done. Every vampire that once sympathized with him and his brothers cause before were now very careful, they didn't want to be found associated with him. News of defeat and death of his brothers had also spread like wildfire and it was all any vampire could talk about. It was being said that Mason had finally removed the gum on the heel of his sole. The insinuation irritated Hector, but fighting those saying it would mean creating more enemies for himself and that, he didn't need.

He couldn't shake the feeling that if Sebastian was now Mason's enemy, then Hanna and Sebastian might have reunited. Another news he didn't need. He wanted Hanna for himself, especially now that he didn't have his brothers to hold him back anymore. His mind went to the time he spent with Hanna in Harrogate when she searched for her mother. His memories drifted to the wonderful kiss they shared, and how it made him feel. Then, he remembered the abrupt way she had ended it claiming her love for his nemesis. As if Sebastian had not taken enough from him, he got the girl as well. Just then, an idea popped in his head; he thought perhaps he could find Sebastian and hand him over to Mason; maybe then Mason would show him clemency for his past wrongs. He hated Mason as much as he loathed Sebastian, but using one stone to kill two birds seemed like a great idea. It was risky; Mason could kill them both, but if he presented Sebastian in the presence of all the vampires that had gathered as a gesture of goodwill, Mason might forgive him, especially now that his brothers were dead. Hector told himself that he would crawl and beg for forgiveness and then when enough time had passed, then he would look for Mason's lieutenants one after the other and avenge his brother's death.

Hector immediately got to work and set up eyes around Sebastian's house in Grosmont. He wasn't sure if Sebastian would be crazy enough to return, but if he did, he wanted to be the first to meet with him. His mind went to Hanna; he knew that if they were truly back together, she would pose a problem, but he would handle her. All he had to do to break their union would be to sow a seed of doubt in Sebastian's mind about her.

****

Two Days later,

One of his human informers reported seeing a dark-haired girl at the house. Hector knew that Hanna's hair was blond but she could be in disguise, he thought. Knowing that Mason also had eyes watching the place, Hector quickly made his way to Sebastian's house after sunset. The doors were locked, but he could smell Hanna's familiar scent. He should know; he was with her only a few weeks ago. Hector broke into the house through the back door. He carefully looked from room to room, but they were both nowhere to be found; their scent was heavy everywhere. He was annoyed with himself; they had obviously been there, and he must have just missed his chance to capture Sebastian. He stood in the living room, wondering where next he needed to look when before his face, two bodies appeared out of thin air.

He couldn't believe his luck; the shock of it all made him immobile for a moment, and the second the three of them recognised each other, Hector made his move. He tried to grab Sebastian before Hanna could use her powers on him, but he was too late; before he could reach him, Hanna sent him reeling to the ground with a wave of her hand.

Sebastian looked at Hanna and said, "No leave him to me. I will destroy him myself and send him to hell to meet his brothers." Sebastian did not wait to hear her response. He was tired of Hector popping up in places he was not wanted. Hector was on his feet; he cracked his neck and smiled sadistically.

"Now, that you don't have others fighting for you, let's see how you will fare with me," he said, and he grinned,

"Wait. You two shouldn't fight," Hanna protested Hector looked at her for a moment. He wondered if she didn't want them to fight because she cared for him, but once he saw the way she looked at Sebastian, he knew the only reason she didn't want him fighting Sebastian was because she feared that he would kill him.

"Hanna, stay out of this," Sebastian said sternly without turning to face her. Hector looked at how full of concern she was for Sebastian.

"Don't worry Hanna; for your sake, I will not kill him which is against every fibre of my being. I will beat him to stupor though, and then I will personally hand him to Mason. I hear he is quite famous now," Hector said sarcastically and turned to face Sebastian.

Sebastian rolled up his sleeves in preparation for combat.

"I would like to see you try," he said as he began to position himself to attack Hector.

"I mean it you two; I will not let you fight," Hanna warned.

"Sebastian, listen to me; look at me now, please!" Hanna yelled. Sebastian refused to take his eyes off Hector.

Hanna said, "We didn't come here for Hector; you are angry at him because he and his brothers attacked my family, but I'm not dead. If anything, he did me a favour and you can't still be angry at him for that. His brothers have paid for what they did; you made sure of it. Isn't that enough?" Her defending Hector made him furious. When Sebastian didn't say a word, Hanna turned her attention on Hector, hoping to talk him down from fighting Sebastian.

"And you, I thought you were better than this. Have you lost your mind? Do you think you can just waltz in here and announce your intention to take him to Mason? Do you have a death wish or something? I thought you were cleverer than that; I hear Mason hates you more than he hates Sebastian. Do you think he is just going to let you walk out freely? Think, you two; you hate each other now; you can keep acting stupid and fight, or you can join heads and fight a common enemy; which will it be?" Hanna asked, and she moved to stand between the two. Sebastian turned to look at her, still furious because of her attachment to Hector.

"What is this thing you have with him?" He asked. "Why are you always against me, fighting him, and don't tell me all that rubbish about him helping you. I have a feeling there is more?" Hanna looked away from Sebastian and shot her eyes in Hector's direction knowing that he would be thinking of their kiss. The kiss meant nothing to her, not like when she kisses Sebastian, but how could Sebastian understand this? She hoped that Hector would not mention it, and she pleaded with him with her eyes, but he looked away from her. Hector wanted her for himself, and if he could he would keep the kiss a secret, but seeing the way she was around Sebastian hurt him. It reminded him of the hurt he felt when she rejected him after the kiss. Even more so, he knew that if he told Sebastian of their little escapade, it would wound him knowing that he'd had his girl in his arms.

"Shall I tell him or would you do me the honour?" Hector asked looking straight at Sebastian and enjoying the effect of his words. Hanna looked helplessly from Hector to Sebastian. Sebastian's eyes narrowed as Hector's words penetrated his ears.

"Tell me what?" He demanded. Sebastian feared the worse. He had always felt that she defended Hector too much, and he wanted to get to the bottom of it.

Hanna turned to face Hector. "Don't Hector please, if I ever meant anything to you?" Hanna pleaded. Sebastian's irritation at the situation unfolding before his eyes turned into rage. He couldn't stomach the fact that Hanna had a secret she shared with Hector knowing how he felt about him. He could see the smug look on Hector's face as Hanna pleaded with him not to tell him.

Sebastian wished he had pressed Hanna for answers before; he felt her react each time he mentioned Hector in the past. And now he felt like whatever would be said would no doubt humiliate him.

"If there is anything to be said Hanna, tell me now," Sebastian pressed.

"S, listen to me. It's nothing; he is just trying to cause a fight between us. I will tell you all about it later; let's concentrate on why we came here," Hanna said moving towards Sebastian to try and calm him down. Hector beamed as he enjoyed the friction he had caused between them. This was the opportunity he was waiting for, he thought. Sebastian was breathing hard, and doing his best to control his anger. Hector smiled knowing he had him just where he wanted and he knew that if Hanna didn't tell him then he would do him the honour of telling him how delicious her lips tasted, and how soft she felt in his arms. Sebastian looked at Hanna; he knew he had to control his anger; he knew he was letting Hector get to him. He wanted to listen to Hanna and trust that she would explain it all later, but the grin on Hector's face made him even more furious.

He looked away from Hector and faced Hanna, "I know that you love me," he said, "but is there any chance that you have some feelings for him too? Is that why you want me to spare his life?" Sebastian asked, not wanting to believe that he had asked that question, and he was desperate to hear her tell him that there was no truth to it. He felt a hard slap on his face.

"How could you even think such a thing? I have loved, and I am in love with only you," Hanna said fiercely and turned to hear Hector laughing.

"If that is true, then why did you kiss me, Love? Did you tell lover boy here that we were together a few weeks ago? That we spent time together in that hotel? Or did you just omit that when you two were making up? Well, I don't blame him; you do have a way of messing with one's head. You had me fooled. I thought perhaps you loved me, too. The way your lips moved urgently against mine as though your life depended on . . ." Before he could finish, Sebastian looked at Hanna sadly.

"Tell me none of the things that worm is claiming is true?" Sebastian asked fuming. Hanna looked away feeling helpless. She knew now that she shouldn't have kept it a secret; she should have told him and trusted that he would understand, but she didn't know that their paths would cross Hector's so soon.

"Hanna, look at me and tell me he is lying; were you with him like he claims; is any of this true? Tell me now," Sebastian pressed her further for the truth. Hanna held his face so that he was looking at her and said.

"It's true; I was with him; we were together briefly but . . ." Sebastian only heard the first two words. His mind went blank. He had tried to control the urge to kill Hector earlier and now, all he wanted to do was rip him apart. He walked away before she could finish; she reached for him, but he shook her off. Hanna ran in front of him as she tried to explain her side of the story.

"Listen to me; it meant nothing; plus, we weren't together you and I. I don't know why it happened, but I have only ever wanted you; I was missing you; it was you I wanted, not him. I was at a low, and I made a mistake," she explained. Hector smiled, although inside he wished she cared for him half as much as she cared for Sebastian.

"You kissed him; Hanna, of all the men in the world, it had to be him," Sebastian said.

"I'm sorry; I don't know what else to say, I needed him to help find my mother, and when I found out that she was still alive and that you didn't kill her, all these emotions came at me. I was crying and he walked in to comfort me and then . . ." she broke off,

"And then what Hanna?" Sebastian pushed.

"We kissed, for a mad minute but then I came to my senses," Hanna said.

"That's not how I remember it," Hector cut in.

"Shut up Hector," Hanna snapped.

"I'm just saying, you held me; I held you close as you pressed your body against mine. We couldn't help it; we had tension building for days. It was only natural that it happened. We both felt that kiss; you can't deny that Hanna," Hector said knowing his words were cutting Sebastian deep.

"I said shut it, Hector," Hanna warned. "Don't listen to him, S; he's just saying it to get at you. Believe me S, Love, look at me; it meant nothing to me. I told him I didn't want him. Ask him; I told him it was you I love. Hector please, tell him the truth, please, I beg you," Hanna pleaded. She had never seen Sebastian look at her with such disappointment.

"Please, Hector; the least you can do is tell him the truth," Hanna said turning to Hector seeing that she was losing Sebastian. Hector toyed with the idea of helping her out; he didn't like what he had done to her, but if it meant infuriating Sebastian, then he couldn't say what she wanted him to say.

"I don't remember you wanting to stop; I had to push you away because you wanted more. If I didn't mean anything to you, why were you whoring yourself away with me; one would think that he has never satisfied you like real men do, with the way your hips moved under me; you were insatiable . . ." Hector lied, but before he could finish speaking, Sebastian charged at him and lifted him off the ground and then slammed him right back to the floor. Hector felt weightless in his hands. Frustrated, Hanna stood and watched the two of them wrestle.

First Sebastian was on top of Hector, throwing deadly blows at him, and then Hector kicked him off with some force and managed to overcome him; he held Sebastian by the throat and tried to strangle him, but Sebastian grabbed Hector's fingers and pulled them off with ease, and then he drove his knee into Hector, shoving him off of him with force. Hector crashed into the sofa shattering it; his eyes widened at the effortlessness with which Sebastian was taking him on. Perhaps he had underestimated the boy; after all, it was he who killed Zacchary. With this information surfacing to his mind, Hector was filled with rage once again, and he bounced off the floor to meet Sebastian, who had already aimed his feet at him intending to send him back to the ground, but Hector managed to twist Sebastian's feet; he held them with both hands so that Sebastian had to back flip to get away from Hector's grip.

Gaining some respite, Hector got on his feet before Sebastian could turn and landed a hard blow on Sebastian's jaw sending him sideways; he landed another kick on Sebastian's back so that he fell to the ground. Sebastian turned before Hector could connect with him again blocking Hector's fist with one hand and grabbing his throat with the other forcing Hector to his knees. Sebastian held on to Hector's throat, as he got to his feet and pulled Hector up with him. The rage in his eyes as he thought of Hector touching Hanna made him increase the force with which he strangled Hector. He was annoyed at Hanna for not telling him the truth, and as he could never harm her; he was going to take it all out on Hector. Hector's hands moved frantically, as he tried to free himself, but Sebastian was too strong for him.

Tears rolled down Hanna's cheeks as she watched the two of them fight. She didn't want Sebastian to kill Hector and she knew that Sebastian knew this. She didn't know why Hector lied to Sebastian saying she moved her hips under him, but she also knew that she had rejected Hector, that he was still hurt, which explained why he had abandoned her at Harrogate. Hanna couldn't allow Sebastian to kill Hector, as he was still the only one who could identify her birth mother.

"Please S, don't do it. Please for me, I beg you," Hanna pleaded for Hector's life. Sebastian looked from Hector to her; it annoyed him even more that she was still pleading for his life. He felt the rage of jealousy flow through him, and he wanted to end Hector once and for all, but he knew she would never forgive him. Giving in to her request, he lifted Hector off his feet and flung him across the room. Hector crashed into the wall and remained where he landed; he had never felt so much strength from such a young vampire. He had thought that fighting Sebastian would be easy, but he was wrong and had Hanna not begged for his life Hector would have died.

Hanna ran over to him to check that he was alright; Sebastian stopped to look at the two of them; he couldn't stomach the fact that she cared for Hector still even after the way he spoke about her. As he looked at them, he imagined them kissing, and he instantly wanted to throw up. The rage he felt inside increased; he wanted to be anywhere but here. Sebastian wished he could go where he couldn't see her until he calmed his anger. He left the living room and made for the kitchen, although, the kitchen didn't seem far enough away; he could still hear her asking Hector if he was alright which only added fuel to the fire burning in him. He left the kitchen immediately and went upstairs to his room; he hoped she wouldn't come after him, not after nursing Hector.

Chapter 17

This was meant to be an in and out operation, although they knew they could be walking into danger, but never in a million years did Sebastian think that Hector would be the one they would first meet. Sebastian paced his room not knowing what to do with himself. He wanted to leave so badly, but he knew he couldn't go anywhere without Hanna and her face was the last thing he wanted to see right now. He never thought there would be a day he would say that or even admit it to himself. How could he look at her the same way now, when each time he closed his eyes all he could see was that worm's hands all over her, kissing the woman that he loved. In annoyance, Sebastian destroyed every piece of furniture he could lay his hands on. He knew he needed to calm down, his behaviour would raise alarm and any vampire around would know that someone was definitely in the house, but as much as he tried, he couldn't turn off the rage he was feeling inside.

Hanna got up from beside Hector; she heard the commotion Sebastian was making upstairs and the guilt of the kiss and the way he found out ate at her. She wanted to go and console him, but she also knew her face was probably the last he wanted around him.

"What did you do to him? He's an animal," Hector said; he placed one hand on his neck as he massaged the strain Sebastian caused when he strangled him.

"Don't tell me that behaviour is what you like in a man," Hector joked as he managed to get on his feet. Hanna threw him a hateful stare.

"Shut up Hector; this is all your doing. Are you happy now?" She retorted.

"Well, I had to do something for the way you rejected me. I mean you've got to agree it was quite cruel the way you went on about loving that animal knowing I had a thing for you," he said, trying to straighten his shirt.

"Really, and you think by doing this I will somehow end up with you? Even if Sebastian decides he doesn't want me anymore, which is highly unlikely, I will never be with you, Hector. I don't want you; get that through your thick skull," Hanna said angrily.

"Okay, I think we've already established that; by the way, I didn't mean all those terrible things I said about you earlier. I was craving a fight and I got more than I bargained for," he said.

"And you deserved it," Hanna added. Hector chuckled and then took a deep breath. He looked around at how he and Sebastian had destroyed the place when they fought.

"It's a good thing you won't be staying here; it's pretty much trashed now," Hector commented. Hanna ignored him and walked toward the stairs where she could still hear Sebastian destroying everything in his vicinity. Hector looked at her longingly as he wished it were him she cared for like that. He looked away, telling himself it was pointless to hope for her love. Just then his eyes spotted something in a bag.

"What's that?" He asked, picking up the bag with Patrick's head. Hector's eye widened as he discovered the severed head of a vampire in the bag.

"I take it that this is his doing, and he would have done the same to me had you not stopped him?" He said as he held the head in his hands and walked toward Hanna. She reluctantly dragged herself away from the stairs and snatched the head from Hector.

"Give that to me," Hanna said. "Sebastian brought it as a warning to vampires like you who think because of their age they can take him on." She placed the head on the shattered chair.

"Well, I think if you really want others to see it, you have it in the wrong place," Hector said going to take the head and placing it on the mantle in the living room. Hanna looked at the severed head and then turned her attention to Hector.

"You need to leave now; you've done enough damage," she said to him.

"I'm not going anywhere; I came here to use your raging boyfriend as a bargaining chip, but due to the events that took place minutes ago, I have changed my mind. That head there says if I align myself with the two of you, I have a fighting chance of staying alive," Hector declared.

"Well, you messed that up when you decided in all your wisdom to mention the kiss; there is no way we can work together now, so get out of here; I need to go fix my relationship with him, and I can't very well do that with you hanging around now, can I?" Hanna said.

"Fair point; I will go and give you time to do that, but I won't be far; if you need me, I will be right here. Good luck with mending the crack I masterminded. Tell your boyfriend about my plan, let him think it over. Hey, that does not mean we are buddies, but for now, I am willing to put our conflicts to one side until we defeat our common enemy," Hector said. Hanna took a deep breath; she could see how that could work, but talking to Sebastian about Hector now seemed wrong even if it was for the right reasons.

"I will try, but don't hold your breath. I am not promising anything. Now go please," Hanna said moving Hector toward the door.

"Okay, I will go, but . . ." Hector was saying when the front door opened. From where they stood, they couldn't make out who the intruder was. Hector and Hanna looked at each other, knowing it could be Mason or one of his goons. Hector nudged her to hide until they knew who it was. Hanna didn't really see the point in hiding; she listened for Sebastian who seemed to have calmed when the intruder came in. Before Hanna could decide what to do, Hilda Denali's face came into view. Hanna was taken aback; she wondered what Hilda was doing here in Sebastian's home. Especially now that they were in the middle of a dangerous war. She didn't want Hilda getting caught in the crossfire.

"Hilda!" Hanna said. Hilda's face looked stern. Confused, Hanna wanted to understand the reasons why she came. She knew to not trust anyone anymore; she'd been burnt too many times, but Hilda used to be like a little sister to her.

"Hilda, what . . .what are you doing here? How did you know I'd be here?" Hanna asked, moving closer to her to get a better look. Hilda scoffed and looked from Hanna to Hector and then focused on Hanna.

"I have come to undo my father's failure," she smirked as Hanna approached her. Hanna stopped in her tracks; the words that fell from Hilda's mouth alarmed her.

"Undo your father's failure. I am uncertain as to what that means Hilda," Hanna said, unsure now if Hilda was a friend or a foe. Hanna was no fool; she remembered clearly what Hilda said the last time she visited Suzan when Suzan was about to be taken to Scotland where the rest of the wolves resided. But now wasn't the time to deal with Hilda's issues; clearly, she couldn't have this many enemies at one go.

"My family failed the tribe because of their weakness, but I won't make the same mistakes," Hilda said. Hanna felt like she was speaking in parables; she smiled and wondered if Hilda knew the implications of what she was saying.

"I'm afraid you have to break it down for me, so I know exactly what you are saying. So, I ask again, what is the meaning of your words?" Hanna questioned.

Hilda moved a step closer to Hanna and said, "I told you the last time we met, that the next time I see you, one of us will die." Hilda began to charge her powers within. She had not counted on seeing Hanna today; what a fortunate turn of events. A member of the tribe had brought it to her attention that occupants were inside. Hilda had thought she would find squatters, but as luck will have it, the very person she was after had been handed to her on a platter of gold, and all she needed to do was show Hanna who was boss.

"Um," Hanna voiced; she remembered the threat, but she really didn't think Hilda meant it.

"Were you really serious about that? Listen, Hilda, I am in the middle of something dangerous and you can't be here, or you will get hurt. This issue you have with me; we can sort it later. I will come over to your house and we can sit down and talk about it," Hanna said.

Hilda laughed callously. "You still think me a child; you think you know what danger is? Hanna today you will pay for all the pain you have caused my people, my family." Hilda's hands were now glowing red. Hector noticed and alerted Hanna. Sebastian listened to their conversation on the stairs. He stood there not wanting to give himself away just in case Hilda brought more people and Hanna needed backup. Until her hands turned red like fire, no one saw Hilda as a threat. Hanna smiled sadly knowing there was no talking Hilda out of what she came to do.

"I don't know what you have been told Hilda; I am not the enemy. I didn't place the curse on your family. And I won't be used to cleanse it. Think carefully before you act," Hanna said gently not wanting to engage in a fight with her.

Hilda said, "You really think you can talk your way out of this, eh, like you did with my weakling of a father. This is what will happen: I am going to subdue you; then I will take you back to my house, where as we speak, all the elders are gathering every tribe

148

member both human and beast for the sacrifice. We will hold you until the next full moon, and then I will sacrifice you to appease the curse. You don't get to live when half of my tribe are living as wolves. After the sacrifice, they will all become human again and you will die like you were always meant to." It was Hanna's turn to scoff; she had noticed the fire brimming in Hilda's hands. Hanna now knew this wasn't going to be an easy challenge, but she was certain in her mind of victory.

"Well, let me make one thing clear, Hilda; you are not taking me anywhere with you so that sacrificial lamb you are after, you may have to look elsewhere for it. I'm sorry." Hanna had taken a stand.

Hector looked from one girl to the other; he had seen powerful witches before, but he wasn't sure what category Hilda fitted in. If he were betting, he would put his money on Hanna after she took out Ruth, the only other powerful witch he knew; he was aware now that Hanna was not to be messed with, hence the reason Mason was after her, but he wondered if this new girl would surprise him. Sebastian moved closer now that he knew none of the girls was backing down. He wanted to be close in case Hanna needed his help.

"I'm sorry," Hilda said, "did I say that I needed your approval? I think you heard me wrong. I am not leaving here without you; it is your choice; follow me voluntarily or I will kill that thing standing over there." Hilda gestured to Hector.

"You will have to go through me first," Hanna replied. Hector chuckled softly as the girls squabbled about him, although he didn't enjoy being referred to as 'That thing' by Hilda. What amused him was the fact that Hanna was willing to fight to defend him.

"I didn't come here for him, but I will kill him just to make a point," Hilda threatened. Hector didn't like being in the middle; he wondered if Hilda thought he was Hanna's boyfriend.

"I would like to see you try," Hanna said, calling her bluff. She noticed Sebastian was closer now, and she tried not to give away his presence. Hilda smiled sarcastically, and raised her hands, folding her hands into fists. She generated two fireballs in the palms of her hands. She had been itching to use her powers on Hanna, and here she was standing before her, but first she wanted to incite some fear into her. Before Hanna could block her, Hilda threw the fireballs at Hector; he dodged in time, but the second one scrapped him by the chin.

"Wow," Hector cried. "Another girl with too much power beyond her years," he lamented.

"Hey, I'm not the enemy. You don't even know me; what's wrong with you? Why . . ." Hector yelled at Hilda, but before he could finish speaking, Hilda sent another dose of fireballs his way. Hector tried to block with his arms and his shirt caught fire. He quickly peeled off his clothes before the fire spread. Hanna looked on in horror at the display of power. She never thought that Hilda had such abilities.

"Hilda! Stop it now," Hanna yelled.

"You wanted me, and now that you've shown me what you are working with, see if you can really take me on," Hanna challenged.

Sebastian looked on with concern; he wanted to move in front of her, but Hanna stopped him with her eyes. Hilda grinned wickedly as she charged and directed another set of fireballs in Hanna's direction. Hanna closed her eyes as the fireballs made their way to her. It was as if everything was in slow motion.

Hanna chanted, "Let water consume away the fire before me." Then bubbles of water appeared from thin air and engulfed and quenched the fireballs. Hilda had not anticipated that, and she threw more fire at Hanna, but none of it touched Hanna. It was as though Hanna had a shield that protected her from all of Hilda's efforts. Realizing the fireballs were pointless, Hilda opened her mouth and a huge cloud of gray smoke escaped and encircled the place where Hanna stood. Hanna smelled it and her eyes opened.

Sebastian looked at her with worry; he didn't know what the smoke circling Hanna would do to her. He wanted to move her away from it, and as he moved closer, he noticed Hector do the same, but they couldn't reach her. An invisible covering stretched out around her protecting Hanna, and it seemed the smoke was fighting to gain entrance into it. Hilda, tried to force her way inside with her powers, Hanna smiled then she looked at her and said, "Reveal," and a froth of radiance shone around her so brightly that it was impossible for Hilda to penetrate. Hilda looked stunned; she had thought this was going to be easy; she had given her soul for this day, and now it looked like she had failed again like her father before her. Hanna noticed the defeat written all over Hilda's face.

"You have to try harder than that if you want to take me on, don't you think?" Hanna asked, and then she added. "You are not welcome here." Hanna looked around her, and saw the evil resident in the smoke encircling her shield.

Hanna warned: "Take this evil with you and be gone from here. I hope that you have learned a lesson. In case you haven't, the next time I set eyes on you, one of us will surely die, and I promise you, it won't be me." Hanna then shoved her hands out, and the front doors opened. Then a force hauled and threw Hilda out from the living room toward the door until she was outside the house. Sebastian and Hector heard a loud screech as the creature in the smoke followed her out of the house, and then the door slammed shut. Hector clapped his hands respectfully in applause.

"I'll say, wasn't that something. Incredible!" He said and added "Believe me, I have seen my fair share of power, but I have never seen anything like what you just did and the ease with which it was done as well. Wow, I now truly understand why they all want you." Hector marvelled.

Hanna sighed and looked from him to Sebastian. "Not now Hector, I can't do this now," she said. The truth was that she wanted to cry. A little over three years ago, Hilda, Suzan, and Hurrit Denali had all been like her family. Hilda was like a little sister to her and now she was an enemy, and this wasn't over yet. The girl had gone in search of power and had found it, and Hanna knew she would return for her with more force in the future. When that would happen was uncertain, but when she returned, Hanna was sure she would have no choice but to kill her. She would not be used for any sacrifice. Not by the wolves, nor by the vampires, and definitely not for empowering and resurrecting dead witches.

"Hector, you need to go now please," Hanna reminded him as she focused her attention on Sebastian. Hector saw the way they looked at each other; he could see the relief on Sebastian's face as Hanna asked him to leave and it irritated Hector.

"Yeah, I know when it's my cue to leave," he said, and then he stopped next to Hanna but his eyes rested on Sebastian.

"Don't forget what we discussed Hanna; talk it over," Hector said as he walked out of the house. Sebastian looked away, not wanting to get himself in a rage again. Just witnessing another psycho coming to attack Hanna brought him back down to earth. What was important now was making sure she was alright even though she had handled the situation brilliantly. He knew he had to force himself to forget the situation with Hector; for now, there were more important things to worry about.

"I'm sorry," they both chorused; Sebastian chuckled, and Hanna smiled.

"No, you have nothing to be sorry for; if I found out that you kissed another girl, there is no telling what I would do. I can't even bring myself to think about it. It's unfair, I know, especially because it happened to be with Hector," Hanna said as she tried to comfort him.

"Can we not mention his name again please? It drives me up the wall," Sebastian said as he looked around at the mess that used to be his sitting room. He was finding it hard to look at her and not see Hector with her.

"You can't even look at me," Hanna noted. Sebastian scoffed and forced himself to look at her face. He placed his hand on her temple and tucked her hair behind her ear.

"It's hard, but I am trying," he said. Hanna took a deep breath; he noticed her eyes were cloudy with tears, but he didn't know what to say to make it alright and he didn't want to lie to her that he was over it. "How are you feeling after that episode?" He asked referring to the situation with Hilda. He couldn't bring himself to talk about anything other than the battles ahead and for the first time, he was grateful for the fights. They would help keep his mind sane until he could get over the constant image of her kissing Hector.

"I'll live," she answered and then she said, "It's not over though. She is going to come back, but I'll be ready when she does. I don't know where she got her powers, but that's no longer Hilda; something else resides in that girl." Hanna could tell that Sebastian was avoiding talking about the situation with Hector. She wondered how she would broach the subject of joining forces with Hector and if he would agree. The way she saw it, Hector was an asset at least for now until Mason was defeated. There was no time to waste; she must tell him, but she knew that now clearly was the wrong time to raise the subject.

Chapter 18

Mason Benedict

Mason paced about in his great room as he awaited word from his subjects on their findings about Sebastian. The influx of vampires coming to join his army was beginning to become a problem. Their congregating in one city meant more humans would die than was necessary. It was a cause of concern to him; to maintain order, humans must be unaware of the existence of vampires. With so many bound to disappear due to the arrival of many of his kind, it was critical that Sebastian and the child of power be found as soon as possible. That was not the only thing that worried him; he had instructed Patrick to call him daily and it had been more than two days since he last heard from him. It would seem that he had underestimated Sebastian; he had thought he would easily crush him and he was wrong.

His mind was disturbed; Sebastian threats had begun to haunt him. He knew now beyond doubt that it was Hanna that came to Sebastian's rescue in Mexico, and if he was right about that, then the damage and havoc they could inflict would be great. Hence the reason why it was paramount that they be found. The quicker the situation was handled, the better he would come out, he hoped. Thomas and Henry arrived in England with their groups with three dozen more vampires that came with them to support Mason's army. With so many eyes on the ground, Mason knew it was only a matter of time before he found Sebastian.

As he awaited news of their sightings, the double doors opened; Henry bowed and then walked in. Mason could tell by the look on his face that whatever tidings he had, they weren't what Mason wanted to hear. Henry mentioned that the sorcerer Anchor was here; he didn't explain further. Mason sighed with trepidation; he knew if Anchor was here then something had gone wrong in Mexico. He gestured to Henry to bring him to his presence. Mason's mind feared for his wife's body; Mason managed a smile as Anchor approached him.

"I'm sorry, I haven't come with any news worthy of your ears," Anchor said, and Mason's eyes narrowed as he braced for the worst. Sebastian's threats rang deep in his mind.

"You're here now, so speak," Mason demanded.

"We were attacked, and I'm afraid it's bad news. I did everything in my power to stop her but . . . she is unstoppable . . . I barely made it out with my life. He was there also, the boy you seek, and she protects him. As soon as I escaped, I tried to re-enter, so I could take your wife's body to safety, but I couldn't gain entrance. Her powers were too strong; there was an impenetrable shield. Each time I tried, I lost more of my powers. I'm sorry; I don't know what happened to her body, but I watched as the whole place was scorched to the ground. Nothing was left unturned," the sorcerer said; Mason looked at him in disbelief; his eyes popped, and his jaw clenched as fury took hold of him.

"What about Patrick? Perhaps he escaped with his life. Did you see what happened to him? I left him in charge of her body. Is it possible that he got her out in time?" Mason suggested.

The sorcerer looked down and then up at Mason and said. "If he has any magical powers of his own, more potent than hers, then that may be possible." Mason couldn't believe what he heard; he looked about desperately and then paced around trying to process what he was told. Then he walked back to the Anchor.

"You must know what happened to her body? You can't be this useless? Where is my wife's body?" He cried as he grabbed the sorcerer by the collar.

"I don't know, but she wasn't there when I returned; there was nothing left," the sorcerer said doing his best not to look fearful of Mason. Mason looked at the man as anger at his failure reached another high. Truth be told, he was angrier with himself for underestimating Sebastian and not bringing Annemarie's body with him. Admitting that was tough, and he could only direct his anger at another so he could feel better now.

He looked at the sorcerer and shook his head disappointedly.

"Anchor," he said, "you failed so miserably. How you have fallen; to think that you once strove with Annie to show strength. Your name Anchor means bringer of trouble; I suggest you change that now. You are nothing but a joke." If Mason didn't need his help to perform the ritual that would bring Annemarie back when he found her body, he would have killed him this minute, he thought. Anchor could read his mind; he laughed softly and said.

"You need me, and I need the girl to stay alive. I may not be a match for her, but I am still strong enough to destroy you, so be careful of your devices toward me Mason," he warned. Mason, scoffed and then released his hold on the man.

"Get out of my sight," Mason yelled in defeat; his veins popped out and spit splattered from his mouth. Anchor quickly retraced his steps and exited the room. Henry and a few other vampires re-entered the room, and Mason turned toward them furious and fearful over the fate of his wife's body.

Mason commanded: "I want Sebastian found now! Today, not tomorrow; this night; I want every hole he may be hiding in searched; anyone that helps him will be put to death immediately. Henry, get Thomas. Call him back to me; tell Nicholas to get himself ready now. If you all don't know it yet, we are at war. Get the cars ready. We are all going to the place she was last spotted." Mason shouted this in anger; just then the phone rang and everyone's attention was turned. A female vampire picked it up and listened to the person on the other side. Mason looked at her curiously; she placed the receiver on the table as she tried to relay the message back to Mason.

"And?" Mason urged impatiently.

"You are right, Master," the female stated. "I have just been informed of a situation at his house in Grosmont. He has not been physically sighted, but they are positive it's him. A fracas is happening as we speak, and they want to know if you want them to attack and take him or wait for you to arrive?" Mason, rubbed his hands together gladly; finally, news worthy of his time.

"Tell them to do all they can to delay whoever is in that house; they must attack now before they disappear. I will be there soon," Mason instructed, and then he faced the rest of his subjects.

"Forget the cars; get the choppers; we need to get to Grosmont now. I want everyone available with me in Grosmont," Mason commanded and everyone scattered about beginning their preparations to go to Grosmont.

As everyone departed, Henry entered with Nicholas. Mason turned to look at Nicholas who still appeared beaten and it angered him more.

"Did you hear what that useless sorcerer said? Sebastian has your mother's body. Without her body, nothing matters; all of this will be for nothing. Do you understand, Nicholas? Now, get it together; enough of this impudence. We have a war to win; now is not the time for your childish whimpering, it is disgraceful. Get yourself ready for battle and meet me at the chopper.

Chapter 19.

Sebastian and Hanna.

"We need to leave now; all that commotion will not go unnoticed," Sebastian said as he gazed at Patrick's head on the mantle.

"Did you put that there?" He asked Hanna. She followed his eyes until her gaze fell on Patrick's severed head.

"No, I didn't," she said. Sebastian sighed knowing it was Hector; he was doing his best to forget him, but he knew it would be hard. He grimaced as the thought of Hector with Hanna came flooding to his mind again, and then he looked at her.

"We need to leave now," he reminded her; she nodded, and then reached her hand toward him, but before their hands connected, the door flew open and to their astonishment, they were immediately surrounded by more than a dozen vampires.

Sebastian looked at her; they were stuck. He had hoped to avoid this and the only way out now was to fight. He looked around; there was no one he knew amongst his assailants. Sebastian walked in front of Hanna to shield her from their attackers.

"What do you want?" He asked the intruders, making sure he appeared fearless regardless of their number. Their attackers smirked as they began to close the gap between them. Sebastian looked at Hanna. "If it gets too bad, get yourself out of here and don't come looking for me ever," he whispered although he knew all the vampires present probably heard what he said. Then he faced them and warned, "Look, I don't know you, but if you leave now, you may not end up like that fool who thought he had a chance with me." Sebastian hoped that he could scare them into leaving.

The one that appeared to be the leader said, "That is unlucky for him; we are more in number and whatever happens here tonight, you are not going anywhere until Mason gets here." He wore a white shirt tucked nicely into skinny jeans, and his brownish dark hair roughly fell across his forehead to his shoulders. Sebastian cocked his head to the side, making a mental calculation of how many he could take at a time, and how he could slow them down and allow Hanna time to escape.

"Then you are making a very big mistake," Sebastian said. You are fighting a battle you can never win and you will die here tonight because of your stupidity."

The leader smiled sarcastically, and then without any warning, he rushed toward Sebastian. Sebastian had anticipated his move; he caught him mid-air and used his momentum to push him into a couple of vampires knocking them to the ground. Three more rushed him immediately; he pushed back and they all fell to the ground. The others watched as they rolled on the ground, and a few of them started to close in on Hanna. Sebastian punched his way out quickly so he could get to Hanna. As he rushed toward her, a hand pulled him back. Sebastian flipped backward in rage, encircling his attacker's neck with his arm and breaking it with one sharp move. Then he tried again to get to Hanna, wondering why she had not left; He felt a hard punch on his side that knocked him sideways.

"Go, Hanna, what are waiting for?" Sebastian yelled across the room.

"No, not without you," she returned. It frustrated him; by now another vampire had joined in; in their attempt to subdue him, they kicked and punched him from all angles, but all he could think of was Hanna's safety. From where he was he could see at least six vampires closing in on her. And it looked liked they were exercising caution, someone must have warned them to be careful. Sebastian tried punching his way out; by now he had four or five on him. He kicked, punched, strangled and bit off their flesh with his teeth to gain freedom. As soon as he gained a bit of respite, two other vampires descended on him. Angered; Sebastian shoved the two vampires away as though they were two flies perched on his shirt. The strength Hanna had put in him made him feel untouchable. He flew high so he could reach her on time before they could get to her. When he landed at her side, he noticed that the six vampires that surrounded her had become like statues. Their eyes danced around in their head, but they could not move their bodies. Hanna's eyes were closed as she pointed her hands at them. Without thinking, Sebastian began kicking the stone-like vampires to the ground and smashing their bodies into smithereens. Hanna opened her eyes as the sounds of their breaking bodies reached her ears. The other vampires looked on in shock at what was happening; they came in pairs to try and stop Sebastian, but Hanna stretched her hands in their direction, and their bodies were quickly frozen. As Sebastian continued to destroy them, Hector walked back in and stood by the entrance to the sitting room observing the sight before him.

"Wow, I missed a lot by the looks of it," he said. Sebastian was angered by his return; he wanted to leave what he was doing and throw him out, but he knew better than to let his personal feelings get the better of him now. The remaining vampires were petrified; they gathered at the entrance blocked by Hector as they tried to leave.

"Not so fast; this party only just began," Hector said as he pushed the closest vampire toward Hanna and Sebastian. Two vampires came at him from the sides, and Hector pushed back, holding the two as the three of them rolled to the ground. With Hector, out of the way and Sebastian shattering the rest of the vampires that Hanna had frozen, the remaining four vampires rushed outside to escape dying, but before they could reach the door, it slammed shut on their faces. They pulled at the handle desperate to escape, but it did not budge. Then they rushed to the back of the house to find a way out, and as they ran, they were stopped in their track as Hanna approached them and froze them all where they stood. Their eyes were still moving and their ears were still functioning.

Hanna walked over to them so they could see her, and then she said, "I considered letting you go, but if you had, the chance is that you would come back again to fight me. The fewer of you there are today, the better for me tomorrow, so you die."

And then Sebastian came to join her and did with them as he did with the others in the living room. By the time, Sebastian and Hanna returned to the sitting room, Hector had disposed of one of the vampires that strove with him, and he and the last remaining vampire wrestled. Sebastian thought about going to help relieve Hector, but he couldn't bring himself to go. He folded his hands and smiled as the vampire tightened his hold on Hector's neck. Hanna looked at him and shook her head.

"Why are you smiling? He came back to help us; he didn't have to S; the least you can do is help him too." She said it like an order, and Sebastian reluctantly moved his feet to go and help but before he could get to him. Hector tossed off the vampire. Sebastian grabbed the vampire; it was the same one that had led the others into his house.

He smirked as he looked at him and said, "I warned you, didn't I? This is not your fight, but you are too moronic to understand your place. I have half a mind to take that useless head off your neck.

But I will let you live so you can tell the other stupid air heads like yourself that are foolishly flocking in to join Mason's army that they will all die if they don't go back to where they came from. Tell them that I spared you just so you could relate the truth, and if you see Mason, tell him all that happened here. Let him know that I am not afraid of him and I am coming for him." Sebastian then pushed the vampire out the door. The vampire fell but quickly scurried out of sight. Sebastian wiped himself down; the room before him was in complete anarchy, but he was glad that he and Hanna were fine. Then his eyes met Hector's.

"No one asked you back here; you weren't needed," Sebastian hissed.

Hector chuckled lowly. "I know, but I wanted to help anyway," he said in defence.

Hanna looked from Sebastian to Hector and didn't want a repeat of what happened earlier, but she was glad that Hector came; if only she could make Sebastian understand that if Hector joined forces with them, it would be to their advantage. Hanna knew that Sebastian wouldn't listen, so rather than argue, she decided to take matters into her hands.

"Okay you two, stop. I have had it today; it's been one fight after the other and I can really do with some rest. Come here you two," she said.

Sebastian furrowed his brow wondering what she was doing; he sincerely hoped she wasn't about to tell them to shake hands; he would die before shaking hands with Hector. He stood his ground and refused to go to her. Hanna shook her head in frustration. She walked toward Sebastian and took his hand and then dragged him to where Hector stood, and before he could open his mouth to complain, the three disappeared and reappeared in their little cottage in Wales.

Sebastian looked before him and saw that Hanna had brought Hector with them to their little cottage, and he was immediately angry. He looked at her. "What is the meaning of this?" He questioned Hanna bitterly; she looked at him, and she knew she shouldn't have done what she did, but the three of them needed to be working together. They couldn't exactly remain talking it out in Grosmont where it seemed everyone came looking for them.

"S, listen, let me explain . . ." she began, but he couldn't bear to be in the same room as her; he felt in that moment that he didn't know her anymore. It was as if she wanted to keep hurting him. It was bad enough that she had kissed Hector while claiming that it was because she missed him. Then she kept it a secret so that Hector got the chance to stab him in the heart with the news of their frolicking, and now she brought him to their secret safe house. *What did she want from him?* Sebastian wondered. Did she not think that he had feelings, too, or did she think it was all right to keep hurting him because he had always let her get her way? Clearly, she had feelings for Hector, and he was not going to allow her to rub it in his face again.

"S, please wait. I need to explain," Hanna pleaded.

"No, don't please. I clearly don't know you anymore. You want him; you can have him," Sebastian said and walked out of the cottage.

Hector stood, still amazed by how they had arrived there in a matter of seconds but pleased that the two lovers fought over him. And for the first time, he agreed with Sebastian. He thought to himself, "She must have some feelings for me.

Chapter 20

Hector stood grinning as Sebastian stormed out of the cottage. Hanna turned and saw the stupid grin on his face and she was infuriated. Although she believed that she had good reasons for bringing Hector with them, looking at him enjoying the spat between her and Sebastian made her regret her decision immediately.

"What's so funny Hector?" She snapped. Hector shrugged and stopped grinning at once.

"Nothing," he replied knowing he didn't want to get on her bad side. Hanna knew she should have discussed things with Sebastian, and she understood his anger, but she hoped that he could see that she didn't mean any disrespect toward him. There was no telling what he would do next; he had trashed the whole top floor when Hector mentioned the kiss. She knew she had gone about it all wrong; the moment they arrived back in the cottage. She had given him no time for respite and now this.

Hanna took a deep breath, took another look at Hector and then said, "Wait here; don't go out; I'll be back." And then she stormed out in search of Sebastian.

She found him standing on the cliff, staring into the sea; she walked cautiously toward him knowing she wasn't his favourite person at the moment. It turned her stomach, knowing she was the reason he was so angry. Sebastian did not turn around; he had smelled her presence the minute she left the cottage to come find him. He didn't want her around, not now. As she got closer, he contemplated walking away, but he didn't want her to accuse him of being infantile. He never thought that there would be a day or a time when he didn't want to be near her, and as much as he loved her, he couldn't stand looking at her. It was too much, and her bringing the evidence of her disloyalty to rub in his face was all he could take.

"S," Hanna called, stopping a few yards from him. He didn't acknowledge her call with a reply. Before now, when she called him "S," it made him smile inwardly but not this time. He felt betrayed by her, and he felt justified in that feeling.

"Please, let me explain," Hanna begged. Sebastian sighed; he couldn't bring himself to face her; doing so would only remind him of the inevitable, not that it helped looking away either when the kiss was all he could think about. When he didn't respond, Hanna decided to carry on with her explanation regardless.

"I'm sorry, I wasn't thinking, or should I say, I wasn't thinking about your feelings when I brought him with us. All that was on my mind and still is; even now; is how we can come out on top of all this chaos. I know we have been doing well on our own, but I just feel another set of hands in this war won't hurt us," Hanna tried to reason with him. Sebastian scoffed, not wanting to respond afraid she wouldn't like what he would say.

"Please Love, look at me; I know it's difficult for you now, but can you not try and put that other business with Hector to one side. Try and see it how I see it," she pleaded. Sebastian, forced himself to face her; the expression on his face was unyielding.

He chuckled softly, "I am glad you can separate the two. I think that is probably because it was you that kissed him. You know what I see, each time I look at you or . . . him? The image of the two of you at it. You gave me no time to process it all, and then you threw him in my face. Perhaps you're right, but I can't reason like you do now, and I can't see beyond this problem." He paused, and moved two steps away, and then he said, "I know we were not together then, but I would think you would know if you cared about me like you claim, that he was the last person you would have done that with. So, pardon me if I can't work hand in hand with your new boyfriend."

Sebastian could see he was hurting her, but she couldn't be as heartbroken as he was at that moment. He began to walk away; Hanna hurried after him. "Wait, please," she said. It's not like that. I don't know why it happened either, but my head wasn't right then; I really missed you and I was lonely . . ."

Sebastian cut in. "So, you run into his arms instead? Did that make you feel better?" Hanna bit her lip nervously as she tried not to let her tears run down.

"I can't imagine you with someone else, let alone him; why him Hanna? You knew how I felt about him; if I meant anything to you even if we were not together you should have considered that. You won't admit it, but right from the beginning, you have carried something for him. You tell me it is not true, but each time I say we do something about him you are against it. So, forgive me if I am not doing what you want right now. If you never wanted anything to do with me again, then you should have carried on with whoever pleased you, but you tell me you wanted me still and then you . . . do that with him, and as if you hadn't punished me enough, you bring him here to my face. I'm sorry. I can't do this, and talking about it makes me feel nauseous. I need to be alone. I . . . I never thought there would be a day that I wouldn't want to gaze upon your beautiful face, but right now, I can't bear . . . to look at you," Sebastian said and walked away.

Hanna stood by as the one she loved most in the world walked away from her; she could no longer hold back her tears. It felt like what they had was over and she hated that feeling. She blinked once, and when she looked again, he had vanished. He was jealous, and he had every right to be, but she wished he understood that she felt nothing for Hector.

The tears wouldn't stop falling; she had never seen him so cross, and the way he looked at her—like she was someone else. She knew now how he must have felt when she walked away from him three years ago; she felt rejected and it scared her that he wouldn't be able to get pass it. If he couldn't, not having him in her life would crumble her; she was sure of that. Not wanting to return to the cottage, Hanna sat by the cliff and cried to her heart's content. If she returned to the cottage, Hector would offer to comfort her, and she didn't want him involved in her relations with Sebastian. She sat until she began to shiver from the cold. She hoped Sebastian would return and find her still waiting, but she didn't have such luck.

It was late, close to midnight; everywhere was quiet, with only the noise of the sea crashing over the rocks for entertainment. Sebastian did not return; neither did Hector come to find her. Hanna felt exhausted; the fights had taken a lot out of her, and the situation with Sebastian had drained her even more. She needed a good sleep; she got up and wiped her eyes, feeling so alone; she walked back inside the cottage. Hector had stretched himself on the sofa with his hands supporting his head as if he owned the place. His eyes were closed. Hanna stood and watched him; he didn't open his eyes, and she wondered if he was pretending or sleeping. She thought about covering him with a blanket and immediately knew that was a bad idea. She tiptoed up the stairs. She briefly checked Sebastian's room to see if he had returned, but there was no one in it; his absence crushed her. Getting into bed and covering herself, she fantasized about him coming back and getting in bed with her and cuddling with her until she slept.

Exhausted, she dozed off, and when she opened her eyes and looked over at the side of her bed, it was empty. Feeling depressed, she got up and showered and then dressed. She could hear someone rummaging downstairs; she knew it was Hector; she considered going downstairs to tell him she had made a mistake. Right now, she would do anything to be with Sebastian again and earn his trust and forgiveness for that kiss. The best way to do it was to get rid of the very vampire he couldn't stand.

"Morning," Hector called as she made her way down the stairs.

"You look like a ray of sunshine," he commented.

"Stop it," Hanna said.

"Looks like someone is in a foul mood this morning. Whatever is the matter?" Hector asked playfully, Hanna eyed him, ignoring his comment. Hanna was dressed in a white off-shoulder maxi dress.

"White definitely suits you; you look stunning I dare say," Hector continued to compliment. Hanna smiled and noticed that he looked especially handsome as he stood by the entrance to the living room, but she said nothing to him.

"Are we fighting? May I remind you that this was your idea?" He remarked; Hanna finally turned toward him.

"Morning Hector. I'm sorry but I think this was a very bad idea. Clearly, you can see it's not going to work and I can't afford to lose him over this . . . I think you have to go Hector; we will manage on our own," Hanna explained; she noticed the cheerfulness he had earlier suddenly disappeared. Hanna still felt they were stronger with him around, but she couldn't please the two of them without losing Sebastian for good.

"Okay, I understand; I won't say I'm not disappointed, but I want you to be happy," Hector said. Hanna, looked away.

"I love it when you smile Hanna, and I can see my presence here has not helped," Hector said. Hanna took a deep breath in relief, glad that Hector understood. As they both stood in the hallway, the back door opened and Sebastian walked in observing the two of them for a moment. He had overheard their conversation. He noticed how breathtakingly beautiful Hanna looked dressed in white. It showed off her icy blue eyes, and the way her hair fell to the side of her face made him want to reach for her, but then he saw the bags under her eyes. He knew they were there because of him; she had cried herself to sleep, and it killed him inside. He never thought he would hurt her, and even though she had wounded him, he didn't want to reciprocate that feeling. He had a hard time overnight, thinking and talking himself into looking at things the way she saw it, and that meant a lot of mental and emotional blockage of what was causing him a great upset. In the end, if Hector behaved himself, Sebastian thought that he could put his personal feelings to one side and work with him to fight Mason until they won the battle. And then he hoped to never see him again.

"You don't have to go," Sebastian said to Hector. Hanna's eyes dashed toward him in confusion; she didn't understand; was he testing her, or was he now onboard or even worse was he saying that because he would be leaving? Her eyes begged him; she was fearful that he had made up his mind to leave her. Hector looked from Hanna to Sebastian and wondered what was going on in Sebastian's head. He could see how his absence had affected her, plus her love for Sebastian was written all over her face. It moved him with jealousy and it made him want her even more. Hector knew that what he felt for Hanna would be to his own detriment. Knowing she would never feel for him what she felt for Sebastian upset him greatly, but he did his best to hide it. He looked away so as not to give away his emotions.

"We have spoken about it; we agreed this was a mistake; it clearly won't work," Hanna said trying to convince Sebastian that she was now seeing things his way.

"No, he can stay if he wants. I am a big boy, and I think I can tolerate becoming allies with an enemy to eliminate a bigger one. So, if you think you still want to work together, then I am in," Sebastian said and noticed the twitch of happiness playing on Hanna's lip although she did her best to mask it. He sighed inwardly unsure if the happiness was because he came around to her point of view or simply because she was glad Hector wasn't leaving.

"I'm in," Hector declared,

"Good, then it is settled," Sebastian replied.

Sebastian focused his eyes on Hanna; he had missed her dearly; all through the night, he battled with himself, wanting nothing more than to be with her. He had come home when she slept and watched her, and for a moment he wanted to swoop up next to her and hold her in his arms. Then she turned, and the mental image of her in Hector's arms returned to haunt him, and he fled.

"Thank you," Hanna said allowing her joy to show through with a smile. Sebastian nodded and walked up the stairs past her and Hector. He went into the shower straight away. He had slept badly, and he wanted to wash and smell fresh. Hanna didn't know what to think; she had hoped he would smile at her. Although he said Hector could stay, she didn't know what that meant for their relationship. If they were alone, she would have gone to meet him, but she didn't want Hector to think she was desperate for attention. Hanna looked down and felt Hector's eyes on her.

"So, what now?" Hector asked.

"Uh," Hanna responded absent-mindedly.

"Now that your man there has authorized my stay. What's first on our agenda?" Hector asked.

"I don't know; I guess we will take each battle as it comes," Hanna replied.

"Okay," Hector said knowing her mind was elsewhere. He looked away, and Hanna could tell he knew she wasn't present.

She sighed and then said, "Don't worry, Hector. I have something in mind for you. I just have to run it by Sebastian first," she said.

"Alright," he said in frustration and then told himself to get used to her running everything by the golden boy. Hector felt famished;

he hadn't exactly counted on being brought here by Hanna, and he knew he had to go and hunt.

"Talk to lover boy and when he approves of whatever it is you have in mind, then we will talk. In the meantime, I must go out immediately after the sun sets. We aren't all as lucky as your man, prancing about in daylight. I need some breathing space; I don't do very well cooped up in tiny places." He walked toward the window wishing with every fibre of his body that what Hanna had up her sleeve had something to do with him walking the day. Looking through the window enviously at the trees as they soaked up the sun, he closed his eyes and imagined he was that tree being warmed up by the sun.

Hanna noticed he didn't want to be disturbed, and she didn't want to ask him where he was going later for fear of being told something she didn't want to hear. She looked up the stairs and could still hear the shower running. She contemplated waiting in the room for Sebastian, and then decided against it. She knew he wasn't ready to be around her yet, and she didn't want to hang around with Hector either. She had been picking up on his feelings for her even though he was doing his best to hide it.

Hanna walked out of the cottage and hoped the next time she saw Sebastian he would want her near him.

Chapter 21

Mason Benedict

Three choppers carrying Mason, Thomas, Henry, Nicholas, and fifteen other vampires that had joined him, landed on Sebastian's property in Grosmont Yorkshire. As they approached the house, the vampire that Sebastian spared during the last fight ran over to meet them. He looked defeated and scared; stopping in front of Mason, he bowed in obeisance.

"Did you manage to capture him?" Mason demanded, half dreading the response he would hear. The vampire looked up, afraid to reiterate the horror he had witnessed—how Sebastian and Hanna had destroyed seventeen vampires without breaking a sweat.

"I don't know what to say, Master. I think you need to see for yourself what took place inside," the vampire responded. Annoyed but fearful of what he would see, Mason thrust him aside and hurried inside, followed closely by his entourage. On the floor, he saw piles of stones that looked like ice shattered into tiny pieces. He walked from the entrance of the house following the trail of disaster into the sitting room and out onto the hallway and the back of the house. Abruptly, he turned in anger and called for the vampire that met with them.

"What happened here?" Mason demanded. "I see a lot of stones like relics shattered. What's this to do with anything? Where is Sebastian?" He commanded. The vampire looked away,

"Speak now before I crush you myself," Mason ordered.

"He . . . he and the girl did this; we didn't stand a chance," the vampire said. Thomas then bent to examine the stone-like pieces on the floor and observed that some parts were carved in the human form.

"What are these?" He asked himself, but the vampire replied.

"The remains of those they destroyed," the vampire said. Thomas looked up at him, and then his eyes met with Mason's doubtfully.

"What do you mean by that? You will do well to explain it more plainly." Thomas required.

Mason and his entourage turned their attention to the vampire in question.

"It's the remains of the other seventeen," he confirmed, and everyone was quiet as dread befell them.

"The girl did it; I have never seen anything like it; there were eighteen of us. Half of us were at least more than five hundred years old, but he, he was too strong to subdue. She froze them and turned them into stones and he smashed them to pieces. It was brutal. I fought and he would have killed me as well, but he wanted me to inform you all that this is what awaits you if you don't stop hunting him." He looked from Mason to the rest of the group. The others looked petrified; Mason could tell that he was inflicting fear into them just as Sebastian had wanted, and he wasn't going to have it.

"Enough with this nonsense; you will have me believe a two-hundred-year-old vampire did this? What did he promise you to make you turn on me?" Mason said grabbing the vampire by the throat and lifting him off his feet.

"It's the truth Master, I am not lying," the vampire protested.

Mason laughed and looked at the others, and he mimicked the vampire's voice. "It's the truth Master." The others laughed nervously.

"You are lying and you will pay the price traitors pay. You turned on your own kind and helped him escape. There is no way a mere two hundred years old vampire has enough power to take out seventeen vampires." Mason threw the vampire to the ground and looked at Thomas.

"Take this liar out of my sight and put an end to him before his deceitful tongue poisons us all," Mason commanded and Thomas took the vampire out of Mason's hands.

The vampire yelled his innocence as Thomas dragged him away, and then shortly afterward he was silent. The others knew what had happened to him; they choose to believe Mason, knowing to believe the girl could do the damage claimed would be preposterous. It would mean that they were on a suicide mission.

"Don't let his lies scare you; I could not allow him to perpetuate such deceit. Sebastian is barely two centuries old; he cannot do what he claimed. Look around for clues that can help us find where they may be hiding. Make no mistake; he is in hiding only because he is afraid. If he were as powerful as that traitor mentioned, then he would not run." Mason motivated his subjects, as they dispersed to search the building.

Nicholas remained at Mason's side as the others dispersed about the house. Mason regarded him for a moment, and then he hunkered down to inspect the shattered pieces of stones on the floor. He knew the pieces were the remains of the vampires killed in battle with Sebastian and Hanna, but accepting such truth would lose him followers. Now more than ever, it was clear that he needed every hand he could find. He figured the more his army grew, the more difficult and impossible it would be for Sebastian to triumph. Hanna was definitely a worthy opponent as was Sebastian, he admitted, but capturing and defeating them would make for an even sweeter victory. Now that Mason knew that Sebastian was more than capable of everything he had sworn he would do, Mason knew he had to find a way to outsmart him or he would lose the war before the battle even began.

As he plotted in his head, Henry interrupted his thoughts,

"You need to see this master." Henry was alarmed. Mason rose and walked purposefully toward the sitting room dreading what he would find. He followed Henry's gaze until his eyes rested on Patrick's severed head.

"He knew you would come here; he left him here for us to find," Henry said.

***

Thomas walked in to see what the commotion was all about; he noticed Patrick's head and looked away. A part of him was proud of Sebastian; he never believed that he had what it took to crush Mason, and now it seemed with each passing day Sebastian was proving everyone that underestimated him was wrong. Thomas knew Sebastian couldn't have pulled this off on his own. He had help; he had Hanna, and they had no one that powerful on their side. Although he was here doing everything Mason commanded, Thomas did not feel loyalty to Mason anymore, not since he ordered the death of Margret, the woman he loved. He detested Mason now, and he knew that if he got the chance to side with Sebastian again, he would take it without a moment's thought. There was a time when Mason could do no wrong in his eyes, but all that changed when Mason proved that he cared for no one but himself.

Thomas remembered his human life all too well. Then he used to be homeless, and he begged on the streets. There was a terrible winter; the blizzard was bad; Mason had found him on a street corner where he lay freezing to death. He took him in and gave him to his wife Annemarie as a servant. Thomas ran errands for her, and she took a liking to him. She must have spoken highly of him to Mason because Mason began to take more notice of him; Patrick was already a vampire then, but Thomas didn't know what that was. He only observed that he never saw Patrick eat with the rest of the servants. One day, Mason asked Patrick to bring him to the field. That day he announced that at the behest of his wife, he had decided to give Thomas the gift of immortality. Unsure of what that meant, Thomas happily accepted. The next two years were years of training. Mason would take him into the thick woods and teach him how to hunt and track humans. After those two years passed, he was eventually bestowed his gift and made him a vampire. Then Thomas would have accepted and done anything to stay close to Annemarie. Even though he knew he had no chance with her, still she made him feel special. She was a beauty. Thomas remembered fantasizing about her loving him like she loved Mason, even though she was his master's wife, he couldn't help the way he felt. Annemarie died a long time ago, and when he least expected Margret showed up only to be killed at Mason's say so as though she didn't matter.

What Mason and Nicholas did he found unforgivable, but for now, he would go along with everything until the right time presented itself and then he would strike. Thomas took another look at Patrick's head and felt nothing; he enjoyed seeing the pain on Mason's face as he stared at the detached head.

"Oh, my dear Patrick," Mason muttered to himself. "I will see that he pays for this; there is no rock that can hide him from me and with these two hands, I promise you that I will destroy him." Mason turned to look at the vampires around him.

"I don't care what it takes; you will find that boy for me; double your efforts. Sebastian must be found and made to pay," he commanded, and then he took another look at the severed head.

"Henry see that he gets a good burial. Let's get out of here," Mason said. Henry, picked up Patrick's head and placed it in a bag. Then they all filed out behind Mason and headed for the choppers.

Chapter 22

Hilda Denali,

Hilda raged; she was disappointed with her poor performance when she came face to face with Hanna. Her whole body glowed red as though she were about to break into fire.

"I should have done better. I am better than her," she said into the empty room.

"Shame, shame," an eerie voice replied.

"You let me down. You promised you would beat her," Hilda argued.

"You disappoint and ridiculed me. I am more powerful than she is, you shamed me," the voice responded. Hilda screamed and banged her head repeatedly into the wall.

"I did my part, you let me down," she cried.

"No! You failed; you have not learned how to use the weapons I have given you," the voice said and laughed at her. Rage grew within her, and she covered her ears to stop the voice from speaking to her. Then there was silence; she could feel her body heating up as the humiliation she felt surfaced to memory. She tried hard to control the fire brewing inside. Her skin dripped in water, as every pore on her body opened.

"We must teach her a lesson," the creature spoke.

"Yes, we must," Hilda agreed with gritted teeth.

"She must learn to respect her betters," the voice said.

"What if she wins again," Hilda asked in a childlike voice.

"Quiet," the Eerie voice roared and Hilda whimpered.

"Help me be strong." Hilda whispered.

There was silence again and then the creature spoke. "You are stronger when I'm in control, let me out and I will consume her, I will destroy her." Suddenly Hilda's hands began to brim with fire. As she remembered the ease with which Hanna had thrown her out the door and the fire began to spread all over her.

Hilda felt she could have done better; failure was not an option, not when she had declared herself the tribal leader. Clenching her fist together, she knew she had lost control of the fire that was now lit all over her body, and she needed an outlet. In that anger, she looked around the empty castle; her mind fluttered back to times when parties were held there, and her brother Hurrit, who was the most handsome of all the boys in the tribe, lived here as a human. Her sister, Suzan, flirted with boys, and her parents played host to their numerous guests. Then there was laughter; then there was love. It was a time when she had no worries; when she didn't have a clue about the curse placed on her tribe centuries ago.

Now, as she looked about her, she saw none of that; instead, she carried the shame of her defeat. The confidence that she once felt about her newly acquired powers had drained. Hilda closed her eyes, and as she did, she heard the voice in her head telling her she was a disappointment.

"Let me out; give me control; unleash me, and I will bring her to her knees," the creature tormented. Hilda tried to shut the voice out as the fire burned through her body. The more the fire raged, the better Hilda felt. She opened her eyes and took another look at the home she grew up in and decided she couldn't take another minute of the torments of past bliss.

Hilda laughed as she threw fireballs at everything and anything she could see. Breaking and burning everything in her path, her body crackled again and burst into flames; she cackled with joy as she took in the scene before her. Then she walked past a broken mirror and noticed her body sparkling with fire and she loved it. She twirled in the fire; the crest of each burning object grew into a bigger fire until everything and every part of the home she used to love erupted into violent flames. The fire screamed as all that her family once held valuable consumed in the blaze. Her voice continued to cackle violently until the only image visible was an outline of her body as it sparkled in red. Hilda burned in contrast to the fluorescent orange glimmer of the fire and the smoke that brimmed to the top.

***

Half the tribe was already gathered outside of Hilda's home to meet with her, as she had instructed, but to their horror, they witnessed the disaster as the house of their leader broke into a blaze of fire. And as if that weren't enough of a bombshell, they watched in shock as she walked out of the burning castle, brimming all over with fire; a few individuals stepped back in fear while others were in awe of what was before them.

Hilda stood before her tribe; she had forgotten that she had asked for the meeting, but it was also good that all those present, could witness her power. If they had any doubt of her leadership, she was sure that it would now be put to rest. Still brimming with fire, she tried to control her anger. As she looked at her subjects and noted their awe, she suddenly felt the rage dissolve. Then the fire calmed and vanished, and her body resurfaced unharmed by the blaze. She stood naked, unashamed as another round of awe's, and ha's chorused from the lips of her subjects. They had never seen anything like it; two women from the gathering tied their scarves together and wrapped them around her to cover her nakedness.

Hilda smiled and thanked them; then she turned to face the tribe and, she suddenly felt confident again as she stood before her people.

"Don't be afraid. I won't hurt you," she said turning around to look at what used to be her home.

"That was the past," she said as she pointed at the burning house. "Together we will forge a new future for the tribe; that house reminded me of all the failures that brought our tribe so much pain. From now on, there will be no more mistakes; from now on we will not take what others hand out to us; we will forge our own destinies. We will fight and destroy whatever stands in the way of victory and die if that is what it takes. But we will not lie down and be dictated to, or fold our hands while our loved ones live as animals. Yes, we are magical, but our magic will not be used against us. You've all heard the stories of how our ancestors were betrayed by a witch like Hanna. She took from us our humanity and cursed us with the moon, but no more. We are no longer going to roll over and play dead; we will take back our lives, take back our humanity. But first, you all must join me in this battle. We must all wage war against our mutual enemy to prevail." There was rapt silence as she spoke; everyone listened attentively, nodding their heads in places as she filled their heads with hopes of victory.

"Who is ready to join me in the battle?" Hilda asked as she made an end of her speech. She looked from person to person, but no one said a word.

Then suddenly a man at the back nudged his way through the crowd until he was before Hilda. He knelt and bowed his head in reverence; then he looked up at her and said. "I will fight; I will join you in battle my chief."

Hilda smiled; then another man stepped up, kneeling and bowing and declaring his pledge to the fight. Two women came forth also and stepped up to the plate, and from then on, almost all the men stepped forward, and half the women and teenagers that were gathered vowed to fight with her and pledged their honour and life to the cause. Hilda smiled with contentment; she now had her army.

"Thank you all for believing in me. Go to your homes now and prepare; rest; you will need it, but be ready to answer when I call. The battle will not be easy, but I promise you that together and with force, we will take victory and rid ourselves of the curse."

Chapter 23

Sebastian and Hanna Greene

After showering, Sebastian dressed and sat in the garden. He had heard Hanna telling Hector that she needed to run something by him, and he was curious to know why she needed his approval. He smiled to himself as he thought of the irony of the situation; as far as he was concerned, he had always done things her way. No matter how strongly he felt about something, she always talked him into doing what she wanted. A classic example was his agreeing to have Hector around. As angry as he still felt inside, he didn't want to fight with her anymore, not when he knew that the time they had together was no longer certain. If ever the battle became too fierce and they were overcome, he knew she would have to do what she must to save her life and the human race. His only regret was having to spend the time they had left together, however long or short, in the presence of Hector. Sebastian noticed Hector lurking about in his sitting room, flicking the remote control from one TV channel to another. It was hard for him to accept Hanna's decision to make Hector a valuable ally. The mere sight, sound or thought of Hector rekindled jealousy in him and made him furious all over. However, for Hanna's sake, he would do his best to get along. The knowledge that he and Hanna were not together when she kissed Hector didn't help. The way he saw it, he didn't even bat his eyes at other women, even when he didn't think she would ever take him back because there was no way he would give himself to anyone but Hanna.

He shook his head as another mental picture of her and Hector kissing tried to surface. Sebastian knew that for their relationship to work, he had to force his brain to stop constantly reminding him of the kiss. He missed being alone with her, even though it had only been a day since Hector became the third wheel. Seeing her this morning made him want to scoop her up in his arms, but then that parasite was there too, and he couldn't bring himself to say what he had in mind. He couldn't touch her like he wanted.

Hanna entered the garden and sat next to Sebastian. He hadn't heard or sensed her coming. Her scent filled his nostrils, and he drew it into his lungs as he took a deep breath. He looked at her; she smiled nervously, forcing him to smile, too. They stared into each other's eyes and saw how much they had hurt each other and how much they had missed being close.

Although it had only been a night, it felt like years.

"I'm sorry," Hanna muttered. Sebastian nodded; her heart was beating wildly as her eyes held his.

"Me too," he said after a while and looked away breaking the intensity of the electric sensation he felt as he beheld her face.

She has suffered enough he told himself, and then he got up from where he sat and said, "Walk with me."

Hanna followed him, and they walked side by side in silence. When Sebastian felt, they had walked far enough away from Hector, he turned to face her; he wanted to take her face in his hands and kiss her senseless, but he restrained himself.

"How are you?" He asked concerned as he traced a finger on her cheek.

"I have been better," she replied. Sebastian, regarded her briefly then drew her into his arms, resting his chin on her head. She grabbed onto him, pressing herself into his embrace. It had only been for one night since she had snuggled up to him. After a while, he pulled her back to gaze at her face. "I don't want to fight anymore, not when I miss you like I do," he said, and she smiled happily.

"I missed you more." She said it was his turn to smile happily. Suddenly, he wasn't filled with all that rage that tormented him earlier.

"I don't know what made me angry the most, but I think it was mostly because he told me and not you. Not that I will ever be cool with that scenario, but perhaps if it had come from you I would have received it better. Tell me again, how did the two of you end up together in the first place?" Sebastian asked; he needed to be sure that she was not carrying any feeling for Hector. It would devastate him to think that she did.

Hanna nodded and said, "Okay, I will tell you everything." And she explained how Hector had found her working and living with Ruth and how he had warned her that Ruth was an aged witch whose sole purpose was to siphon her powers. She also let him know that Hector had told her about her birth mother, Hope Lane, and the story of how her birth mother had gone to Hector for help even before she was born. Sebastian listened quietly doing his best to understand her attachment to Hector. He knew now that Hector had always been a part of her life even before he was, and a part of him envied that. Hanna relayed how she had confronted Ruth about the truth and how Ruth had confessed to wanting to kill her when she was an infant and committing her mother Hope Lane to a mental hospital.

Sebastian knew the rest of the story because Hanna had filled him in earlier on how Ruth's apprentice, Angelica, had stolen her from Ruth and was taking her somewhere else and it was this apprentice Sebastian had murdered when he thought that he killed her mother.

Hanna paused to check if Sebastian understood all that she was telling him. She then told him how she fought with Ruth and defeated her and then decided she wanted to find her birth mother, but the only person who could point her in the right direction was Hector. She also told him how Hector and she had gotten connecting rooms; she wasn't aware of that until after they had checked in. She narrated everything that took place from then on and how she felt after she found out that her mother was still alive—the overwhelming guilt she felt when she realized that she had caused Sebastian great pain for nothing. "I felt vulnerable; I felt alone, plus I had received this letter that you sent to me, which I had not opened for fear of what it would say. I was missing you and I wanted to be held; I was crying; I was a mess; nothing made sense. I was happy and sad at the same time; my mother was alive, and I still didn't know how to find her. I couldn't connect to you like I did in the past, and I feared that you had killed yourself, and if you had, it would have been my fault and there . . . there he was, Hector, he heard me crying and he came into my room through the connecting doors. And if I'm honest, at that moment I was glad he was there; I wanted comfort, and he wrapped his arms around me and at first that was all I needed but then, something crazy happened and we began to kiss but S, your face was all I saw in my head and I broke it off. It was a moment of madness and stupidity, and it will never happen again I promise you because I don't feel for anyone what I feel for you, and I know I should have told you but . . . we only just got back together and I was afraid that if I told you, it would spoil things for us. But I was clearly wrong, and I deeply regret not telling you. Please forgive me; I know I have said *sorry* a few times, but I will say it again, *I am really sorry S.*" She pleaded and waited for him to say something.

Sebastian was quiet; he was digesting all that she went through in his absence, and he felt silly for lashing out over a mistake she made; at least that's what he chose to believe.

"There is nothing to forgive darling, I understand better now," he said; she smiled in relief and leaned her head on his shoulder. There was silence again, and then Sebastian said, "Hanna, I want us to find your mother; if she is still alive, I want you to meet her before we get into any more fights," Sebastian said Hanna looked up at him, her eyes beaming with happiness.

"You have me now; we will find her together. They say everything works together for good; it seems it's a good thing that Nob Hector is here; we will definitely put him to use since he's the only one that knows your mother," Sebastian said, pulling her head into his embrace.

"So, we are okay?" Hanna asked.

"We're more than okay?" Sebastian replied. "Come, let's go back home; we need to plan where to search for your mother next." Hanna circled her arm around his waist, and they began to walk back to the cottage.

The sun shone brightly; Sebastian looked up at the sky as the sun soaked and warmed his face. He smiled with contentment; he seldom revelled in the gift she gave him to walk the day. He was happy, he had everything he ever wanted, and he had Hanna. She felt his joy; she swelled inside with delight as well; she had gotten her Sebastian back and not only that, they were going to find her mother just as she had hoped to do from the beginning.

Everything was well; she didn't want to think of anything else; the day was not a day for planning battles, but it was a day to enjoy the company of the love of her life and to put into effect a plan to finally find her mother.

Hector stood behind the curtains by the window; his stomach dropped as he watched the two lovebirds approach the house hand in hand. Hanna seemed very happy, and so was Sebastian. He knew they had settled their differences; he swallowed hard but that was not what he envied most. As much as he wanted Hanna for himself, what he wanted more was to walk the sun like Sebastian.

Watching Sebastian bathe in the glory of the sun made him green with envy, but he knew to get that gift he had to be on his best behaviour.

He faked a smile as his eyes met Hanna's, and he looked away and moved from the window. He was bored out of his eyes; the only thing that had kept him sane was knowing that after the sun set he would be able to go hunting. The boredom made him lonely; the loneliness made him miss his brothers Anton and Zacchary, and that made his blood boil with vengeance. One way or another, Hector assured himself that he would avenge his brothers and that meant killing Sebastian. However, for now, he would play nice and bide his time until the perfect opportunity to strike presented itself.

Hector sneered as he thought about his original plan to give Sebastian up to Mason. Sebastian was clearly too strong for him to fight; the only way for him to come out clean and on top would be to outsmart him without Hanna being any wiser. It was the perfect plan; he would use one enemy to eliminate the other. Hanna would be so bereft, she would avenge Sebastian's death by killing Mason and then, he would have her to himself.

He rubbed his hands with glee; he had to be patient. Hanna's mother Hope Lane had shown him his future; he had seen himself basking in the glory of the sun. And he wasn't going to let anyone get in the way of that dream and his ambition to have Hanna Greene to himself.

Chapter 24

Hanna had noticed Hector watching her and Sebastian from the windows; she felt pity for him knowing he must feel alone with no one in his life to love as she loved Sebastian. Sebastian noticed when she looked at Hector, but he looked away and said nothing. Hanna's countenance changed; she became quiet the closer they got to the cottage. Then she stopped him abruptly before they entered the garden.

"Wait, S, before we go inside, I wanted to run something by you." Sebastian creased his forehead; he knew that whatever she had to say would have something to do with Hector. He understood a little now why she appeared so attached to him; however, understanding a situation did not mean liking it. Earlier Sebastian had heard her tell Hector that she needed his approval for something she intends to do for Hector. He knew now that she would ask it, and he would have to say *yes* to keep the peace. It was funny how she liked to pretend that his opinion mattered, but then, each time they were faced with a situation, especially where Hector was concerned, she always won. He hoped it's not what they had fought about in the past.

"Okay tell me," Sebastian said looking at the window where Hector had stood a moment ago, and then returning his gaze to her.

"Listen S, you may not like what I'm about to say," Hanna said.

"Well, I'm getting used to a lot of things I do not like," he replied bracing himself for what she would say.

"I think that if we are all going to work together to fight Mason, I mean you, me and . . ."

"Hector?" Sebastian cut in.

"Yes, Hector," she confirmed

"Hmm, go on," Sebastian pushed.

"I think I have to make it so we are sure of victory," she said.

"How do you mean?" Sebastian questioned; his heads tilted and his eyes narrowed into slits as he wondered what she wanted to do with Hector.

Suddenly Hanna couldn't find the words to tell him what she had in mind.

"Darling, you were saying?" Sebastian pressed.

"For that victory, then it is right that I do what I think is necessary for Hector," she said.

Sebastian chuckled softly, trying to hide his disapproval. She didn't need to say it out loud; he already knew what it was. He sighed and looked at her; he could tell that she was having difficulty putting together her words to mean what she meant to say.

"So, here's what I'm thinking you want to say the long and short of it is that you want to make Hector a day walker?" He asked, and she nodded.

"Yeah, you read my mind. That's exactly what I meant to tell . . . I mean to ask you." Sebastian was quiet; he knew his opinion didn't matter; he just didn't want to fight anymore even though he knew making Hector a day walker was the worst thing she could ever do.

"Think about it; we would move faster; we wouldn't have to wait till sunset to venture out with him. We need to find my mother and we need him. Even when the time comes to fight Mason, we will have the upper hand because all three of us will have the element of surprise. We may choose to attack during the day and let the sun kill most of them and weaken the rest. Think about it, the more of us, the merrier," Hanna explained, looking at him eagerly expecting him to say something.

Sebastian looked away; he didn't like it at all; first there was no way he would attack vampires at day time; that would mean alerting humans of their existence, but he wanted to make her happy; he wanted her to find her mother and if that meant Hector got to walk the sun, then so be it.

He turned to her; he could tell she wanted him to say *yes*. His head and heart screamed at him to say *No it's a bad idea.* But he was done with fighting over Hector. He touched her cheek with the back of his hand, and instead he said. "Okay, it seems practical."

She smiled and embraced him. "I'm glad you understand my love."

He held her close for a moment, but his heart was troubled. Hanna's tummy rumbled, and Sebastian managed a soft laugh.

"Okay let's get you inside; you need food; your tummy is reverberating," Sebastian said and Hanna laughed.

"Yeah, I know, I missed breakfast, I wasn't hungry for food then, but now I could eat a whole house," Hanna joked.

"Good—as long as it's not this one," Sebastian teased. Hanna laughed and punched him hard on the shoulder, and then her eyes widened as she quickly retrieved her hand and held it to her chest.

"Let me take a look?" Sebastian said concerned.

"No, I'm fine; it hurts, but I know I deserved it," she said.

"Don't say that," Sebastian scolded as he examined her hand.

"But I do; I have put you through a lot, and still you love me. I'm blessed to have you. Even now you are unhappy with my decision, but for me you will do anything," Hanna said looking into his eyes.

Sebastian didn't meet her gaze. He drew a deep breath and said, "Still, never say that. Especially not where I am concerned. It needs ice," he said, referring to her hand.

"No, it doesn't; I can make it go away. I don't know why I did that; perhaps I wanted to punish myself," Hanna said.

"Stop it; no more talk of that," he said in annoyance; he didn't like that. "I'm sorry darling. I do not like it when you say things like that. I am with you because I adore you; I belong to you. Do you understand?" He asked, and she nodded.

"Okay, do what you must to take the pain away," Sebastian said. Hanna nodded and closed her eyes and then reopened them as the soreness on her hands disappeared.

She looked at him, and he said. "Better, now let's go see about that food."

They entered the cottage and Hanna immediately set about opening a can of Spaghetti Hoops, while Sebastian observed her. She poured the hoops into a pot and began heating it on the stove. The odour made Sebastian very uncomfortable. Hector was in the living room which meant Sebastian had nowhere else to go but his room. He excused himself and went to lie on his bed. He closed his eyes; he hadn't rested the previous night, and his body felt tired; he had wanted to warm a blood bag, but it could wait; his body needed rest more, so he shut his eyes and shut down his body for the night.

When Hanna finished eating, she went to the bathroom to brush her teeth not wanting any food remnant in her mouth. She knew that the smell of human food repulsed Sebastian. She noted that he had not kissed her today, not even the day before. She wondered if there was any reason behind that; she could think of many, Hector being one of them. The last time he kissed her was just before she strengthened his body, and that kiss had felt like their last. Hanna knew her mind would not rest until she knew the reason for sure.

Hector had mentioned he was going out after sunset, and she planned to wisely use that time alone with Sebastian.

Hanna popped into Sebastian's room; to her surprise, he was asleep, and he looked peaceful and innocent. So beautiful, so handsome, she thought. She moved closer, on her toes not wanting to make noise, and she watched him as he slept; her heart skipped within her as she took in his beauty. Before now, she had never had a chance to watch him sleep and ravish his face with her eyes. She was tempted to touch him and caress his lips with hers but she didn't want to risk waking him.

Reluctantly, she left him to sleep and went to join Hector in the living room. Seeing her, Hector turned off the telly and dropped the remote control; he sighed with exhaustion, then he stood up. Hanna waited at the entrance with the light in the hallway giving her the perfect glow. Hector smiled softly at her and Hanna smiled in return and said, "I know what's on your mind. You are bored."

Hector admired her beauty and it saddened him that he could not tell her how she made him feel inside. He laughed instead and said, "I have never watched a truckload of garbage in all of my existence, and I still have an hour before the sun sets; I need to get out of here before I lose my mind," he announced; Hanna laughed at the way he threw his hands about to explain how dire he felt.

"I'm sorry; this is my fault; I dragged you here. I really didn't think about how it would affect you. I mean the two of you hardly look at each other. Anyway, I hope that the end will justify the means. And maybe one day the two of you will be friends," Hanna said. Hector scoffed.

"I won't hold my breath love," he responded.

"Well, never say never. Who knows what the future will bring," Hanna said.

"I admire your optimism," Hector replied.

"Well, when it comes to the two of you, that's all I can do. As you know, we must fight together to destroy a common enemy," Hanna stated and took her seat on the sofa; then she patted the seat next to her.

He looked at her; sitting next to her would be the closest he had been to her since that kiss. It felt like torture, being this close when all he wanted was another taste of her lips. He reluctantly sat down next to her; he felt nervous although he masked it with a smile. It was difficult for him; he loved the way she smelled, he looked at her neck as she spoke and the shape of her cupid bow lips, the swell of her breast drove him crazy. He fought the will to touch her and quickly looked away. Hector swallowed hard and asked. "What do you have in mind?"

She took his hand, and an electric bolt sparked through his body as she did, but he did his best to hide it. Hanna noticed that his hands were a little shaky at her touch.

"Calm down I am not going to bite," she smiled as she teased him. *She is messing with my head* he thought. Hector looked away; he was feeling things he hadn't felt before.

"What is this?" He asked. Hanna looked on in shock at his sudden outburst.

"What is what?" She questioned. Hector looked at their hands and said. "If your boyfriend comes down here and sees you holding my hands like this, he wouldn't like it," Hector quickly added. Hanna shook her head and laughed softly.

"Don't worry. He knows what I am about to do; I already ran it by him." Hector's mind raced within him, he wondered what she was referring to.

"Do you mind telling me then?" He asked hoping it was what he had always dreamed of.

Hanna smiled and said. "All good things come to those who wait."

"I think it is time I pay that debt my mother owed you," she added.

Hector opened his mouth in shock; before he could form any words to show how grateful he was, Hanna said. "Now listen, I must warn you; it's going to hurt a lot; maybe it depends on how much pain you can take, but I'm not going to stop until it is done, all right." Hector nodded still dumbfounded.

"Now let's do this, while we still have the sun out there. I want you to go to the window where you stood before; open the curtains and let the sun in and leave the rest to me," she instructed. Hector got up, still in shock; if anyone had told him that this would happen to him this day he would have called it a lie. He wanted to jump up in elation; his dream was coming true. He wanted to pull her to him, kiss and hug her so she felt how grateful he was, but he knew that could ruin everything. Instead, he went to the window, stood where she pointed, and pulled the curtains.

Chapter 25

Hector yelled out in pain as the sun burned his skin; he couldn't see Hanna; a bright translucent light was blocking his view, and then suddenly all that light rolled into a ball and hit him at once. The intensity of the pain increased as he yelled, and he dropped to his knees; his body was on fire, and every hard-dead cell burst painfully to life. He had never felt such excruciating pain; he started to doubt her intentions; it felt like she was killing him; he raised his hands to ask her to stop, but the pain grabbed hold of him, and he crumbled to the floor and cried out loudly waking Sebastian from his sleep. Hector's body was covered in sweat as his pores opened; the light subsided and his eyes focused again on Hanna. Then, he started to shiver from the cold, and he felt a rush of freezing wind embrace him and then—nothing.

Sebastian, rudely awakened by Hector's screams, ran downstairs to see what was going on; he saw Hector whining on the floor; Sebastian's eyes darted toward Hanna as he witnessed her turning Hector into a day walker. Sebastian knew they spoke about it, but he never thought she was going to do it so soon; he took a deep breath, then observed Hector's whimpering body on the floor; he remembered that feeling very well. He sighed and wished he felt good about what was happening, but he didn't. He sighed, he had promised himself that he wasn't going to fight anymore, not over

Hector. He didn't want to be there when they finished; Hanna had not noticed his presence; she was too busy making Hector a day walker. Sebastian left for his room; at least there he could think rationally.

Hector got up slowly after the pain stopped; he examined his body, and gazed up at Hanna; it didn't seem like anything had changed. He still looked the same, but he felt different. He smiled and then turned toward the sun streaming through the window. Hector felt the sun's rays bounce on the surface of his skin and for the first time in seven centuries, he wanted to cry as the sun warmed his body. In that moment, he thought of his brothers, Anton and Zacchary; he had wanted to share this feeling with them. He told them it was possible even though they didn't believe him, and now look at him standing in awe of the sun. He forced himself to turn away; his eyes found Hanna and he said, "Thank you. You did it! You did it, I don't know what to say, or if I'm ever going to be able to thank you for this." He returned his eyes to the rays beaming in. Hanna smiled happily; it made her happy that he was so happy.

"Go on; go outside before it sets; go and enjoy it," she encouraged.

"Are you sure?" Hector asked reluctantly.

"I promise; you will be fine," she assured him, and before she could blink, he was outside in the sun. She moved closer to the window and observed him. Hector removed his shirt; he wanted to feel the sun all over. Hanna watched, bringing to memory the day she saw him bare-chested at the hotel. He looked fit, she admitted, and quickly looked away. As Hector celebrated outside, her mind went to Sebastian; she had felt his presence earlier, but when she opened her eyes he wasn't around. She wanted to check to see if he was awake, but then she remembered that she had to warn Hector not to misuse the gift.

She ran out to meet Hector; he was acting crazy. When Hector saw her approaching, he ran and grabbed her and swung her around in appreciation.

Sebastian watched the two of them from his window; he had been watching Hector as he rolled about in joy; then Hanna came out and Hector grabbed her. He knew she was innocent and he also knew that the bastard Hector would not miss the opportunity to hold her close. Sebastian always knew Hector was up to no good and he wished that Hanna would realize it as well.

Hector's eyes and Sebastian's met; Hector smiled knowingly to himself as he drew Hanna closer. She pushed him away playfully and said, "Hector, I forgot to tell you, there is one condition to this gift." He stopped his celebration.

"Tell me anything and I will do it as long as you never take this gift from me," he said, his eyes twinkling with joy.

Sebastian stepped away from the window and returned to his bed.

Hanna looked up towards Sebastian's room and saw no one; she had felt someone looking; she sighed and returned her attention to Hector.

"You can't kill humans; I know you are not like Sebastian, and I am not trying to turn you into him. When you feed, take what you must, wipe their memories of it and let them go. You must not kill any human to feed; the day you do that, that is the day you will lose the power to walk in the sun and that very sun will be your destruction," Hanna stated. Sebastian could hear them; she had never given him that condition, he thought. Maybe because she knew he didn't feed on humans.

Hector took a deep breath and smiled, "That sounds good enough; I will take it, I promise you; I won't kill any human on purpose; I will be careful I promise you, Hanna Greene," he said.

She smiled and said, "Okay, erm . . . another thing, please do not tell anyone; I don't need to remind you of the dangers of confirming that I can make your kind walk the day. So, I know you're happy, but don't go shouting about it to the world," she warned.

"Don't worry Hanna; I want you safe; I don't want any harm to come to you darling; you can count on me," Hector promised.

Hanna smiled. "Okay let's shake on it," she said and he pulled her to him and kissed her cheek. She moved away awkwardly.

"I'm sorry, I didn't mean to embarrass you," Hector said. He felt her heartbeat; he couldn't tell if it was because of him or because she didn't want Sebastian to see him kiss her. Hanna looked away but not before her eyes caught sight of his toned body. She swiftly moved her eyes; Hector noticed she felt awkward. He looked up toward the window to see if Sebastian was still there; Hanna's eyes followed his, and she sighed in relief because Sebastian had not seen Hector kiss her on the cheek.

Sebastian had heard him promising to keep her safe and it infuriated him because Hector was claiming to care about her as he did. Maybe he did, maybe not; Sebastian didn't like that Hector was suggesting to Hanna that he cared for her.

"Okay, that is all; you may go if you so wish," Hanna said. Hector smiled; he was going out to hunt and drink to his heart's content to celebrate his new gift. It was a shame he had no one to celebrate with, but he also knew he had to be careful and not over indulge. Hanna's warning rang deep in his head like alarm bells. He had no intention of dying, not now when he had every reason to fight for Hanna's love, but first he must ensure Sebastian's death.

Hanna returned to the house; something told her that Sebastian was awake; she went to his room and found him lying on his back with eyes opened. She walked in and lay next to him; he didn't say anything, but he didn't have to; she knew him well enough to know that he wasn't very happy.

"Do you want to talk about it?" Hanna asked Sebastian; he turned his head in her direction.

"Talk about what?" He requested.

"Hector becoming a day walker," Hanna informed.

"You forget that you told me an hour ago of your intention to make him a day walker; I just didn't realize it was an express request," he said, trying not to sound bitter.

Hanna knew he was unhappy about it; she knew that when she decided to make Hector a day walker, but she felt the decision was right to prove to Hector that they were a unit. She wanted to be fair to Hector, not to talk of the added advantage it would give them in battles to come.

"Look, I know he is not your favourite person in the world. The timing just felt right; I wanted to get it over with. You said we would go look for my birth mother; you know that we need him," she explained.

Sebastian sighed and puts a hand out to embrace her as he drew her in for a cuddle. He had promised himself he wouldn't fight over Hector, no matter what; the deed was done now, and there was no reason to cry over spilled milk.

"It's all right, it's not a problem, and he is never going to be a problem between us. You had to do what you felt was right; I may not like it, but I can tolerate it. I see the bigger picture, and that's all that matters," Sebastian said and kissed her neck delicately. A surge of current ran through Hanna's body as he planted kisses on her neck. She closed her eyes and bit her lip at the pleasure of his touch. Then he stopped suddenly and rolled her back on her side, and then he got up from the bed. Hanna had thought that he would kiss her; she had been longing to kiss him, and he just teased her and left her craving his kiss. She wanted to speak to him about it but couldn't summon the courage. She was too embarrassed to say anything, not when she had informed him that all they could do was kiss.

Hanna's mind ran; she wondered if it was still because of the news that she kissed Hector, or if it was simply because kissing her was too uncomfortable to bear. Sebastian made his way downstairs without turning to look at her; Hanna wanted to cry; she wanted him close, and it felt like he didn't want her around. She waited and hoped he would return to her, an hour went by and nothing. A sharp pain surged through her heart, it felt horrible not being wanted by the one you love even when you knew they wanted you too. To stop herself from crying out, she closed her eyes and let sleep claim her body and she was thankful when she drifted off into a state of unconsciousness.

Chapter 26

Sebastian knew that Hanna didn't want him to leave her side, but he had promised himself that he would limit the temptation to kiss her. As much as he longed for her, he didn't see the point in constantly torturing himself when his body always yearned for more. He had lost count of how many times he had had to break away sharply from her kiss because he craved more. He didn't blame her; it was just too hard having her close. *She is what she is,* he thought, and if they were to have any chance at winning the war ahead, he had to learn to keep his hands to himself.

The temptation to return to her was greater than he could bear; to avoid it, he walked out of their home and went to stand on the top of the cliff. He forced his mind to think of other things; he reminded himself that he needed to train hard. Thus far, they had been lucky, but soon it would get harder than they expected and he wanted to be ready. He was stronger now, thankfully, but that was no guarantee that he could beat whatever storm was coming. He wished he had someone to train with; nevertheless, he closed his eyes and imagined himself surrounded by two assailants. Then he began to fight, defending and attacking as he went along. In his mind, his attackers increased from two to four and then six; he moved with grace imagining with his mind's eye how they might move, anticipating their actions, blocking their moves, yanking them off him and killing swiftly and then moving on to the next.

He moved and jumped in a flash as he dodged imaginary blows, bending and kicking to repeal the attacks. He flipped his body forward and backward with such ease and grace and spun around to avoid being held. Sebastian knew it would be difficult for anyone to break him, but it wasn't impossible if the number of attackers was high enough. The trick was to never get caught, he told himself.

Like Thomas had taught him in the past, the best warriors are those that move like ghosts; they are not seen as they fight their way through a host of enemies, and when they attack, it is decisive, premeditated, smooth and with precision. The greatest trick, Thomas always mentioned, was to survive in the end. Sebastian knew that if he wanted a future with Hanna, then he had to become a ghost and survive.

He trained until his body became exhausted; then he went back home. He was hungry; he got out two blood bags and warmed them in the microwave; the house was exceptionally quiet. He knew Hanna was upstairs; while he waited for his meal to heat up, he wondered if he should pay her a visit, but then he decided against it. If she was sleeping, he didn't want to wake her; he poured the contents of the bags into a teacup and went and sat in the sitting room. He took a sip out of the cup and then downed the contents. Feeling a little better, he wondered where the snake Hector went now that he had gotten what he'd always wanted. Sebastian wondered if he would even come back, and he hoped that he wouldn't but regretted his thoughts because he knew Hanna wouldn't be happy about it.

Sebastian placed the cup on the side table and sat quietly thinking. He wondered if anyone had spotted them since their arrival. The place was remote enough; still, he didn't feel sure they would be safe living there for too long. He closed his eyes and tried to relax, not wanting to go upstairs. He wasn't sure why he didn't want to go upstairs; he knew deep inside that he was angry, but he wasn't sure if it was at her, or at the whole situation. He couldn't quite put his finger on the reason he was avoiding her, and it pissed him off. Many thoughts ran through his mind. Could it be because of the kiss, or because she made Hector a day walker, or because he had noticed that she enjoyed Hector's company? Or could it be because of the fear of not existing in her life if she erased him from her memory to become stronger in battle? If that happened, and he had become nothing to her, he feared that she would fall for Hector. Hector would pursue her love and might get it.

Sebastian clenched his fist and bit down on his jaw at the cruelty of fate. His whole life, both as a human and now as a vampire. The joke had always been on him; whomever he loved he never could keep. He always got to be happy at first, and then that happiness was ripped from his hands. First, his mother murdered by the person she loved, and now he must sacrifice his love for the good of the humans.

"What's wrong?" Hanna's voice came from behind him as she interrupted his thoughts. She stood by the entrance of the sitting room. He turned his head in her direction; she looked worried; he hadn't heard her come downstairs, but then again that was always the way it had been with him and her.

"Nothing for you to worry about." He said,

"Then why do you look so sad?" Hanna probed further.

Sebastian sighed, his heart beating rapidly as his gaze met hers. In his mind, he had already lost her; even though she stood before him, he dropped his gaze and said, "Don't worry about it."

Hanna moved closer to him, and Sebastian refused to meet her eyes.

"Can't you see that whatever it is that worries you, affects me also? Are you avoiding me?" She asked.

He smiled softly, but she was right. He looked at her and said, "Seriously, I don't know." And then he looked away. Her heart broke; she knew he wasn't happy, and she didn't know what to do to help him. Earlier today, they had settled their quarrel and she had thought that things would go back to normal and now he was avoiding her.

Hanna would do whatever it took to fix what was broken in them. She wondered if she could fix his pain by listening to his thoughts. She was tempted but decided not to invade him in such a manner.

"S, it's still me; I am still the same girl you fell desperately in love with; I know we've had a lot of hurdles, but it hasn't changed how I see you, what I feel for you," Hanna said sitting next to him and turning his face to look at her.

Sebastian was quiet; the problem was not because he didn't love her; it was the fear of not having a future with her that killed him.

"Please my love, tell me, what troubles you; your eyes are brimming with pain; share them with me. Is it me? Do I make you unhappy?" She questioned. Sebastian held the hand she placed on his face.

"I . . . I don't know; I wish I could point at one single thing, but the truth is that I don't know," he said, and then he removed her hands from his face and got up; he made to leave the sitting room. Hanna's heart sank; this wasn't what she expected when she wished to be alone with him.

He looked so depressed.

"Wait, S, wait . . . please." He stopped and turned around. He knew he was pouting like a child, and he didn't like it, but he couldn't help the way he was feeling. What was the point in playing happy couple when she was going to forget him? No memories of him would remain with her when he died. He wished there was a way he could accept that fact. At that moment, Sebastian knew the only way to deal with losing her would be to break away from her now. He loved her too much to continuing hurting her. The thought of letting her go terrified him; he only just got her back and now he himself was playing with an idea he never thought possible in a million years.

"Darling, none of this is your fault, if I am truly honest. I am not happy; it is not because you have wronged me; it's the cruelty of life and I am at the centre of its spitefulness. I love you and yet I can't touch you the way I desire; I have only just got you back; however, it seems that there is a great probability that I will lose you again and none of it is your fault, Love," he said. Hanna wanted to say something, but he put his hands out to stop her.

"Yes, I have been avoiding you, and not just because of Hector; he doesn't factor where you are concerned. I am avoiding you, only because being so close to you is too much of a temptation of what I desire but cannot have. I want to hold you, hear your heart beating; I want to smell you and watch you laugh; I want to bury my nose in your hair and fill my lungs with your scent and then I want to kiss you slowly at first, teasing you every inch of the way until I can't get enough of you . . . and, yes, I can do that now, but I want that forever with you, with only you, but it isn't wise to think of a future such as that. I feel like I am living a fool's dream. So, I think, I think . . . it's better for us . . . for me . . ." Sebastian spoke, struggling with the words he wanted to tell her,

"No! No! I disagree. No! Sebastian, do not say it," Hanna begged; he looked at her; he was causing them both pain and he wished he could avoid it; was it not better now to rip out the plaster and face the pain than for him to delude himself into something that would only end up bringing him a greater pain.

"I don't have a choice; we . . . don't have a choice," he whispered.

"No, S, I disagree; we do. Do not coward out on me; I need you more than I have ever needed you. Listen to me; it will not get to that; I will not allow it; you and I, we will have a future together I promise you, Sebastian," she pleaded. Hanna stood in front of him and held his face with both her hands; tears rolled freely down her face.

"Please, S, my love; you are my heart; I beg you; don't destroy what we have; others may think they can, but let it not be you. I beg you, my love. I will do my best; I will fight for us, but if you leave me now, I'm sure my poor heart will not bear it. We would have lost the fight even before it started. Please, my love, do not give up on us; don't give up on me. I will do anything you want. I will send Hector away if it makes things better. I want you, only you."

Sebastian wiped her tears with the palm of his hands.

Hanna continued to beg, "Can we not pretend like I never told you? Please my love, for my sake be strong. I'm dying inside at the thought of you leaving me. I know I've wronged you; those three years you tortured yourself when I left you. I could never make up for it. All that time we could have spent together, but I am here now; please don't let me go," Hanna said, her hands shaking, her heart beating so fast, her face sweaty as the fear of losing him consumed her very soul.

Sebastian realized quickly how selfish he was being. He had promised himself that he would not bring her pain, not on purpose, and he was doing exactly what he said he would not do. He felt guilty as he wiped her tears, and other tears soon filled her eyes. He pulled her into his arms knowing there was nothing he could say to justify making her feel this way.

"I'm sorry love; I don't know what I was thinking. Forgive me. I don't know what got into me; it was selfish; I realize it now," he said.

"I just want us to be happy; I want us to focus on now and take each day as it comes," she said.

Sebastian, nodded. "I know, you're right and I'm sorry," he said as he held her trembling body close to his chest.

"I know it's hard for you; the temptations, the wants and needs, but I feel it too. When this is all over, I just want you. I will give away all the powers in the world to just have you. But now, we can be happy still; tomorrow will take care of itself," Hanna said and pulled back from his hold to look at him.

"Kiss me, please," she whispered; he regarded her pleading eyes and felt awful that he had reduced her to begging him for a kiss. He pulled her to him gently and clamped his lips around hers, and just as he had told her earlier, he nibbled at her gently, at first. The touch of their lips surged a vibrant heat to his head and hers; she held on to him tighter melting into his arms. Sebastian couldn't believe how much he had missed kissing her; their breath was fast and hard; he moved her from where they stood to the love seat and laid her on the sofa not breaking the kiss. Hanna quickly wrapped her legs around him, pulling him even closer to her and they kissed until they couldn't handle the feelings coursing through their bodies. Sebastian finally found the strength to break away; still breathing roughly, he stared at the beauty before him; and he smiled with satisfaction.

Hanna placed her hands on the back of his head and played with his locks. She couldn't believe she almost lost him; now she knew exactly why he repeatedly tried to kill himself when they were apart. The love they felt for each other was not ordinary. If he had left her. she would have wanted to die. She was bound to him for life and that's how she liked it.

They lay on the sofa in silence, content in each other's company. Almost half an hour later, as Hanna was about to drift into sleep, Sebastian whispered into her ears, "Darling, I will never put you through that again."

Hanna smiled with sleepy eyes. "You better not," she responded and then welcomed sleep. Sebastian carried her up to his room and laid her next to him and watched her as she slept.

Chapter 27

Hector Sayers

Hector rushed back to the cottage having fed on three humans in the neighbouring village; he had to make it three to stop himself from killing; he also stopped for a spot of shopping and bought himself a few changes of clothes as a form of distraction. Normally, when he felt so famished, he would only need to drain one healthy looking human, but now, he knew that if he killed a human it could lead to his destruction. The problem with eating from different humans was a question of flavour; each tasted different from the other.

Usually, when he hunted, he took his time to select the very best and to feed to his heart's content. A couple of the humans he fed on today were slobs; he could taste their filthiness in the blood. However, he took consolation in the fact that his situation wasn't as bad as that of Sebastian who fed from a bag, and as if that weren't terrible enough, the blood in question was nauseating animal slop. The inconvenience of finding sources of food did little to dampen the joy of becoming a day walker.

As Hector made his way back to the cottage happily humming an old Spanish song his mother used to sing to him many centuries ago, he heard Sebastian's voice as he spoke with Hanna. Hector stopped far enough away to hear what they were saying and not be detected. He held his breath when he thought Sebastian was about to end things with Hanna. At that moment, he wanted to jump for joy, but then he heard Hanna, the woman he loved, begging Sebastian not to leave her. Hector's heart sank; she was in a state; he could hear the pain in her voice as she pleaded for Sebastian to remain in her life.

Jealousy stirred in his heart; he wanted her to need him like she needed Sebastian. He wanted her to love him with everything as though her life depended on it. Instead, he got to hear her pant after another. Hector wondered why things couldn't just go his way for once. As if he didn't already hate Sebastian enough, his hatred for him went to another level.

Then he heard Hanna say to Sebastian that she would ask him to leave, Hector closed his eyes in rage. All the joy he had been feeling drained when he heard her discard of him like a piece of gum beneath the sole of her shoes. He wondered why he had to love her too; it felt like a curse the more he saw her throw herself at Sebastian; the more he wanted her, the harder he fell. It was painful to be in his shoes; the cruelty of it all was preposterous, and he wanted her to feel the pain he felt. And as if he were a sucker for punishment, he then heard her beg Sebastian to kiss her. And then the torturing sounds of both their lips moving against each other and their breathing drove him mad with rage. He clenched his jaw as he tried to control the fury raging in him. He wanted someone or something to punch. His mind brought him the memory of their kiss; opening his eyes, he imagined her in his arms and it brought to remembrance how supple, warm, and beautiful she felt in his arms when he kissed her. Supreme feelings coursed through him as her lips met his.

Hector wanted to feel that way again with her, and he knew he would do anything within his might to make Hanna his.

He waited outside; he couldn't bring himself to go inside; the last thing he wanted to witness was Sebastian kissing her. After what seemed like an agonizing eternity, he saw Sebastian's silhouette carrying Hanna out of the sitting room. He waited until they were upstairs before venturing inside.

He paused to see if they were going to continue what they started downstairs. and to his surprise and utmost relief they were quiet, and then he heard her breathing with the consistency of someone that was asleep. He sighed with content as he settled himself on the sofa. Then he jumped to his feet immediately realizing that he was lying where they had been kissing. He looked at the floor and decided it was a better option.

Hector placed a cushion on the floor, lay down, and rested his head. It wasn't comfortable but it suited him just fine. It wasn't easy to shut down the uncomfortable thoughts that roamed through his mind. His heart was filled with desire for someone he couldn't have, at least not yet, he told himself. Although he could hear Hanna breathing, he reassured himself that one day, he would be the one lying in her bed. He tried welcoming sleep, but for someone that had walked the path of darkness for so long, his body didn't seem to understand that he needed to rest in order to live as the humans. His rage had calmed, and he knew he needed to put it in check.

Hector knew that he couldn't allow his emotions to control him, or he would give himself away each time they paraded their love in front of him. He closed his eyes and tried to force the hand of sleep; seconds turned into minutes and minutes into hours. After about three and a half hours of his mind constantly forcing him to relive the kiss he shared with Hanna and the whole conversation he had overheard between Hanna and her man, his body finally shut down and he welcomed it with open arms.

A few hours later, he opened his eyes. It was morning; he could hear birds chirping. The curtains were still open and the first morning rays were streaming in. He went outside. It had been so long since he'd walked outside so early in the day.

****

Hanna forced her eyes open; as she woke up, she stretched her body and noticed the bed was empty; Sebastian was already in the shower. The top that he had worn the day before was on his bed. Hanna drew it to her and inhaled his scent and smiled happily. Then, she got up and went to her room; there was only one shower in the cottage, which meant that she had to wait her turn. She would have preferred to share the bathroom with him, but for now, that thought would remain a fantasy. She took off her clothes and put on a robe; she wanted a cup of coffee; she went downstairs to put on the kettle. While the kettle boiled, Hanna went back up the stairs to brush her hair. Sebastian had finished showering by the time she got back; the door to his room was opened and she saw him bare-chested as he dried his hair. She stopped to admire his body and then reluctantly moved her eyes away. Staring at him made her want him and that would bring nothing but trouble.

After Hanna finished brushing her hair, she decided to shower. Sebastian dressed and waited for her upstairs, not wanting to go to the living room in case he bumped into Hector. Hanna's shower was quick; she dressed and met Sebastian and together they went straight to the kitchen. Sebastian noticed Hector outside by the cliff, bare-chested with his arms stretched out as he soaked in the sun. He smiled; he knew that feeling very well, and if they weren't enemies, he would have been happy for Hector.

Hanna made coffee and sat in the living room. Sebastian joined her, and she snuggled next to him. His breathing was bumpy as the aroma from the coffee turned his stomach; but he didn't want to leave her. So, he stayed. Hanna noticed her coffee was making him uncomfortable and she teasingly placed her cup by his nose. Sebastian grabbed the cup from her hands and placed it on the floor; then he pulled her close and tickled her. Hanna laughed out loud, begging him to stop; her laughter rang in Hector's ears as he entered the cottage.

As Hector approached the living room, Sebastian moved, not wanting Hector to witness him being intimate with her. Hanna got up as well and straightened herself. Hector walked in as if he had not noticed anything.

Sebastian looked from Hector to Hanna and said, "I will be in my room; we should probably discuss leaving tomorrow to find your mother. All of us." He said it out to Hector's advantage so as to let him know his plans without speaking to him directly. Sebastian understood now that having Hector around was important to Hanna and also important to successfully finding Hanna's mother. Hanna nodded her head approvingly and smiled at Sebastian in appreciation. She understood what he meant by *all of us* and it made her happy that he no longer wanted her to send Hector away.

Hector smiled as he looked at Hanna's flushed face and the jealousy of what took place on that sofa the night before stabbed at him.

"You seem very happy," Hector commented as Sebastian's footsteps receded to his room.

"Yes, I am. I couldn't be happier," she responded to Hector still not wanting to give away anything.

"Why is that? Don't tell me it's because we are going in search of your mother. A decision I assume you are both forcing on me. Does my opinion actually matter here? Do I have a say whether I come or not?" He asked sceptically.

"Of course, Hector. I wouldn't force you to do anything you don't want to do; I mean you are free to go, but I thought you wanted to be part of this team until we defeat Mason. I assumed you would want to come," Hanna explained. Hector was quiet; he decided the best way to beat Sebastian was to find out all he could and the only way to do that was to be close to his enemy.

"Okay, if we are to find your mother, then I'm in. They say one good deed deserves another. You gave me a massive gift; the least I can do in return is find your mother for you. I will do anything to make you happy," Hector said. Hanna smiled in appreciation; her eyes beamed with joy.

She got up from where she sat and walked up to him; held his hands, his eyes were fixed on hers and she said, "Thank you for this Hector."

His heart rose in him, and he had never wanted her more than he did in that moment. Then he broke his gaze from her; his eyes dropped to their joined hands and he said, "You are welcome."

Hanna let go of his hands and patted him gently on the shoulder then said, "Okay, see you later." And she exited his presence and went upstairs to join Sebastian. Hector listened as they laughed and played with each other, and he knew he couldn't bear to be in the same space, not with the way he was feeling. He put on his top and exited the house and he didn't return until very late when both Hanna and Sebastian were asleep.

Chapter 28

The following morning, Hector was up before Sebastian and Hanna. He hadn't slept more than two hours; his body still struggled to adjust to his new state. The morning warmth beckoned to him. He smiled happily and stepped out and allowed himself to enjoy the freshness of the morning. Hector felt reborn. His mind twitched and took him back a very long time to when he was just a boy, and he lived in a little village with his mother and father. He remembered he had a little sister who was about five years of age; she was the cutest thing ever. It felt strange how memories of his human life seemed to be dripping in. They were a happy family, but he remembered not having a friend of his age he could mess about with. The children in his village were either too old to be his friends or too little. But he was loved by all; his father then was the hero of the town. He was a warrior and Hector remembered wanting to grow up to be exactly like his father. To earn the peoples', love and respect as his father had. When Hector turned seventeen, while his father was away on his travels, a strange sickness afflicted his village, and the plague wiped away more than half the population. His mother was afflicted with the disease also, but it was his little sister that had died first. Hector's mother died a slow and painful death. He remembered the pain filled bloody cough. She struggled to breathe, to stay alive, wanting to wait until his father arrived back home. She didn't want Hector to be alone, but her body became too weak and the loss of his sister was too strong a grief; in the end, his mother, too, left him.

Hector remembered going into the woods in the evening to fetch firewood to help keep the house warm. His father had always told him that in his absence Hector was the man of the house; he had to be responsible for the girls. When his sister died, Hector felt like a failure. He struggled to come to terms with her loss, but he had wanted to be strong for his mother; he couldn't let her see him cry even though his heart was broken. His father had been gone for two seasons now, and the winter was bitterly cold; everyone in the village mourned their deaths so no one had time to see what happened in other peoples' homes.

As he gathered the wood for fire that evening, he saw the shape of a boy about his age, standing afar watching him. He stopped to look; as he rose to his feet, he saw the boy's face briefly but before he could blink, the boy disappeared from view. Rattled, Hector gathered the wood and hurried back home; he lit the fire, hunkered down, and warmed his freezing hands by the fire, and then he warmed some water to take to his mother.

While the water boiled, Hector called her; normally she would answer with a soft groan, but that evening there was no response. He got up cautiously afraid of what he would find. A part of him always feared that she would leave him, but he hoped against hope, as he moved slowly towards her bed. He hoped that she was sleeping, but when he finally got to her, her eyes were closed and he knew she was no longer there. He tugged at her body, and there was no response. Tears rolled down his cheeks; he didn't know what to do; he hadn't prepared himself for her death; now he was all alone. For days, he sat by her side, holding on to her corpse and hoping for his father's return, but he never showed. Hector remembered wanting to die too; he wondered why he was spared, why he didn't get sick like his sister and mother. On the third day, his mother's body began to ooze as her body decomposed. So, late in the evening, he got up and covered her corpse. And went out to find help; as he went from house to house, he noticed the boy he had seen when he went to fetch firewood; he was standing by the woods and watching him. Hector wondered why he was being watched, but now was not the time to make friends. Hector went from house to house; most of the survivors of the disease were busy nursing their sick or mourning their dead. It seemed that most able men had been killed by the plague.

Hector returned home and wrapped his mother's body in cotton and then took her body out; he then began to dig the ground near where he had buried his sister. Just then, the boy he had seen watching him appeared out of nowhere. Hector stopped digging and looked at the strange boy and then he continued to dig.

"You look like you need help," Anton Doyle mentioned steely. Hector ignored him; he was too grieved to make friends. Anton walked closer to Hector.

Anton had been watching Hector for more than six months. It all began when he hunted down a man that had tried to kill him. This happened close to Hector's house. Anton had killed the man just before he could enter his home. At first, Anton had wanted to wipe out the man's family, but then he saw Hector catering to his little sister and he was moved. He wanted him as a companion; he needed him for a brother.

Anton had been alone for a century; he had always wanted to make himself a fellow comrade, but he kept deferring it until the day he clamped eyes on Hector Sayer. Hector was a good boy; he helped his mother with the house chores; he played with his little sister and he was loved by all.

Anton was taken by him; he wanted to be friends and so he started putting together a plan to entice Hector; he was going to give him the immortal gift of becoming a vampire. To do this, Anton decided he would first befriend Hector, and then kill his mother and sister so Hector had no ties left in the human world, but as fate will have it, a fatal plague beat him to it. Now with all of Hector's family gone, Anton knew he could finally make Hector his family.

Anton jumped in the grave that Hector was digging and took the shovel from Hector's hands. Reluctantly, Hector let him have it; truth be told, he was grateful for the help.

"Who are you?" Hector asked, without looking up.

"Someone who hopes to be a friend," Anton replied.

Hector was quiet; he didn't know if a friend was what he needed, but he knew there was no harm in talking if that would help take his mind off the pain in his heart. He had lost his family; his father might as well be dead, too. He had been gone for too long, and all Hector wanted to do was to die. He would hang himself on a rope, he decided, and hopefully someone would find him and bury him next to his mother and sister.

"Thank you, but I don't need a friend; I'm no use to anyone. I'm no longer for this world," Hector said sadly.

Anton scoffed. "Ending your life does not take away the pain; making meaning of it is what you need to do my friend," Anton said and continued digging.

"And what meaning can a life that is full of woes and despair bring? It would be a constant reminder of what was once loved and brutally snatched. Make friends with another; your good cause is lost on me," Hector said as he proceeded to drag his mother's body closer to the grave.

Anton regarded him and offered, "Your sadness clouds your mind and impairs your judgment. There is a lot more to gain in life even after one has suffered a loss so great in magnitude. What would you say if I told you I could make you better? You will forget this terrible pain that grieves your heart, and you can have another chance at life."

Hector looked up and said, "If only that were possible, but nothing can stop the bleeding in my heart. Don't waste your time on me friend; you have done well for me. Even though I don't know you, yet you've shown me great kindness, but I cannot take more of your time as I cannot repay you with anything."

Anton smiled because Hector had referred to him as a friend. Pretending he didn't know who Hector was about to bury, Anton asked. "Who is it you lost my friend?"

"My mother; she died three days ago, killed by the plague, and the grave next to her is my little sister Lily. And I intend to dig one for myself next to theirs as soon as I am done burying my mother."

Anton pretended he didn't hear Hector's last statement. "And what of your father?" Anton questioned.

Hector shrugged and stated, "I don't know whether he lives or not." He looked at the grave Anton was digging and decided the pit was deep enough.

"That should do it, thank you," he said. Anton got out of the hole with graceful ease, Hector noticed, but this was not the time to give out compliments.

"And what if your father lives? Would you like him to be greeted by three graves of the family he loves?" Anton said; he knew the father was dead because he had died at his hands, and he felt no remorse about it. However, he wanted Hector and he would lie a thousand times to ensure he gained his friendship. Anton didn't want to make a companion that wouldn't remain at his side for life; he wanted someone that would become his family.

Hector stopped to consider what Anton had argued, "It's been two seasons; he had never been gone for that long." Hector was trying to convince himself that his father was dead so he could end his own life and join his family.

"But you could be wrong; the winter has been brutal; I hear the seas have frozen over. Is it not possible that the weather delayed him?" Anton tried to persuade Hector, as he helped him pick up his mother's body and lay her in the ground.

"Look, I just don't want you to be in a hurry to leave this world. I can help you forget the pain you feel now, and this life will be a thing of the past. If you agree, I will be your family, your brother for life. I will not leave you as your family has done, and together we will become untouchable." When Anton said this, Hector smiled awkwardly.

"But I don't know you. How can we be a family when I only just met you?" Hector argued.

"I am here now. Who else do you see around you? If you say *yes* to me, then I will make you like me, indestructible; you will be strong and no plague that ails the humans will ever befall you." Anton said.

Hector, creased his forehead. "What you say is not possible," Hector argued and climbed out of the pit leaving Anton still inside.

"You will do well to climb out now; I need to fill it with earth," he said, and Anton flew out of the grave and in a blink, he was by Hector's side. Confused and amazed at the same time Hector opened his mouth to say something but before he could. Anton held him by the shoulders and looked him in the eye.

"There are a lot of things possible, a lot of things considered myths by humans," Anton said, "but as you can see there is more to me and much more to be gained if you want. I am not human not anymore and I can offer you a world without pain; all you have to do is say *yes* and I will take away the pain you feel now and the memories of it and together we will begin life again. We will take on the world and conquer it as brothers. Say *yes*, and all of this will be a long forgotten memory."

Hector thought about a life with limitless possibilities; he had known nothing but this little village, and here was a boy like himself offering to take his pain away and show him the world. He looked from Anton to his mother's dead body, and then back at Anton and he heard himself utter the word. "Yes."

The rest was history; he and Anton had been together since then, travelling together and fighting for territories until they came upon Zacchary and two brothers became three brothers.

As Hector marvelled under the glorious sun, the sudden rush of past memories and pain reminded him of his brother's death. The pain hit him afresh, further deepening his hatred for Sebastian. Hector closed his eyes and willed his anger away. He had lived for so many centuries and survived great battles, but conquering Sebastian and winning Hanna's love was all he lived for now, and that for him would be the greatest win.

Chapter 29

Sebastian and Hanna Greene

Sebastian found it difficult to sleep; he got himself ready for the day and sat down on his bed while Hanna slept. He could hear Hector outside and it made him fell unsettled. Sebastian knew the reasons why he couldn't sleep. He didn't trust Hector; having him so close was wrong. He wished Hanna would understand why they could never rely on Hector. Sebastian knew that because he had killed Zacchary, Hector would never forgive him, for this reason, he would surely come for him. When? He didn't know, but there was no point pretending Hector would wait until after Mason's death. He wouldn't wait if he were in his shoes. Sebastian had single handedly ripped Zacchary's head from his neck, and Hector had witnessed it. There was no forgiving that, and he was not looking for forgiveness. He only did to them what they had done to Hanna's parents, Joan and Joseph, when they helped Isobel fulfil her evil desires.

Sebastian watched as Hanna, on the other hand, slept in peace; she had brought Hector close and created this worry for him, and here she was looking like she had no worries in the world. He admired her hair as it glowed like the golden sun as the morning rays streamed into his room. Sebastian wondered if she was dreaming and what dreams she was having. He never dreamed; he didn't even know what dreams were like anymore. Hanna opened her eyes and yawned; she stretched her body out and turned to face Sebastian who had been watching her for the past hour.

"Morning," he said, and she smiled.

"Morning," she echoed.

They looked at each other for a moment and then Sebastian said, "Did you sleep well?" Hanna nodded.

"Good, you have to get ready; we need all the time in the day," he said.

Hanna arched her brow in confusion, "All the time in the day for what? You are talking about finding my mother, right?"

"Yes Love, what else would I be referring to?" Sebastian responded.

"I don't know; I was thinking maybe something like this," Hanna moved in to plant a kiss on his lips and then his neck.

Sebastian closed his eyes. "Yes, I was referring to that as well." He laughed softly and held her at arm's length, but Hanna wiggled her way back into his arms.

"Okay temptress, we have to get moving. Do you have a plan?" He asked Hanna, lifting her head up from his neck.

"Plan? I don't have one, but, I was thinking we go back to that mental hospital. I don't know if we would find anything. I've already been there; there was no new information. Come to think of it Hector gave me an address when we were last together. He said he had given that address to my mother; that was where he would have taken her and me had he gotten the chance, before Ruth's apprentice kidnapped me. I have a feeling we should probably start there. It may lead nowhere, but it's worth going there just to be sure. What do you think?" She asked.

"Me? I don't think anything. Your plan sounds like a good idea. We go to the house and check, and if she is not there, we make a new plan," Sebastian said, and then quickly added. "Do you still have the address?"

"Yes, I have it somewhere amongst my stuff, but Hector is here; even if I can't find it he will direct us there," Hanna said.

"Or since he now has a part of you in him . . . " Sebastian suggested hoping Hanna would connect the dots.

"Mm-hmm . . . how does that help us?" Hanna requested.

"You can connect to his mind like you did with me when we went to Mexico and Grosmont. We should be in and out in a matter of minutes," Sebastian suggested.

"Yeah. Why didn't I think of that? This is exciting. I have to go get ready right away." She leaned forward and planted another quick kiss on Sebastian's lips and ran out of the room.

Hanna's excitement was infectious; Sebastian found himself chuckling with anticipation as Hanna dashed out of the room and into the shower. He was also eager to know that the woman he killed was not Hanna's mother even though Hanna had insistently told him so; still he had to see for himself to be sure. Sebastian looked out his window and saw Hector soaking in the sun; he turned away and went downstairs to the kitchen. Hector could lead them into a trap for all he knew. Sebastian wanted to feed so he was ready for anything.

He warmed two blood bags and quickly downed the contents; then he went back to his room; he had thought he would find Hanna waiting, but she was getting dressed in her room. Sebastian decided he would wait in his room until she was ready.

Then he heard a knock and he overheard Hanna speaking with Hector; he had not realized that Hector had come upstairs until then. Sebastian tried not to make anything of it; he trusted Hanna, even though he knew Hector going into her room was done deliberately to upset him.

Hanna had just finished dressing up when Hector knocked on her door; she opened the door to find his grinning face staring at her.

"You look happy," she commented.

"Well, I woke up to the glorious sunlight all thanks to you," he said. "May I come in?" She smiled and hoped Sebastian would not be annoyed.

"Sure, I was just trying to apply a light makeup. Have a seat," Hanna said pointing to the armchair in her room.

"Well, if you permit me my opinion, that stunning face doesn't need makeup. You are beautiful just the way you are," he complimented, and he meant every word.

Hanna smiled and blushed. "Stop it."

"I only speak the truth. I don't flatter. You know it; anyone with eyes knows it. You are breath-taking," he said as he moved closer into her space.

Hanna stepped back to create space between them and smiled awkwardly. "Thank you," she said. What girl does not like to be complimented, but she also knew he had a thing for her; he had told her that much.

"You're very welcome," Hector said. Hanna moved away quickly before she gave him the wrong impression; she had just managed to save her relationship with Sebastian; she wasn't about to let anything or anyone ruin it again.

Even though Hanna didn't think she could love anyone other than Sebastian, she had formed an attachment to Hector. It was a strange friendship that Sebastian may never understand. She didn't understand it either; perhaps it was because he had offered to help her mother, or because he had fought so that her body was not touched by his brothers when they had come to kill her family. Or perhaps a part of her secretly fancied him, but the thought of that being possible was absurd. Sebastian for her was the air she needed to breathe; so, whatever it was she felt for Hector would pale in comparison to her love for Sebastian. However even though she was a sucker for compliments, she wished he would stop saying things like that when he knew that Sebastian could hear him.

"I was just going to come down to you actually," she said as she glossed her lips, rubbing her lips together for an even cover.

"Oh, I sensed you needed me. That's how much I can feel your connection to me," he said.

She glanced at him and shook her head. "What am I going to do with you?" She said rhetorically. Hector smiled. Hanna admitted he looked handsome, even more so when he smiled.

"I am here now; what do you need from me?" Hector asked.

"You first. You came here. What do you want?" Hanna asked.

"I wanted a shower; the door was locked; I wasn't sure if you knew . . . he was there. This sharing business is tedious, but for you, I will condone many things." He was teasing her with his compliments. Hanna wanted to discourage him from saying such things, but she knew she would only be wasting her time. She also didn't want to upset him because she needed him to take them to the house in Devon.

"I don't think S is in there; he is in his room."

"Oh, okay, I'll leave you in peace then beautiful," Hector said.

"Stop it, Hector," Hanna said frowning at him.

Hector shrugged his shoulders and asked "What?"

"You know what, you know Hector if only you could get along with him for my sake if you like me as much as I think, then please just let's forget the past. You wronged me when your brothers killed my parents; he wronged you when he avenged their death by killing your brothers. We've all been hurt. Let's just put all that away and start again. Together we can do more, please. For me." After pleading, Hanna turned to face him.

Hector was quiet; he knew there was no way he could forgive and let bygones be bygones. His brother's death had to be avenged, but if she wanted to bury her head in the sand and play happy families, then he would give her that for now until the right time presented itself and he would deal her lover a fatal hand.

"What you ask is difficult, but as you have put it clearly, I will try for your sake," Hector said, saying what she wanted to hear. Hanna smiled; she moved closer to him and kissed him on the cheek. Hector closed his eyes and inhaled her scent.

"Thank you; that is all I ask." She turned and picked up a brush from the dressing table.

"So, you still haven't told me why you wanted to come find me," Hector said, placing his hand where she had kissed him.

"Oh, yes, Sebastian and I think that my mother may have gone to your house in Devon; you remember you told me you gave her the address? So, it got me thinking; you said she showed you your future, and you saw that you walked the day, all of which has happened; perhaps she saw more than that. It is likely to think that she knew I would be the one to give you that gift, which means if she is still alive, she is banking on my connection to you to find me. What do you think?" She asked as she stopped to take in air.

"You might be right. But, let's take baby steps, okay? Don't give yourself too much hope; it may be another dead end," Hector warned, noting how excited she sounded.

"I know; but I can't help it. I have this feeling that I will find her soon. Anyway, we, Sebastian and I, think we should all go there today," she said happily.

"Oh okay. I better get ready then. It's going be quite a drive, I should think." Hector stated.

"Drive? Why drive, when I can take us all there in a blink of an eye?" Hanna said,

"Oh, I forget. Pardon me. You mean like how you transported us from your boyfriend's house to this place?" Hector asked to be sure.

"Exactly; all I need to do is to connect to your mind. You have to think of your home in Devon; then I will place my hand on your head and try to see the place through your mind's eye," Hanna explained.

"So, after I let you in, what next?" Hector asked.

227

"Once I can see the place like you do, we can go there," she replied.

"Ah, okay; that sounds a lot better than driving. Truth be told I have been dreading being so close to your man. This way definitely suits me better," Hector said.

"Behave, Hector. I thought we agreed to do better," she said. Hector smiled and raised his hands.

"It takes getting used to, but I will try," he said and quickly added. "I better go get ready for the trip of my life, and then I will be all yours to do with as you please," he joked as he exited Hanna's room knowing Sebastian could hear him; he walked into the shower and smiled with satisfaction.

Chapter 30

Sebastian heard every word exchanged between Hanna and Hector, even though he'd rather he didn't. It felt as if Hector was deliberately talking loudly so he could catch every venomous word that dropped out of his mouth. Even if Hector had whispered, he would have heard them; Hector deliberately raised his voice to try and upset him, but Sebastian promised he wouldn't give him the satisfaction. He waited until Hector was in the shower before venturing downstairs. Hanna met him on his way down the stairs; she jumped on his back and he obliged her.

"I spoke to him about helping us, and he agreed," Hanna said.

"Yes, I know. I heard it all; he was talking so loudly the next village could probably hear if they wanted to," Sebastian said. He crouched down as he got to the bottom of the stairs so that Hanna could get down.

She giggled. "Then you must have heard me telling him to behave," she said, looking at Sebastian to see if he was angry, but he looked okay. Using his current mood to her advantage, Hanna said. "S, I don't want you two to fight anymore, and I know it's difficult and you don't trust him, but just give him the benefit of the doubt for my sake."

Sebastian looked at her; he wondered what pill Hector gave her that made her like him so much, but he wasn't going to argue. He had heard her tell Hector, too, to get along, so if that was what she wanted, he would keep trying to stomach the snake like he had been doing since she forced them to live together.

"Whatever you say, Love," Sebastian responded and Hanna smiled happily.

"I will make myself a cup of tea, and maybe do a fry up, some hot dogs maybe, while we wait for Hector to get ready," Hanna said and went into the kitchen. Sebastian went into the living room; he didn't want to be around her as she prepared her food. As he sat in the living room, minutes later, the aroma of Hanna's food diffused into the room. Sebastian wriggled his nose as the stench of human food visited his nose. Hectors scent had also filled the living room and it disgusted him, so he went out to the garden. He watched their surrounding for a moment for any sign of intruders. Sebastian did not trust that Hector had not given them away when he went out hunting. Everywhere was quiet as normal; he heard Hanna chewing and making sounds that meant she was enjoying what she was eating. She wasn't chewing loudly, but he could hear her.

"Have you eaten? Hanna called.

"Yes, Darling," Sebastian answered, moving closer to the kitchen. He held his breath, and then swallowed hard; the closer he got, the more unbearable the food stench was.

"Are you sure you're not hungry?" Hanna asked again.

"Yes darling. I think I know myself a little better than you do," he said. Hanna could tell he was enduring the smell of her food just to be closer to her.

"You can go back out if this is too much for you. I don't mind," she said. Sebastian wanted to leave at the very suggestion but that would mean that he was too weak, he thought.

Just then Hector waltzed in; he looked from Sebastian to Hanna and he smiled and said, "If I were still human, I would be battling you for that; it looks appetizing I dare say."

Hanna smiled cautiously not wanting the fact that she enjoyed Hector's company to offend Sebastian.

"Does it not affect you?" She asked, wondering if the nauseating effect human food had on vampires affected only Sebastian.

"What?" Hector asked.

Hanna pointed at the food and said, "The smell."

"Oh yes! Very much. It looks so beautiful. But, I can't abide it; I don't understand why something that looks so appealing to the eyes stinks like shit, a very horrible one for that matter. Well, to each their own. To you it's food, to me, it's shit," Hector said, and chuckled.

Hanna's face twisted with disgust at the description of the smell of her food. Sebastian did his best to bite his tongue. Hector's description was perfect, but he didn't like that his lack of decorum had put Hanna off. Still smiling Hector noticed Sebastian bite down on his jaw. He knew it was because he had compared her food to dung; he felt bad for her and tried to apologize.

He said, "Pardon my French. Didn't mean to put you off your food." Hector grinned as he spoke.

Sebastian could no longer hold his peace. "You could have tried harder; you knew calling her food *shit* would put her off," Sebastian snapped.

"I apologized, didn't I?" Hector shot back.

Hanna quickly emptied her food in the bin and dropped her plate in the sink. She had to do something quickly or it could turn ugly, and that was the last thing she wanted. "Okay, boys, now is not the time; remember we are a team and this team has to get on. I've thrown the food away; I couldn't eat it anymore thanks to Hector. Somehow after your careful analogy, each bite tasted like shit in my mouth," she said

"Don't forget it was you who asked. You wanted to know," Hector said defensively and went to the living room.

Sebastian took a deep breath to calm himself; he went back to the garden; he needed the fresh air, after forcing himself to stay close while Hanna ate. Also, he couldn't bear breathing the same air as Hector. Hanna went upstairs to fetch air freshener; she returned later and sprayed everywhere so that the boys would not feel suffocated by the stench of her food.

"Okay, let's get to work," she called and Sebastian re-entered the cottage and made his way into the living room.

Immediately, Hanna addressed the two of them. "Listen, I know the two of you don't see eye to eye and you may never, but we have said we would work together, so let's do that peacefully. Now, first thing on the agenda is finding my mother. When we have done that, then we can begin planning Mason's defeat. Right now, all his followers are busy looking for us, but we have the advantage. We have the witch's body; he can't wake her from the dead without a body," Hanna stated, looking from Sebastian to Hector.

"What witch's body?" Hectors asked,

"Annemarie . . ." Hanna was about to say, but Sebastian stopped her.

"You are saying too much," Sebastian warned.

"Wait, am I hearing you, right? Are you referring to Annemarie, his wife? You have her body?" Hector asked.

"Had," Hanna corrected, and then added, "Sebastian tried to burn it, but it wouldn't take, so he took it over the cliff and threw it into the sea," Hanna explained in spite of Sebastian's caution.

"Look, if we are all going to work together, then we can't keep that a secret. He needs to know what happened to her body." Hanna tried to justify her reason for letting Hector in on their progress so far.

Hector grinned inwardly; he had not counted on having such valuable information. Now his bargaining power had just increased; he would deliver Sebastian to Mason and if that was not enough for Mason, then he could tell him where to find his wife's body. Hector hated Annemarie as much as the next vampire. With that witch by Mason's side, Mason would become untouchable, not that anybody would dare face him as an opponent now, but Annemarie brought his fame to every vampire's ear and forced them all to their knees. However, if giving Mason back his dead wife would grant him favour and take him out of Mason's kill list, then that was what he would do.

"It seems you two have been very busy. I like it. I've definitely chosen the right side," Hector said. "Okay let's do this; let's go find your mother." Hector sat down so that Hanna could have access to his head. He smiled; he would first give her the chance to meet her mother and put a smile on her face before he sent Mason to kill Sebastian. Sebastian noticed Hector's devious smile, and he shook his head; he wished Hanna weren't so trusting and always so eager to throw out his advice. It angered him, but he didn't want to pout about it; if it came back to bite them at least then she would understand and learn the importance of not trusting a scum like Hector.

Hanna looked at Sebastian. "Okay, are you ready? You need to hold me by my waist while I connect myself to Hector's mind," she said. Sebastian nodded and waited for her to place her hands on Hector's head. Then he circled her waist with his arms. Hanna closed her eyes. "Okay Hector, I need you to see the house in your mind's eye so I can see it too," she said,

"Um, okay, it's a white stone house with a thatch roof, and there is a field and a little river about . . ." Hector described.

"Okay, I see it," Hanna cuts in. "Get ready S, here we go," she said and they vanished.

Chapter 31

Hope Lane.

Hanna, Sebastian, and Hector appeared in front of a beautiful picturesque mansion spread over three floors. From the outside, it looked so perfect; it had a few stairs running up to the double door entry, and it was surrounded by trees and crawling vines. From the top of the roof, Hanna counted five chimneys and noted that the closest neighbour was half a mile away. Sebastian's house in Grosmont was remotely located too; it would seem that all vampires loved living away from humans.

"Not bad," Hanna commented.

"Yes, I agree. If I do say so myself. It's a pity I haven't yet had the honour of living in it myself, but I intend to change that after our business together is completed," Hector said smugly. Sebastian didn't say a word; the house was beautiful, but it belonged to Hector and that was about it for him.

"Okay, so we can just go in, right?" Hanna asked.

"Sure, the house is in my name," Hector said walking up to the stairs to retrieve his keys from where he had hidden them.

"It's been a while since I came this way. Just to warn you, I don't know what we will find. It might be quite a mess inside. I accidentally fired my caretaker four years ago, if you know what I mean," Hector said as he looked around for the key under the flower pots.

"And by accidental, you mean you killed him for food." Hanna stated.

"It wasn't intentional, anyway, things happen." Hector answered as he looked for the keys to the house.

"For some reason, I can't find the keys. I am sure I left them here, but then again . . . these flowers look well taken care of; they should be dead by now." Hector took in his surroundings and all the blossoming flowers and plants. He looked from the plants to the house, but before he could say what was on his mind, Hanna interrupted his thoughts.

"If you are sure you left the key there, and now it's gone, perhaps she took it." Hanna said. "My mother, she could have been here. What do you think?" Hanna looked from Hector to Sebastian and hoped they were thinking the same thing.

"Yes, it could be; but, it could also be anyone; let's not raise our hopes. It seems I must find an alternative route into my own house."

"Which is?" Hanna asked.

"Well, there are only two options really; break down the door or find a way in through the windows," Hector said and flew up the side of the house to find an entry.

Sebastian and Hanna backed away from the house and watched him; just then Sebastian noticed a window curtain twitch. Hector was still on the side of the building breaking the window with his hand. Sebastian alerted Hanna to what he had seen.

"I think someone is watching us," he whispered.

"Really, do you think it could be her," Hanna asked.

"I don't know, but there is definitely someone in that house," Sebastian said.

"Oh, wait, should I warn Hector?" Hanna asked Sebastian with concern for Hector.

"No, there's no need. Whoever it is, I wouldn't worry much; he should be able to handle himself," Sebastian said.

"What if it's one of Mason's followers?" Hanna asked anxiously and then quickly added. "What if they already came here, found my mother and killed her. What do we do S?" Hanna began to panic. Sebastian didn't understand why she was suddenly anxious. He thought she knew by now that with everything they did, there were always going to be risks and a chance of being found. He held her to him to calm her down.

"Shush, you don't know that; and Mason will not come to Hector's house to look for me." Sebastian assured her. "He knows I hate him. I went to him to get help to kill his brothers; here is the last place he would ever look. Now calm yourself; you're nervous, and that's okay. If your mother is here, then we will find her; if not, we will continue to look." Hanna nodded and looked up at the curtain where Sebastian said he noticed a twitch. She searched for movement but saw nothing.

"S, are you sure you noticed something up there earlier?" Hanna queried again.

"I did," Sebastian said; just then the front door opened and Hector appeared.

Hanna stepped forward; she smiled and Hector bowed playfully and said, "Your highness, I welcome you to my humble abode." And then he held out his hand for Hanna to take; she looked from him to Sebastian who pretended he hadn't noticed that she wanted to take his hand. Hector took her hand and led her in. Hanna smiled happily at Hector as they stepped inside the living room. Sebastian followed behind cautiously, not wanting to react as he didn't understand the bond between Hanna and Hector. Hanna took in the surroundings, the high ceilings and clean furnishings and no web in sight. It occurred to her that the house had to be occupied to be in such a state. She pulled Hector to the side and told him what Sebastian had noticed earlier.

"Are you sure?" Hector asked.

"Yes, he said he is," Hanna responded.

"Well that is strange. I can't smell anyone down here, but then again the house is exceptionally clean and looked after which means your boyfriend is probably right. If your mother is here, I won't put it past her to have spelled the place. You do know she was a witch of some kind, as I remember . . ." Hector said.

"She is not a witch; she had a gift; there is a big difference," Hanna argued.

"Okay, you say *potato*, I say—you know how the rest goes," Hector said.

"She's still not a witch," Hanna protested.

"Okay. Have it your way. Anyhow, my point is that her gifting allows her to see the future . . ."

"So?" Hanna cut in.

"So, if it's her upstairs, she must have known we were coming," Hector tried to point out.

"If that is true, then surely, she must know then, that I'm her daughter; why hide?" Hanna asked as they argued amongst themselves. Sebastian watched as the two of them exchanged words; then from the corner of his eye, he saw a human, a woman.

"I am not hiding," the woman said, and everyone turned around to see where the voice came from. Hanna's eyes widened, and her mouth opened wide as she took in the woman before them.

"I have been waiting here for you. For three years," the woman said.

"I must be having some kind of dream," Hector said. "This is unbelievable," he continued. Hanna looked from him to the woman in front of her, and Hanna's eyes swelled with tears. She didn't need Hector to confirm whom she was staring at; she could already tell.

The woman smiled, and said, "I have waited every day by that window for you to come find me."

Hanna noted that she looked to be in her early fifties or late forties. Sebastian could see the striking resemblance; the big beautiful blue eyes, the cupid bow lips, and the shape of her head were the same as Hanna's. The first feeling he felt looking at her was relief. Now he knew for sure that he didn't kill Hanna's mother. Sebastian moved closer to Hanna; she was shaking; she couldn't tear her eyes away from the woman.

Hector smiled, and he looked from Hanna to Hope Lane.

"I never thought this possible, but here you are Hope Lane, in my house," Hector said moving closer to Hope. She reluctantly broke her gaze from her daughter and looked at Hector.

"You gave me this address all those years ago; you were going to bring us here, remember? My daughter and I, but something horrible happened and I lost her," Hope said returning her gaze to Hanna. She wondered if Hanna thought that she had abandoned her; she wanted to explain, but where would she start?

"I did my best darling," she said, "but I failed. I tried. I wanted you safe at all cost. But life always has a way of doing things its own way; there was nothing I could do to change our fate. It deprived me of the best years of your life. Still, I wish I had been strong enough to have protect you, to have kept you with me and raised you myself."

Hanna's tears were now rolling down freely; she hadn't thought that it would be this simple to find her mother, and now she was standing in front of the woman who had given birth to her, and even though she could see the resemblance, which was like looking in a mirror, the woman before her felt like a stranger.

Hanna didn't know her, and she didn't know what to do next now that she had found her. Hanna wondered if she should give her a hug or remain where she stood. When Hanna didn't say a word in return, Hope decided to fill in the silence.

"I knew you would come, you see. I saw it in a dream three years ago; you came looking for me; I just didn't know the exact time it would happen. I don't see as clearly and precisely as I once did. My visions now come in pieces. I knew you when I saw you call it a mother's intuition, even though it was a dream. I felt it here in my gut. My daughter is alive in the world somewhere." Hope placed her hand on her and beckoned to Hanna.

"Come to me darling, come let me see you properly," Hope said as she closed the gap between her and Hanna. Sebastian released his hold on her, and Hanna forced herself forward and then looked to Sebastian for help; he nodded at her to go to her mother.

Hope smiled and placed her hands gently on Hanna's face. "You've grown into a beauty," she said, smiling as tears escaped her eyes. "My baby, my precious baby girl, I'm sorry, I'm so sorry for all the lost years. I wasn't there to keep you safe, but look at what you've made of yourself. You look well and strong." Hope placed her hand on Hanna's heart. "And beautiful." She looked Hanna over, and then drew her in for a motherly embrace.

Hanna broke down then, "Mama," she said.

"Yes, I'm here now. I am your mama, Astraia," Hope said, kissing Hanna's face delicately as they both cried. Hanna heard her call the name she had only heard her father call her and hearing that name confirmed she was with her mother. She smiled and melted into her mother's embrace.

"My beautiful baby, finally we get to be together again," Hope said. Sebastian smiled with content and then walked away giving Hanna and her mother space; Hector walked in the opposite direction.

"You have a lot to tell me; I missed everything. Where do you live? Who raised you? Tell me everything my love; don't leave anything out," Hope said. She pulled back to look at her daughter, and Hanna giggled happily.

"Okay slow down. I promise to tell you all I can remember."

"Good. Before you say a word, let me put the kettle on; we should have tea, right?" Hope turned to go to the kitchen, and then she turned back again, "What about your friends? I know Hector isn't human, the other one is he like Hector?" Hope asked, and Hanna nodded.

"Okay, so they wouldn't be needing cups of tea then; it's just you and I. Come with me, baby. I don't want you out of my sight," Hope said and took her daughter's hand as she headed for the kitchen leaving Hector and Sebastian alone in the living room doing their best to avoid each other.

Chapter 32

Hanna sat on the kitchen bench and watched as her mother fussed about trying to prepare a meal for her. Hanna wasn't hungry but she knew she and her mother had been looking forward to a day like this. She still couldn't believe she was in the same room with the woman that brought her into the world. She looked like everything she had dreamed about; Hanna felt at peace. She wondered what Sebastian was doing; she wanted to share these moments with him. Hope placed a flowery cup and saucer on the table and poured hot tea into it; the table was big; it looked like an island with a bench on each side. A main Louis armchair was placed at each end of the table. Hope pulled out a cake she had baked and cut pieces for herself and Hanna. She placed the cake on the table in front of Hanna and poured herself another cup of tea. Hanna noticed the substantial amounts of herbs growing in pots around the kitchen. She wondered what her mother used them for. Hanna moved her gaze from her surroundings as Hope sat next to her. Hanna could see the pure joy on her mother's face as they both sat down to eat together for the very first time.

It was all happening too fast for her to process; one minute she had thought that it was probable that her mother ventured this way and the next, she was sitting next to a stranger whom for some reason she was falling in love with by the minute. Hope took a bite of her cake, but Hanna found herself a little hesitant to eat. She was excited, but at the back of her mind, alarm bells rang and she had to will them away. She remembered the many times she sat at dinner with Ruth; she had trusted that woman like a mother only to find out she had been dining with the devil. She had to remind herself that this was her true mother. Apart from Sebastian, she was now the only other person in the world she could trust.

Hope noticed Hanna was not eating the cake or drinking the tea. Hope smiled because she understood why Hanna might distrust her. Hope knew many people would have let her down. Any child that had to grow up and face this cruel world alone without their parent to love and protect them would distrust humanity—especially one with her daughter's ability. Hope took a knife and cut a little piece of Hanna's cake and ate it.

"See, there, very edible," Hope said. Hanna smiled nervously.

"Did you bake them yourself?" Hanna asked,

"Yes, I did darling," Hope replied. She picked up her teacup and sipped a little then set it down. Hanna was quiet; she still was not eating or drinking; Hope decided it was best not to push her to do anything she didn't want to do. They stared at each other for a while, and then Hanna looked away; she didn't really know how to behave around her mother.

Hope took a deep breath and said, "Would you like me to explain my side of the story? It may help you understand what happened darling."

Hanna looked up at her and smiled. "Okay, I'll love to hear it," she said.

Hope smiled and cleared her throat. "Okay darling," she paused and looked up as she thought of where to begin; then she looked at her daughter and began recounting her side of the story.

"I discovered at a very early age that I had the power of visions; at first, I didn't understand the things I was seeing and I had no one in life I could lean on. You see, I was abandoned as a child; so, I don't have any clue about who my birth mother was or if my gift was genetic. I was raised in a convent the first half of my life before I was sent to a foster home. The woman they gave me to once mentioned adopting me, but that never happened I don't know why. I remember a night when I awoke, crying and talking about something I saw in my dream; the next day someone very close to my foster mom died suddenly. My foster mom's attitude changed toward me; she became very distant and two days later, a woman came to get me and took me to another home. I was told the convent I was raised in had closed; the same thing happened repeatedly; I never stayed anywhere for more than nine months until I was old enough to live as an adult. To cut a long story short, the visions never stopped; instead, they became more precise; if I see it, it will happen; it could be good or bad, but mostly I was known as the bearer of doom. I don't understand it but when a person came close to me, I would see their death or a misfortune that would soon present itself. I don't know why. I decided to keep my visions to myself, but when I see something, and I didn't warn those involved and something happened, I always felt guilty as if I caused it. And when I tried to warn them, they called me a witch and blamed it all on me saying I caused it. I couldn't win either way. I lost the few friends I had, and I felt alone in the world." Hope stopped to see how her daughter was taking what she was saying.

"To sustain myself, I sold herbs to make a living; all kinds, like the ones you see here now; I had a gift with those; I knew what herbs to make to cure many diseases, so that helped a little. I made enough money from that to afford a house, although I had no one to share it with until one day, a man came knocking. He was the most handsome of men, and I knew from the moment I laid eyes on him that I loved him." Hope smiled.

Hanna responded with a smile of her own; she knew that feeling very well; at this point, Sebastian waltzed in to check on his girl.

He could tell they were enjoying each other's company. Hanna looked happy and transfixed on what Hope was saying. For the first time in many days, Sebastian was happy to see his Hanna so content and even more than that was the joy he felt inside that he was with her when she found her mother. Hanna turned to look at him and gestured at him to join her on the bench.

"Do you mind?" she asked her mother.

"Not at all, come sit with us," Hope said beckoning to him.

"Thank you," Sebastian said respectfully to Hope and sat next to Hanna on the bench as Hope continued to tell Hanna about her life.

"We were in love; he helped me around the house; I don't even remember very well what he said the first time I saw him; I knew his lips moved, but my mind was transfixed as I gazed upon him. Something changed in me; the moment I saw him, I was happy and I didn't understand why, none of the things that had happened in my past mattered as long as he was with me. He would sit next to me by the fire and tell me stories of worlds long forgotten. I didn't know at the time how much of the things he said were true until the day he left, and I realized that they must have all been true." A cloud of tears gathered in her eyes and Hope forced them back; today was not a day to be sad; it was a day of celebration.

"Anyway, he was always so meticulous. I would catch him looking at me, but each time I attempted to touch him, he would recoil, like there was something wrong with me, which made me sad at the time. I understood his reluctance because of the men I dated in my past. At least he stayed. He wanted to explain his reasons for being distant, but he couldn't. And for a while that was how it was between us; we knew we cared for each other, and we knew without giving reasons that it wouldn't work. Then on the day you were conceived, it was as if he threw caution to the wind; we had been feeling the heat of the moment for so long; he took me in his

244

arms, and as he did I could feel myself trembling all over and we began to kiss. One thing led to another and he gave me the best gift ever, you; that was the last day I saw him."

Hanna looked away; she already knew what happened to him; she didn't know if she wanted to tell her mother about that part now; the part where Hanna died and met her father. She had not even told it to Sebastian; spilling the beans here would make him feel like she didn't trust him, so she decided not to mention it.

Hope said, "That was the beautiful part of the story. The next phase wasn't as pretty for me. I was pregnant with you. I had just lost the love of my life. You were the only thing left in my life, and I was going to protect you from harm even if it cost me my life. I loved you the moment I felt you inside me, but you were no ordinary child as I know you have found out. My visions increased. I would sleep and see a lot of enemies after you. All through my pregnancy, I saw all the evil that would come to haunt you, to harm you. They were all after your powers, and the terrifying part was that I didn't see myself in that future. How could I protect you if I wasn't in your life? I realized quickly that I had to do something to ensure your safety and protect you, us, from this evil." Hope paused when Hector made his way to the kitchen; he stood by the entrance, arms crossed as he took in the sight before him.

"I see you've made the place your own, still selling herbs?" Hector said. Hanna looked at him and placed her hand to her mouth to shush him.

"I needed a source of income. I made tea, creams and soaps from the herbs and I take them to the farmer's market to sell; it's helped a little," Hope responded. She turned her gaze to Sebastian, who was holding Hanna's hand beneath the table.

"So, tell me, before I continue, I am curious, are you two together?" Hope asked, noticing the way Hanna's body leaned on Sebastian. Hanna smiled. Sebastian looked up at Hanna and then looked away. He felt a little embarrassed; it wasn't the same feeling he had felt when he was questioned by Joan and Joseph; maybe because he knew them and gave Hanna to them. This time around he didn't know if he was good enough in Hope's eyes to be with her daughter. This was the typical meet-the-parent scenario, and he didn't know what to do with himself. Hanna lifted her hand and Sebastian's hand from under the table and placed their clasped hands on the table. She looked at Sebastian and then at her mother.

"Yes, we are together; he is everything to me, and I guess we both have him to thank really, because, the day I was taken from you, he killed the woman that had stolen me and found the family that raised me. My mother and father, they took care of me like I was their own, and they loved me. So, don't worry mama, I was loved, I was taken care of and I lacked for nothing all thanks to him," Hanna explained. Hope Lane looked from Hanna to Sebastian trying to understand how they went from his taking care of her as a child to their becoming lovers.

"So how did this happen? Forgive me; it's the mother in me, I guess. I want to know if you remained in her life after you found her and how you then both got to this point?" Hope pressed.

Sebastian looked down; he didn't know how to explain to Hope how his love for Hanna had changed from that of a father to a lover.

"I don't know; it just happened; I loved her the moment I saw her. I wasn't good for her so I had to find her a family," Sebastian explained. Then he paused to see if Hope was following him so he could say *how* things changed.

Hanna kept quiet and allowed him to explain things; she also needed to hear for herself how things changed from his taking care of her to his loving her the way he did now. Not that anything he said would change the way things were between them.

Hector moved closer, pretending to smell the herbs. He wanted to know exactly what happened between Hanna and Sebastian and how he missed his chance to be the one she could have loved.

Sebastian explained: "When I found her, she was only days old. I was a monster back then. I had lost my mother; she was murdered, and her death took me on a vengeful path. Then, I held the humans responsible, which now I see was a wrong and poor judgment. Anyway, I went on a rampage. I saw this woman by the station; she carried a bag, and all I wanted to do was kill her. I didn't know she had a child hidden in the bag she carried. After I had killed her, I noticed the child and I was immediately remorseful for what I had done; off course at the time, I thought it was you I had killed, so I wanted to look after the child and raise her as my own." Sebastian looked at Hanna, and she furrowed her brow as she listened to him explain his side of things. She wondered about what he had said. If he had kept her and not given her to her parents, then she would have only known him as her father. That felt weird and she quickly erased the thought from her head.

Hector giggled at the change of events; he wanted Hanna and Sebastian to feel uncomfortable. Sebastian ignored Hector and continued; what was important to him was letting Hope Lane understand that he would never have harmed her daughter.

Sebastian paused and continued, "I didn't understand it, at the time. I never wanted to leave her side; she was so beautiful, so helpless and adorable, and I wanted her with me at all times. I thought about hiring a nanny to help nurse her, but at that time it was a bad idea. I had engorged myself with too many human bloods. Having another human around would be dangerous. I didn't want any harm to come to her from me or any creature. So, I went out night after night, looking for a family for her; it was hard looking after a baby all by myself."

He looked at Hanna before continuing. "I was about to give up and raise her myself when I found this husband and wife; they had just lost a child, so I thought giving them Hanna would help ease their pain and they could help me raise her and give her what I couldn't." Sebastian paused now to look at Hope and then at Hanna; she was quiet, and her eyes were glued to the table. Hanna had never known this part of her story. She never knew that her parents had another child; they never mentioned it.

Sebastian continued, and Hope encouraged him by smiling through her eyes. She wanted to hear everything about her daughter's life and how her daughter became smitten by this vampire. "I left her on their doorstep, knocked on their door repeatedly and waited in the bushes; moments later the man, her father Joseph, came out and found her. He looked around for who had left her and then took her in. Initially, his wife Joan found bonding with Hanna difficult, but that was a given because she had just lost her own child. Anyway, to cut the story short, they took her in and loved her as their own. I gave them money anonymously for years so she could have the best in life, and I stayed away so she would have a chance at a normal life. However, distance meant nothing; she was constantly on my mind; no matter where I was in the world, her little face always crept into my mind. I felt terrible leaving her with those strangers at the time, so I went back when she was five, and I learned that she was doing well. They were a family; she didn't need me, so I left again and I did not come back until she was seventeen. When I came back this time, I told myself that I just wanted to see that she was well looked after and then leave as I had done before. I promised myself that I would leave her as soon as I was sure. I always knew I loved her more than my own existence, but, when I saw her again after so many years, she was different beautiful and something changed in me. I should have left, but I couldn't. I loved her even more; the more I saw her, but I did not love her as a father. All I wanted was to be a part of her life, but before I could get to know her, I found out that some other vampires were after her life." Sebastian paused to look at Hector who dropped his gaze and started to walk out of the room, but Hope stopped him.

"Don't go," Hope said. "I saw that part in my vision, which was why I approached you. It's not a coincidence; you were in a group that wanted her dead; your role was always to protect her, and you did and that is why we can all sit together now and share the story."

Hector stayed, still feeling ashamed. Sebastian didn't like Hope's praise of Hector, but at the same time, he hoped that if it were true that Hector did what he did knowing that he was saving Hanna; in that case, Sebastian probably owed him thanks.

"Please continue," Hope persuaded.

Sebastian took a deep breath. "I don't know; one thing led to another, and we found each other again; she found me actually lying under a tree near her house, as I had done every night since I returned to her life. We started this friendship; like you, I wanted to know all that I had missed while she grew up, and we became inseparable. I never thought I could love her more than I already did; then, every day my love for her increased, but I wasn't going to do anything about it; I knew I had no right to expect anything even though I loved her greatly. Then one day, she told me she felt the same way. I felt guilty hiding the truth of her past from her. I felt undeserving of her love and what made it worse was the fact that I had thought that it was you I killed when I found her in that bag. Keeping this secret from her ate me alive. I started to dread the day she would find out. I wanted to tell her, but I was scared. Having known so much love, I was scared that she would reject me." Sebastian's eyes met Hanna's. She held his hand to encourage him.

"Hanna eventually found out, and she left me for three years. I begged for her forgiveness. Those were the most painful years of all my existence living without her; but now, we are together again, and the rest, as they say, is history." Sebastian paused and looked at Hanna, who was now gazing into his eyes.

"I love your daughter; what I feel for her is more than love itself, and I don't know why fate brought her into my life, but I am thankful for her, and I would never harm her." Then he looked at Hope, whose face was both teary and happy.

"I am both very happy and relieved," Sebastian said, "that it wasn't you in that alley that night. I am truly happy that you both get to meet again and I will like to say, 'It is a pleasure meeting you.'" Hope got up from where she sat and took Sebastian's hands pulling him to her; she looked at him and hugged him.

"I have you to thank; it seems you gave her more joy than I could ever have given her. Thank you, for taking care of my daughter and loving her like you have. Thank you so much," Hope said; she pulled Hanna up to join them and beckoned Hector to come. He refused but Hope insisted.

"You have to join us, Hector," Hope Lane pleaded. "You are part of the reason she is alive; you were strong for her when it was necessary, and because of what you did, we all get to meet today. Please come for my sake," Hope Lane continued.

Hector reluctantly joined, and the four of them hugged at her insistence. When she finally broke the hug, she looked from Hector to Sebastian. Hector knew what Hope was about to say; although he had joined in the hug, that was all he was prepared to do, not a thing more. The moment felt awkward for him, and he walked out of the kitchen. Hope Lane quickly followed him.

"I will be back you two; I need to have a word with Hector," Hope said to Hanna and Sebastian as she went after Hector.

Chapter 33

Hope found Hector at the top of the house; she climbed the stairs to the open space outside the balcony and smiled as she watched Hector soaking in the sun. Moving closer, a step at a time until she was by Hector's side, Hope said. "I told you, then, that you will walk the day. Look at you now basking in the sun." Hector turned to face her, he wanted to smile but nothing about today felt victorious for him. Yes, they had found Hanna's mother, but listening to Sebastian tell the story of how he found and took care of Hanna really aggravated him. It made it clear that he never had a chance, not when Sebastian had been in her life for that long and claimed his love for her since her childhood. Hearing Sebastian speak made him irk with jealousy, and he knew walking away might be seen by Hope as infantile, but he could not handle another moment breathing the same air as Sebastian.

Watching Hanna's face filled with adoration for his nemesis was torture. Hector wished in that instance that he didn't feel for her what he felt; many times, he had wondered why his heart longed for hers, especially knowing she loved another. It felt like a curse, and what irked him the most was that the more she threw herself at Sebastian, the more he needed her for himself. And the more he fell in love with Hanna, the more his hatred for Sebastian deepened.

Hector knew he wasn't alone the minute Hope approached the stairs; he tried to compose himself, but the anger and hate he carried in his core for Sebastian could be seen sparkling to life in his eyes. He nodded at Hope to acknowledge her presence; then he returned his eyes to the amazing landscape of rolling fields before him. Hope Lane stood next to him and looked out onto the field.

"It's so beautiful here," she mentioned. Hector remained quiet.

"Each day, just before sunset, I come up here and watch the glorious sight; it's simply stunning," she said, and then she turned to face him.

"You two are more alike than you know," she said. Hector knew whom she was talking about, but her comparing him to Sebastian only fuelled the anger in him. He decided he had to leave and act on his plans before Hanna noticed how he truly felt. It was too hard pretending that everything was fine. For his plans to work, he must get word to Mason; that would improve the outcome for him, he thought.

As he stood watching the rolling hills, Hector wondered if Hope could tell what he was thinking. He turned to face her; she looked at him, put her hand to his face and said, "Hector I may not be able to see like I once did, but the energy I feel between you and Sebastian is not good. I can feel your sadness, and there is no cure for it. You both love her; you took care of her, and so did he, but she chose him way before she knew you, and you must accept that." Hope returned her gaze to the open field as did Hector. There was silence between them for a moment. Hector refused to respond to what she had said.

Then Hope turned toward him. "Look at me Hector," Hope said and Hector gave her a side glance.

"No properly, look me in the eye," Hope insisted and Hector reluctantly faced her.

"Don't be mad, Hector, everyone deserves to have that one great love of their life. Mine was her father, and hers is Sebastian.

Perhaps, if he had died young and they had never met, it would have been you she would love now. Mind you, it would not be in the same way as they feel now, but it would have been enough for you. When the original isn't available, there is always an alternative, a substitute. We all know having a substitute is not the same as the original. I want you to understand that it's nothing to do with you; it's just the way it is. Think of it as a test. How you choose to react will determine if you fail or succeed. Choose well Hector; forgive; bury the past where it belongs, and you may yet be surprised. What I say hurts you, I know, but I don't mean any harm. So, think carefully before you do anything; it's better if we can all be as one," she said and placed one hand gently on his shoulder; with the other on his cheek she added. "I'd better get back now; I don't want to miss another moment with my daughter."

Hector smiled. Hope may not see like she did once, but she still had something; he would give her that. As Hope left, he gazed into the field once more; in his heart, he knew his hatred for Sebastian had gotten to the point of no return. He would no longer wait for fate to throw him scraps when he could take for himself what he needed from life.

The only thing that could bring him peace now was seeing Sebastian's severed head on a platter of gold. At least then, he thought, he wouldn't have to watch him hold the heart of the girl he yearned for. Hope's words rang deep, especially the part where she said, "Perhaps if he had died young and they never met, it would have been you she loves now." He laughed inwardly because he was definitely going to do something about that situation and get the girl to love him.

Chapter 34

Hope returned to find Hanna eating the cake. Smiling, she asked," Do you like it?" Hanna nodded not wanting to talk with her mouth full.

"I baked a fresh one since the day I saw a vision that you would come looking for me," Hope said, looking her daughter over and taking her hand. "We still have a lot to talk about you and me. I know we have discussed most things, but there are still a lot of things a mother needs to know about her only child."

Hope paused and looked from Sebastian to Hanna. "Would you stay here with me?" she asked. "I know you both have a life you probably want to get back to but . . . I only just found you."

Before Hanna had the chance to respond, Hope pressed. "Tell me you will stay. I have saved enough money from selling this herb; if Hector wants his house back, I can rent a place just for the three of us."

Sebastian smiled. Hanna looked from her mother to Sebastian; she also wanted to spend more time with her mother, but she needed to know that she and Sebastian were on the same page.

Hanna said, "I know we have a lot to do. And I know I said we will find my mother and then face the other things we planned, but S, please, I would really love to get to know my mother better . . ." She was pleading.

Sebastian cut in before she could finish. "Hanna stop. Of course, you don't need my permission. If you want us to stay, that is what we will do. You both need this. I'm glad to be here to witness it." Hanna beamed at her mother with excitement dancing around in her eyes.

"We would both love to stay with you, but as you know, this is Hector's house; perhaps we should ask him if he minds," Hanna mentioned.

Sebastian looked away; the part where he had to accept charity from Hector didn't sit well with him. Although he had given all he owned to Hanna should he die, he was not dead yet, and so he was still in control of his own wealth and he could very well afford a better place for Hanna and her mother. He told himself he would tell Hanna about going to the letting office with her mother to look for a place of their own.

Hope was happy with the decision; she stood and said, "Well at least for tonight you get to stay here; let me go and make up a room for the two of you; do you share rooms or do you want separate rooms?" It was an awkward question, Hanna thought, saying they wanted the same room would give her mother a completely different mental image of what she and Sebastian were up to, and although she and Sebastian had always had their own rooms, she preferred sleeping on the same bed as him, but she didn't really know what Sebastian wanted. She wanted to say *separate rooms* just to be safe but Sebastian beat her to it.

"The same room if you don't mind; I love having her close," he said, holding Hanna's hand; she smiled and confirmed his decision to her mother.

"Yes, we want the same room, please," Hanna said as Hector walked in.

"So, I take it, you have all decided to remain as guests in my house," Hector said Hope looked at him with anticipation, afraid he may say no. Hector looked from Hope to Hanna, avoiding Sebastian.

Hector continued, "I'm good with that; at least we won't all be sharing cubicle shower rooms as we did in the past." His eyes fell on Hanna and Sebastian's joined hands. He felt sick to the pit of his core, but he did his best to hide it. He knew he only had to tolerate it for a little while. Before now, he had fantasized about sharing this house with Hanna; now he knew after he got rid of Sebastian and after Hanna had killed Mason for it in vengeance, he would get rid of this house. The last thing he wanted was a reminder of their love.

Hector wondered if staying on Hope's good side would help him win Hanna's love, and the best way to start would be to show her he was a good host. Also, he thought it was best for his plans to have Sebastian close, and after he died he would be there to comfort Hanna through the pain until she realized that she wanted him too. Then she would beg him to love her.

"You don't mind us staying, do you Hector? My mother and I, we still have a lot of catching up to do," Hanna said.

"Of course not; don't be foolish. You will always be welcome in any of my homes including this one. You can stay if you want; you can all stay," Hector said, and then he left the room; he had work to do.

"Well, am glad that is settled," Hope said. "As soon as I have made up a room for you all, I will get dinner started for the two of us. You look like you haven't eaten a delicious meal in a long time," Hope said looking over at her daughter.

Sebastian smiled; he agreed that it was time Hanna had something hearty in her stomach. He decided to go hunting while Hope cooked; his body craved fresh blood from a live animal.

"When I get back, you will tell me what you are in the mood for; let your mama spoil you rotten with some of my cooking," Hope said, cupping Hanna's face in her hands. Hanna laughed.

"I can think of a thing or two," she said.

"Okay hold that thought, dear, I will be back shortly," Hope said and quickly left the kitchen. Sebastian noticed that Hanna had not stopped smiling since she met her mother. He loved seeing her this way, and he wished they didn't have a war to fight. He pulled her into his lap.

Hanna said, "Thank you, my love."

"For what, darling?" Sebastian asked curiously.

"You said we should go find my mother, and now we have, and I'm grateful and thankful that you are here with me to share this moment," Hanna said.

"I'm never going anywhere darling; your happiness is my joy, remember?" Sebastian said. Hanna smiled and lay on his chest.

Chapter 35

When Hope returned, Hanna mentioned she was in the mood for beef casserole; Hope rubbed her hands together with excitement as she set about the preparations for dinner.

"I love me some beef casserole. I guess we have that in common. Right I'm going to get started. Would you like to help? I have some vegetables here you could chop up for me," Hope said as she rummaged through the freezer for some frozen beef. She placed the beef in the microwave to defrost. While the beef was defrosting, Hope joined Hanna to prepare the vegetables. Hanna was peeling onions, and Hope was chopping carrots.

Hanna turned to Sebastian and said, "You don't have to stay; I know this is the last place you want to be."

Sebastian smiled. "Thank you. I think I will look around and acquaint myself with the surroundings. That should give you two time to cook and enjoy your meal," he said as he made his way out of their sight.

Hanna called out to him, "S, you forgot something."

Sebastian returned at once and Hanna tapped her cheek with her forefinger; Sebastian chuckled softly and proceeded to kiss her cheek before exiting the kitchen.

After Sebastian had departed, when Hope was sure that he wasn't within hearing distance, she whispered "He is gorgeous your Sebastian." Hanna looked away shyly.

"And he adores you so. I don't know very much about you two, but I can feel the purity of your love, and it makes me want to cry with joy," she said.

"I have spent all this time worrying about you and the reality is, it seems I shouldn't have worried so much; he's looked after you for your whole life. There is not one part of me that is not grateful that he met you, and no one except me, could possibly love you more than he does," Hope continued, pausing to look at her daughter. Hanna said nothing; she couldn't believe she was standing where she was, making dinner with her mother and discussing her love life.

"You are quiet," her mother noted with concern.

"I'm fine," Hanna said looking up at her mother. "This just feels surreal. I never thought it was ever possible, and here we are together, mother and daughter. It's still sinking in, I guess. I mean this time yesterday, I was thinking about you, but I didn't know that I would find you the next day. I am still getting used to you . . . Mum. Can I call you that?" Hanna asked.

Hope welled up, "Don't be silly darling, of course you can. I am your mother. No amount of time away from you changes that or the love I have for you Astraia. I'm sorry, Hanna. I am still trying to get used to this other name you go by," Hope said and Hanna smiled at the thought of constantly hearing her mom call her by another name.

"Your father, before he left, he told me to name you Astraia, so in my mind, for twenty-one years that's the name I had for you up here," Hope said tapping her temple with her fingers.

"Never you mind; you are Hanna now, and if that is what you want me to call you, then that is what I shall," Hope said and resumed chopping the carrots.

"Mum," Hanna called, putting down the knife she was using to dice the onions. "You can call me Astraia. I like it. If everything had gone the way it should, that would have been my name, and it's still my name, so please call me Astraia; it only makes it more special," Hanna said.

"Okay dear, thank you," Hope said.

They continued peeling and dicing, and then Hope began putting everything together. She browned the beef in a pan and combined everything while Hanna started to peel a few potatoes to roast with the casserole. It felt natural being together; they didn't have to talk much; they just worked side by side enjoying each other's company. When they had finished prepping the food, Hope placed it in the oven, and they left the kitchen and retired to the top of the house where Hector had gone earlier. Hope pulled out two seats, and they sat next to each other as they watched the sun setting over the rolling hills.

"That is spectacular," Hanna said.

Hope nodded. "I agree. I came here every day because of that view, it was the only thing that helped me. I stared at it and for a passing moment; I was not thinking about you. I enjoyed the view and then my mind went back to you, and I didn't see the beauty in front of me anymore. My heart became overwhelmed again with uncertainties and the guilt that I was enjoying life's simple pleasures without you. I was hopeful, but when you wait patiently for something that you are sure will happen and you wait for so long, one begins to doubt one's belief in hope. When that feeling of hopelessness would set in, I would shake the doubts away, and I am glad I did or I wouldn't be here today Astraia, enjoying that very same view with my daughter," Hope said taking her daughter's hand.

"Well we've definitely got each other back now, Mother, and I am not going anywhere anytime soon," Hanna said.

"You'd better not," Hope teased. They were quiet again, and then Hope said, "Three years ago, after I got to this house, a part of me thought that I would find you here, but that wasn't the case. And for about three weeks, I tried to get my gift back; the woman that took you away from me, she siphoned my gift and locked up my mind; it was like a prison without walls. I don't know what happened; all I could think of was that she finally died because I was suddenly free, and my gifts returned sparingly. I could see again but not clearly, not like I had done in the past. All I really wanted to do was to find you immediately by any means possible. I had a bit of your placenta that I had preserved, so I made a potion so to speak with some herbs that I knew will help me connect to you, and I drank it all and fell into a deep sleep. In my dream, I could see you, only parts of you in France I think; I couldn't see your face, but my spirit found you, and you didn't seem fine. You were crying all the time over something; I didn't understand what it was, and you worried about money as well. I spoke to you; I was the voice you heard. But before then, I wondered how I could help. There was a man. In his hands was money and you needed some. I also saw that he would get in trouble and try to kill himself. Then I saw that you helped him, and that he gifted you with some of the money. That was when I called you. I was trying to help connect the two of you. You would help him, and he would solve your money problem," Hope said.

Hanna looked stunned. "That, was you?" she asked as her eyes widened with surprise. "I have been thinking about it for so long, wondering what that was all about; nothing surprises me; most things that happen I can usually make sense of, but I didn't know who it was that was talking to me. Why didn't you tell me who you were?" Hanna asked.

"Yes, I should have, but there was no time to waste; if I told you, you would want more answers, and the potion was running its course. I wanted to help you get out of the situation at the time; that was all that mattered. Well, look at us now; the rest is, as they say, history," Hope said. Hanna was still in shock; she couldn't believe she had been in contact with her mother back then.

"Mum, I don't know what to say. I mean, thank you," Hanna said. Hope squeezed her hands.

They were quiet for a minute before Hanna broke their silence. "For eighteen years of my life, I didn't know I was adopted, although I suspected it. My parents, they loved me, they were good to me, but I didn't have anything in common with them, and they never told me I was dropped on their doorstep. When Sebastian told me the truth, I was just so angry, I cut him out of my life because I thought the woman he killed was you. Before then I was sheltered. I lacked nothing, but after I walked out on Sebastian, I had no money. I had no support. I had no one. And now, you tell me that during the hardest time of my life, you were there. It was you, your voice speaking to me. I don't know what to say, Mum. Thank you again. I'm just so touched. That man. His name is um, Andre. I helped him with his trouble without expecting a reward, but he gave me a lot of money. I took it and came back to England to try and start afresh, but whom was I kidding? I couldn't forget Sebastian. I missed him and wanted him so bad; but I couldn't forgive him. He was meant to have killed you. I couldn't see past that. Then I found you were still alive, and I had to find Sebastian and beg his forgiveness; he forgives me; he always does. I am glad that we are all together now. I don't think I can survive losing either of you again. Mum, I want you to know that I have loved you since the day I learned about you. Seeing you today and talking about all these things makes me happy. I am sorry that my birth had caused you so much pain," Hanna concluded.

"No, Astraia, you didn't cause me pain; the world and their greed for power tried to tear us apart, but their plan failed. I have loved you since the night your father told me that I had conceived you, and I will love you until my last breath," Hope Lane said as she squeezed her daughter's hand tighter.

Hanna smiled; she looked contented; then she shook her head. Hope wondered what she was thinking about now. "Is there something else bothering you?" Hope asked.

"No, not really," Hanna said. "It's just that I can't stop thinking about a girl I used to know. Hilda was like a little sister, and now she blames me for what happened to her tribe, her family. I had a situation with the wolves, her tribe, and her family are all under a curse that turns them into wolves, and they thought sacrificing me would erase the curse. Anyway, Sebastian helped me a lot there. He found out their plans for me and told me. They wanted me dead. They were planning a ritual to sacrifice me when I turned eighteen to cleanse and reverse their curse. My best friend then Hurrit Denali was part of it. He befriended me to keep me close. His family and mine were close, but they were after me. And they waited eighteen years before showing their true nature. Sebastian and I fought them, and we won. I didn't place the curse on them. I don't know why I should pay for it. I wish they were more truthful; perhaps I would have found ways to help. Still, I don't think anyone should be forced to live such a life, so even though they don't deserve my help, I want to help, but I don't know how," Hanna signed.

"Wait. Did you say Denali? I have heard that name before," Hope said, trying to think of where she heard it.

"Do you know them?" Hanna asked optimistically.

Hope said, "No, I don't but . . . um . . . I'm trying to remember where I heard that name . . . wait let me think. Oh, now I get it. I don't know if they are the same family, but Ruth, the witch that stole you from me,"

Hanna nodded, trying not to think about the dead witch. "Ruth, what about her? What does she have to do with the Denali's?" Hanna asked.

Hope answered, "Well, it's not her in particular; she told me of her fights with the dreaded Annemarie. I knew she had powers, but until she spoke about Annemarie, I didn't know how long Ruth had lived. I remember her touching on the story of these orphans, a brother and a sister, twins, they were. Annemarie had taken them in to help raise them or something like that. It was a long time ago. I'm talking centuries ago. Anyway, Annemarie had many enemies; she was a very powerful witch—the most powerful then. These children lived with her and she loved them like her own, but rumour had it that she had been the one that killed their mother because their mother stood against her. Their mother, I was told, was like a sister to her, a very dear friend, so when she turned on Annemarie, her punishment was death. Now, Ruth said that some other witches, who also wanted to kill Annemarie to avenge their loved ones, needed a strand of her hair and they needed someone on the inside—someone she trusted to help get them what they needed. They believed that if they had her hair, they could gain her power and weaken her. To get the twins to turn on her, they decided to tell the children the truth about Annemarie. Once the children, now grown, heard what Annemarie had done to their mother, they turned on her and plotted to get her hair, but she found out. She was heartbroken because she had loved them as her own, and she felt that they had turned on her as their mother did, but she didn't kill them because she said only animals turn on their masters, so she cursed their bloodline. That at every full moon, they will live as animals until such a time when a child of power is born, and when the child turns eighteen, they will live forever as animals. I guess that's where you came in," Hope finished.

Hanna's mouth was wide open. "Wow," she mouthed.

"Yes, I know; at the time, I was pregnant with you; little did I know that you were the child they referred to; I mean I knew you were special, but I didn't know that your birth had been predicted for so long," Hope said.

"So, what happened to the children?" Hanna asked.

"I don't know; my guess is as good as yours. She threw them back on the street; they must have married and had children, and here we are one generation after the other. They are still here living with the curse," Hope said.

"So apart from the obvious, there is no other cure?" Hanna asked.

"No, not that I know of unless of course, as Ruth mentioned, if the witch that cursed them is killed by a supernatural being and didn't get to die a natural death, then the curse will be lifted."

"That means," Hanna said, "I have to find a way to wake the witch up and kill her myself. If she dies at my hand, then the tribe would have their lives, back right?" Hanna looked to her mother for approval. Hope didn't want her daughter in dangerous situations, but she also knew she couldn't talk her out of it.

"Precisely, but you can't save everyone, my dear, without suffering. I know you want to help, but you must be careful. I only just got you back. I don't want to lose you again. Promise me you will always be careful?" Hope said.

"I'll do my best; that's all I can say," Hanna said.

"That's all I ask." Hope smiled, realizing that she had no say in the matter. Her daughter was now an adult and had lived all her life without her guidance, and all Hope could do now was give her motherly advice.

"Now come, you must be hungry. I can smell the aroma of that casserole all the way up here; let's go eat darling," Hope said, getting up and helping her daughter up.

Chapter 36

Hector Sayers

Hector lay on his bed and plotted how he would leave to execute his plans, and he considered who he could trust to carry his message to Mason. For what he was planning, he would need to travel to the next town, but he knew his absence could be explained away when he told them he needed to go and hunt. A tiny part of him thought this might all blow back in his face, but that was a risk he was willing to take. For someone who had lived in darkness for more than seven hundred years, and now could walk the day, he had to tell himself to be patient, but he couldn't adhere to his own advice.

Every bit of him impatiently wanted Hanna, and the sooner he was rid of Sebastian, the better. He got out of bed and took a walk around his field. He was outside, by the river that crossed his land, when he saw Sebastian pass. He knew Sebastian saw him too, but as they had both ignored each other since they had been forced to cohabitate, it was easy to pretend he hadn't seen him.

Hector laughed to himself because he knew that if Mason agreed to his plans, then Sebastian had just a short time to enjoy his so-called existence and Hector would have finally exerted vengeance for his brothers. Hector wished that Sebastian would die at his hands, but he would receive his death with glee, however it came. When Hector was sure Sebastian was no longer within view, he took his Nokia phone from his pocket, scrolled down to the name Pablo, and he typed, "We need to meet soon at the Twins Inn. I'll text you when I'm coming." He pressed send, and returned the phone to his pocket. He thought about what he was going to say to Pablo who was a former ally of Hector and his brothers. Pablo lived not too far from Devon. Hector had not spoken to him in a while, but he had heard from another ally that Pablo was considering joining Mason, not because he was a particularly loyal subject, but the word on the street was that the brothers had been dismantled so any vampire that had any kind of loyalty to the brother's cause realized that he must choose sides wisely.

If Mason succeeded in bringing his wife back to life, then anyone that opposed him will be erased. Hector did not blame them; everyone had to fight to survive, and even he must do what was required to survive. The only thing that he didn't like was the necessity of telling Mason where Sebastian dumped his dead witch Annemarie. No one wanted that witch brought back from the dead, definitely not him but he knew that to secure Mason's trust he might have to give up that location.

He didn't want Hanna to get hurt, which meant he had to stay close and convince her and her mother to run away with him to be safe after Sebastian had been killed. He knew she may not want to stay with him because vengeance would be on her mind. Killing Mason would mean another enemy gone, but, he didn't want to risk losing her to Mason and his witch wife. The only way to ensure she came with him would be to drug her and her mother, he thought. He decided when he went to find Pablo, he had to find something he could use to knock out both Hanna and her mother until he had safely transported them to a location that Mason would never find.

Satisfied with his decision, Hector started back toward the house; as he got closer, he started to smell the stench of human food, and his stomach turned. He then decided to go hunting for food instead of staying home smelling shit.

Chapter 37

On day two of Hanna and Hope's reunion, the two of them didn't sleep much; after dinner, they sat together in the kitchen by the fire and talked about anything and everything. The kitchen was lit by candlelight, and the crackling fire was the only other noise in the room. Sebastian was resting and Hector was nowhere to be found. Hanna had been spending most of her time with her mother since their arrival; she missed being with Sebastian, but he had told her not to feel guilty about wanting to spend time with her mother. Sebastian had other things on his mind, the top of the list being Hector; he had seen him punch something into his phone the day before. Sebastian worried that it could be something or nothing. It worried him being in a house owned by Hector and being required to trust him to keep silent about his and Hanna's whereabouts. He knew he should talk to Hanna about it, but as usual, when it concerned Hector, Hanna had a fabulous way of inventing excuses for Hector's behaviour and then sweeping everything under the carpet.

Her attitude with Hector irked him a lot, but he didn't want to allow his feelings about Hector to ruin Hanna's time with her mother. Sebastian wondered if he was being paranoid about Hector because his thinking would always be clouded when it concerns him, but, he also knew it was better to be safe than sorry. He mentally prepared himself for whatever Hector had planned;

for now, he would lie low and rest. The more rested he was, the stronger his body would be should something spring up when Hector eventually showed his hand.

****

Hanna reminisced about her life before Sebastian; she filled her mother in on the fabulous life she had with her late parents, Joseph and Joan. All the holidays, her father's bad habits and how her mother looked for any excuse to throw parties. They both laughed a lot, and at times Hope wept a little. Hanna touched on how Hurrit's betrayal had cut her, and how she had also trusted Ruth, who had pretended to be a friend.

Hope sighed and said, "It saddens me to know you went through all these things by yourself, but I'm happy you came out on top. You didn't even need me; still, I wish I was there for you."

"I know. Well it all worked together for good, and I hope it will be in the end," Hanna stated. Hope made coffee and refilled her daughter's cup. Hanna continued speaking about the things she went through, but when she noticed her mother starting to tear up, she changed the subject to Sebastian. She told her mother how she had pretended that she wasn't falling in love with him during their initial meetings.

"He accidental bumped me in the head with the door, and when I opened my eyes and saw his face, I couldn't breathe. I literally couldn't stop looking at him; at the time, I didn't know what he was, and I was bleeding and probably in pain, but I didn't want him to let go of me. I think that was when I first fell in love with him." Hope smiled.

Hanna continued. "And then he just disappeared for about a month or so, and every day before I slept, I would think of that guy with the beautiful green eyes and the way he held me and looked at me like I mattered to him. It was pathetic the way I felt about this stranger that I was sure I wasn't going to see any more. Then, one day, I sat in my room like I had done for the past seven weeks since the accident. The scar had gone, but somehow it was as if he left a scar in my heart. I couldn't explain it; I felt this strong pull to be with him. I couldn't tell my mom then; she wouldn't understand it. They never knew about my powers; anyway, I was disturbed. I couldn't sleep. I couldn't forget him, but I didn't know him or how to contact him. I hadn't seen him before the day he bumped into me, but he had invaded my heart and my thoughts. I got up from my bed and I started to walk; as I got outside, I looked up and I knew he was out there somewhere, but I wasn't prepared for what I was about to find." Hanna paused and then said. "As I stood outside my house, my heart felt something close; it pounded in me like a part of my heart was missing and I could feel the other part calling. I almost wanted to start crying because I was longing for something that I thought was impossible to have. We have a willow tree at the right corner of the house. I remember my parents argued about that tree; my father didn't like it; my mother thought it was beautiful, romantic. Then I used to think it was stupid arguing over that tree. That night, I looked at the tree, and I was drawn to it; the closer I got, the more nervous I felt and the more I felt I was close to something important. I don't know why, but I kept walking until I found him lying there; it was like something out of a book. I looked, and I thought I was dreaming or hallucinating. My heart raced within me; his face was as shocked as mine." Hanna paused and laughed softly as she brought to memory the event of that night.

"Tell me more. Did you scream?" Hope asked wanting more details.

"No, why would I? I was happy; it was weird but I kept my cool. I couldn't believe he was there, and I didn't understand what he was doing there. But my heart in that moment felt complete; the ache was gone; I had him within touching distance. We just talked, and I knew then I didn't want to be parted from him again. He was so beautiful to look at." Hanna closed her eyes as she recalled how she felt in that moment.

"I wanted him for myself," Hanna said. "I wanted him around forever, but I was only seventeen and living at home with my parents, and it was only the second time I had seen him. From then on, we just hit it off, but I feared he didn't feel the same. I had fallen too deep; I knew he cared, but I didn't know how much he cared. It was scary for me; there is nothing I can compare that feeling to. We would meet, but before then, nothing would feel right until I had seen him and when it was time to go home, the thought of leaving him made me so sad. I used to sit and daydream about him. I know, pathetic, but I couldn't help myself. I really loved being alone with him. I used to dream of a future with him. I wanted many things, and they all included him. My mom thought it was too much; my dad, bless him, he thought it was adorable. I had seen many movies and read books, Mum, where I'd hear people talk about being in love, but until him, I never knew what that meant; still I don't think that word really covers or explains my feelings for him." Hanna stopped speaking and sipped her coffee. Her mom did too and smiled.

Then Hope said, "Is that it? Tell me more; in case you haven't noticed, I'm a sucker for love."

Hanna giggled, then she continued. "I was so in love and I tried to play it cool. I wanted him to tell me how he felt if he felt anything at all. Mind you, all of this was in the space of about a month or two. If he had asked me to run away with him, I'm sorry to say, I would have said *yes*. Then, one time, I didn't see him for three days; I almost went mad, I missed him too much. At first, I thought he didn't like me; then sometimes I hoped he was missing me, too. When I couldn't stand pretending that we could only be friends, I told him how I felt. In his eyes, I could see he felt the same way about me, but he fought it and it killed me. I couldn't believe that what I was feeling, this powerful love inside me, could

272

be one sided. And if that was the case, that would have been the worst thing that could ever happen to me. I don't know what I would have done if he had not changed his mind. But he did, and now even till this day I still feel exactly the same way about him, if not more. And the amazing thing is even though we love each other, we haven't been close like that," Hanna said and gazed into the fire. Hope's face creased in shock at this last claim. They were both quiet, and then Hope wondered if she heard correctly what Hanna said last. What did she mean by they weren't close like that? To be sure she understood what her daughter was saying, she had to ask.

"You mean since the two of you have been together, you haven't?" she asked. Hanna nodded to confirm Hope's question. Hope didn't know if she should be pleased Sebastian was a gentleman or if she should be worried.

"It's not like we don't want to, with everything that has been going on in our lives, we can't afford to be together like that now. I mean, for now, we are somewhat content with just being the way things are. It can be frustrating, but I can't get into that now; that is a story for another night." Hanna paused and considered how it must look—Two people claiming to be powerfully in love yet they had not expressed the love in the act of lovemaking.

To change the subject, Hanna said, "Let me show you something." Hope smiled and waited for what Hanna was about to reveal, but then Hanna clicked her fingers and darkness covered them. The fire had gone out, including the candlelight's, and then she flicked her fingers again, and the room was once again lit.

Hope smiled proudly, "Amazing! That's my girl," she said.

"I have never used it for fun like that; it's bloody amazing, don't you think? I think it can be used for fun, but then again with power comes big responsibilities," Hanna said; her voice faded off as thoughts of the battles ahead came calling. She looked at her mother and she knew she had to let her know what was happening.

"I need to tell you something, and I don't want you to worry," Hanna said, and then she told Hope of the impending fight between her, Mason, and his vampire followers and his plan to bring his dead wife back to life, not forgetting little Hilda's vengeful attack as well. Hope looked worried; Hanna was worried too, but she had to be strong.

"I don't want you around during the fights; I don't know when it will break out; as we speak, we could be getting surrounded, but I don't want you involved Mama. You need to promise me you won't get involved," Hanna said.

Hope's face was loose with horror; she shook her head and said, "No darling, I can't let you fight alone. I am your mother. I will play my part," Hope argued.

Hanna shook her head in disagreement. "No, I won't allow that; if something happens to you, I won't forgive myself. This is my fight, and I won't bring you into it. I have Sebastian and Hector; they are enough. I will talk with Sebastian; we will get another place. I want you to go there and when it's all over, we will meet you there, I promise you, Mum. I will come back to you," Hanna said firmly Hope wanted to say something but Hanna cut her off.

"There is nothing you can say that will allow me to put you in danger, Mum. Look at me, you did your part already when you made sure Hector took care of me. I am here because of you and I am stronger for it. Please, I don't want anything to happen to you. I need you in my life and I need you to stay alive for me. Please," Hanna begged.

"If anything happens to you, and I did nothing to help," Hope said, "then my life would be worth nothing Astraia. Please. Maybe there is something I can do to help." Hope's tears fell to the ground.

"Don't cry Mama. I already told you with power comes responsibility. There is nothing you can do, but to pray it all comes out well. But I am positive of victory," Hanna said through clouded, teary eyes.

"I will come back to you, I promise." Hanna tried to assure her mother.

Hope wiped her tears with the back of her hand. "Very well then, I shall brew some herbs; perhaps with my vision I can help. I can see the future although I am afraid to look; I may not like what I see," Hope said, getting up from where she sat. At once, she started plucking herbs from the plant pots.

"I wish you wouldn't do that Mom; I don't want you seeing things that may break your heart. Let it alone; what will be, will be, but I promise I will do all I can to ensure that I return to you. You and Sebastian are all I have now," Hanna said placing her hand on her mother's hand to stop her from plucking the herbs.

"Darling, I will just brew it down, just in case. Let me; it won't hurt to know a thing or two. My visions are not as reliable as before; who knows, I may see nothing or something. The brew will take three days to be ready; as you said, we may never even get three days. But I will sleep better knowing I did something to help," Hope said, not backing down. Hanna knew that there was no talking her mother out of it; she must have inherited her mother's stubbornness.

Hanna smiled. "Okay, if it makes you feel better . . . if you see something, tell only me if you think it will help . . . otherwise, I don't want to know," Hanna said.

"All-right darling," Hope said and got to work on her herbs.

Hanna watched her for a bit, and then she said, "Mama, I have to go to bed now. I am tired. I'm sure Sebastian is up waiting for me," Hanna said as she yawned.

"Okay, goodnight darling. I'll see you tomorrow; go and rest," Hope said as she busied herself with the herbs for the brew.

Hanna turned back to watch her mother and smiled to herself. She could feel her mother's genuine worry. It was nice to have another person in the world fighting for her.

"Ah, before I forget, tomorrow, we are going house hunting; remember I said I want you out of here just out of caution," Hanna said over her shoulder.

"Yeah, yeah. I will be ready darling; anything you say," Hope replied without turning away from what she was doing.

"Okay, love you and goodnight," Hanna called and disappeared. Hope dropped what she was doing and turned to where her daughter was just moments ago; her heart felt warm because her daughter had just told her she loved her. She smiled contentedly and continued with her chore.

Chapter 38

Hanna snuck into bed beside Sebastian; his eyes were shut so she assumed he had shut down for the night. She placed her head on his chest and moved closer to him. She smiled as she thought of how easy it was to share her feelings for Sebastian with her mother. It had only been two days, and even though she knew things were going too fast, she loved it; she might never again get the chance to be with her mother and catch up on the past twenty-one years. They both knew it, even if her mother didn't want to believe it. Somewhere hidden at the back of Hanna's mind was the fear that she might fall in battle, even though she put on a brave face. Sebastian moved beneath her and wrapped his arms around her.

"Hey," he said,

"Hey to you, too," Hanna responded, doing her best to shake the negative thought that was surfacing.

"Are you okay?" Sebastian asked.

"Hmm, yeah, I see you waited for me; you should have been resting," she replied. Sebastian took a deep breath and raised his head to kiss her forehead as she looked up at him.

"Yeah, but I didn't want to sleep until you were here with me. I know you and your mother need time, and I am not complaining. I just miss you is all. Anyway, tomorrow I still want you to go out with your mother; perhaps you can both do some shopping. You need a change of clothes. I love you but this dress is beginning to . . . hmm." He stopped himself and wrinkled his nose; Hanna saw his expression and lifted her dress to her nose.

"Yeah, I get what you mean, it's starting to stink. I definitely need a change of clothes, and you are coming with me," Hanna said.

"No, I will find something to occupy my time; I definitely don't want to be the third wheel. Just go without me; spend some more time with your mother; you need it," Sebastian objected; he had planned to find out what Hector was up to, and to do that he needed to track Hector's movement.

"No, I'm not having it; I love spending time with my mum, but I miss you too; I miss being around you. I was just recounting our love life to her downstairs; I'm sure she will understand having you tag along. Moreover, I want to go house hunting, too, and I was looking forward to doing that with you," Hanna said, Sebastian was quiet; he didn't want to disappoint Hanna, and he didn't want to tell her what he wanted to do with regard to Hector either. Arguing about Hector was out of the question; he couldn't stomach how she managed to side with Hector and tell him he needed to give Hector the benefit of the doubt. However, if he said he wouldn't go out with her, then she would want to get to the bottom of things, so he caved to her demand.

Sebastian kissed her forehead again and said.

"If you insist, then I will come with you. I agree we need to find another place. I was thinking about that, too, when the fight is over and we can finally rest from all this chaos, you and I and your mother can live in a house of our choosing as a family," he said.

"Won't that be lovely," Hanna responded. They were quiet as though they knew that they were thinking of a future that was uncertain.

Then Sebastian said, "If I were human, Hanna, we would have lots of babies and make your mother a grandma. I know you would make a great mother."

"Yeah, wouldn't that be just perfect, a little me and a little you running about the place. How many would we have?" Hanna asked living the dream with him.

"Well, quiet a bunch I should think, but it depends on you really; how many can you handle?" Sebastian asked.

"Hmm, let me think, I think quite a lot, as I can't keep my hands off you. I wouldn't let you rest, and I predict that I will be pregnant every nine months," she said, and Sebastian laughed out loud.

"Darling, I wouldn't do that to you, not every nine months, perhaps every year," he teased.

"What difference does that make?" Hanna asked.

"Well, at least you would have three months of rest from being pregnant. Seriously, tell me, if I could give you children, how many would you want?" Sebastian pushed.

"I don't know. I can't tell. If I could, I would have a dozen with you, but I think I could settle for four or even six," Hanna responded,

"Not six or seven?" Sebastian joked; they laughed happily.

"Who knows, as long as they are mine and yours, I already told you a dozen kids are doable," Hanna joked. Sebastian was quiet; he remembered a time just before he was turned when that was his dream. To find a girl he loved and be loved back and have children he would adore and bring them up with all the love in the world. However, lying next to Hanna, he had no regret that he was turned; if he hadn't been he might never have known or felt such great love.

"Wouldn't that be something? To have children? If seven, four boys and three girls just like their mama; if six, three of each," he said as he stared into space and imagined himself surrounded by their beautiful children.

Hanna laughed softly. "Yeah, I could just see it now, what a lovely family we would make."

"Indeed, my love. Indeed," Sebastian said; he took a deep breath as he tried to tear himself from dreaming about a life he knew would never happen, but he wished that he had with Hanna.

"Rest now, darling, according to you; we have a lot to do tomorrow," Sebastian said. Hanna smiled as she dreamed about the impossible; but it felt good to think about what could have been if they had met in a different world and they were both human. Lost in a dream world, within the gentle grasp of Sebastian's arms, Hanna drifted off to sleep.

Sebastian noticed that her breathing had slowed a bit and was more regular while sleeping. He brushed his hands gently on her hair being careful not to wake her, and then he shut his body down and welcomed his rest.

****

The next morning, he showered and waited in the room for Hanna who had gone downstairs to join her mother for breakfast. He could hear them chatting to Hector who was informing them that he would be going out for some air later. Hanna had asked him what time he wanted to go out, but Hector was evasive. He said he wasn't sure, but that he would leave the house when he felt ready. Hector went outside and stopped by the door where he could still hear Hanna talk. She looked at her mother and said, "Those two just can't get along. I don't think he likes Sebastian being here, but he is being a gentleman for both our sakes. So is Sebastian, too, but for now, I'm glad they are trying; maybe one day this hate they have for each other will die and they can be friends. I don't think that will ever happen, though, but I will never stop hoping," Hanna said.

"You don't need to tell me about them; I can see it for myself," Hope said, "They have barely stayed in the same room together. You can't force this thing darling. Just let it be."

"I can't, I love Sebastian with everything, but I like Hector, too. He has grown on me these past months. If I choose sides with Sebastian, then Hector automatically becomes my enemy. I don't see him as one and I don't want him to be my enemy. I have enough of those already. But I live in hope that one day the two of them, for my sake, will make up for past wrongs. Right now, it seems impossible," Hanna said.

Hector scoffed, as he started to walk off. "She must be out of her mind," he muttered to himself; he didn't want to think of her as naïve. She herself had said it would be impossible and she was right. There was no chance in hell he would forgive Sebastian for his brother's death. He brought out his phone and texted Pablo.

"Change of plans. Let's meet at your home. I'll let you know the time soon." Then he pressed send, and a few seconds later, he received a text from Pablo. "Busy, busy, except the cause is good. Won't be home."

Hector sighed in frustration, then he wrote, "Need you to carry a message to Mason. Still busy?"
He waited a few minutes before his phone buzzed again and Pablo wrote, "Ok, I'll be home; let me know when."

Hector smiled with satisfaction and placed his phone in his pocket.

***

Sebastian heard every word Hanna had said to her mother and shook his head in disagreement. About this, at least, he and Hector agreed; they would never be friends. He saw Hector as a snake, and he would stop at nothing to prove to Hanna that he was right about him. Sebastian wondered where Hector was going later. Sebastian thought about calling off the shopping and staying at home so he could track Hector's movement as he had planned earlier, but he knew Hanna wouldn't hear of it. His fist was clenched in anger as he battled with himself on the decision not to follow Hector. Then he heard Hanna coming up the stairs to find him. He unclenched his fist and sat on the bed and tried to relax. She entered and went straight into the bathroom to brush her teeth. As she came out of the bathroom, she popped a mint into her mouth to help erase the smell and taste of toothpaste; then she came nearer.

"Okay, mum said we should give her half an hour to get ready; what about you, are you ready?" she asked as she leaned in to give him a quick kiss. Sebastian drew her into his embrace; he wanted to let her know he changed his mind about going out with them, but then he saw the excitement dancing in her eyes, and he couldn't bring himself to destroy it.

"Only if you show me how badly you want me there with you," he said.

Hanna raised her brow and leaned in closer. "I have got a few tricks in my bag," she said as she tenderly planted a kiss on his lips, then another, and another in succession. Sebastian laughed softly beneath her kisses. He grabbed her waist.

"Is this what you call tricks?" he jested. He took control of the kiss and he began to slowly kiss her building up in intensity by the second until they were both breathless." Hanna struggled to break away, but he pulled her back into the kiss until she collapsed in his arms with contentment.

It was her turn to laugh softly. "Mr. Sebastian Francis, you've got some skills; you know how to leave a woman breathless and wanting more," she said.

"It's always my pleasure to please you, darling," he said as he got up and pulled her to her feet.

"We better get going; we don't want to keep your mother waiting," Sebastian said. "By the way, do we have any cars, or are you zooming us there?" Sebastian asked jokingly.

"Ha, ha, very funny. Mum already called a cab; there is a car in the garage we could take, but it's Hector's; he just changed the batteries this morning. I didn't mention it before because I knew you wouldn't want that," Hanna said. Sebastian nodded in agreement.

"Good girl, cab it is," he said as they made their way down the stairs to meet Hanna's mother. The cab arrived a few minutes later and Sebastian, Hanna, and her mother went to town.

Chapter 39

Hector Sayers

.

Immediately they were gone, Hector knew now was his time to act. He didn't know how long they would be gone, but he was counting on Hanna and her mother to make the shopping trip lengthy. Girls always love shopping he thought. The sun was going to set around five, so he decided to quickly text Pablo,

"I will meet you at yours 6 pm."

Hector drove his car out of the garage. He was thinking it was a good thing the windows were still tinted because it meant no one would suspect him of being a day walker. Though he wanted Sebastian dead, he dreaded bringing any harm to Hanna; giving away that he was a day walker would not help her cause. Hector looked at the time; it was just a little past eleven in the morning. He knew if he left now, he would get to Pablo by 2 pm. Although he had told Pablo to meet him in the evening, he didn't see the need to wait now, especially because he had other errands to run. He needed to get the drug he would use on Hanna and her mother. Hector reasoned that if he was quick enough, he could get to Pablo, send him to Mason, run his other errand and be back before Hanna and the others got back home.

Three hours later, he was at Pablo's. Pablo had a darkened-out garage like every vampire he knew. He brought out his Nokia and wrote, "I'm here. Sorry. I was in the neighbourhood."

Now, most vampires would be resting, but he was hoping Pablo was awake, especially because he had told him that he had a message for Mason. He waited and wondered if the risk he took coming early would pay off; if not, it meant he would have to wait around until Pablo was awake. After waiting for five minutes, Hector was about to drive off, when the garage door opened.

Hector smiled happily as he drove in and killed the engine. He waited for the garage door to shut as he would have done had he not been given the gift of light by Hanna. Then he came out of his car and was faced with a nervous looking Pablo. Hector knew immediately that something wasn't right. His instinct told him to leave immediately, but he was locked in. There was no going back out now. He sighed, and looked at Pablo.

"What's wrong Pablo; what have you done?" Hector asked. Pablo looked towards his house without speaking. Before Hector could make sense of what was happening, he heard a voice he hadn't expected.

"Hector, imagine us meeting again like this." Out came Thomas, closely followed by Henry. Hector's heart sank. He looked from his new companions to Pablo.

"Why? I trusted you. What is this?" he inquired through gritted teeth.

"I'm sorry Hector, but it is important that we all act as one, Pablo said. "What I did, I did for the good of our kind. Someone said they spotted you outside the Grosmont house; they thought you died there, but when you texted me, you confirmed to me that you were still alive, and you were not seen leaving, so we figured you went with them. This isn't personal, but if you know where they are, you have to tell us; you have to tell them."

Hector hissed. "You snake, you're a viper. So, you called them right after I contacted you! Is there no loyalty anymore?" he asked more to himself. Hector took a deep breath; all was not lost, he thought; he had planned to send a message to the Mason camp and this would only serve to fast forward his plans.

He looked from Thomas to Henry, purposefully avoiding the traitor Pablo. "Believe it or not, my business here today was to get a message to Mason. I can help him get Sebastian, but I want a deal that he and the rest of you will pardon whatever atrocities I committed when I was still with my brothers. They are dead now thanks to you two; I have no one else; no allies, and I just want to be left alone," he said throwing Pablo an evil look.

Hector said, "I just want a peaceful life. So, if you agree, then I will help you get what you want." Everyone was quiet; then two more vampires appeared and stood behind Henry and Thomas. Hector was frightened; he had expected them to jump at the opportunity to get Sebastian; he didn't know what to make of this situation. He knew he couldn't fight them all. They were all aged vampires, all experienced warriors. He tried not to look nervous.

Then one of the two that appeared said, "Mason said to bring him in."

Hector didn't know Mason had come too. The two vampires stepped forward and held him by his arms and pushed him forward. Thomas, Henry, and Pablo stepped aside as Hector was forced inside the house.

He followed reluctantly as the rest of the vampires that were in the garage followed behind. As they entered the living room, Hector's eyes clamped on Mason who stood in the middle of Pablo's living room. Mason turned to face him, and smiled sarcastically; he then proceeded to sit on the armchair and face him. He flicked his hands and the two vampires that held him, released their hold on Hector. Hector looked nervously at Mason and turned to count the number of vampires in the room with him; from the corner of his eyes, he could count at least twelve, and those were the ones he could see. He knew that at least another twenty or so would be hiding somewhere. It seemed every vampire was now on Mason's team. There was no fighting his way out of this; there was only dying if he didn't corporate. He took a deep breath and focused his gaze on Mason. Mason gestured his hands majestically into the air and asked him to speak. "I heard you said you wanted to help?" Mason asked.

Hector was quiet; he wanted his delivery to sound like he had all the power and to show that he wasn't afraid at the same time; he didn't want to sound too arrogant in Mason's eyes.

"Speak boy; I have a lot on my mind," Mason persuaded,

"I know where he can be found; I mean Sebastian, but I want assurance that you will leave me be. I apologize for my trespasses in the past and ask your forgiveness. My brothers have paid with their lives, and I just want a simple and peaceful life now." He paused to see how Mason was taking his proposition. Mason's expression didn't change; his eyes bored holes into Hector who had to look away in defeat.

Mason cleared his throat. "If I understand you, you are offering me Sebastian, who I know hates you as much as I do and wants you dead because he came to me to arrange for help killing you and your brothers. A fight in which you managed to escape death. Now, you want revenge. Hmm let's say I believe you; how would you know where he is; you two clearly hate each other; he would not confide in you; he isn't stupid and I am no fool," Mason said firmly.

"No, no, I am not lying to you; why would I? It's true I hate him; that is why I contacted Pablo when I heard you were looking for him. I wanted Pablo to get the message to you, to arrange this very deal. Believe me, when I say, I know where he can be found," Hector said.

"He lies; it is a trap; you have been sent here to lure me out," Mason accused.

Hector tried to convince Mason: "No that is not true. I have no reason to lie; I told you my only motivation is my own survival. I bear you no grudge, not anymore. I just want to be left alone to live out the rest of my existence in peace." Mason scoffed.

"Take him out of my sight and finish what you started," Mason instructed Thomas. Hector realized he had to do all he could to ensure his neck was not separated from his head. "No! No! You are making a mistake. I know more than I am telling you, believe me. I am telling you the truth."

Mason got up and walked closer to him. "Then make me believe you," he said, standing toe to toe and bearing down on Hector.

"They took your wife, Annemarie's body. I know where you can find it; they tried to destroy it but they couldn't; if you promise to leave me alone in the presence of all these witnesses here, then I will tell you where she can be found. If you don't believe me, then destroy me now." Hector didn't want to be killed. But, he managed to look as fearless as he could.

Mason stared him down; he could tell Hector was telling the truth, and he didn't know how he came by his information, but anything was better than nothing. However, if Hector wanted his freedom, then he had to do more than share information; he must give more. To help resurrect his wife, Mason needed only a drop of Hanna's blood spilled on the ring that Annemarie had given him to empower and bring his dead wife to life; then Mason could bind and weaken Hanna, putting her under his control. The ring would only work until his wife was restored, meaning Mason had a short time in which to wake his wife and then slit Hanna open so that Annemarie could consume all her powers with the help of his sorcerer.

Mason said: "If you want my forgiveness, you will do more than tell me where I can find Sebastian. I will not ask how you know this if you give him to me and tell me where Annemarie's body is kept; but to gain your freedom, you must bring me a drop of Hanna's blood."

Hector looked shocked; he didn't know how he could do that without being found out. He said, "Surely if you believe that I can do that, then you really must want me dead. I said I knew where they could be found; I never said I live with them; how do you expect me to carry out what you request; it is ludicrous what you want from me. I am willing to give you Sebastian and your wife; I cannot get what I cannot get." Hector dug his heel in; he knew that he couldn't get Hanna's blood without losing her trust; what Mason was asking was impossible; also, doing so would put Hanna in harm's way and that he would never do.

"You will do as you are told if you want to carry on with your useless existence," Mason roared. Hector smiled sarcastically; he knew he couldn't do it, and if he must die then he brought it upon himself with his devious plotting.

"Then do what you must, if that is your intent. We all must die one day, no matter how long we live. I have told you the truth, and I will not tell you I can do what you ask. You know very well that I will be killed before I can get to her. My information is good; when you find Sebastian, you will find her, and you will find your wife's body. How you get the blood you need is your cross to bear, not mine. No one else knows where they can be found; so, if you want me dead, do it now and find Sebastian yourself," he bluffed. He knew this could all end so badly for him and he was ready but he would not die, signing Hanna's death.

Mason backed away and went back to his seat; he looked at Nicholas, who stood at his side, and then at Thomas and Henry. Then he looked at Hector; he knew if he killed him, then he would be no closer to getting what he wanted. He reckoned that he had enough army now to take Hanna on; almost all the vampires from all over the world that have heard of what he was about to do for their kind had joined his crusade. They had searched high and low and found nothing and now Hector walks in saying he has all the answers. Mason knew he had to take the chance.

"Okay, tell me where they can be found, and where my wife's body is kept. If I find it all to be true, you can have your pardon and go live your life free from me," Mason, said.

Hector wanted to shout in relief; he had thought that he would die. Instead, he held himself together; now was not the time for celebration. He always knew his plan to take out Sebastian was a high risk, but it had paid off. Soon Sebastian would be gone, and he would have his revenge for his brothers Anton and Zachary and more importantly, the girl of his dreams. He felt victorious, there was no way, Sebastian would escape death now. However, he also wasn't a fool; Mason might yet change his mind and kill him after he had told him all he wanted to know.

"Okay, promise me in the presence of all that are present here that you will not change your mind as soon as I divulge what I know," Hector asked.

"I am nothing if I do not keep my word; you have my word Hector; no harm will come to you if what you say is found to be so," Mason said. Hector smiled and looked about him; he felt more relaxed now.

"I will give you an address where they will be two to three days from now; when you get there, you will see a cliff. I was told by a very reliable source that Sebastian threw your wife's body over that cliff. I suggest that you go there; you will find her body at the bottom of the sea. If you go now, it will give you time to find her before they arrive," Hector said.

Mason fumed inside; he wanted to tear Sebastian apart with his hands for dumping Annemarie's body at the bottom of the sea.
"You have done well; give Thomas the address, and we shall go see for ourselves," Mason said; then he looked at everyone around, "Gather everyone together; we are going to war; every hand will be needed. We shall all be there waiting when they come."

***

Thomas had been undecided about what side to take, but with the influx of vampires from around the world, he knew he could not oppose Mason now.

He decided to leave his vendetta alone for now; he reckoned walking the day was a bigger cause for all their kind, and he had believed in it before Margret was killed, and he still believed in it now. Moreover, he didn't think Sebastian would want him on his side now, as it looked like Sebastian would not come out of this. The only way out of this for Sebastian would be if he and the girl were powerful enough to destroy Mason's legion of an army. It seemed impossible.

After Hector gave him the address, Mason instructed Thomas to allow him to leave. As Hector got in his car, he still could not believe he had been spared; if he were in Mason's shoe, he would kill him now. Still, he knew he could be followed, he thought. As he drove out of Pablo's garage, his heart was in his throat.

He decided to drive to another town instead of returning to Devon. He wished that finding Sebastian wouldn't lead to Hanna, but if it did, he knew she was powerful enough to subdue them. Still, he would rather she was not involved; that meant he still had to get the drugs. Forty-five minutes later, Hector parked his car in an underground car park. He had not seen anyone trailing him; still, he knew he could be wrong. He got out of the car, took the lift and entered a hotel lobby. Still nervous, he looked around to see if anyone was watching him; then at the reception desk he requested a room. Hector got his room keys and then pretended he was going to his room. He found a chambermaid in the corridor and asked about a back exit. The chambermaid pointed him in a direction, and he made his way into the street.

The time was about 4.20 pm; the sun had not set; he put on his sunglasses and hailed a cab. Then he ducked inside and asked the cab driver to take him back to Devon. Half way through the journey, he was sure that if he was being followed he would have lost them by now. He relaxed and thanked his stars that the risk he took paid off; he was still in one piece, but then he remembered he had forgotten to buy the drugs he needed. Hector heaved a sigh and decided he would do that the next day; he smiled foolishly at himself and almost patted his own back for a job well done.

Chapter 40

Hilda Denali.

"It's another full moon tomorrow, and all I am getting is nothing; she needs to be found; get more people out there and find that witch fast. Do you want your freedom? Do you want our tribe to be healed?" Hilda asked.

Her subjects roared, "Yes."

"Then how can there be no one with any useful news. You all look to me to do something; well I can't very well do anything if I can't find her, or do you expect me to do all the work on my own?" she asked. Everyone was quiet; no one dared look up at her.

"There must be something that can lead us to her; anything out of the ordinary; think all of you; think!" Hilda shouted at the tribe as they gathered in circles. Hilda stood in the middle of the tribe as she addressed them. They were gathered on her land, in front of her ruined castle. Her subjects ranged in age from twelve year old boys to seventy-year-old men and women.

"Still nothing; no one here can think of something?" she said fuming. Hilda had searched everywhere, but it was as if she had gone blind, and she was hoping that someone in the tribe had tried as much as she to find Hanna. She had also brought back all tribe members including her family already living as wolves in the Scottish forest. All that remained was to lay hands on Hanna and perform the sacrifice that would change and erase the curse. A few of the tribe's elders told her that even if Hanna were brought back and sacrificed, they were already sealed to the curse when Hanna turned eighteen, which meant killing her may not cure those that were already wolves. Hilda refused to entertain their advice. She was certain that she could turn the curse. No one dared to argue; they had been told what befell the grey-haired man that laughed and argued with her.

As Hilda looked around the circle for help, a young girl stood up; she was about sixteen years of age. Hilda focused her eyes on the girl.

"Yes, do you have any idea how we can lay hands on her," Hilda asked; the girl shook her head timidly.

"Then why are you wasting my time?" Hilda said irritated.

"I . . . I . . . have just noticed something unusual; I told it to my ma, but she . . . she got a cold and couldn't make it here tonight," the girl said.

"What is it? Spit it out already; we don't have all night," Hilda said firmly.

"I don't know if it will help, but I have noticed the arrival of a lot of the undead, the bloodsuckers. My father used to tell me about them before he turned into a wolf. You see, I have a gift, and I'm not too sure if it will help, but I can tell the undead from the real humans by just looking at them. I have noticed more of them around lately; I overhead they are also looking for someone who has the power to make all undead walk the sun. So, if this is true, I wondered who that could be; such a person must have lots of power to make them walk the sun. Then I wondered, what if we are all after the same person?" The girl finished speaking and her eyes remained on Hilda, who was in deep thought. Every eye moved from the girl to Hilda trying to connect the dots.

Hilda looked at the girl, and asked, "Can anyone here verify that you have the gift to tell those bloodsuckers from humans?" Hilda knew what the girl said could lead to something, but she'd rather not waste time chasing the wind. The girl nodded and looked at her sister, who was only about a year older.

"My sister knows about my gifts; she can tell you," the girl said. Hilda looked from the girl to the one sitting next to her.

"Well?" Hilda asked looking at the girl's sister. "Is it true what she said?"

The sister stood up and said, "Yes, there is a coven that lived not far from us, but each time they had visitors that are like them, Amari could always tell. She would point them out to us and we sometimes tracked them close to their home. She knows them apart," the sister confirmed.

Hilda smiled. "And how many did you say you've seen recently?" Hilda questioned.

"More than usual; in the past, one or two came to visit in six months, but in the last week alone, I have spotted more than ten. They are arriving from all over and I think if we follow them, it may lead us to her if she is the same person they are after," Amari explained. Hilda understood perfectly what the girl suggested.

"Very well, if what you say is true, then we have a bigger fight on our hands; we will follow those bloodsuckers; where they go, we go, and when they draw her out, we will battle them for her and take her for ourselves. We need everyone, and we need all the wolves brought from Scotland. Everyone must battle so that we can be liberated from this curse. This is going to be a fight to end all fights. Tomorrow is the full moon, so let's hope they make a move soon. Tell us where to find the coven you speak of; we will get everyone ready, and we will watch from afar, and when they move, we move and when we attack, they won't see us coming. Understood?" Hilda asked looking at the circle.

Everyone said, "Aye," in unison; each man beat his chest and the women made whistling noise.

"Soon we will take back our freedom to live as we were created and send the curse back where it belongs; we will fight for our lives even unto death if that's what it takes." The crowd got on their feet; chest beating followed and the gathering made a bigger noise as Hilda inspired and motivated them for battle. They screamed in agreement and stamped their feet in one accord in response to the call to battle.

"Go to your homes; prepare yourselves for battle, prepare to take back our freedom, and I will deliver her to you. There will be no more curse; together we will be victorious. Go now; get your cars ready; fill your tanks; and prepare for victory."

The women yelled even louder; their men were eager to fight, their noses were flared, the jaws tightened and their chests bloated with pride. Hilda kept quiet as the uproar increased; she liked what she heard; her body started to tingle with fire as the excitement of the battle ahead seduced her powers. Then, Hilda lifted her hands to quieten her subjects and the crowd immediately fell silent.

"We have no time to spare; as we speak they may already have found her and all this will be for nothing; our future depends on her; we cannot waste time; go now and get ready, and let us meet again at Amari's house." Then she pointed to five men randomly from the crowd.

"Amari, you will show these men where the coven you spoke of live; they will go with you now and stake out the place while the rest of the tribe prepares. Your family will get for you what you will need so that you can journey with us immediately. Your job is to tell us immediately when you see the coven move; if they have found her, we will know; when they all leave, we will not be far behind. Be careful; you must not be seen. Now get going; something tells me we don't have long." She said to Amari and the five men she chose. Then everyone bowed in obeisance and hurried away.

296

Chapter 41

Sebastian and Hanna Greene

Hanna planned to drag her mother and Sebastian into every clothing store possible, but before they started shopping, Sebastian suggested they sort out their living situation. So, the first port of call was at the estate agent's office. They gave the agent their brief list; they all added bits of what they wanted. Hanna asked for a traditional house with many rooms and no wooden beams; her mother wanted a large kitchen and a garden big enough to accommodate a greenhouse; Sebastian wanted a modern home, soaring ceilings, acres of land, and it had to be remote.

His other specification was that the house have stunning sea views and cliffs. The agent asked about their budget. Hanna looked at Sebastian and they laughed when they said, "There is no budget, and we will pay over and above the asking price if you can deliver our perfect house," Hanna said; she knew now what Sebastian was worth thanks to the documents he had sent her which named her as the sole heir to his fortune in case of his death. She smiled at Sebastian; the estate agent looked at the three as if they were time wasters.

"I don't mean to be rude, but you are not giving me any budget to work with. I sincerely think you have come to make a joke of my work, and I must tell you, I am not in the business of dealing with jesters. I run a . . ."

Before he could finish, Sebastian shook his head, "What is it about us that makes you think we are here to waste your time. We want a house; we've told you what we need; why do you have to be so difficult?" Sebastian said.

The man cut in "I am not being diff . . ."

"Shush," Hanna interjected, and said, "He's still talking; it's rude to interrupt; now let him finish and then you can decide if we are jesters or not."

Sebastian said, "As I was saying, this is not some fantasy. We know what we want and we can afford it. Now, we have stated our requirements. Unless you want us to take our business elsewhere, you will search high and low until you find for us the perfect house. One more thing; we don't have long to wait, so if you can't do it, we will look to others hungrier than you to serve us." Sebastian placed his card on the man's desk. The estate agent nodded and picked up the card. Sebastian raised his arm and Hanna coiled hers into his, as they reached the door, Sebastian turned his head toward the man and said. "You will do well to call us immediately when you find something of worth." Then they walked out of the office and into the street. Hanna laughed; she was delighted with her man.

"Has that happened to you before?" she asked.

Sebastian knew what she was referring to. "A few times and it gets tiring; they look at me and think I can't afford a room. There's only so much I can take.," Sebastian said."

Hanna joked, "Perhaps you need to start dressing the part."

"Hmm, why be so superficial and fancy? You are either what you are or not. I will not be dictated to by people's reaction to me," Sebastian stated.

"Do you think he will call," Hope asked Sebastian, and he shrugged his shoulders.

"I honestly don't know; I mean I know Hanna and I may look like we are teenagers but we had you; surely you are old enough to buy a house?" Sebastian joked. Hope laughed softly.

"Perhaps he can sense that I am not exactly loaded with money; someone that can afford the house we require would look . . . you know . . . better than I do," Hope said.

"Mum, you don't look bad at all; if he was thinking that, then he must have a screw loose in his head; let's just hope he calls. Okay, enough of that. Let's go shopping and Mum, I am giving you a whole new look. You are dressed like the year you birthed me; you have to move with the time's Mama, I'm going to change your whole wardrobe," Hanna said, moving from Sebastian to her mother.

"We shop for you first Mum; then me, and then I will start on you and get you looking your worth," she said pointing to Sebastian.

"Hey! What's wrong with the way I look?" Sebastian protested.

"Nothing, I just want to pick out something for you. you know add a woman's touch and all that," Hanna said Sebastian knew there was no changing her mind so he gave in.

"Okay, whatever you say, your highness," Sebastian said.

"I'm doing you a favour; people pay for a stylist, and you are getting my help for free," Hanna joked.

"Is that, right? Whatever you say, Mum," Sebastian replied. He had thought he wouldn't like being around Hanna and her mother while they shopped, but already he was loving it. It felt like they were normal; he had not thought about Hector or Mason, and it felt good to just be normal. Sebastian feared that they may not survive the fight, or worst Hanna may have to erase him from her life, but in this moment where they could enjoy life's simple pleasure, he wasn't going to let anything get in the way of that.

He stood by as Hanna piled clothes on his arms. Then, she and her mother went into the fitting room to try them on. She soon returned with more clothes. They took the clothes she chose to the till and paid, and then it was on to another store. Hanna bought more clothes for her mother and a few for herself.

When they arrived at the third store, she bought a few more things for herself and for Sebastian some shirts and fitted cardigans, ranging in colours from sky blue to olive with sage undertones. He had no choice; he had to take what he was given. He tried a few on at her behest, and both Hanna and her mum agreed he looked beautiful in them. They all changed into some of their newly bought attire; Hanna binned the dress she had on this morning; she was now wearing a mustard-coloured dress. Sebastian thought she looked stunning. He then found a white hat in the store and placed it on her head. They both admired her look in the mirror, and then she got herself sunglasses to complete the look. Hope looked on with joy as the two of them carried on like there was no one else in the universe. Hope felt like the third wheel, but she was glad to have a front row seat as she witnessed her daughter's happiness.

Sebastian went in search of a cab to take them back to Hector's house while Hanna and her mother went for a little bite of lunch. When he returned, they had finished their lunch and the three of them got in the cab and were on their way home, then Sebastian's phone rang; he picked up the call and listened for a while; then he said, "Thank you, we are on our way; we'll meet you there as soon as possible." Then he hung up. Hanna looked at him. Sebastian smiled and said, "I guess, he's taken us seriously."

"Who?" Hanna asked confused.

"The agent, the estate agent. He said he's found a house for us to view. I told him we would be on our way. Would you like to go to this house, or do you want to head home?"

"Sure, if Mum doesn't mind." Hanna looked at her mum,

"No, not at all. I will like to see what he found us," her mum said.

"Okay, driver, could you please take us to Torquay," Sebastian said.

The driver nodded and said, "It will cost a lot more."

"Yeah, don't worry. I'll make it up to you. Also, if you don't mind, you will wait for us and bring us back home. I promise you won't regret it," Sebastian said to the cab driver, who made a U-turn immediately.

"Well, that was fast. I guess he took us seriously after all," Hanna joked, referring to the agent.

"I guess so," Sebastian agreed.

They made the forty-minute drive to the house the agent wanted them to view. One look, from the outside, and Hanna fell in love. Sebastian couldn't enter as he didn't have permission, it wasn't his house and the agent couldn't authorize his entrance either. Hanna and her mom entered the house with the agent. Sebastian viewed the grounds; he hoped Hanna didn't like it because it didn't have enough land and it was not remote enough.

Every time he heard her say, "Wow I love it," he felt a stab in his chest; he didn't want to have to compromise on this one, but then as luck would have it, the kitchen wasn't big enough for Hope and they rejected it. Once they were outside, Sebastian pulled the agent to the side and emphasized the need for the house to be remote.

The women got back in the cab, while Sebastian thanked the agent for his help; once he was in the cab, they began the journey home. Hanna still gushed about the things she loved in the house, but Hope kept insisting the kitchen was too small. Sebastian was grateful he didn't have to put his two pence in and crush Hanna's excitement over the house, but he felt thankful to Hope for rejecting the house. He loved how excited Hanna was over life's simple pleasures, and he couldn't wait until the next day to do it all again. In his mind, he knew this was the calm before the storm, and he very much wanted to enjoy every bit of it.

Chapter 42

As soon as Sebastian, Hanna and her mother arrived home, Hector's cab pulled into the drive. Hanna was still outside, getting the rest of their purchases out of the truck, and Hope had run inside to use the loo; Sebastian had gone inside, with some shopping bags. Sebastian had paid the driver double what he requested. Hanna turned toward Hector who was at that moment paying his cab driver.

She waited for the cabs to leave before asking Hector, "What happened to your car? Didn't you take it?" Hector hadn't thought of what to say to her or anyone that asked about his car, so he decided to stick to a version of the truth. "I had to get rid of it; I had a feeling I was being followed; I couldn't be sure, so I abandoned it in a hotel's car park and exited the hotel through the back. I don't know; perhaps I was being paranoid, but it was better to be safe than sorry." Hector omitted the part where he met with Mason and bartered Sebastian's life for his freedom.

"Well, it's always better to be safe than sorry. That was the right call; we never know; anyway, we should be going back to the cottage soon. If anyone did follow you, they will find this place empty," Hanna said.

Hector nodded; he tried not to meet her eyes in case she suspected that he had been up to no good.

"So, I take it you had loads of fun; a shame I couldn't be there. I can tell you bought the whole store," he said, looking at the shopping bags littering the floor.

Hanna giggled. "I don't know how this happened. I only wanted one outfit, and then I found these lovely, beautiful dresses and I just couldn't resist," she said.

"I see you're wearing one already. You look . . . very beautiful. That colour suits you," Hector complimented. His eyes let her know how he felt as he looked at her. Hanna could tell that he wasn't just flattering her; she could tell by the way he looked at her that it was deeper than that. She smiled awkwardly; his eyes held hers and she broke her gaze. She reached for the rest of the shopping bags, but Hector reached for them also, and his hands touched hers as he took the bags from her.

"Let me. A lady shouldn't be burdened with lugging heavy loads," he said. Sebastian was on his way out to get the rest of the bags, but he observed the awkward situation between Hanna and Hector and walked back inside heading straight for the stairs.

Hanna smiled and said, "Thanks" allowing Hector to carry her bags. She walked inside the house. Hector followed her closely smiling as he thought about how his life would change soon when all that he planned fell into place. Hope met them in the front room, and Hanna locked arms with her mother and said, "We did some great lots of shopping, for mum too, loads of new things; she is sure not going to know what to do with all her new clothes, but I have to go to her room and remove all the old ones."

Hector asked, "Where do you want these?" referring to the shopping bags.

"Oh, those are Mum's; thanks, I will take it from here," Hanna said but Hector refused.

"No, allow me," he said, and he took the bags to the front of Hope's room. Hanna was still in the living room with her mother when Hector returned. Hanna quickly excused herself; she could tell that something wasn't right with Hector. She wasn't sure what it was; he was flirting with her and she didn't want Sebastian to witness that. They had had fun together today and the last thing she wanted to do was to be the one to destroy the rest of his day. He must not find her cosying up with the one person he hated as much as he detested Mason.

"I'm a little tired, I'm going to rest, Mum," she said and kissed her mother on the cheek; then she turned to Hector and said, "Thanks for the bags. I'll see you later."

Hector knew she was avoiding him because of Sebastian; he smiled, and thought to himself, *His days are numbered and she will soon be all mine.* Hector excused himself from Hope and made his way to his room. For someone who nearly died today, he needed the rest too and thanked his stars that Mason had not had him killed. He hoped that Mason would already be headed to the cottage in Wales as planned. Hector wondered how he would keep Hanna away when the fight started. He had not been able to get the drugs he wanted; he needed a plan B. He tried to think; but his body needed to rest; he had not slept well since their arrival at Devon due to making plans to get rid of Sebastian. Now staying awake was not an option as he found his body shutting down for a well-deserved rest.

As Hanna returned to her room to join Sebastian, she just wanted to nap; she wondered why Sebastian didn't return downstairs for the rest of the bags. As soon as he entered, Sebastian got up from the bed and told her that he needed to go and hunt. Hanna lay on the bed and looked at him as he spoke. She nodded at the things he said; her eyes were tired; she heard the words, *hunt* and *feed*. Sebastian noticed her eyes closing and he lovingly kissed her on the temple and left her to rest.

It was dark when he returned three hours later; as he approached the house, he saw Hector leaving. He wondered where the snake was headed now. Sebastian scoffed and reminded himself he couldn't worry about Hector's plans; he already knew Hector couldn't be trusted. When Hector finally played his hand, then he would finally prove to Hanna once and for all, that she was foolish to trust him.

Hanna was still sleeping when he entered their room; Sebastian decided to shower and wash away the smell of blood and woods. When he came out of the shower, he heard clattering downstairs in the kitchen. He wondered what Hope was up to now, and he hoped she had already prepared dinner for herself and Hanna when he went hunting earlier. Sebastian dressed and was heading downstairs when a familiar scent hit his nostrils. Immediately, he knew they had been found; as he was about to turn back to get Hanna, he heard Thomas say, "I wouldn't do that if I were you." Thomas had his hand around Hope's neck.

"Thomas," Sebastian said.

Thomas said sarcastically, "Yes, imagine this. I would never have put it together, you and Hector living under the same roof; that is a wonder in itself." Sebastian wondered if Hanna was awake now and if she could hear what was going on.

"What do you want Thomas?" Sebastian asked; he hoped to distract Thomas so he could find a way to save Hanna's mother; the last thing he wanted was for Hanna to lose another parent.

"Well, now that you ask, I want you and I want your little friend. Remember, you and I had a deal, and you disappeared before I could make good on mine; now, a deal is a deal; you said if I helped you, you would help make me a day walker," Thomas said.

"Well you didn't help me," Sebastian said. "You left me there for weeks so that deal whatever it was it's off. Thomas, you were a friend once, and although sometimes we butted heads, I respected you. Whatever this is, it's between you and me; she has nothing to do with it, let her go and we can settle this amongst ourselves." Sebastian did not want Hope to become a casualty of war.

"You get me wrong Sebastian. I mean the little woman no harm but if you promise to listen to what I came to tell you, then there will be peace here today and no one has to die, not even her," Thomas said. Sebastian was quiet; he wondered what Thomas had to say that didn't have to do with Mason.

"Okay, let her go and I will listen, but not here; wait for me by the river," Sebastian said.

Thomas laughed softly. "You mistake my proposal for stupidity. I will let her go, but you will come with me and take her place; that way no one gets hurts. Hurry up, I don't have all night," Thomas said, tightening his grip on Hope.

"Okay, easy now. Do not hurt her. I am coming," Sebastian assured, moving slowly until he got in front of Thomas. Thomas placed his free hands around Sebastian's neck and then he released his hold on Hope.

"Now, you and I need to have a little chat," he said as he took Sebastian, and before Hope could blink, they had vanished from view. Hope was in shock, but at the same time she worried for Sebastian; she didn't know if she should go and wake Hanna and get her involved or if Sebastian could take care of himself. She knew that if anything happened to him and she didn't do anything she may never again be able to look her daughter in the eye.

***

"Okay, now you have me; what do want? Are you taking me to him to show your loyalty?" Sebastian asked Thomas.

Thomas released his hold on Sebastian.

"If I were taking you to Mason," Thomas said, "We wouldn't be here. Look, what I'm about to do could backfire on me, but I have struggled with this decision for a while. I can't forgive Mason for what he did to Margret, and I want him dead. You and I made a deal when we were imprisoned together. I couldn't come true on it then because Mason had someone on my tail. There was no way I could get you out of there. One of us or the two of us would have died. However, here we are, and I am here to make good on that deal."

Sebastian, wondered if he could believe anything that came out of Thomas's mouth.

"Thomas, I want to believe you, but, you could be setting me up. Why should I trust you?" Sebastian questioned.

"Trust that we have the same goal. You knew what Margret meant to me. Your girl, if someone laid hands on her, would you be able to forgive? If I were on Mason's side, we wouldn't be having this conversation. Listen, I am on your side if you want, but for now I have to pretend to stay with Mason. It's not going to be an easy battle; every vampire on planet earth has arrived to join forces with Mason. They all want his promise of the sun. You have a serious battle on your hand son," Thomas said.

Sebastian looked to the ground; he already knew that Mason would have quite an army at his disposal, but what Thomas just described made him afraid.

"If I say *yes*, how is this going to work? What can you do for me?" Sebastian asked.

"Tell me that we have a deal and I will give you something in return," Thomas said.

Sebastian clicked his tongue as he wondered what use Thomas could be in all of this.

"I don't know Thomas, I can only say *yes* if what you have to trade is good enough," Sebastian countered.

"Trust me; you are going to want to hear this," Thomas said.

"Okay go on then, tell me. I can only decide after I hear what you have to say," Sebastian said.

Thomas scoffed, but he knew he had no choice; it was either this or continuing as Mason's lackey. "Well, you got me. Listen good," Thomas said. "I don't know what you have going with Hector; you and I know you hate him; whatever situation you have with him will backfire on you if you don't act quickly. I saw him today and he gave you up to Mason." Thomas watched Sebastian's reactions.

"What! Did you say you saw Hector today?" Sebastian asked shaking his head in disgust and anger. "I always knew that rat couldn't be trusted," he muttered to himself.

"Tell me everything Thomas; don't leave anything out," Sebastian said with a clenched jaw.

Thomas smiled and said, "I knew there was more to this; he contacted an old ally; his name is Pablo. Pablo had already sworn loyalty to Mason and he's one of Mason's lackies now. Anyway, they were meant to meet later today. Pablo called us immediately, however; before then, someone already mentioned that Hector was seen in your house in Grosmont, so now he became a person of interest. Although at the time, we couldn't connect the two of you as allies, we all know how much you detest each other. But Mason didn't want any stone left unturned, so we came to Pablo for answers. Hector showed up early and we surprised him. I'm not really sure why he came to see Pablo, but the short story is that he gave you up for his freedom and he told Mason where to find the body of his wife, too. We figured for him to know the things he said, you must have given him that information. Mason wanted to be sure it wasn't a trap."

"So, you followed him?" Sebastian asked.

"Yes, at Mason's behest. He asked that I follow the rat. He tried to keep his tracks clean, but I am too old and clever to be outsmarted by him. However, what shocked me most was seeing him walk the sun," Thomas revealed and watched Sebastian's reaction.

"Why are you shocked? I told you then that if you side with me, I would help you become a day walker," Sebastian stated.

Thomas advised: "Yes, you said, but hearing a thing and seeing it with one's eyes are two different things. Now that I am sure, I understand better, and if you agree to keep that deal, I will help you however much I can on the inside. I don't know how powerful that girl of yours is, but you are going to be facing a legion of vampires all wanting a piece of her. Joining your camp is risky business. I may not survive it, but I will take that risk if it means Mason's destruction. So, if we are going to do this and live, we have to really pull something big or run now."

Sebastian was quiet as he contemplated Thomas's advice. As sensible as it sounded for them to run, he knew that would be the wrong decision. His mind went to Hector again, and he wondered if Hanna would admit her wrong when he broke it to her that Hector was the scum he had always suspected him to be. When Sebastian didn't speak, Thomas pressed him for answers.

"Listen, if you give me your word now, I will help you if you decide to fight. It won't be easy because Mason always keeps me on the side, but when it comes to it, I will help and if we live, and Mason dies, I will come to collect what you owe me," Thomas said.

Sebastian, regarded him for a second. "And what about Henry, and Nicholas? The others may be easy for you, but would you kill those two if it comes to it?" Sebastian asked to test Thomas.

Thomas was quiet for a moment, he looked down then up at Sebastian, "If it came to it, I will do what I need to do. I know if I don't kill Henry, he will end me; he's too loyal to Mason. As for that shell Nicholas, I will gladly put him out of his misery," Thomas assured Sebastian.

Sebastian sighed and said "I know that was hard for you. But if we are to survive, you must take out Henry, Nicholas, and any other vampire old enough to be a hindrance. With them out of the way, Mason will be reachable for Hanna to kill, and you and I can deal with the rest. Do we have a deal?"

Thomas smiled. "We do indeed, boy; we have a deal," Thomas said. "Once upon a time, I never thought you were made for this world of ours, but hearing you talk now and seeing how far you've come, I admit I got you wrong; you are one of a kind; never forget it." Thomas patted Sebastian's shoulder, "Now I am going to go meet Mason at your cottage in Wales and tell him I didn't find Hector; what you do with Hector is up to you, but see that he doesn't become a problem," Thomas warned. He took another look at Sebastian and then said, "See you on the battlefield."

The wind caused by Thomas's departure hit Sebastian's face. With Thomas gone, Sebastian turned his gaze to the house. It was time Hector faced judgment for his treachery; if he had to fight Hanna to kill him, then so be it. Sebastian knew there was no way Hanna could talk him out of killing Hector this time.

Chapter 43

Sebastian returned to the house to meet a worried Hanna and Hope as they stood by the entrance to the house. Hanna was being held by her mother as she tried to go look for Sebastian. When she saw him returning, she let out air in relief; removing herself from her mother, she ran straight into his arms.

"What happened S? Tell me; Mum came and woke me up; she said someone was here, and he took you with him," Hanna asked, checking him over. "What happened? Who was it? Tell me S. I was so worried. Why didn't you wake me?" She questioned.

"I am okay; don't worry," he said, and then he looked at her and placed a finger to his mouth to quiet her.

"What is it? Is something wrong? Tell me S, is there trouble?" Hanna asked nervously; she wanted answers immediately. Sebastian shook his head.

"No, have you seen Hector? Has he come back yet?" he asked, looking from Hanna to Hope; they both shook their heads.

"No, I haven't seen him since we came back," Hope said. What is it? Did something happen to him?"

"No, and that is the problem," Sebastian said as he turned to Hanna who looked alarmed.

"I want to tell you both something, but not here; let's get inside," he said.

"What is it S? What happened? Tell me now?" Hanna pushed. Sebastian put his arms round her as he led her inside.

"I will, in a moment; just come with me," he said, and then he led them to the kitchen. Once they were all in the kitchen, he excused himself and went to check around the house to ensure Hector was not hiding somewhere eavesdropping.

By the time, he returned to the kitchen, he looked at both Hanna and Hope and gestured to the kettle.

"You might want to make yourselves something," he said to Hope.

"No, we're fine. Speak already," Hanna pressed.

"Hanna, please sit," Sebastian said. Hope put the kettle on, and then she turned to hear what Sebastian had to say that was so important. Hanna sat down reluctantly thinking it was better if she sat down for whatever news Sebastian had to reveal.

"Okay, the vampire that came here today was Thomas," Sebastian said looking at Hanna and hoping she remembered him mentioning him to her before.

"Before you saved me from that dungeon, he and I had a deal. I offered the deal to him at first; I told him that if he helped me escape I would ask you to make him a day walker," Sebastian said. Hanna shook her head disapprovingly.

"Wait let him finish," Hope said to Hanna to calm her down.

"Anyway, after Mason released him, I didn't see or hear from him, so I thought that he had abandoned me. Anyway, he said it was impossible to reach me, and I kind of believe him. Now that isn't what I really want to tell you both. He just informed me that he saw Hector today." Sebastian waited for the meaning of what he just said to sink in but they both looked at each other as if they didn't understand what he was getting at.

Sebastian said, "Thomas said that Hector made a deal with Mason, he gave up our location and where I dumped that witch's body for his own freedom. Don't you see, he has been playing us

312

all along. I said he couldn't be trusted and now here is the proof." Sebastian watched Hanna carefully as she got up from where she sat. She looked at him, shook her head in disbelief, and argued Hector's innocence.

"That . . . that . . . can't be true, he won't do that . . . why would he do that? Are you saying they know where we are now? Why would Hector do that? What does he have to gain, when he lives here, too? Have you considered that perhaps this Thomas has lied to you? Think about it; if they come between us and Hector, then they weaken our force," Hanna said defensively. It annoyed Sebastian that the first thing she chose to do was defend that snake.

"I can assure you, Thomas is not the liar in this situation," Sebastian responded disappointedly. Hanna knew she should believe her man, but believing that would mean that she had single handedly put his life at risk when she believed Hector to be a friend.

"I don't know what to believe, I mean, is that why he has disappeared? Did Thomas say they are coming here now?" Hanna asked confused, by the news of Hector's betrayal.

"No not here; he gave them the address of the cottage in Wales, and they have all gone there now; if Thomas had not followed Hector, we wouldn't have known and we would have been walking into a trap," Sebastian explained making sure Hanna understood what could have happened.

"He wants me dead and he wanted Mason to do his dirty work, so you won't have to look at him differently. Now, listen Hanna, you know you mean the world to me, but this bond you have with him, it ends now because I will kill him with my bare hands the moment he comes back into this house, and I will enjoy doing it." Sebastian watched Hanna's eyes cloud over with tears. She couldn't blame Sebastian and there was nothing more she could do for

Hector, but she wanted to be sure that Thomas was telling the truth.

"How sure are you that what Thomas said is true? Is there any chance, he is lying? Please, just let's make sure; that's all I ask. Please." Hanna pled.

"I am sure Hector has betrayed us, and I am not going to wait until he hands me over to satisfy your conscience," he said irritated. He couldn't allow her to win, not this time. Anger built up inside him, as he saw tears spilling down Hanna's face for Hector.

"Look, Hanna, I know a part of you feels something for Hector; you won't admit it and it pains me to say it. I don't want to be that guy that tells you to choose, but you must choose now, Love. You must know this day was coming. It's either him or me; you can't have us both. I know what Thomas said is true; how else would you explain how they know about the cottage in Wales and where I dumped Annemarie's body? I warned you not to trust him, but, you always had to get your way. How much proof do you need before you realize that Hector is no good? I will fight and kill him tonight, and you won't get involved."

Hanna had never seen Sebastian this angry; she had hurt him and she was sorry, but she couldn't help how sad she felt about Sebastian's decision to kill Hector. Sebastian made to leave, not able to watch her cry for his enemy any longer.

"Wait S, wait I'm sorry. I'm not against you doing what you have to do. I just want us to confront him, and hear what he has to say—that's all. I can't help thinking there must be an explanation, a misunderstanding. And if it's true, I will really love the opportunity to look him in the eye and find out why he chose to betray my trust, please Love, for me," Hanna pleaded. Sebastian stopped to look at her; he wished for once, she just allowed him do things his way, but if she wanted closure before he killed Hector, then he would give her that.

"If that will help you, you shall have that time with him, but after you have confirmed for yourself what a low-down dirty rat he is, I will send him to hell to meet his brothers," Sebastian said and then he walked away; he went upstairs to pack his things; there was no way he would remain in this house after he had killed its owner. He had always felt uncomfortable living under the same roof as Hector, and now that the truth was out there, he couldn't wait to be away from the house. Then he heard voices downstairs; he could make out Hanna's voice; he left what he was doing immediately to go see what was happening.

"Is it true Hector?" Hanna yelled at him as he entered the house.

"Is what true? What are you talking about?" Hector asked.

"Tell me what you did?" Hanna said and pushed his chest.

"What is this? What is wrong with your daughter Hope Lane? What is she accusing me of?" Hector said, turning to Hope for an explanation, but Hope said nothing; she shook her head as she watched Hanna push at him. There was nothing Hope could do to stop what was going to soon explode into a violent scene before her, and she knew that if what Sebastian said was true, then Hector deserved whatever he got for putting her daughter in harm's way.

"Calm down Hanna, please, and talk to me in a reasonable way. What's gotten into you? What am I missing here? What am I meant to have done?" Hector lamented; he was sure there was no way they could have known about his meeting with Mason earlier. So, whatever had her reeling was something else he didn't know about.

"I trusted you with my life, Hector; why did you throw that trust away?" Hanna yelled again. Hector furrowed his brow, still sure she couldn't be talking about his plans with Mason.

"Hanna, please stop yelling and tell me what I am meant to have done to get you this bothered?" He held her hands to stop her from hitting his chest.

"You sold us out; is it true? Did you sell us out? Did you tell Mason where the house in Wales is? Did you tell him where to find the body of his wife?" Hanna fired questions at him. Hector was in shock; his mouth dropped open as he tried to think of something to say to lie his way out of the mess he had created. Hanna could tell by the look on his face he was thinking, but she wanted to be sure that whatever came out of his mouth was the truth; She decided it was the time she broke that rule about not listening to his thoughts. She closed her eyes and penetrated his mind; she could hear him debating what to say to cover the truth.

"You are debating what to say to me?" Hanna said out loud. Hector opened his mouth to say something, but Hanna shushed him, "It's true then, isn't it? You sold us out. You are a turncoat. Sebastian was right all along but I foolishly chose to trust you," she said as the tears freely flowed down her cheeks. "You break my heart Hector. I thought we were friends. I thought you cared about me; why Hector? Why? You could have had anything you wanted. I even made you a day walker. Why did you do it?" Hanna pushed harder at his chest as she demanded answers.

He could see he had hurt her; this wasn't what he wanted to do. Whom was he kidding; he always knew that having Sebastian killed would hurt her, but he didn't want to destroy the trust she had in him. He couldn't even bring himself to look her in the eye, but he was not sorry he tried to take Sebastian out; he was only sorry that by so doing he brought her pain. "I didn't want to lose your trust, but I had to do what I had to do. That's just the way it is; nothing you could have done or said would have changed the inevitable or affected how I felt," Hector said; he knew after this, Hanna would choose her boyfriend over him, so he wanted all his cards on the table.

"I don't understand; why do it? What would this achieve?" Hanna asked.

"Isn't it obvious?" Hector replied; he looked remorseful.

"What? What am I missing?" Hanna asked. Hector smiled sadly.

"I did it for you," he said. She looked at him as if he had gone mad.

"Are you out of your mind? How is exposing us logical to you? How is that for me?" Hanna questioned.

"No Hanna, you still don't get it. I did what I had to do because . . . because I love you. I am in love with you, and I wish I weren't, but I can't help the way I feel. I am in too deep, and I know you don't feel the same way about me now, but that is only because you have him in your life. He took you away from me; your mother came to me for help, not him. It should have been me in your life; it should have been me you love the way you love him. I hate him, and I know you want us to get along, but I can't. I detest him; he gets to kill my brothers and live, and he still gets to have you. You are the love of my life. I want you to know that. So, I did what I had to do to get him out of the way. I'm in love with you, and I am not ashamed to say it out loud. The only way we can be together is if he dies. I knew if I killed him myself, you would never want anything to do with me; hell, you might even kill me yourself, but if Mason killed him then, I thought that maybe I would finally get a chance at happiness and we could end up together. I don't know what happened to me, but I couldn't rest until I had put my plans into motion. Like I said, I did it for you; I did it for us. Do you understand that?" Hector asked, knowing Sebastian could hear him declare his love for his woman. Hector knew now that all bets were off.

He could tell by the anger in Sebastian's eyes as he stood on the stairs that tonight they would fight to the death for Hanna's love, and he was determined to win. Hanna looked at Hector in shock; she knew this was all her fault; being friendly with him had made him hopeful; she turned to see Sebastian's hurt-filled face. "I'm sorry," she mouthed. Then she turned to face Hector; she knew whatever she said now, she had to convince Sebastian that she didn't encourage his behaviour.

"But you knew I don't feel the same way as you do, Hector; how did you suppose this would end? You were just a friend. If you had succeeded, you would have rid me of the love of my life and you would never have gained my love, not in this life or any other," Hanna said.

Hector was embarrassed. He smiled and said, "You only say that now for his benefit; when you kissed me that day, I could feel how much you wanted me. I'm not a deluded fool; I see how you look at me when no one is around, but I can tell that deep down you feel something for me too, maybe not as much as you claim to love him. But it is not a rarity to love two people at the same time. I just don't want to share you with him. I need you for myself. It kills me inside each time I watch you two parade your love before me. So yes, I plotted to get rid of him, but not to harm you. Never to harm you, and don't look at me like I'm some evil person; that is what loving you did to me. So, if you are sure you don't love me, if you are so sure you don't feel anything for me, take my life now; it's useless without you in it anyway. You have all the power; kill me now and let's be done with it; you will only be doing me a favour." Hector stretched his arms wide in surrender, and Hanna looked from him to her mother and then to Sebastian, and it seemed everyone was waiting for her to do something.

Sebastian couldn't take it anymore; he knew Hanna wouldn't do what Hector asked, and he wasn't sure why, but he didn't want her to take the joy of killing the rat from him.

"That won't be necessary; it is me you wanted dead after all; you want to die; I will be the one doing the killing, and I will enjoy doing it," Sebastian said stepping forward; he didn't look at Hanna. He just wanted the business with Hector over.

"You want him to do it for you, Hanna; look at me; kill me now and I will know I meant nothing to you," Hector urged.

"No," Sebastian said, "You won't leave this world so easily thinking you died for love. You will fight me, and I will kill you, and that will be the end of the matter and no one will remember you or talk about you; you will be like the grass of the field that once was here and now it's gone."

Hope pulled Hanna to her and told her to leave them to settle it amongst themselves. Hector noticed Hanna's closed eyes; Sebastian hoped she wasn't already grieving the loss of Hector; that would mean that Hector was right about her feeling something for him.

"I will fight you, if that is what you want Sebastian. I'm not afraid of you. I will fight you for her and for my brothers and, like you, I will enjoy every moment," Hector said

Sebastian scoffed. "I would like to see you try. Step outside; we won't do this in front of the ladies," Sebastian said.

Hector, stole one last look at Hanna knowing it might be the last time he saw her. She looked like she was in shock. He heaved a sigh and then said, "Fine by me. Prepare to die. You might want to say your good-byes now."

"Don't worry Hector, I'm sure, I'll be back."

They both stepped out of the house. Sebastian rolled up his sleeves, clenched his jaw and focused his eyes on his opponent.

Hector smiled sardonically. "I have been secretly waiting for this day, and I am glad to be the one to send your damned soul to hell," Hector said through gritted teeth.

Sebastian tilted his head to the side; he was ready; he knew what Hector was doing, and he wasn't going to be distracted by fear. If he could kill Zacchary when everyone thought he couldn't, he was definitely looking forward to destroying Hector once and for all. There were no words necessary to convey the hatred between the two of them. They leaped at each other and met mid-air. Tumbling back to earth, each fought to gain the advantage; deadly punches and lethal kicks were thrown from all angles as they wrestled to the death.

Chapter 44

Sebastian stood over Hector's dead body; he had not enjoyed killing Hector as he had thought that he would. A small part of him felt remorseful because he had taken him away from Hanna. He wasn't jubilant, and he didn't want to return to the house to face her disappointment. It killed him to know the woman he loved had also loved another. The fact that she hadn't killed Hector when he requested it told him all that he needed to know. It wasn't an easy fight; Hector could have easily been the one standing over his body, but there was no way he could let that worm win. At the end, just before he killed Hector, Sebastian thought about showing mercy, but that squirm had to say the words that ensured his death.

"You know it; she loves me, and when I kill you, it will be me making love to her," Hector said as he laughed hysterically; his laughter brought out a blind rage in Sebastian that powered him to rip his head off and finally finish what he had started. The strength Hanna put in Sebastian gave him the upper hand, but he would like to think that with or without that, he would have killed Hector anyway.

Hope came to meet Sebastian where he stood, as he stared into space, with Hector's dead body under his foot.

"Sebastian, come inside now; you have stood there long enough. You didn't have a choice; if you didn't kill him, he would have killed you and from where I'm standing the better chap won. Come on in now, don't worry about it," Hope said as she gazed at Hector's lifeless body. "I will see that he gets the burial he deserves," she said as she pulled Sebastian toward the house. Sebastian had hoped that Hanna would come instead of her mother; not seeing Hanna confirmed his worse fears. He nodded at Hope and followed her inside. Hanna wasn't in the room when he entered; his heart sank; he sat on the bed; nothing made sense to him anymore, and he started to doubt for once that she was worthy of his love. Every fibre in his body wanted to get away; love was meant to bring joy, not pain, not betrayals and disappointments. He wondered if she would have preferred it to be him lying in Hector's place. Perhaps she didn't know how much she felt for Hector until she was faced with what happened today. Not seeing her made him think that she hated him for taking Hector's life. He lay on the bed as he thought of what to do next. If there was any truth in his thinking that she loved Hector too, then he didn't want to be around her. Then he sensed her presence, the door opened and she entered; he didn't lift his head to look at her.

"You are here," she said as she came into the room.

Sebastian didn't know whether to scoff or laugh. *What did she mean by that?* he thought.

"S, I'm sorry," she voiced; he wanted to know exactly what she was sorry for; although he didn't want to look at her, he had to force himself to sit up; he raised his head and her beautiful face filled his vision.

For a moment, he was quiet as he gathered his thoughts.

"What are you sorry for Hanna Greene?" he asked, and she looked away. "Are you sorry that you can now admit to yourself that you had always loved him and that because of this love, you didn't care how it made me feel when you sided with him at every turn. Are you sorry that your blind trust could have had me killed? Tell me? What are you sorry for? I hate to be the one to say I told you so, but in this case, I beg to differ. I told you from day one he couldn't be trusted, but you never listened. You always looked for reasons to justify wanting him around. I don't blame you; love makes us all do stupid things. I had always worried that I didn't deserve your love, but I just realized today that I was wrong. Tell me this. If I had not stepped forward, would you have killed him? Would you have ended his life when he said, 'If you don't love me, kill me?' You couldn't do it, and I had to save you from making that decision. The funny thing is, now that he is gone, a part of me wishes I had not killed him because now I know how you truly feel about him. For that I am sorry. I am sorry I lived and he died. Perhaps Hector was right; if he had met you first, it might have been him you love like you say you love me," Sebastian scoffed. Then he continued. "I don't understand it; I may never understand you, but I understand this: I deserve better than you and I may never love again like I love you, but at least I know if I ever do, it will be someone that loves me and only me. Call me selfish, but I have only loved you; I have only kissed you and I never think of anyone else or put anyone else before you." Sebastian could tell she was heartbroken, but so was he; he was tired of putting his feelings last. Hanna wanted to say something, but he stopped her; he got up from the bed to put more distance between them. He went and stood by the window. "So," he said, "This is what we are going to do; together we will fight Mason, and I will do my best to ensure your safety; if you can, then you must do all that is within your ability to kill him while I do my best to keep the others away, and should you require . . . what we spoke about . . . then you must do what must be done to gain victory. After that you will be free to live your life away from me. Like you said, it would be as if we had never been. Now, whatever you are thinking of saying, I beg you not to say it; it does not matter at this point. Not anymore; respect my decision. That is all." Sebastian turned his back to her.

He could feel her pain but whatever she was feeling he felt it triple fold.

"I know you are annoyed . . ." Hanna began to say.

"Hanna please, just go," Sebastian interjected. She swallowed hard as she tried to control her emotions. She had never seen him so infuriated, and she knew that he meant every word he just said.

"I will give you space if that is what you want, but you don't get to end this. You don't get to say what's on your mind and leave me hanging. I need to say my piece. S . . ." Hanna began to say.

"Please, don't call me that," he said.

Hanna's heart sank even more; she could tell he was beyond hurt, and she wished she could have listened when he warned her about Hector. Hanna swallowed hard as she tried to control her emotions so she could get her words out. "I know I hurt you, but I never did it deliberately. If it helps, I never loved Hector, not like you think. Just because I couldn't bring myself to kill someone I considered a friend does not mean I wanted him over you. You are being stupid throwing what we have away; can't you see this is what Hector would have wanted, the two of us fighting over him. I know all of this is my fault, and I should have listened to you. I am so sorry I am constantly causing you pain. I am sorry for many things. I am sorry I kissed him; you know it meant nothing to me, despite what Hector said. I am sorry you feel I chose him over you, but in my heart, you always came first. I never intended any of this; you must believe me. You, you are the reason my heart beats, and you will be the reason it stops beating. You may not want or need me anymore, but I will always need you. I will always love you, and I may not say it always, but I am glad for each day I get to spend with you. Please think again. I know you love me; you don't want us to end, but I will go away if you insist that is what you want or need from me now. Tell me, is that what you want? Please, turn around and tell me again."

Sebastian turned toward her; he wanted to tell her he didn't mean it, but he wasn't sure he believed her claim that she never loved Hector.

"Honestly, right now, I don't know what I want Hanna." He could see the disappointment on her face, but he couldn't lie to her.

She ran out of the room; he considered going after her, but then he knew he needed some space to sort out his own head before he could face her again.

Chapter 45

Sebastian heard Hanna sobbing; it took all his strength not to go find her and comfort her. It had been three hours since they had the talk; there had not been much sleeping, and he felt drained and tired of everything. This was not how he had thought everything would be; he wished he could be okay with knowing that she loved Hector even though she said she doesn't. In his head, he had concluded that she did, and feeling like he only had a part of her love didn't seem fair when he had given all of himself to her.

Then again, he wondered if he had misjudged her; he wondered if it was his hatred for Hector that made him so paranoid about her. But then, his mind would bring to focus all the times she sided with Hector over him and how she had been unable to kill Hector even after he confessed to plotting his death, and he was convinced all over again that he had done the right thing. Sebastian heard Hope, trying to comfort Hanna, and he didn't know what to do. He had promised her that he would never hurt her again, and he had broken that promise, and he didn't know how to fix it or if he wanted to fix it.

How could he be so in love with her and not want to be with her? How was that even possible? Perhaps love wasn't enough; he wanted more from her or perhaps he was using this situation to help himself later when all hell would break loose and she had to do what she must to survive. He couldn't decide the real reason he wanted it all over. However, he knew he could no longer take hearing her weep; with each tear, she stabbed at his heart repeatedly. He got up and walked outside the house; he wished there was somewhere he could go; if they didn't have the fight with Mason, Sebastian was sure he would have left. As he walked outside the house, he felt like he had left his heart inside; he knew why. Sebastian hit himself repeatedly in the head and muttered to himself, "What am I doing, common think." He turned toward the house unmoving, undecided about what his next move should be. Some fresh air would do him good, he concluded, and it would make him think more clearly. As he turned around to leave, he heard a creak by the front door; he hoped it was not Hanna; he was not ready to face her yet because he still didn't know what to do. He spun around and, to his relief, it was Hope. She didn't look happy; Sebastian promised Hope that he wouldn't hurt her daughter, and he was doing the thing he promised not to do.

Hope had a cigarette in her hand; she looked at him and said, "I didn't know you were still around." Sebastian knew what she meant by that; anyone with ears could hear Hanna crying her eyes out.

"Yes, um . . . I'm sorry. I need air," he said, avoiding her eyes; she was doing her best not to accuse him of hurting her daughter.

"Can I come with you?" She asked. Before he could say anything, she closed the gap between them and locked her arm in his. Sebastian had never felt so awkward around Hope. They walked quietly until they got to the bank of the river on Hector's land. Then she stopped and looked at him, forcing him to halt. He knew she would have questions about what happened, and he was ready to be reprimanded for his part in all of it. "I remember, when I met Hanna's father," Hope said out of the blue. Sebastian turned his head towards her wondered where this was going. "You know most people don't believe in love at first sight. I am not talking about the type seen around today when people confuse lust for love. I am talking about the real thing in its purest form; it only takes one look, and you will know it. That was how I felt when I saw Hanna's father. He didn't speak; he didn't have to; he was so beautiful," she said looking away from him. "My heart stopped, and I wished in that moment that he was mine; I wanted him to love me, to be mine forever. Well, that didn't happen, but as fate would have it, he kept coming back to my shop. At first, I thought there was something wrong with him; surely, he must have heard of my reputation with men; they run for the hills. But here he was, day after day. I was in love and he didn't even know it; for a while, I kept it together. But the way he looked at me, the way his face would light up when he saw me, it made me melt inside. He was gentle when he spoke, very polite and when he left, it was the saddest moment in my day. I constantly daydreamed about him. I used to imagine us together, married with children. He made me so happy and so sad at the same time, and I didn't think he even knew it." Hope laughed softly. Sebastian chuckled as he observed her happy face as she recalled her life with the man she loved. He knew the feeling she was describing very well.

Hope puffed at her cigarette and then continued. "Then one day, I told myself, I owed it to myself to tell him how I felt; he was practically at my store every day. I had nothing to lose and everything to gain. I thought, he must like me too or why would he want to be around so much? So, I plucked up a bit of courage after downing a few shots of whiskey. As I walked up to him, my heart was pounding and my feet nearly gave way, but I kept moving toward this beauty of a man. It was now or never, I told myself. I was love sick; he had to know. I couldn't keep it in for another second. I stood in front of him and poured out my heart; he stared at me as I poured out my feelings to him, as though he never thought I would say such a thing to him. Then he opened his mouth to say something, only nothing came out, but I could see it in his eyes, his love for me beneath the surface. I just needed him to tell me that I wasn't alone in this. I tried to touch him and he recoiled; then he got up and ran out like I was some plague or something. I didn't understand it; after that day, I didn't see him for a week, and I cried myself to sleep every night. I wanted to die. I loved him, but it seemed I made a fool of myself, but that didn't matter; it was the feeling that he had rejected my love that was killing me. Another week passed and he was still a no show, and when I had accepted that I wouldn't see him again, he walked through my door. I was in shock. My heart stopped as soon as I saw him. He apologized for leaving like he did. I felt sure he had only come back to let me know he didn't feel the same way. Then he said we could only be friends; he said he liked me but that I shouldn't ask him for more. I said, 'Okay, I will try.' My days were better with him around. We continued as we were, but who was I kidding? Being his friend could not work; my feelings intensified; I was constantly pulled to him; it was torture. He would leave and I would sit where he had sat and breathe in his scent. He was careful not to touch me, but I wanted more; just to feel his touch; sometimes, I would intentionally graze his hands when I poured him a drink. He never liked it when I did that, and he found a way to gently tell me not to do that. I would agree, but then this feeling would take over and I would do it again. Then, he left again, and this time, I didn't see him for a month. Perhaps it was for the best, but how could it be when my heart yearned for his daily? To cut the story short, one day I was closing up; he was the last person I expected to see. I had not been myself for a while, as you can imagine not being with him made me exceptionally empty. My back was turned when he entered my shop. At his sight, my mouth ran dry. I was over the moon; my heart leaped for joy. But he had this look about him. I could tell he was struggling. I didn't know why he looked like he was debating within himself; he also didn't look like his proper self, you know. Still, I couldn't control the joy within me; I ran into his arms like I had not seen him in years, and for the first time, he held me." Hope paused to take in that moment as the memory flooded back. Sebastian didn't say a word; he listened quietly.

"I literally broke down in tears. I had longed to be touched and held by him and then to my surprise, he kissed me." Hope laughed happily. Sebastian couldn't help but chuckle too as he shared in her joy.

"I was on cloud nine; nothing made me happier than that moment. He was mine at last. He told me what I had always wanted to hear. He said he loved me deeply and that he couldn't run from it anymore. One thing led to another, as it goes; they were all beautiful and happy things and we made Astraia. I mean Hanna as you like to call her, my gorgeous daughter. However, sadly for me, after that night, I never saw him again. I only have her to remind me that I hadn't dreamed it all. But you know what? Even if it was only for one night, that night, he was mine, and I was his, and he made sure that I felt every ounce of his love. It felt incredible to be loved the way he loved me." Hope paused, puffed at her cigarette one more time before saying, "That kind of love doesn't come around very often Sebastian; some people will never feel that way about anyone. Don't throw it all away; somehow Astaria's father and I couldn't manage it, but if you walk away, then you threw it all away for nothing. Hector is gone, and I know she never loved him. I am her mother. I would know. She only has eyes for you; each night when we stayed up, she told me how madly in love she is with you, only you; her heart belongs to you, Sebastian and Hector never shared in that love. Her only crime is that she trusted the wrong person, and I know you feel bruised, but it's not enough to throw away a love so beautiful. Don't be a fool; think hard, and then do what is right," Hope said; she threw down her cigarette stub and squashed it to the ground with her foot.

"Bad habit," she said. "I only do this on exceptional occasions. I'd better go back and check on her," she added and patted Sebastian on the back before leaving him alone with his thoughts.

***

Standing there by himself, after hearing what Hope had to say, Sebastian realized what a fool he had been. He had allowed Hector to get into his head. He couldn't believe he was ready to throw it all away; they'd been through so much together, and he had no proof she loved Hector. Even if she did, she chose him over Hector. So why was he so angry at her? Why was he hurting her? He knew the answer even though he didn't want to admit it.

The fight ahead, him fighting over a thousand vampires it was going to be an impossible task, and he knew that at some point, she would be taken and she would have to erase him to overcome them. That must be the real reason he wanted to break off things with her, and he wasn't being fair.

Suddenly, a light came on in his head, and he found himself running toward the house. He met Hope on the way; he stopped for a moment and said, "Thank you for the talk, I appreciate it," and then he resumed his run to the house. Hope smiled; she stopped and retraced her steps to where they had been standing a few minutes ago; she didn't want to be in their way.

Sebastian ran inside and went straight into Hope's room. Hanna was on the bed, her face covered with the blanket; she peered up to see what the matter was; she was shocked to see him. He walked to the side of her bed; her eyes were swollen from crying. "I'm in the wrong," he said as Hanna sat up to hear him.

He continued, "I can't begin to tell you how wrong I've been . . . I . . . I've hurt you, the one thing I said I wouldn't do, and . . . I am so very sorry. I don't know what came over me. I was jealous and scared . . . I wasn't thinking clearly. And I know that nothing that comes out of my mouth now can make up for what I put you through. But I'm here to beg your forgiveness. Please Hanna, can you forgive me . . . um, if it's not too late darling? I didn't mean what I said; how could I? I clearly can't live without you. I admit it was foolish of me not to have trusted you. Please, if it's not too late . . . forgive me. I will work toward forgiving myself for putting you through this pain. I said I wouldn't. I promised you, but I will do my best to make it up to you," he pleaded. Hanna was quiet as more tears flowed down her cheeks. Sebastian wanted to wipe her tears, but he wasn't sure she wanted him to do that He had to take the risk. He moved closer and wiped the tears with his hands and then he said, "Please love, say something."

Hanna got out of the blanket; she was shocked to see him; he had broken her heart when he told her she didn't deserve him and he didn't want her, but he was with her now asking her forgiveness and that was all she needed. She threw her arms around him in relief, as another round of tears filled her eyes and she sobbed into his shirt.

"I forgive you S; it was all my fault; I did this to us; I made you doubt me, and you were right to be annoyed, but not right in your thinking that I loved another. It had always been only you, please, you must believe me," she said as she pulled away to face him.

Sebastian nodded and wiped at her face gently again. "I believe you," he said and Hanna smiled.

"Then, I'm glad you are here now." she said.

"It was a moment of madness, darling. And I'm glad I came to my senses in time. What will I do with myself if you are not in my life?" he asked, and she laughed.

"You will be miserable without me," she said.

"Tell me about it. I know that feeling all too well, and I am sorry I inflicted that on you," he apologized again, wiping her tears and stroking her face tenderly. She looked down.

"I think we have inflicted enough pain on each other. I just want us to be happy. We know our love is stronger than any opposition; that is why we always end up back together," Hanna said. Sebastian held her face and began kissing the remaining tears off her face, Hanna laughed as his kisses tickled her and she said, "I love you so much, Sebastian Francis."

"I know you do my darling," he said; their eyes locked for a moment, and he said with all seriousness. "Thank you for taking back this ungracious ass; I will forever be grateful, Ms. Hanna Greene. Now let's leave your mother's room. I'm taking you to where you belong." Sebastian pulled her to him and carried her in his arms into his room.

As he opened the door to their room, he said. "Even though I hated the owner of this house, this room, and its occupant, missed your presence." He laid her on the bed, and then climbed in next to her. They faced each other; he could see the swelling around her eyes from all the crying. Sebastian traced his hand delicately over her eyelids, and then he kissed both slightly. She could tell he was feeling guilty; she didn't have to read his mind to know; it was written all over his face. He opened his mouth to apologize again, and she placed a finger on his lips.

"Shush," she said. Don't say it; it's in the past now; from here on we only talk about the future. I know what is disturbing you; I know it; you don't have to tell me. I can see it in your eyes, the fear that I may die, or the fear that if we live I may have erased you from my memories. I think of it, too, my love; you are not alone there, but we can't let what may not happen stop us from living our lives now. So, what if we die? At least we loved more than most people ever dared. We hurt and we felt so much pain from this wonderful love we feel for each other. But if we are lucky and come

332

out of this alive, and I have erased you from my memories, then our sacrifice would be for something bigger than us because we would have done it for the greater good, even if no one else knows it. Somewhere beyond the clouds, the love that we feel would be written down and if not, who cares my love, we came into the world; we loved greatly and we conquered," she said.

"When did you become so wise?" he asked.

"I don't know, but I think it's because I've been hanging around a two-hundred-year-old fella; I think he rubbed off on me," she said.

Sebastian, chuckled and said, "So today, we sleep and rest well; tomorrow if you feel up to it, you and your mother can go and check out another house. I got a text from the agent; he said he found just what we asked for. If you can't go, perhaps your mum could go for us. Whatever she decides, I will agree," Sebastian said. Hanna nodded in agreement.

"Why don't you want to go," Hanna asked.

"Darling, I need to go hunt, I need to be strong for what we will face," he said. Hanna nodded again in agreement. As they stared at each other, Sebastian said. "You were wrong about one thing," he said.

 Hanna blinked and asked, "What is that then?"

"That wisdom you have; you got it from your mother; she is a very special woman," he said Hanna, smiled.

"Thank you," she responded. She closed her eyes as if she were about to sleep, and then flicked them open again. "So tomorrow, we fight; I'm tired of waiting; I want it over with. Since they are expecting us, we will not disappoint. We will go at night just you and I and we will battle for our lives to the end or forever," Hanna said.

"To the end or forever," Sebastian repeated; she smiled and closed her eyes and welcomed a peaceful sleep.

Chapter 46

The next morning, Hanna decided to go with her mother to look at the house while Sebastian went hunting; when he did not find something big enough to sustain his strength, he decided to buy two male oxen from a farm. He brought them home while Hanna and Hope were out, drained their blood and fed. He then cut some pieces of meat from the dead animals and placed it in the freezer as food for Hanna and Hope. The rest of the animals, he buried next to Hector's grave. He showered, dressed, and sat in the kitchen waiting for Hanna and Hope's return. Half an hour later, Hanna and her mother burst into the house. They found him in the kitchen; Sebastian noticed they were both grinning and gushing happily.

Before he could say something, Hanna said, "I wish you could have seen it for yourself S; that is the perfect home; it has all the things we all wanted; Mum didn't want to leave the kitchen; it had an indoor Olympic-sized swimming pool; it had tennis courts, the gardens are to die for, and there was a secret garden you could only find after going through a maze. This house is everything you could hope for, beautiful; the ceilings are so high it's like living in a palace. I just imagined the three of us living there. And oh, the stairs were gorgeous S, just breath-taking. I didn't want to leave. I felt at home immediately when we stepped inside."

Sebastian was impressed, he really wished he had gone to see it for himself.

"It was really that good?" Sebastian asked; he'd seen a lot of houses in his time, and watching them so happy reminded him of a time when he used to go house hunting with his mother, Elizabeth. She would gush and grin when she saw a house she thought she couldn't live without. They would buy it, do it up, and then they would travel to another city, and then his mother would find another. That was how he ended up with a collection of over eighty homes, including an island in Fiji, and they all came with very high price tags. He had a feeling this one Hanna and her mother were raving about was going to cost a pretty penny, too. And he knew he would buy her that house a hundred times over if it made her this happy.

"It is our dream house S; I found Mum hugging the kitchen island like she had never seen one before; it was so hilariously beautiful to watch her be that way about the house, and I know you would love it," Hanna said.

They both seemed content; although Hanna had not let her mother speak, he could tell that Hope too was in awe by the expression on her face.

Without asking if the house was remote or if it had enough grounds, Sebastian said, "Okay, I hope you said we are taking it."

"S, I wanted to, but then he said, wait for it, asking price surplus of twenty million pounds. I almost choked when I heard the price, but then, I remembered we had said no budget, still I couldn't make that decision without you," Hanna announced and quickly added. "Mum almost fell to the ground when she heard the asking price. Anyway, I controlled my urge to say *yes* and told him I had to discuss it with you first." Hanna said.

"Darling thanks for considering my feelings, but you didn't need to; I asked you to look for a house, and you've found one you love.

That's all I wanted; call him and tell him we are taking it," Sebastian said as he reached for his phone in his pocket.

Hope looked from Sebastian to Hanna, and then said, "Really! We can afford it? When you two said no budget, I never thought you meant for it to stretch that far; did you not hear her Sebastian, that house is worth over twenty million!" Hope repeated the price louder; she had thought visiting a house like that, pretending to be able to afford it was just her and her daughter fulfilling a fantasy.

Hanna giggled and looked at Sebastian. He went to Hope, and drew her into his arms and then said, "Yes, I heard right and I am worth so much money that I don't know what to do with it all. If you and Hanna love this house, then you shall have it. What's the use of all that money if we can't spend it as we like?" Sebastian said.

Hope's mouth widened with astonishment. "Really? Are you serious or are you having me on?" she asked looking to Hanna for confirmation.

"It's true Mama, and oh S, I forgot to mention the house is remote; our nearest neighbour would be almost a mile away and that's not all; the land surrounding it and the forest come with the property, too. He even said that if we wanted more land, the neighbour would consider selling some; but I think the land is more than enough for us. I mean a hundred and thirty acres is pretty big, wouldn't you agree?" she said, watching as he became infected by her excitement.

"I think it's pretty spot on; I was considering farming some animals you know; well I guess this house is truly the perfect home for us. What are you waiting for? Call the agent back; we are taking it. Hope, if you don't mind, I will transfer some money to you so you can sort all this out for us if it's not too much. I have an interior decorator. I will call her, and she knows my taste. but feel free to add your input; all your inputs and ideas are welcome; it is our house after all," Sebastian said; he got up and walked out the door, then he stopped to think and went back to the two excited women.

"I just thought of something; if you don't mind, I will like to put my estate in your name, just for now," he said to Hope. She looked confused.

"You know just in case I don't . . . I mean in case we run into problems. You will be the best person to look after it all. What do you think?" he asked. Hope looked from him to Hanna.

"But S . . ." Hanna wanted to say something, but Sebastian cut in.

"Believe me, it makes sense; when we come back, should we make it back in one piece, I will take back control, but this way is better for now. You never know; it pays for one to be ready for any eventuality. It's important to me, and it will help you a great deal, I suppose, don't you think so?" he said looking at only Hope now, avoiding Hanna's face.

"If, if you think it's best that way, but I am only agreeing to do this because you say it's important to you," Hope said,

"It is. Thank you. It's settled then. I will go talk to my lawyer and accountant and sort it right away." He could tell Hanna didn't like the morbidity of the whole situation. It was as if he were saying he was sure he and she would die. He wanted to put her mind at rest and not spoil the excitement.

He turned to her before leaving for his room. "Hanna, I know you don't understand; I am setting our house in order. We will come back darling, and when we do, everything will be as it was meant to be, but for now, don't think about it. It's just what it is; paper works. Now call the agent please before someone else puts an offer on our home." Hanna smiled; she understood he was only looking out for her interest as he always did. Sebastian left to tie up the loose ends and make sure Hope had all she needed. He felt hopeful; buying a house together represented the future and as long as he focused on it, there was hope he and Hanna would have that future together.

Fifteen minutes later, Hanna joined him in the room.

When Sebastian finished speaking on the phone, he turned to her and said, "Have just spoken to my lawyer and accountant; it's all taken care of; come to me, darling." Hanna moved closer and wrapped her hands around his neck.

"How are you feeling, I mean apart from the excitement of the most incredible house you've ever seen?" He asked.

She shrugged. "I'm good, all things considered, a little nervous about tonight but that's to be expected. What about you?" she asked,

"I feel the same way," he replied, and then they stared at each other.

"Have I told you today how beautiful you are?" he asked; she smiled and shook her head.

"I don't recall hearing those words lately," she said.

"Well, then, let me correct that; there are no words on earth that can adequately express how extremely stunning you are Hanna Greene," he said noticing a twinkle in her eye; she was glowing again and he felt a little sad that he might never be able to do this with her gain.

"May I have the honour of dancing with you?" he enquired.

"You may, but I don't hear any music," she said.

"Don't worry; I will hum it to you if you don't mind," he replied.

"I can't exactly turn down such an attractive proposal," she responded. Sebastian then began to hum the song he had written for her; she recognized the tune even though it had been three years since she heard it. He took her right hand and led her to the middle of the room; then he placed his left hand on her waist, while she placed her other free hand on his shoulders and they moved slowly and smoothly to the melody he hummed. Sebastian led and she followed until the song ended. Hanna smiled; she had remembered the song being sad; even though it felt sad, it was the perfect song for what they had been through.

Sebastian bowed his head at the end of the dance.

"Thank you for the dance. I hope we can do it again one day, preferably to live music," he joked.

"I hope so too, but I enjoyed dancing with you; it was perfect," she said; he looked at her with adoration as her glow filled his presence.

"Well, this was the first dance I ever enjoyed. I am glad it was with you," he said; she was quiet; his scent intoxicated her, and she wanted desperately for him to kiss her.

There was a morbid feeling in the air, and none of them wanted to spoil the moment by mentioning it. Then he tucked her hair behind her ear as he used to do and pulled her closer to him. Slowly he tilted his head to meet hers and their lips met. The kiss was slow, and gentle and honest; with every movement, the passion deepened; they knew they wouldn't get this chance again. Sebastian could hear her heart beating faster as their kiss intensified; he wanted to remember this moment forever; he had one hand on her back and the other hand buried in her hair. She moaned softly as they kissed; hearing her breath mixed with his and hearing moans escaping from her, his body wanted more; she clenched her body tightly to his and he felt like he was going to explode. He pulled back from her; gently he released his hold on her; her eyes were still shut and her cheeks were flushed. She opened her eyes.

"I couldn't help myself," she said.

"Neither could I, but we can't lose control," he said.

"I know, I couldn't resist you," she said, he smiled awkwardly.

"Come here," he said circling her in his arms. "You are the one I find irresistible; if we didn't have battles, I would have said to hell to everything, and show you with every touch just how much I love you." and then he kissed her on the forehead.

"Okay, so we have about an hour before we have to go; what do you want to do? Do you want to talk with your mother before we go?" Sebastian suggested. Hanna looked at him; she was ready for war, but another part of her feared losing him. She nodded.

"I will go spend some time with her and then tell her we are ready. Are you sure you are ready for this?" she asked.

He took a deep breath. "No one is ever ready for what we are about to face, but I am ready for whatever comes. What about you? Are you sure you want to do this? You know, we can run," He said.

Not wanting him to see her fears, she nodded again. "No, I can't forever look over my shoulder. It's now or never," she said.

"That's my girl, okay, I will be waiting here for you. Run along now," he said and watched as she left the room to find her mother. While she was away, Sebastian reached into his pocket and brought out a necklace that belonged to his mother, he placed it in an envelope, along with the bracelet he gave to Hanna when she first declared her love for him. Then he addressed the envelope, leaving instructions for Hope to give it to Hanna, if he never made it back. He hoped, in the future, that the bracelet would serve a purpose and help her remember him.

Chapter 47.

Hanna spent half an hour in her mother's company. They spoke about a few things, but she avoided talk about the battle ahead. Her mother knew what would happen later; she too didn't push; she was scared and she knew she couldn't talk them out of it. They had to face their demons and conquer them. When Hanna returned to meet Sebastian, she changed into a comfortable juniper dress; Sebastian was holding a steel rod he found in it Hector's garage. The tip was shaped like a wooden stake; he wondered what Hector had planned to use it for; probably on him, he thought. Hope stood at the entrance of their room; she knew they had to go, and her heart was broken. When Hanna was ready, Sebastian stood up and faced her. She couldn't bring herself to look at her mother again; she held her hands out to Sebastian, and he took them in his and before Hope could blink, they vanished from view.

They reappeared in the middle of the living room of their cottage in Wales. They knew that they would be surrounded, and at first, they thought they might have gotten it wrong. Standing back to back as they took in their surroundings, they couldn't hear anything or see anyone; even though no one was visible, Sebastian could feel eyes on him; his nose was bombarded with all sorts of scents.

"They are here," he whispered to her. "Take no chances," he warned.

"I know; you too be careful," Hanna replied. She could feel them moving closer, but she couldn't see them, and then she heard Sebastian flinch.

"I can't see anything or anyone, but someone or something is moving close to us," he said.

"I know, and I'm going to do something about that," she said.

"Let all that is hidden be revealed," she said, and immediately their eyes opened. It felt like scales falling off and they could see what they faced. They were surrounded. Sebastian could not count the number of assailants cramped around the cottage and hungry to attack.

There was nowhere to run now. He noticed them eyeing Hanna, and he knew to get to her they first had to mob him. He looked for Mason, Thomas, Henry and Nicholas, but he couldn't see beyond those in front of him. Sebastian held his breath and reminded himself he had known it would be this bad. "I can't see Mason," he said; their attackers now realized that the cloak Mason's sorcerer made to give them the upper hand had been uncovered. They moved in quickly. Mason's instructions were for them to grab Sebastian. Mason knew Hanna would surrender to him if he got his hands on her boyfriend. As they moved in to get Sebastian, he willed the steel rod to keep them away and Hanna created a demarcation with fire to create more difficulty; a few broke through the fire. Sebastian hacked at them with the steel sending them toward the fire, but the more he knocked them back, the more other attackers broke through the fire. Sebastian knew they couldn't win in such a tight space.

"Listen, we need to get out of the house; we need to go outside," Sebastian yelled as he fought another set of vampires that just crossed through the fire. While he pushed back with the rod, a few more charged through the fire and Hanna threw them back with a swipe of her hands. Hanna noticed that the fire was not helping; the more vampires they knocked back, the more they charged through the fire to attack. They all looked hungrily at them. Sebastian had said no one had to die if they could get to Mason, but if she didn't do something now, they may not make it back alive. However, she thought, she owed them a warning.

"Listen, I mean you all no harm; as it stands, I haven't killed anyone so far and I won't if you all leave now. We are not here for you, so back off; if you come any closer, it will be your death, do you hear me? You have been warned," she said. Sebastian wondered if her little talk would help, but it had the opposite effect; the vampires ran toward them at once; Sebastian reached for Hanna as vampires broke through the fire. He had not anticipated this, and he didn't know what she could do other than her zooming them out of the place, and then, to his shock, he heard her say the word. "Stop."

Hanna shut her eyes and willed everything to a stop, and everything froze; she opened her eyes again and more than fifteen vampires had their hands stretched out to grab them with the fire burning through their clothes. They were falling over one another to get to them; some vampires' bodies were off the ground. Everything, including Sebastian, was frozen in time. She tapped Sebastian and pulled him into her time warp. Unfrozen, he looked around him and was amazed at what he saw; he had heard her say the word "Stop" but that was the last thing he heard.

"You could kill them now where they stand, or I could turn them all to dust; which would do you prefer?" she asked.

"I like the version when they all become dust. It's faster," he responded.

"My thinking exactly. Let all frozen before my eyes become as dust, and let the wind disperse and blow them all away until there is nothing left." At once a strong wind shook the cottage and began to form within the room, throwing open the windows and smashing all the vampires through the roof; suddenly they turned very dark grey and just as she had said, their bodies began to break apart and dispersed as dust; the wind scattered their ashes and pulled them out of the cottage. Sebastian held Hanna tightly until every vampire that had surrounded them vanished with the wind.

"Wow! Okay, let's get out of here. I know there is still more to come. We can fight better outside," Sebastian said.

"I agree," she said as they walked out to the garden. About two dozen vampires were there, frozen. Sebastian smashed them with the steel in his hands knocking off heads and limbs, and thrusting the steel into their hearts. Job done, Sebastian and Hanna moved toward the cliff; everywhere was quiet. There was a feeling of eeriness in the air. The moon was full; they knew there was more fighting to come. Mason was hiding somewhere and didn't want to show himself. He must have seen what happened to his first horde of vampires, and they knew that whatever he threw at them now would be greater than the first batch.

"Where are they? Where is he?" Hanna asked.

"I don't know, but I am tired of playing his games," Sebastian said.

"Show yourself, Mason, you coward; you want me, come and get me," he yelled. He could hear the echo of his own voice as he spoke; then as if catapulted from the sea; another influx of vampires flew up from the base of the cliff.

They were once again surrounded; the numbers increased as the vampires kept flying in. This time around, the number of attackers had tripled. Sebastian tried to spot Mason. When he couldn't find him, he shouted, "I see you've sent these fools to die for you; show yourself or they all die." This time around, they wasted no time; just as Sebastian finished yelling and before Hanna could blink, a vampire sprung out of the crowd and yanked Sebastian from her side.

"Sebastian!" Hanna cried but heard no response; half of the vampires that surrounded her now started to move in cautiously. "Sebastian, can you hear me? Talk to me," she yelled nervously; she wasn't scared of the vampires approaching her, but she needed to know he was all right. She heard nothing; her blood boiled within her; then she heard a struggle. There was a fight in the middle somewhere; she saw a few bodies tossed into the air, then she noticed Sebastian leap into the air, stepping on the shoulders of the other vampires as he made his way toward her. Another Vampire leaped up and grabbed him taking him out of her sight. Hanna heard hard pounding as more vampires descended on Sebastian, and her heart skipped with fear; time slowed down as the ones coming toward her hastened their steps. They leaped up aiming for her. All she could think of was helping Sebastian; the thrashing continued. Hanna looked up just as the first attacker got to her; she stretched her hands to the side and sent them reeling.

Then, she moved purposefully toward the hungry-looking vampires, moving them away with the force of her power. They fell on each other as she cleared a path. She needed to see that Sebastian was still alive. As she cleared her path, others flocked toward her; there were too many. She kept hearing pounding, which fuelled her anger. Her only focus was to get help for Sebastian; he had been on the ground too long. Her worry for him made her lose focus; she moved faster, throwing and slamming anyone that came near her.

She noticed one or two vampires flung into the air only to be replaced by another. Sebastian couldn't get away; too many of them were on top of him. She was distracted; he was being held down by five vampires who punched him repeatedly in the face, as he fought hard to defend himself. Hanna flicked her hands and pulled them away from him.

Just then, Sebastian noticed someone behind her. "Hanna!" he yelled; she turned, but before she could see who or what it was, she felt a sharp stab on her neck. Sebastian got on his feet, carried her and flew high, taking her from the midst of their attacker; he landed in a clearing. The vampires were not letting up; they rushed in toward them; Hanna held her neck; whatever pricked her was causing her to bleed.

"Are you okay?" Sebastian asked.

"I'm fine." she said, "How many do you think they are?" she asked.

"I don't know about five hundred, give or take," Sebastian said.

"Everyone wanting blood," Hanna stated as she pressed hard on her neck. It wasn't a big wound, but it felt like a needle was drawing blood from her.

"I knew they would be this much, but I thought at least we would see Mason," Sebastian said as he quickly examined Hanna's neck.

"He's too much of a coward, I guess," Hanna replied. Sebastian looked ahead, and they were once again encircled. He sighed and looked at Hanna,

"If we get out of this, will you marry me?" he asked.

"What!" she asked; she heard him, but she thought she was mistaken.

"Will you marry me, Hanna Greene?" Sebastian proposed. Hanna looked at him and shook her head in awe. She couldn't believe he chose now to ask her to marry him. "I'm waiting Love; we don't have all the time in the world," he said.

"Well, do you want the answer now?" she replied,

"Now will be nice, darling; it doesn't look like later is guaranteed," he said, as the host of vampires charged them.

She smiled and yelled, "Yes. I will."

He smiled, "Thank you, love; it's nice to know what could have been," he said as he rushed toward their attackers; he pushed them back with his body to keep them away from her. Sebastian disappeared into the crowd again.

Hanna looked up and said, "Let night turn into day; let the sun stream down upon this evil and strip it away from this world." Sebastian looked up, he was beneath a pile of vampires, and he noticed movement of the clouds and the moon. The night became clearer as it gave way to the sun. Everyone stopped at once and looked to the sky fearfully. Then, he suddenly heard screams as the vampires surrounding them ran in search of shelter. He smiled at the ones on top of him; as they hurried to get away, he pulled them closer to himself so they couldn't run. From every corner, their attacker burst into flames and the sun consumed them. A few lucky ones jumped into the water; some combusted on their way to finding shelter, but not all were so lucky; more than half of their attackers were destroyed by the sun until no one was standing but him and Hanna. They looked around and saw no one, and hoped that Mason had met his end too, but they knew he was still alive somewhere.

Hanna heaved a sigh as Sebastian held her in his arms; then she looked to the sky and said, "Let the night return and the moon be as it was before." And everything moved into place again. Hanna suddenly felt tired, as if she had used all her powers to summon the sun. She wanted to say something to Sebastian, but before she could open her mouth, they heard someone clapping. They looked at each other as a pack of wolves appeared; Sebastian knew the fight wasn't done, but never in a million years did he think they would also fight wolves tonight.

He shook his head, and looked at Hanna. "It's a full moon tonight, and we still haven't found Mason," he said. Hanna decided not to mention being tired; it would worry him unnecessarily.

"Tell me about it," she replied, as she watched Hilda approach. Hanna knew Hilda wanted blood, and if Hanna didn't have to fight vampires as well, she would have welcomed the challenge.

347

The wolves were about sixty in number, and forty human foot soldiers followed her.

"I see you came prepared; how did you know where to find me?" Hanna asked as she observed the angry wolves surrounding them.

"I followed the undead; it was rumoured that they found a way to walk the day; I knew it had to be you they were after. The original plan was to fight them for you, but you have helped us so far; there is no one to fight except you now. So, it's time for you to die, Hanna," Hilda said coldly. Hanna looked at her; she knew this was not the little girl she once played with; she looked from her to the angry faces of the wolves, and wondered which one of them was Hurrit or Suzan.

Hanna had promised Suzan she would do her best to lift the curse; she remembered what her mother had told her about lifting the curse, and she wanted to let them know there was a solution.

They didn't need to fight her.

"Wait, we don't have to do this." She looked from Hilda to the angry faces that surrounded her and Sebastian. "I know how to help you now; the witch that cursed you, she is here, she is not dead not really. If you join me and help me fight these vampires until they are all destroyed. I will kill her for you and once she is dead, I mean properly dead this time around, I assure you, the curse will lift and you can all resume your lives. What do you say?" Hanna asked looking from Hilda to her army. Hilda let out a wicked laugh.

"You lie," she said. "You are not going to get out of this easily. You think we are fools; you will die today and your blood will be used to cleanse the tribe. Don't believe her; she is trying to deceive us; we have come this far; don't fall into her trap," Hilda warned her tribe.

"I'm not lying; I promised that I will help; that is the solution you've been looking for; if you stop now, I will help you kill that witch, and you can all go back home and live a normal life. You wanted a solution, a real one. I have given it to you. You can either take it or you can fight me; but if you do, I will kill every one of you before I let you take me. If anyone of you have any doubts, now is the time to leave," Hanna said hoping that her speech would deter a few of them. She noticed a white wolf come out of the pack; it turned around urging the others to follow, but no one did. Then, the wolf turned on its heels and left the battle ground. Hilda laughed.

"Suzan, always a coward, run for your life; when I finish with her, I will come for you. Are there any other cowards?" Hilda asked; no one stepped forward.

"Good, now let's destroy this bitch and take back our lives," Hilda said. Sebastian was ready for this one; humans weren't as strong as he was, and wolves were just animals. Killing them was more his thing than fighting vampires.

"Well, you came looking for a fight; show me what you got," Hanna said as the wolves moved closer. Sebastian leaped forward immediately, picked them up two at a time and crushed their necks in his hands. The others jumped on his back, and tugged at his legs and arms; they bit him, but his skin was tough. He shook his body to get them off him, and he yanked the ones grinding their teeth at his back. He kicked and smashed their heads with his foot. The human foot soldiers had wooden stakes in their hands; a few threw stakes at him as he fought with the wolves that had piled on him. A wooden stake brushed past his ear and Sebastian caught the stake and used it to gut the wolves. Hanna wanted to help, but she had a bigger problem. Hilda's body spit flames toward Hanna who forced the flames back to Hilda; with both hands she pushed back, but Hilda's force thrust at Hanna. Hanna felt wearier now; her neck was stinging where she had been jabbed with a needle earlier; it was draining her power. She had used a lot of her power today, but she knew she had to be strong. From the corner of her eye, she saw a few of Hilda's foot soldiers closing in.

Sebastian couldn't help Hanna; he had too much on his hands. Hanna waved one hand and sent the foot soldiers reeling. Hilda took advantage of her distraction and sent a fireball toward her chest; Hanna staggered and fell to the ground on her bottom. Hilda sent waves of fireballs at her; Hanna pushed herself up, and stood her ground as she formed a dome around herself to prevent the fireballs from hitting her; she looked around for Sebastian, but he was nowhere to be seen. Hilda's human foot soldiers continued to gain ground; as they moved in on her, Hanna knew she could either block Hilda's attack or take on the people closing in to grab her. She brought down her shield and waited for Hilda to attack again. Hilda threw spits of fire at Hanna, and Hanna redirected the fire with her hands sending it toward the foot soldiers. The fire burned them, and they yelled out in pain. Hanna looked around for Sebastian again but Hilda wasted no time; she used Hanna's distraction to her benefit again as she threw another set of fireballs at Hanna sending her reeling to the ground once more. Hanna's face smashed into the dirt, but the fire did not burn. Hanna looked up as Hilda approached; then she noticed Sebastian; he was on the ground covered by an overwhelming number of wolves. Things weren't looking great, and just when she thought things couldn't get worse, she heard a voice that sent chills down her back.

Chapter 48

"Who brought wolves to a vampire's fight?" Mason asked.

"Hands off, she's mine," he said to Hilda who laughed sarcastically.

"I don't think so; you want her; you have to fight me," Hilda said. Mason smiled; he looked at Hanna's wide eyes as she lay on the ground.

"Aren't you something spectacular? We finally meet," Mason said quietly to Hanna before looking at Hilda.

"You want to fight? I will fight and kill you for her," he said, and then he clicked his hands and the rest of the vampires that were in hiding began to fly in until Hilda and her fighters were fully surrounded. Sebastian pushed through the wolves yanking him at the sound of Mason's voice, and to his surprise he saw Hanna on the ground. He ran toward her; he knew what she must do, but before he could get to her ten vampires stood between him and her creating a border. He pushed through, but he too was tired; his strength couldn't break their force. He looked around for Thomas. He really needed Thomas to help now.

The wolves sneered, bearing their teeth at the vampires, and the remaining foot soldiers from Hilda's camp held out their stakes as Mason's army enclosed them in a circle.

Sebastian's eyes were on Hanna who tried to get up, but she was too weakened, and it felt like she had used up her powers; she needed strength, and she couldn't see Sebastian from where she was.

"Don't let him get to her," Mason commanded as Sebastian pushed through the vampires blocking him. Sebastian fought his way through but as he got to her, he was yanked off and brought to his knees. He felt so many hands on him as another vampire held his neck to snap it. Hilda didn't care much what happened to Sebastian; she had come for Hanna, and she was not leaving until she got what she came for.

"Bring him to me," Mason commanded; the vampires holding Sebastian forced him to his feet and led him toward Mason. Sebastian struggled to break free, Hanna's face was tearful as she saw him struggling, but she felt spent and empty inside.

Sebastian looked at Hanna and he mouthed, "Erase me now." As Sebastian was being dragged toward Mason, Hilda thought it best to attack while they were distracted.

"Attack," she shouted, and the wolves and the foot soldiers leaped toward the vampires; Sebastian used the commotion to his advantage and broke free racing toward Hanna. Mason caught him mid-air and brought him to the ground with one blow; Sebastian lifted his hands toward Mason's throat, but his hands could not reach. He pushed Mason off him with his knees, but Mason shifted and adjusted his hold; Sebastian looked for Hanna from the corner of his eye; she was running away from a pack of wolves.

Angered by what he saw, Sebastian pushed forward and threw Mason off of him, and before Mason could return, Sebastian flew toward Hanna, hotly pursued by Mason. Sebastian grabbed Hanna and moved her behind him. While the wolves circled them, they were soon joined by Mason, Thomas, Henry, and Nicholas and as if they weren't enough, Hilda appeared, too. Sebastian looked at the group in front of him and then he looked at Thomas; he wondered if Thomas was going to back out on their deal now. Thomas winked at him, and in a split second he grabbed Nicholas and snapped his neck off his body to Mason's horror. Henry couldn't believe what he witnessed, and before he could react, he heard Thomas say, "Join me now Henry or I will have to kill you too." Mason furiously looked from Henry to Thomas wondering what had brought such disloyalty. Henry threw himself at Thomas and landed a hard blow, punching Thomas in the face in fury as he tried to avenge Nicholas's mindless death. Thomas blocked the next punches and the two wrestled to the death. Everything was happening at once; chaos and death ruled on the cliff.

Hilda turned her attention to Mason, "I told you before that she's mine. Are you ready to die?"

Mason laughed and said, "I have been around far too long for you to kill."

Hilda scoffed and ordered the wolves. "Keep her there," she said to the pack of wolves that surrounded Hanna and Sebastian. The wolves moved closer toward Sebastian and Hanna sneering and baring their teeth. Sebastian backed away with Hanna behind him as he looked for an escape for them.

In the distance, Sebastian saw the bald sorcerer he and Hanna had met back in Mexico. He was with a red-haired woman; on closer inspection, the woman looked exactly like the dead witch he had thrown into the sea. Annemarie had been resurrected somehow; he knew that was due to the blood taken from Hanna, which explained why Hanna was suddenly weak. He called Hanna's attention to the witch. "How is this possible?" he asked Hanna who shook her head.

"I don't know, but I can see the witch is alive. Whatever they did to wake her has taken a lot of my powers. No wonder I feel weak," Hanna said.

They looked about them as war raged before their eyes. The vampires and the wolf tribe fought on, but Mason and his army were clearly winning.

Sebastian asked, Hanna., "Is there something you can do?"

353

"I don't know; I feel too weak like someone is sucking the life out of me," Hanna explained. Sebastian was afraid for them.

"Can you zoom us away?" Sebastian whispered realizing if they didn't go now, they would die here.

"I'm sorry S, but I don't think I can. I feel empty," she said sadly. Sebastian heaved a sigh; he always knew it would come to this.

"It's okay, look at me, do what you have to do now. Erase me; take what you need from me and save yourself. It's okay with me, but don't let them take you," he said holding her hands. Hanna's eyes watered; she knew Sebastian was right. She had hoped it would not come to this.

****

Hilda was fighting Mason for Hanna; she threw fireballs at him, but Mason managed to dodge a few times until the bald man arrived with Annemarie. For someone that had been dead for centuries, she looked very much alive. Sebastian knew now why Hanna was so spent; whatever they did with the little blood they took from her had worked wonders on Mason's wife. Annemarie flicked her hands and fought off the fireballs Hilda directed at Mason.

"I see we have a little problem on our hands." Annemarie spoke her first words to her man as if time hadn't passed since she last saw him. There was no time for reunions between her and Mason. She was used to this type of battle and all this time away felt like she had been sleeping. Mason looked at her and smiled proudly, and then he walked toward Sebastian, leaving his wife to deal with Hilda.

"Give her to me," he said. "As you can see, there is no way out for either of you," he added. Then he pulled out the ring and pointed it at Hanna. The ring forced her toward him; Sebastian pulled her back, but the force was too strong.

Sebastian held her hands and said, "Take the strength you put in me now, Hanna; take it now and use it." Hanna closed her eyes as she willed the strength away from his body to hers. Current passed from his hands to hers, and when she opened her eyes, she felt stronger. Hanna flicked the ring away from Mason's hands, and Sebastian ran for the ring and picked it up. The wolves descended on him; he pushed through as they tucked and tore at him. Hanna moved her eyes from Mason to Sebastian as he shrieked in pain. The strength she had taken from him made him weak; he felt almost human; he bled as the wolves tore at him. Glimpses of their lives together flashed before her mind as her memory of him began to fade. She shoved the wolves away from him as Mason ran toward Sebastian to get the ring back. He needed it to complete the ritual, but Sebastian managed to get up, and he threw the ring over the cliff into the sea. Enrage and shocked, Mason reached over and grabbed him. Hanna turned to look at what was happening before her as she struggled to keep her memory of Sebastian. At that very moment, Mason looked at her, making sure she witnessed what he was about to do; then before Hanna could do anything, he snapped Sebastian's neck, twisting him around and throwing his body to the ground. Hanna looked on in horror.

She ran to him; she wanted to call his name, but she couldn't remember it. Still, she felt a huge stab to her heart, and she screamed in pain. If she couldn't remember his name, Hanna knew soon all memories of him would be wiped. In a flash, she recalled all the precious times they spent in each other arms. She tried to remember the kisses, the number of times he said he loved her. Tears poured from her eyes as she mourned his death; her heart broke and crumbled within her as the pain of his death consumed her being. Her body shook violently, and she screamed trying to wake him up, but he was gone.

He was dead; she knew it, and Mason was to blame. Her scream brought her to everyone's attention.

Thomas was shocked when he saw that Sebastian had been killed. He had just finished killing Henry, and now he knew he had done it for nothing. Thomas looked at Mason, the originator of all this carnage, and the hatred he felt for him pushed him to attack. Thomas ran toward Mason as he made to grab Hanna, who was beside herself with grief as she cried over Sebastian's body. He pushed Mason away from her toward the cliff, and they rolled downwards. Mason broke the fall by kicking Thomas off him.

"You must be truly mad to think you can take me on?" Mason yelled as he flew up to the surface. Thomas held on to the edge of the cliff and pushed himself up, and then he flew upward to attack Mason. His hand formed a fist that he aimed towards Mason's face. Mason dodged and clutched Thomas by the neck lifting him in a show of strength. Thomas wrapped his legs tightly around Mason's neck forcing him to let go of him. Thomas flipped backward with Mason in the firm grip of his thighs.

Mason choked.

"Thomas, what has come over you?" Mason spurted.

"This is for Margret and for Sebastian and all the innocents you have killed in the name of that wicked witch you call a wife. It's time for you to pay," Thomas said tightening his hold on Mason. Understanding now that Thomas resented him, Mason forced his hands between Thomas's legs, peeling them away from his neck, and throwing Thomas off of him. Thomas tried to stand up, but Mason was faster; he grabbed him and twisted him around so that his head was locked under his shoulders. Thomas tried to fight him off, but Mason was clearly the stronger of the two. Thomas moved his hands about fitfully trying hard to grab Mason so that he could free himself, but nothing could be done now.

"I gave you everything; you were my right hand; I took you from the streets and made you a king, and this is how you show me loyalty," Mason spat out; then he looked across the field and saw

Henry and Nicholas's dead bodies, and in that anger, he lifted Thomas high and broke him in two.

Everything had slowed to a stop for Hanna; she looked up to see only a few wolves left; the vampires seemed to have slaughtered most of Hilda's tribe. Hanna got on her feet; there was pandemonium all around her; dead bodies littered the ground and still she could see Mason's armies gathering round towards her. However, she only wanted Mason; he was coming toward her; Hanna stretched her hands to her sides and wind started to gather around her, twisting in response to the rage she was feeling inside. Mason leaped toward her; at the same she saw two of the wolves that had attacked Sebastian leaping toward Mason, without looking away from Mason, Hanna waved her hands, and she sent the wolves over the cliff.

If anyone would kill Mason, then it would be her. She stopped Mason mid-air and pulled him up with her eyes; she wanted him to feel every ounce of the pain he had caused her; her eyes turned red. As she started to heat him up and cook him from within, his eyes popped with fear as he began to choke; he was drying up; he yelled in pain as she got inside his head and transferred the pain within her into his mind. He was in excruciating pain, and he knew he would die at her hands if no one came to his rescue now. Nothing was going the way he had hoped; he had the number, a thousand against two, and yet more than half his army had been slaughtered on this night and it looked like he would be joining them soon.

****

Annemarie had been pinned down my Hilda; she could do more if she had Hanna's power and fight fire with fire. Anchor came to join her and together they tried to resist Hilda. When Annemarie heard Mason's voice as he cried out in pain, she spun around and saw what Hanna was doing to her man. She wasn't yet strong enough to defeat Hanna, but she knew if she tried hard, she could stop her and buy Mason time to escape. She left the sorcerer Anchor to deal with Hilda and turned toward Hanna. Using all the force within her, she knocked Hanna to the ground with the will of her mind.

****

Hilda's power overcame Anchor's, and he knew if he didn't run he would be killed; Hilda gained more ground and surged at him with full force, falling to the ground; Anchor vanished before she dealt him a final blow. Hilda didn't bother to look for him; the vampires were moving toward Hanna.

Hilda looked around and saw nothing but carnage; all her people were dead but she was not done; she had come to make Hanna pay, and she was not going to leave until she had avenged every member of her tribe.

Hanna got on her feet; Annemarie stood between her and Mason and a couple hundred vampires remained standing. They were not going to give up until they got what they came for. Hanna welcomed the attack; she was full of rage, and she needed to unleash it on everyone in her path. She noticed Hilda coming closer; Hilda pushed Annemarie away with a flick of her hands and put herself between Mason's army and Hanna.

"She dies at my hands," Hilda yelled.

Hanna looked from Hilda to her other attackers. Sebastian's body was still beside her feet; the pain she felt at the sight of his lifeless body made her want to explode. She knew she would kill them all. The wind circled around her fiercely. Hanna pushed her hands forward and forced Hilda back, but Hilda dispersed into a swarm of bees. Hanna looked up and Mason and his witch were no longer in her sight, but Mason's army surrounded her still. They began to converge on her as Hilda's body came back together. Hanna waited; she was going to show them all the height and depth of her power. Hilda attacked with fire, but Hanna stopped the fire with her hands and redirected it toward the vampires gaining ground on her. Another dose of fire roared out of Hilda's mouth. Hanna used the force of the fire to push Hilda back and trap her in her own fire to buy time for what she needed to do.

Then, Hanna closed her eyes and uttered the words she had dreaded saying for so long. "I break the bond I once knew; let it be as though I never loved; let all memories of him I loved above all others fade, and let power return afresh to conquer and see this evil away." Hanna's mind raced down the past from the moment she saw his body fall, flipping through every important page of memory of him and her, the kisses, the joys and the pains they shared right down to when he stood in her room when she was only five years old and then there was nothing.

As she finished, she opened her eyes, and she heard a great thunder clap and lightning struck the ground; the wind around her lifted her off the ground and every muscle in her body received power. Lighting came out of her hands, and she turned her gaze on her attackers. Hilda had broken out of the bubble of fire that had entrapped her and ran forcefully toward Hanna breaking out in all the glory of her power as her body transformed into flames of fire. Hanna remained where she was not taking her eyes of Hilda who roared as she got closer; Hanna moved her hand out to stop Hilda from getting closer; then she lifted her with a finger; Hilda opened her mouth wide as her hands fell to her sides in surrender and the creature that had taken shelter in her body emerged.

Three heads engulfed in flames; the creature screamed as it whipped about with his tail; dark smoke filled the surface he occupied as he bellowed at Hanna. His body raged as he tried to free himself from Hanna's hold. Then Hanna spoke, "Hear me now, you foul creature; I banish and cast you back to the hell from whence you came. Be gone and never be seen again." The creature thrashed about as he tried to fight Hanna's will for him, but she repeated what she said until he evaporated into dark smoke and vanished from view. Hilda's body fell to the ground lifeless.

Mason's army had witnessed what she did; she turned toward the vampires; she couldn't see Mason and his wife, but the bald man stood in front of her chanting. Hanna looked at him purposefully and said, "Let it be unto you as you have spoken; let all the evil your tongue crafted wrap itself to your soul as a garment until you be no more for this world, and let your blood be on your own head." As Hanna spoke to the bald sorcerer, he began slowly walking backward before breaking into a run, but he didn't get far as he started to lose strength in his limbs until he was crawling on his belly.

Turning around to face her remaining attackers, Hanna held her hands out to the sky; a strong wind the strength of a hurricane began to blow lifting them all up; they tried to fly away but Hanna bound them to the wind around her, so none before her could move and then out of her two hands came bolts of lightning. Hanna pulled her hands together forcefully; as she did so, she gathered the vampires toward her; a few escaped, flying over the cliff; then Hanna dropped to her knees and struck the ground. As the lightning struck the ground, it gave way. She was going to bury them all alive. Using the wind, she hurled them into the earth; there were screams and yelling as they tumbled unwillingly into the open ground; there was no going back now. They fell in one after the other; they plummeted into the pit. Hanna heard their harrowing cries of turmoil, but she felt no mercy. She closed her eyes and began to speak to the ground. "Let fire break out and burn . . ." As she spoke, fire descended on those inside the ground, but before she finished speaking, she heard and felt a sudden loud bang to her head. Her eyes rolled to the back of her head and her body fell to the ground.

When she came, she felt a raging ache in her head. Hanna forced her eyes to open slightly, but she couldn't see. She tried to move and felt bound by chains; her hands were tied; her mouth was gagged so that she was unable to speak. She couldn't see because her eyes were covered. She could hear voices; she felt wetness coming from her wrist, and she immediately knew what it was; her blood was being drained. Hanna didn't know how long she had been held; she felt so weak. They were taking from her all that she was, and she knew she was going to die; there was only one thing to do now. Call her father to help save her; although she couldn't see, she knew if she really tried her spirit could reach him.

Chapter 49

Hanna's father was in turmoil; he felt every agony Hanna was going through. He had a dilemma on his hands; he could not leave if he hoped to gain forgiveness from The Highest in the highest. However, to stay meant that he was letting her die. He lifted his eyes to the heavens and cried out for mercy. He begged for help with each agonizing pain he felt through Hanna. He knew if he left for earth without permission to save her, that would be the end of him and the hope of ever returning to his position as an archangel to serve humanity at the pleasure of The Highest would be lost. He had been forbidden from visiting earth after what he did having carnal knowledge of Hanna's mother, Hope Lane.

Once upon a time, he was one of the warriors called upon to help free the sons of men from evil. It was his disobedience and greed for what was not given to him that had brought him to this hell he now lived in and called home, and now he was useless and he couldn't even help the child he loved so dearly. He tore at himself and held his face, bowing his head and knees as the torture of her cry ripped through him. To go to her rescue would mean he had rebelled for a second time. Surely, he was being tested again, he thought. To gain an ounce of favour and pardon for his sins, he knew he could not disobey again, even though his heart was broken by her hurt.

As he lamented over his failures, three angels appeared before him, one in black, another in white and the third in red. Their wings were two meters long on each side where their hands would be if they were human. Their feathers toppled to the ground, and with the tip of their wings each clutched a sword. The swords shone brightly; it looked as though they had been forged in ice, but on closer inspection, they glowed as though they were on fire. Their faces shone so brightly—glorious to behold. Hanna's father looked up in disbelief; once upon a time, he would have been arrayed like they were, and now he feared he had lost all hope of ever returning to perform his true purpose.

He didn't know what to make of their presence; he had not received such visitors since his banishment. He got to his feet, and bowed his head in reverence; he didn't look up for fear of the news they brought.

The angel in white said, "Don't be afraid; you have found grace and your sins are now forgiven, but you have work to do. Together we will destroy the evil that has plagued the earth. The child that you bore with the human has been taken; her powers have been devoured, but do not fear, she has fulfilled her purpose on earth. Now you will return to us and together we will rid this evil from the children of men."

Hanna's father could not believe what he heard; he looked up, his eyes filled with the utmost gratitude. A light shone down on him as his body began to transform back to its former glory. His wings sprang back to life; the feathers were pale in colour. His wings extended above, gracefully reaching up as he bowed his head to the ground and worshiped. The three angels also bowed their heads and worshiped The Highest; then the light disappeared and they got to their feet. All four, in their regal glory, flew to the sky as they made their way to earth.

****

Annemarie had drained off all the power in Hanna's body, and her body sparkled with current, as her beauty and youth returned to her fully. Mason held Annemarie in his arms as they stood in Hanna and Sebastian's cottage and celebrated their victory. Daybreak was approaching, and the surviving vampires rejoiced. Mason had promised them that they would all walk the sun. To demonstrate, her newly found power, Annemarie fulfilled his promise and displayed her supremacy and made Mason and his surviving army day walkers.

Mason made a speech to encourage all those that stood by him and fought to the death for their victory.

Mason said, "Don't fret, the worst is over, and we have conquered. I know you lost loved ones today, but it was not all in vain. I too lost a great deal in this fight. Some that should be standing next to me now died as heroes today. They will be greatly missed. But I rejoice even in this sadness because together you and I have done something special today, and we will go on to do remarkable things henceforth. I promised you the light and now you have it; at the first influx of daylight, you will all be free to walk the sun as humans do. A new age has come, and we will take this world for ourselves and rule over the humans; they will obey and cave to our every bid. We have hidden in the dark for too long, and now our time has come. You shall make for yourselves more companions to replace those we lost here this day. The earth is ours for the taking; no longer will we hide in darkness. When the dust has settled, we will host and celebrate the first centurion feast in honour of my wife, Annemarie and our fallen comrades, and we will celebrate our new-found gift." They cheered as excitement about what they would achieve together filled the air. Mason lifted his hand, and everyone was silent once again.

"Allow me," he said; he lifted his eyes as the first rays of sun hit the ground.

"Behold the sun as it arrives," Mason said; they all looked up; a few stepped back in fear that they would be consumed.

"Don't be afraid; welcome it," he encouraged. The vampires looked up as the first streams of daylight hit the ground.

Mason wanted them to see that there was nothing to fear; he stepped out into the sun, and the others gushed as they saw the rays bouncing off his body. He turned to face them as Annemarie joined him. All the vampires began rushing outside to enjoy the sun, they cried and gushed and thanked Mason for the gift of the day, but as they celebrated, visitors arrived amongst them.

***

Four angels landed and crouched on the ground as the vampires celebrated. The angles got to their feet, pulled out their long swords, and immediately began cutting down the vampires around them. The swords split the vampires and set their bodies on fire. There was yelling and screaming; Mason and Annemarie looked about them to see where the attack was coming from; everywhere they looked someone was dying.

At first, Mason thought the sun was destroying them. "It didn't work," he said in a panic. He pulled his wife to himself and tried to run inside for shelter, but Hanna's father got in front of him; Mason was stunned to see such an image before him and before he could blink, the angel swung his sword and split him in two; Mason's body sparked fire and burned away. Annemarie looked on in shock; Hanna's father retracted his sword and swung it severing Annemarie's head from her neck. Her body fell and burned until there was nothing left.

The vampires flew and ran hoping to escape the wrath that had come upon them, but they were no match for the angels. They were all cut down until none was left alive.

Hanna's father walked to where his daughter's body lay and untied the chains that bound her. He had been forgiven and she had fulfilled her purpose. As he stood and silently mourned her death, he heard a voice. He bowed his knee in worship as he listened.

"For her sacrifice, she will be returned to live her life as a human, she and the one she loved because he sacrificed himself, so she could fulfil her purpose. He will be given another chance to live as a human and for the love they shared to blossom once more. Go now to the child's mother; tell her to fetch them both to her." And then there was silence.

Hanna's father was pleased that she had been given another go at life. He knew now he could no longer claim her as his. She would be human and he had to cut all ties once he delivered the message to Hope Lane. Meeting Hope again was a test that he would not fail now.

****

Hope Lane had drunk the brew she made, and she'd had a terrible dream; she had seen a future where her daughter and Sebastian died. Everyone died in her vision and she cried out as she woke up in torment. She knew no one was coming back when the morning came, and the birds began to chirp their sad songs; she knew it was for her, the woman who had lost it all. Hope stood by her window and stared out into space, her mind blank, her heart hollow. She crawled back into her bed, wanting to sleep and wake no more. A deep sleep took her over, but she felt like she was still awake. In her room, a presence shimmered to the surface and spoke to her. The voice sounded familiar; she tried to look up, but a bright, blinding light surrounded the being before her.

"Do not be troubled woman for I have been given good news," she heard. "Get up now; the body of your daughter and the boy to whom she gave her heart await you in Wales, where they fell in battle. Go now and bring them to you; they have been given a second chance to live as humans. When you arrive home with their bodies, at the right time, their souls will return to them. Go now quickly." Then he disappeared and returned to the site of the battle, where Sebastian and Hanna's bodies had been laid next to each other.

All evidence of the battle had been wiped out, and the cottage was restored to how it looked before hell broke loose.

****

When Hope woke up, she immediately knew what she had to do. She hired a van and drove to Wales. Hours later, she arrived at the cottage and saw her daughter and Sebastian's body as they lay next to each other. Although she had been told not to be afraid, seeing her daughter and Sebastian lying lifeless made her cry. Hope set about moving them and wondered how she would get their bodies to the van, but as she thought about it, although she couldn't see the angels around her, they made light of her worry and made the weight manageable for her to bear. She carried them to the van with ease; she looked around her, and the devastation she had seen in her vision was as though it had merely been a dream. But Hope knew a greater power was at work; Hanna and Sebastian's lifeless bodies were proof of what took place. She got behind the wheels and drove back to Devon.

After Hope Lane departed, the angels reappeared; they had fulfilled their work; they flew into the sky together and turned into birds as they flew away from view and into heaven.

Chapter 50

Hope washed their bodies with wet towels and set them on the bed next to each other in their room. It had been a full day since she brought them back from Wales and nothing had happened. She noticed the envelope Sebastian had left her, she opened it and saw the jewelleries inside. Hope, took the envelope and kept it with her, then she sat on the chair next to their bed and waited for them to come back to life as she had been told. Hope was tired; her body needed food, but she wouldn't dream of leaving them alone. Soon sleep claimed her body, and as she slept, warmth and life returned to Hanna and Sebastian's bodies. Their hands twitched at first and then their eyes fluttered open.

Sebastian turned his head and saw a beautiful girl lying next to him. He wondered who she was; he had no memory of her nor of how he came to be next to her. Hanna felt his eyes burning through her as he stared at her; slowly she moved her head to look at him, and her heart skipped a beat. But she didn't know who he was or how they came to be in the same room and in the same bed. They sat up and looked at the woman seated on the chair next to their bed. Hanna recognized her immediately.

"Mama," she said; Hope's eyes fluttered open; she wanted to cry out in joy at their sight.

"You are alive, the two of you. Praise be to God Almighty. Thank you so much. Thank you so much for giving them back," Hope said repeatedly. She rushed to their side and engulfed them in a strong embrace.

"I can't believe it; you are here; you are back," she said repeatedly in amazement. Sebastian and Hanna looked at her with confusion. It seemed only Hope understood what she was talking about. Hope pulled back and looked at them. "You do remember what happened, right? The fight with Mason?" she asked. They looked at her as if she were talking crazy. "You don't remember the fight? Don't you remember any of it?" she asked in wonder. Sebastian looked at the crazy woman and then at the girl next to him; he wondered what fight he was supposed to have been in. Then, he questioned how he knew the two of them, but nothing came to him. "I don't know what you are saying. I don't know you," he said to Hope, "and I don't know her," he said turning to Hanna. He wished that he knew her because he thought that she was very beautiful to look at and even though he had no memory of her, his heart felt pulled to her as he gazed at her. Hope smiled; she knew she had her work cut out; it was up to her to ensure they ended up together as was intended.

The End.

The saga continues in Sebastian 4: The call of hearts.

Sebastian Francis.

Sebastian packed up his bag after eating some of Hope's delicious breakfast. The food tasted divine. For some reason, each time he ate, it always felt like he had not had that experience in a long time and everything tasted great. But that taste quickly turned sour when he had heard Hanna say it was best if he left. He knew he didn't have any right to her but he had hoped that she felt something for him like he did towards her. However, hearing what she said made leaving somewhat easier for him as he knew he would be doing her a favour by getting out of her hair. Picking up his packed bag, he looked around his room once more. He didn't have much to take with him and that which he most wanted; he couldn't have.

He left the room and headed for the stairs. It was close to mid-day. He hoped to see her face before leaving to let her know he was leaving. Perhaps, I will see her in the kitchen, he thought and stole one last look. As he made his way down the stairs, he heard clattering sounds in the kitchen. He held his breath in hopes of seeing Hanna. Cocking his head into the kitchen, he looked around and saw Hope on her knees sweeping something off the floor. His heart sank with disappointment, but he quickly adjusted his appearance as soon as Hope looked up.

"Oh, Sebastian it's you. I see you are ready to leave," Hope uttered.

Sebastian nodded. "The earlier I leave the better, I thought," he replied.

Hope looked down sadly. She had hoped that Hanna would have talked him into staying but since her talk with her daughter at breakfast, Hanna had refused to leave her room. "Well then, come inside. Sit please and let me explain a few things to you. I won't keep you, I promise."

Sebastian sat on a chair by the dining table and placed his bag on the floor next to him. Hope brought out a file and placed it on the table before Sebastian. Opening the file, she said, "There, everything you need to know about your finances are in that file." Sebastian looked at her questionably. "It's the details of your account, assets, all of it. Your money is back in your name. And at your request, as you mentioned yesterday, I kept a million for Hanna and I. I know you didn't exactly specify how much we can have but I hope you don't mind that I took that much for us."

Sebastian looked through the statement of account and judging by how much he had left, a million pounds was like peanuts. Sebastian furrowed his brow.

Hope felt nervous, "I know it is a lot, but I can put some of it back if you think I have taken too much?"

"No, don't be ridiculous. You barely took anything at all. I don't think a million is enough."

"Oh!" Hope let out an air in relief. "For a moment there, I thought you were upset."'

"Yeah, that you only kept back a little for yourselves. I can send you more money. I have too much money than I know what to do with it. Do you need more?"

"No, no, no, we will be fine. A million is more than generous. I will get us a little house and start a small business."

"Why do you feel the need to work at all? You must take more for both your upkeep. I insist upon it," he said.

"No," Hope insisted. "This is just temporary, remember? Until then, we will be fine. We will be here until I find us another suitable place. As long as you don't abandon us in the end, we will always be alright," she stated.

Sebastian smiled thinly.

"Write to us, so we know you are all right. And when something triggers, call me, I will do the same as soon as Hanna remembers anything," she assured him.

Sebastian placed the file in his bag. Picking up his bag, he got up and began walking out of the kitchen. He stopped momentarily and looked up at the stairs, his heart felt torn like he was leaving a part of him behind and he could feel his eyes clouding over as the pain of not seeing Hanna before leaving hit home. He questioned if the decision to go was the right one if he felt this way about her. He glanced back at Hope and nodded.

"Well, I must leave now, while it's yet day," he said.

Hope was doing her best to hold back her tears, something told her she may not see him again for a long time but she was hopeful that he would return one day for Hanna.

"Let me call you a cab," she said.

"No, I best be going. I think the fresh air will do me a bit of good," he responded.

Then, without turning back again, he walked out of the house. After walking a few yards, he turned around and looked up at the window to Hanna's room. As he did, he saw the curtain pull shut. He took a deep breath, understanding now that she really didn't want him around and him leaving was the best decision for them both. Then he continued walking, forcing himself to take one step after the other until the house was nothing but a speck of dot in the distance.

Enjoy more books from this superbly talented author.

The first book in this Vampire romance saga is:

 Sebastian: A Vampire's Torment, followed by:

Sebastian 2: Dark Times Arising.

Other brilliant books by the author include:

Hasina: My Great Escape

Jana: That Plague called Love

Harry Moon: The Blue-Eyed Wolf

Jaekeal: The Hunter Boy

And watch out for Sebastian 4: The call of Hearts. Coming soon!

Read more about the author on her website,

Or visit her on Facebook, Twitter, Goodreads